WHAT NOT TO FORGIVE

LORING WALAWANDER

LiveLarge Books

Paperback ISBN: 979-8-218-38241-4
Ebook ISBN: 979-8-218-38242-1

Cover and interior design by Jess LaGreca, Mayfly book design

Library of Congress Catalog Number: 2024905079
First Printing: 2024
Printed in the United States of America

Praise for *What Not to Forgive*

"Characters of different means and backgrounds each carry their personal burden: a leg lost in war, an unjust sentence served, a life wasted by drinking, a child withheld and a spouse dying alone. They each come to terms with help from unexpected sources as they make their own life journeys through Montana, Switzerland and upstate New York. Loring Walawander brings new twists to unravel throughout the emotion packed novel *What Not to Forgive*."

James Strauss, Montana Newspaper Association

"*What Not to Forgive* is a war story, cowboy story and love story all in one. Readers will recognize in its engaging characters people they know . . . and even themselves. It's a very good read."

Stan Cohen, Montana publisher, author and historian

"*What Not to Forgive* is the novel I've been awaiting eagerly since Loring Walawander's *Montana Epiphany: One Man's Journey to Wisdom*. With Montana in his heart in this book as well, *What Not to Forgive* delivers on that memoir's promise. It, too, is disarmingly honest and by being so becomes the moving, engaging and relevant story it is. It is a portrait of ordinary people, yes, and yet Walawander's characters are, unlike many, trying to do the best they can. They are, as William Faulkner put it in his famous Nobel Prize acceptance speech, characters that will, because the human spirit is real and needs our celebration, 'not merely endure, but prevail.' *What Not to Forgive* is a wonderful book."

Bruce Mcallister, author of *Dream Baby* and *The Village Sang to the Sea*

"To understand everything
is to forgive everything."
—Buddha

Also by Loring Walawander

Montana Epiphany: One Man's Journey to Wisdom

Acknowledgements

In my first book, *Montana Epiphany*, a memoir, I wrote about my six uncles and father, all of whom served in World War II and all of whom returned home. As a boy, I was a hero worshipper and had hopes of serving in the military too. In college ROTC, I was recognized for my leadership potential and academic achievement. But a pretty dramatic neurological condition got in the way of my military dreams.

I can't explain why my life's travels have been drawn by a mystical force to those places where the sacred blood of men was spilled. Omaha Beach . . . Gettysburg . . . Pearl Harbor . . . Verdun . . . Monte Cassino . . . and so many more. But I have been.

On Veterans Day in 2018, I was inspired to write this book after watching a young Army veteran who served in Afghanistan sprint two hundred meters on his prosthetic running blade at my gym. I was disabled by my "neurodiversity" and he by serving our country. He was inspiring because what he had sacrificed did not hold him back.

What Not to Forgive is a work of fiction, but of course it's autobiographical too, in the ways that novels often are, by the people we have known and cared about, and cities and towns where we've lived our lives.

I've learned over time that many veterans don't want to talk about their time in war. In writing this book, I was lucky to find two who could. I wish to thank these two men profoundly for their service and for being willing to be interviewed: SSG. M.H.W., who served in Operation Iraqi

Freedom and Operation Enduring Freedom; and SSG. R.C., who served in Operation Iraqi Freedom and was awarded the Purple Heart for his service in Operation Enduring Freedom in Afghanistan.

While researching my family tree, I discovered that I had three Tekla Walawander grandmothers dating back to 1750 Poland. It's in remembrance of them that I chose that name.

I also wish to thank Lori Abramson, Co-Director of the Montana Amputee and Limb Different Group for helping me understand the daily life of a woman amputee.

Not everyone reacts to traumatic events in the same way or experiences the same symptoms. I wish to thank both C.J. and L.K. for helping me understand, to the degree that I can, what life is like living with and healing from PTSD.

I also wish to thank Missy Lacock for her early input as my developmental editor.

It took six years to write, *What Not to Forgive*. The world changed with the COVID pandemic during those years. After thousands of words were added or deleted to this book in the way that novels are so often written, and whole chapters found their way to the recycle bin (or were resurrected in other, better forms), and the novel was the best I could make it, I was fortunate to find an incomparable line-editor and proofreader, Sandi Corbitt-Sears, whose masterful touch has given the book the polish it needs to speak as well as it can. "Thank you" isn't quite enough to express my gratitude to Sandi.

My life has been blessed, too, with an old friend, Bob Holland, a Vietnam Navy veteran, whose support of this book and its author has been unflagging.

And, of course, a houseful of thanks to my wife and biggest cheerleader, Jacque. During the days I spent in my office writing, you never flinched, Jacque, when I said, "Hey, how does this sound?"

Contents

Acknowledgements vii

Chapter 1 1

Chapter 2 7

Chapter 3 10

Chapter 4 16

Chapter 5 18

Chapter 6 22

Chapter 7 25

Chapter 8 27

Chapter 9 31

Chapter 10 34

Chapter 11 38

Chapter 12 41

Chapter 13 47

Chapter 14 51

Chapter 15 62

Chapter 16 66

Chapter 17 69

Chapter 18 74

Chapter 19 82

Chapter 20 88

Chapter 21 92

Chapter 22 98

Chapter 23 103

Chapter 24 111

Chapter 25 116

Chapter 26 124

Chapter 27 128

Chapter 28 132

Chapter 29 139

Chapter 30 149

Chapter 31 154

Chapter 32 160

Chapter 33 166

Chapter 34 172

Chapter 35 177

Chapter 36 180

Chapter 37 186

Chapter 38 193

Chapter 39 201

Chapter 40 209

Chapter 41 214

Chapter 42 224

Chapter 43 229

Chapter 44 236

Chapter 45 244

Chapter 46 250

Chapter 47 254

Chapter 48 257

Chapter 49 260

Chapter 50 263

Chapter 51 267

Chapter 52 270

Chapter 53 273

Chapter 54 276

Chapter 55 279

Chapter 56 282

Chapter 57 284

Chapter 58 288

Epilogue 293

Chapter 1

Beads of cold sweat trickled down Frank's cheeks, and the bulging veins in his neck pulsed with each heartbeat. His mouth twitched before his throat produced a violent and unprovoked grunt . . . and then another.

He shouldn't be there. He'd done nothing wrong. But there he sat, in a prison-issued neon-orange jumpsuit. Matching sneakers cramped his toes, and his fingers clutched a paperback Gideon Bible. His only comfort was that he was free of handcuffs and manacles.

When he heard his name, Frank's half-shut eyes opened, and a thin smile fled from his face. Another grunt escaped his throat when his defense lawyer, Chase DeMers, entered the austere interview room in the San Francisco County Jail. Frank grunted twice more after Chase took a seat across from him.

The lawyer unfastened his briefcase and removed a manila privacy folder holding several legal-sized sheets of paper and a photo. He loosened his tie and then gestured to the document. "Listen up, Frank. I just spent an hour on the phone with the district attorney, and this is the deal she offered."

Chase worked a crick out of his neck and stood. He turned his back to Frank, looked at his Rolex, and nodded.

Frank watched every move. He noticed the attorney's typical defensive stance, slightly crouched with his weight on his toes. The posture reminded Frank of the old boxing photos he'd found of Chase on the Internet. No matter Chase's stance, Frank would not enter a plea bargain if it meant doing time in prison.

Chase spoke again. "She is willing to reduce the charge from first-degree to second-degree murder." He slid the folder across the table. Frank let it slide over the edge and fall to the floor.

The attorney frowned and said, "I've got strong advice for you. Take the deal." He emphasized the last word by pounding a fist on the table.

Frank abruptly touched one eye and then blinked both eyes like a set of Christmas-tree lights. His mouth opened wide as he gasped for air.

"Frank, are you okay?" Chase asked.

He was about to call the bailiff when his client's breathing returned to normal. Although Frank appeared winded from the event, Chase wondered whether the facial tics, grimaces, and grunts were just an act.

Could there be something about them he didn't understand? It had sure seemed real when Frank stopped breathing. Maybe all those socially unacceptable habits were involuntary.

Chase sensed a quiet, haunting intelligence beyond the man's grunts and odd behaviors. So what had jaundiced his attitude toward this client?

Chase felt icky about the man, particularly after he had tried to smell his hair during their previous meeting. For whatever reason, Frank's actions had created a distance between them.

As soon as the strange episode ended, Frank regained his composure. He retrieved the documents from the floor, gave them a cursory review, and slid them to the side. "Not good enough, Chase," he said with a smirk. "You're leaving me to believe my fate is clear."

Whatever Frank was up to, Chase wished he would stop. Those tics—or whatever they were—disturbed Chase's ability to think clearly and poisoned his attitude. Worse, it derailed what Chase considered a proper attorney/client relationship.

Frank was not an easy man to like. Something about him bothered Chase, and it wasn't the man's tics. Perhaps it was the sense that he was putting on an act.

Frank did not disguise his anger when he scowled at Chase, his twitches and eye-blinking on full display. He looked his attorney in the eye and said, "No. Listen up, Chase. I'm not copping to a lesser charge. That won't happen."

Frank felt his attorney had failed him, and he didn't understand why. Did his tics and grunts make him less important to fight for? Did Chase think he wasn't intelligent enough?

Frank's voice held menace when he said, "You're supposed to be the best. But you're not doing the job my mother is paying you to do. You say you used to be a fighter." Frank snorted loudly. "Then fight for me. I'm innocent. So what if my record's not clean? It's all small shit. I did not push my wife off that cliff. I don't plan to spend my life in prison for something I didn't do."

Frank tried to keep his fierceness in check, but that meant his tics would erupt in other ways. Whatever bad juju fueled them, he couldn't keep them under control. They ruled him. They kept him isolated from people, even his wife. She once threatened to shake him until he stopped grunting.

Frank's attention rotated between Chase, the documents, and the large clock on the wall. The minute hand ticked off time in a jerky motion, the movements emphasizing the awful truth: even though he was innocent, all he could do was grunt his life away one second at a time.

Chase's voice interrupted Frank's thoughts. "This is your last chance. Take the deal for second-degree murder. Twenty-five years is better than a life sentence." He glanced at his watch. "With good behavior, you can get out in twenty-one. You're twenty-five years old, Frank. You can still have a life after you've served the time."

"Kiss my ass, Chase!"

The attorney ignored Frank's comment and continued. "I can argue that your actions were not premeditated. I can argue that all the evidence is circumstantial. I can argue that your wife provoked you. But your history of angry outbursts and lack of contrition will make it hard to convince a jury of your innocence."

Frank clenched his fists. "Why should I act contrite? I didn't do it! A public defender would fight harder for me than you do."

Chase crossed his arms and rolled his eyes.

Frank continued. "My wife and I weren't arguing that day in Yosemite. Sometimes, I get excited and talk loud. Her dog had crapped on the trail, and she told me to pick it up. I refused. The dog was very protective of my wife and didn't like me yelling at her. He jumped on me, and I pushed him away. The mutt got tangled in my wife's legs and over—*grunt*—the cliff they went. I'll admit to that. Accidents happen. I'm sorry it happened, but I'm not a touchy-feely guy. What else is there to say?"

Chase held up an eight-by-ten color photo of the dead dog. "Is this the same dog your neighbors observed you kicking?"

"What's your point, counselor? Are you saying I'm guilty of kicking my dog? Sometimes I played too rough with him, but I didn't kick the dog. In the ring, you smashed men's faces. Does that mean you're capable of murder?"

Chase ignored the analogy and said, "When someone testifies before the jury that they saw you kick a dog, the jury will view it as the potential for violence." He glanced at the wall clock again. "There is also testimony that you said you'd be better off if your wife got out of your life. Other witnesses will testify to violence in your prior relationships."

"Listen, Chase. I'm not a violent man. Like I said, I sometimes play too rough—with my dog and with the people in my life. It doesn't mean I'm guilty of murder."

"Here's my point, Frank. If jurors see you lose control in any way, it will be game over."

"Wait a second. The judge ruled the prosecutors couldn't use those statements against me. He said there was no connection between my alleged past and my present conduct."

Chase shook his head like a metronome. "Let me handle the legalities, but there is something you can do. This jail offers a class through the Resolve to Stop the Violence Project. I think you should enroll in it." He pulled a pamphlet from his briefcase and gave it to Frank. "It could help you become a better man, and it may even help your case."

Frank waved his hands toward Chase's face, dismissing any notion of seeking behavioral help or taking classes. Looking away, he said, "I'm a good man."

Chase returned to his concerns about the jurors' perception of his client by reading from Frank's deposition. "You stated you wished your wife would have left on her own, but she didn't." He sent the document sailing across the table toward Frank with a flick of his wrist. "I've heard no remorse from you," he said. "You've never told me you regret anything you did or express any desire to change your behavior."

No grunts came from Frank in response.

Chase tried a different approach. "Why didn't you leave your marriage if you weren't happy? I'd like to believe your story, but the judge won't buy it if you don't show some remorse. Saying you're sorry it happened is just not going to cut it."

"I already told you I don't have any remorse, because I didn't do it. I may only have a high school diploma, but I'm not stupid!" Frank said. "All the prosecution has is—*grunt*—circumstantial evidence. It's like those hikers who claimed my wife and I were arguing. We were not arguing. Don't you get it? Can't you hear what I'm saying?"

"What about your record, Frank?"

"Yeah, I did a year in the LA county jail for a stupid high-school prank. My friend and I heisted some fat cat's Porsche for a joy ride around the city. I ended up a felon for making a dumb mistake." Frank jerked his head.

"It's all that's on my record. A stupid one-timer. What happened with my wife was—*grunt*—an accident. Yeah, I wish she would've left me a long time ago. Should never have married her to begin with. Now, if I'd had that wife of yours. I saw her on television with the mayor when he cut that ribbon . . ." Frank's voice trailed off, and he smiled, hugging an imaginary lover.

"Frank, please. Let's leave my wife out of this."

Frank noticed that Chase didn't so much as flinch at the mention of his wife or his pantomimed cuddling with her. He said, "Or what, Chase? You'll push me over a cliff? You're no different from me, are you? You just wear a fancy suit."

Chase gathered and reorganized his papers before placing them in his Italian leather briefcase. He looked directly at Frank and said, "I'm through

with you. Think about what I said. I'll need your answer in the morning."
He tightened his tie and rang for the bailiff.

As Chase turned to walk away, Frank hammered the table with both fists and issued a parting shot: "I'm innocent. If I go to prison, I'll get you one day."

Chapter 2

Chase had tried staying at his ranch house, but it wasn't working. Some days, he barely wanted to live another day. Nothing ever changed, and that was a hard truth to bear. He needed to get out. He just had to.

The anniversary of her death was approaching, which made being in the house they had shared intolerable. He didn't know whether to scream, hit the speed bag until he collapsed, or do both. Getting out of his home was his primary goal, so he grabbed his hat, the old Stetson with the turkey feather.

When he reached for his truck keys on the rack, they were missing. No worries; he had a spare in his wallet. Chase was halfway out the door when a silver pickup truck pulled up to his house. A tall, thin man sat behind the wheel smoking a cigarette, sunglasses hiding his eyes.

Chase threw his hat to the ground in disgust when he recognized the driver. "I'll be the son of a duck!" Chase's unfriendly greeting boomed loud enough that his estranged half-brother, Garet, heard it as he opened the truck's door.

Ten years his junior, Chase had been locked in a battle for decades over Garet's scamming, reckless lifestyle. In his younger years, Chase tried to accept Garet for the way he'd been wired, but he could never accept him for the grifter he became. The man had shamed the DeMers name. What pissed Chase off the most was that Garet kept a discreet distance from the family name but not the family money. He had no problem borrowing from Chase to fund his newest business venture, which would disappear when Garet was on a bender or lost it to an ex-wife.

"Well, what brings you to the Paradise Valley, Garet?"

Chase watched his brother's face, with its wide forehead and bloodshot eyes. The mask-like grimace told him his brother did indeed want something. He'd learned long ago to read Garet's tells.

"Fishing?" Chase asked. "Naw, you never did like Montana outdoor adventures. I'd guess it's money that brought you here. How many shots of courage did it take? You think you can get money from me when you never repaid Dad for the cash you creatively acquired from the family trust? For some reason, he forgave you, yet you never found the time to visit him in the nursing home. Want me to go on?"

His brother did not look down. There was no shame in him. After a calculated silence, his brother said, "You're wrong about the money and the shots." Garet's voice grew in volume as he said, "I'm needing a donation. You hear me? A donation!" Then he paused and looked down. Chase figured it was for dramatic effect.

"You think it's easy for me to come here?" Garet looked up. "You think I like always living my life in your shadow?"

Again, Chase felt he was watching an actor at his craft.

Garet wiped a hand across his brow and sniffed. Was it theater? Probably. It was the kind of theater a drug-addicted, alcoholic gambler uses to feed his habits, though the act didn't fuel those in Garet's case.

"A donation, Garet? Well, that's a horse of a different color. What type of donation, may I ask? Another too-good-to-be-true hedge fund?"

"Chase, look at me. I suffer from acute renal failure, and I'm dying. You're my only hope for a kidney, damn it."

Was his brother serious? Or was he lying, telling one more tale to get what he wanted? Chase stared at him and said nothing, waiting.

"It's true, Chase."

"Why don't I believe you?"

"Because you had the good fortune of being Dad's favorite. You've never wanted the best for me." He spat on the ground. "That's what Mother said."

"That's a horse-shit narrative, Garet. She never said or thought that."

His brother looked away. Then he said, "Okay, you're right. But the renal failure is real. I need your help, Chase."

"So you're saying you want me to donate a kidney to you?"

Memories of JoAnn washed over him, stealing his breath. He steadied himself and said, "I can't deal with this right now, Garet. I need to go into town. I need to think. Let me think, please."

Without looking at his brother, Chase headed to his truck. Behind him, Garet said nothing. He made no sound at all, and Chase didn't know what to think.

Chapter 3

With every bump he hit on the graveled county road, Chase clenched his teeth. He hoped the ten miles to town would shake a decision out of him. Hopefully, there would be enough bumps to shake out the memory of Garet's visit. A living-kidney donation was an extraordinary gift, an act of pure self-sacrifice.

He finally relaxed, knowing he did not have to decide after all. His doctors would never approve a kidney donation after his past heart surgery and the immunosuppressant drugs he still had to take.

As Chase approached town, he prepared for acquaintances to ask how he was doing. People meant the question as a courtesy. They didn't know it compounded his grief every time JoAnn's death came up.

"How does it look like I'm doing?" he'd growl. People gave him space then. Reminders of his grief spurred a hasty retreat to the ranch, and he'd often forget what he'd intended to pick up in town.

Chase winced when the pinging alarm told him he'd let his gas tank get down to fumes. The low-fuel warning light blinked red, confirming the urgency of the matter. He was running on empty and not just in his gas tank.

Gas pumps had always been an exercise in patience. He couldn't remember if he was supposed to slide the card or insert it in the kiosk. He'd filled the tank on the first of the month. Or was it last month? His days blended together into one dull pattern.

The Conoco station was just down the street, but he had another stop to make first. He pulled up to the post office and sat in silence. Several moments passed before he released his chokehold on the steering wheel.

He realized it was Monday afternoon. Phyllis, the postmistress with the new pixie hairdo, would have all the mail boxed by then. The thought of emptying his post office box of the political mail from crazy politicians, followed by the men's catalogs, all featuring executive suits and silk ties that he no longer wore, brought a smile to his face.

His smile faded when he walked inside and saw the overflowing-box notice. His late wife used to pick up the mail. She enjoyed chatting with Phyllis, but Chase had a limited appetite for small talk.

He scowled at the wanted posters on the wall, expressing his irritation with a throaty *harrumph*. The posters conjured up a memory of his former law office. They had notified him by mail in March about Frank Oglesby's early release from a minimum-security prison in California. Chase had read the letter twice, believing that Oglesby had been in San Quentin.

The prison had a practice of notifying law firms about any inmate who had made threats against the firm's defense lawyers before or while incarcerated. At Oglesby's sentencing, he'd promised Chase he'd "pay him back" one day. Due to good behavior, Oglesby had served twenty years of a twenty-five-year sentence for the murder of his wife. He was a free man.

Chase had served as the lead defense attorney representing Oglesby. The lack of remorse his client presented in court had gotten him convicted. His defense strategy, which was weaker than it should have been, haunted him. Had he held back because Oglesby's motor and vocal tics distanced him? Did they prevent him from fighting harder for his client? He had never been able to put his doubts to rest.

Chase's legal career had been marred by his pet peeves, which included defending the guilty, prosecuting the innocent, and billing hundreds of hours for divorce cases because people didn't talk to one another.

Working eighty-plus hours a week had increased his blood pressure and strained his heart. Those conditions became turning points in his life, and he considered them wake-up calls to change his lifestyle. He'd taken his wife's and his doctor's advice and retired from the law in his late forties.

Chase stuffed one first-class letter into his vest pocket, tipped his hat to Phyllis, and hoofed it out the door.

Inviting smells wafted from City Bakery, where Flo baked the best sourdough bread and pastries in town. The sharp aroma of sourdough mixed with the spicy fragrance of cinnamon buns and fresh-brewed coffee always tickled his nose, but he never indulged in the buns. The sourdough was another matter.

Daisy Grimble waited at the counter for her bag of buns, one foot tapping on the scarred wooden floor. Beneath her blouse's half sleeve, the lower part of a state of Texas tattoo sagged in the folds of skin on her right bicep. Her grizzled curls bobbed with the beat to a Willie Nelson song. A hideous splotch of dyed red hair blossomed in the center of her bangs. Chase had first seen that style on women in Europe twenty years earlier. He wasn't a fan.

Daisy's gaze locked onto him with a sunny smile, one that could melt the icing on the pastries. It was almost enough to send him back out the door, but he didn't scare easily.

"JoAnn never told me you craved Flo's buns," she said, her voice uncharacteristically silky. "It's so not you, but you need to eat more than granola bars and protein shakes. Maybe I can come over and cook you a good Texas-sized barbecue."

Remembering how he'd suffered twinges of acid reflux the last time he'd ingested Texas barbecue sauce, he waved off the notion like a referee stopping a fight.

"No buns or dinner, Daisy. I've come for my loaf of sourdough bread, so you see I'm getting my carbs."

Chase had never liked Daisy, who had the figure of an ice cube from years of eating Flo's buns. Now that his wife had passed, Chase had to keep his guard up against Daisy's more insistent onset of friendliness.

"I miss my daily chats with JoAnn about all of your travels," she said, resting her hand lightly on his forearm. "You two sure had an adventurous life together. And my goodness, all those countries—some I never heard of." Her face closed in on his as she said, "Your heart must ache, with you out there on the ranch all by yourself."

If she's hoping for a mercy kiss, she'll have to keep hoping, he thought.

Chase rounded his shoulders and shot a glance toward her that would've neutered a cat. "Life is never the same," he said, shrugging, "when you lose a love of fifty years. You're a widow, Daisy. Clayton's been gone now, what, four years? I just need to learn to adjust to the time alone, like you did."

Every time they had crossed paths during the last year, she'd sidled up to him with suggestive questions, and he was tired of hearing them. Her nasal voice made the hairs on the back of his neck stand up, and her lips reminded him of the pet goldfish he'd cared for as a boy. He wanted nothing to do with the woman.

When Flo handed him a loaf of sourdough, Chase sniffed the warm bread's freshness and then resealed the brown paper bag. He headed toward the door to finish his errands, eager to get back to the sacred solitude of his ranch.

Daisy tailed him through the door. "Maybe I can come to the ranch some evening," she said, pleading. "You could tell me more about your adventures. I would love to take trips like that someday."

"Google Perillo Tours," he replied. "They'll take you wherever you want to go."

He threw the loaf of bread onto the passenger seat, and it bounced to the floor. He left it there. Daisy's self-invitation had unnerved him. It reminded him how difficult it was to find a suitable travel companion. He wanted someone to help him get out of Montana and fulfill JoAnn's wish. Chase considered her wish farsighted to the point of prescience.

He'd used great discretion when he sent out feelers to past associates for recommendations. Nobody understood what he wanted: an experienced woman to help him navigate the difficulties of foreign travel, but nothing touchy-feely.

He'd always prided himself on his cool, calm demeanor, but that had vanished after JoAnn's death. He leaned back in the seat to let the warmth of the black leather soothe his arthritic back.

Feeling more relaxed, he pulled the letter from his pocket before buckling his seatbelt. Postmarked from Los Angeles, it came from a business that specialized in matching couples for the situation he had in mind. He ripped open the letter to find an itemized bill for the three contacts they'd selected.

None of the women they'd referred to him were his cup of tea. Mary Jane was a retired military JAG officer from Colorado. He tossed her because she insisted on equal time to do her own thing.

Next was Flora, a practicing doctor of Chinese medicine from San Francisco who could not step away from her practice during his timeframe.

He also dumped Barb, whose self-description focused on her divorced husband's very successful financial career on Wall Street. And then there were her seven grandchildren.

The company had failed to provide a suitable match, and he was so ticked off that his hair throbbed. He crumpled the invoice and letter and tossed them on the floor next to the bread.

The traffic on Main Street zoomed by. They all knew where they were going, as if heading to a fire he didn't know about. He powered down the window for a blast of fresh air and then started his truck.

Chase had once taken pride in his decisive problem-solving ability, but now his brain's hardware had short-circuited. He stared at the truck's navigation screen to discover which way to turn. When he cranked the wheel hard to the left and stomped on the gas, his right rear wheel clipped the curb.

. . .

It had been a year since JoAnn, Chase's loveable wife, had died from cancer in a Butte hospital. He wasn't there the moment she sucked in her last breath. He had brushed off the nurse's hand when she tried to comfort him by saying, "Many times, patients choose to let go when the room is empty."

His guilt became an unbearable burden that tugged at his heartstrings. He had left his wife's side for five measly minutes to get one of Butte's gawddamn pork-chop sandwiches.

After she died, he worked out more, read more, and fished more. But sleep would not come, and his despair manifested in haunting howls. The sensation of stones lining his gut curbed his appetite.

JoAnn had fought hard to survive cancer, but she didn't last three rounds. Childless and alone for the first time in his adult life, Chase mourned deeply, staggering under the weight of sorrow and grief. JoAnn's battle had been unfair. Chase knew all about unfairness. As a young boy in Butte, taking his lumps in a 16 x 16-foot boxing ring, he learned that nothing in life was fair.

Before leaving town, Chase forced himself to fill the truck's empty gas tank. It wouldn't help his mood to get stranded halfway home.

Chapter 4

By the time he reached the ranch, his energy was almost as empty as the gas tank had been. He settled into the rocker on the big deck, his personal oasis where JoAnn's memory encroached in a steady stream of consciousness.

He popped the top on a can of his favorite energy drink, so chilled it numbed his fingertips. The first sip perked him up enough to come up with another plan for finding a travel partner. He shifted in his seat, adjusted the cushion, and increased the rocking tempo in proportion to the caffeine buzz.

When the late afternoon sun gilded Emigrant Peak, he reached for his aviator sunglasses. The sun warmed not only his face but the fresh, green grass in the valley below.

Thanks to the pair of grooves left by thirty years of rocking, the rocker moved almost without his help. The matching set of grooves next to him stirred the familiar ache of loneliness, but the sun on his face and the rhythmic rocking lulled him into a trance-like state.

Chase retreated into his memories and dreamed in living color of the trips he had taken with JoAnn. He remembered the magical quality of twinkling lights in Paris along the Seine, the exhilaration of trekking across the snow-swept Aletsch Glacier in Switzerland, and their cuddling inside a yurt in Nepal. An involuntary smile formed when he remembered the choking smoke of burning yak dung that interrupted the intimate moment and forced them into the fresh Himalayan air.

Memories of the verdant valleys of Switzerland faded until he was left with a view of the long stretch of gravel driveway bridging the privacy of his ranch and the county road to town. That ten-mile trek was the farthest he'd traveled in the last year. There were no more decadent Swiss veal-and-mushroom ragout dinners. His standard meal was ramen from a package.

He'd sunk far into his solitude. And then he'd awakened to a Montana epiphany, as if his eyes had snapped open after one of the state's long, dark winters. He knew the time had come to fulfill JoAnn's last wish. She had asked him to cast her remaining ashes into the wind high atop the Aletsch Glacier in sight of the three big peaks: Eiger, the Oger; the Mönch, the Monk; and Jungfrau, the Maiden. That part of the Swiss Alps was nothing short of spectacular. They'd found it imposing and rather eerie. Residing at the Top of Europe, the place was so close to heaven that JoAnn had sensed angels in the air.

Chapter 5

Left—right—left. Chase worked over the speed bag, keeping his life's rhythm pulsing. Hands up and in front of his face, the style he'd been taught, let him launch a quick jab. He was still fast enough to catch it with a cross. It all came from muscle memory gained during his Golden Gloves days in Butte. An autographed picture of Sugar Ray Leonard smacking the bag during his Olympic trials hung on the wall. The now faded and crinkled photo served as a constant reminder of his own glory days of flashing leather in the ring.

Chase neared the end of his three one-minute rounds on the bag, knowing the bursitis in his right elbow would flare if he continued. Three years ago, he'd viewed the Rawlings black-leather speed bag as faceless and nameless. But it had since become an ugly cancer cell that he pummeled into submission.

The phone rang inside his wireless-enabled hearing aid. Any conversation would be interrupted by his heavy breathing, so he let the call go to voicemail. Panting, he pulled the tabs to remove his gloves and checked his phone. The call had been from Sean, an old friend and longtime chartered financial analyst on Wall Street. Chase had initially done business with Sean's father, the manager of a hedge fund that bore his name. He'd bonded with Sean years before because of the monetary wizardry that ran in his family. Chase hit the recall button and waited for the other man to answer.

"Good gravy, Sean, no country club golf today?" Wiping the sweat that rolled into his eyes, Chase gave a hearty sniff.

Chase had adopted the expression "good gravy" instead of saying, "good God," a statement JoAnn had frowned upon because it went against her faith to take the Lord's name in vain. When he uttered "good gravy," it was emphatic, coming from the lowest depth of his throat. Sometimes he failed to stick with the gravy part.

"You make me laugh," Sean said, chuckling. His voice turned serious when he said, "I called because you haven't returned any of my calls. Our quarterly meeting update is a month past due. How the heck are you getting along these days?"

"You didn't call just to remind me of a quarterly meeting."

"You're right," Sean said. "There have been acquisition proposals I wanted to go over, but they seemed untimely."

"I've given you the authority to make any moves."

"One thing," Sean said quickly. "After dealing with you all these years, I've learned to punch back." He paused. "The board of directors for that clinic you helped fund on the Rocky Boy Reservation is on my ass."

"About what?" Chase heard the irritation that crept into his voice. "You can take care of it. That's why I pay you Wall Street boys the big bucks."

"You've always been a little eccentric about your wealth. Any philanthropic plans now that JoAnn's will has been read?"

"Not today." Chase cast his eyes to the fly rod in the corner. He cleared his throat. "Definitely not today."

Chase had kept a low profile since JoAnn passed. He wanted his work to be noticed and appreciated but his identity kept close to the vest. He'd stopped maintaining any social media platforms, a good way to disconnect from the digital world. It didn't matter. People still found a way to mine for information about him. A single fact could erode his anonymity. He was fighting a losing battle with technology.

"I don't need any recognition. I'm busy planning a European trip." Chase rolled his shoulders to relieve the sudden tension that mentioning The Trip evoked.

"With JoAnn gone, your identity should become known."

Chase paused, wondering if Sean had an agenda he wasn't revealing.

"Wharton never taught you when to throw in the towel." Chase had pulled no punches about his desire to keep a low profile. "I've bigger fish to fry than having my name on a bronze plaque that no one reads."

"All right, all right. I got the message. Her Hershey inheritance was a big kiss to both of you. Big Sky, bigger problems. Is that what I'm hearing now?"

"You're pissing me off." Chase's voice became heated, and he needed to chill. "I can solve my own problems."

"Glad you calmed down," Sean continued after coughing loudly. "Today you're sounding like—uh—how do they say it out there in the West? An ornery old cuss."

Chase was finicky about anyone referring to his age and scowled at the mention of him being old.

"I'm planning to honor JoAnn's last wish." He took another swipe at the beads of perspiration on his forehead. "I need some assistance though. Damned eyesight and hearing."

"Have you considered taking a tour?" Sean asked. "I hear Perillo has a good one."

What had begun as a courtesy call from Sean had become uncomfortable for Chase. "Good gravy! They'd throw my ass under the bus."

"I hear they do that to ornery cusses."

"You got me off track," Chase said. "Where was I?"

"Somewhere in the middle of Montana," Sean replied. He laughed hard then and hummed the opening notes of "Home on the Range."

Chase ignored the jab. "Here's the deal. I want to find an educated woman, someone trustworthy. No escort service. Just someone to keep track of my damned hearing aid batteries and warn me about tripping hazards."

After a moment of silence, Sean proposed an alternate plan. "How about an old guy friend? Drink a few brews and shoot the shit for old time's sake. You could use the company of old men. Why not ask me to go? I've flown across the puddle with you before."

"Here's why: I want the essence of a free-spirited woman, someone strong and compassionate. Somebody who will notice when I need help and won't leave me wallowing in helplessness. Someone who can understand my heartache."

Chase had to take a timeout. His voice was quivering. He had just described JoAnn. That made him feel hopeless, and he wiped his eyes with his handkerchief.

"Maybe you need a grief counselor, not a travel partner." Sean said. He spoke in a tone that was accustomed to offering empathy. "Let me throw you a bone. My brother's daughter, Tekla, just returned home a few months back after working in the Middle East. She's not planning to go back there. Want me to email her?"

"Whoa, do you know her well?" Chase questioned whether such a call would be good for him.

The first time Chase and JoAnn had traveled to Europe, they hadn't been intimate for long. Being together in a foreign country tested them in a way they had never experienced back home.

"She's solid. Her experience might be just what you are hoping for. I could sure reach out and have her send you an email."

"Yeah, thanks. Time for the evening caddis fly hatch on the Yellowstone. I spend more time fishing these days. Adios, Sean."

Chapter 6

A welcome sprinkle fell during the night in drought-stricken Montana. Chase had maintained accurate rainfall records to help him predict fire danger ratings for the forested acres of his ranch, covered with lodgepole pine and Douglas fir. Record low levels of snow-pack within the past year had him on high alert.

When Chase checked his rain gauge in the morning, the nerve-wracking cawing of magpies interrupted his measurements. Coupled with his severe tinnitus, the noise grated on him. Then the bark of a squirrel on his roof captured Chase's attention. Squirrels had been working their way into the attic where shakes were missing.

He'd have to keep them out of the attic, so he called Jed Hutchens, his longtime ranch hand and general jack-of-all-trades. Winter was over, and Chase needed Jed to get back to work. He needed his company too.

"Hey, partner, almost noon. You out of bed yet?" Chase teased Jed mercilessly but always kindly.

"I wake up earlier in the spring just in case you call. What's up?"

"Ready to come back to work?"

"I'm so ready. I can be there in the morning if that works for you."

Chase detected a spark in Jed, as if he'd been awakened from winter hibernation and was hungry.

"That'll work. I need you to start on my roof ASAP." Chase chuckled and said, "The squirrels are moving in."

"Those shakes looked bad last year. Nate's available this year if I need an extra hand."

"Your call, Jed. Your boy's a good hand."

"I gotta get back to work. These Montana winters are getting longer," Jed said. "Or I'm getting older. April's been giving me housework. I stay busy out in my wood shop, but I'm at the point that my calluses have softened, for God's sake. Any luck finding a travel partner?"

"No luck yet." A wave of sadness overtook Chase. He knew the difficulty in his search had turned personal. He had always been a decisive and results-driven man, and this issue grated on him.

"Why are you putting yourself through so much hell?" Jed asked with a chuckle. "It's as clear as the nose on your face that Daisy Grimble, who lives just two miles from you, would jump at the chance. She'd even bring some buns to pack for your flight."

Most of the time Jed's shtick either left Chase hooting with laughter or madder than a bag of badgers.

That day, Chase busted a gut. He knew Jed was aware of the way Daisy kept trying to cuddle up to him after JoAnn's passing. Chase could not get past the woman's grating personality, bad hair day every day, lack of intellectual evolvement, and the fact that she seldom traveled beyond the aroma of City Bakery.

Chase needed to change gears. "How's April? I miss her laugh and her music in the house."

"She's ready and anxious to throw open your windows, let the sunshine in, and crank up her new greatest hits from Toots and the Maytals for you."

"Great," he said. Apparently, Jed had forgotten that Chase wouldn't know whether she played Toots or Alvin and the Chipmunks. "See you both tomorrow."

Chase was never fooled by Jed's talk of retiring. He wasn't even close to Medicare age. Besides, what would he retire to? At the end of every year, Jed told him his back was beat up. And then Chase would read in the town's weekly paper that Jed and April had taken top honors at the Valentine's Day square dances.

Six years sober—some days more, these days less—Jed needed the work. He didn't require the money as much as the activity so he could keep his distance from Mr. Jim Beam, his old Kentucky friend.

It would be good to have Jed and his wife around the ranch again. Chase liked having April bustle around the house, cleaning in dancelike movements while listening to the sweet soul vocals and rock guitar of reggae. She would turn it way up when she cleaned the seldom-used guest house, blasting her favorite tunes until the walls trembled.

With her green thumb, she might even be able to revive the rhododendrons she'd forgotten to cover before winter. But the lavender bushes were her signature plants.

Chapter 7

Later that day, Chase sat in his beloved rocker, outlining the season's projects on a legal pad, when his cell vibrated and interrupted his solitude. Ticked off, he left the shade of the porch for his office where he could read the email in a larger font. At first, the message appeared to be spam. He couldn't recall anyone with the name Tekla O'Neill, but the sender shared Sean's last name. The subject line included one word: "Introduction."

Then he remembered Sean telling him about his niece. There probably weren't that many Teklas in the world. It surprised him that Sean had remembered to touch base with her. Sean could blow smoke up his ass on matters not pertaining to money. It would've been just like him to space out mentioning a possible travel opportunity to his niece.

While searching for his missing reading glasses, Chase grumbled. "Damn it, where did I leave my specs?" After a few minutes of fruitless searching, he discovered his glasses atop his head.

Tekla's message took up one page and included an attachment. The letter opened with "Dear Sir," a somewhat formal greeting for the occasion. He scratched an ear and paused reading. Although he tried to accept the new generation, sometimes they made no sense. The email gave him enough information to suggest that she would be a good candidate to interview.

She wrote that she'd been born in the Finger Lakes region of New York and graduated from Boston College with a degree in international studies and a minor in Arabic. She'd starred for four years in varsity soccer. After college, the Army recruited her to be a linguist. She'd been on active duty for four years, some of it in the Middle East. After retiring from the Army, she had been hired as a civilian by defense contractors in Baghdad. Her contract had ended, and she was in the process of a career change back in the States.

Tekla's email revealed that outside of the work arena, she was a devout gym rat who loved snowboarding in the Catskills and reading the works of Gabriel Garcia Marquez. Adopting her father's music preferences, she wrote that she was a fervent fan of John Mayall & the Bluesbreakers. Chase found it amusing that someone in her generation had even heard of the British blues boom of the sixties.

He opened the attachment to see a candid photo of a woman in her young thirties, stylish in designer jeans, knee-high brown suede boots, a white blouse, and a brown leather jacket. Her fiery tresses were swept up into a loose bun that exposed a pretty face, more beautiful than glamorous. Prominent lips, lightly glossed, completed her appearance. She projected a certain confidence and grit that appealed to him.

Chase enjoyed watching great boxing movies, and he swore that Tekla could've been a stunt double for Hillary Swank. He grinned at the likeness and decided to attach a picture from *Million Dollar Baby* on his return mail.

Chapter 8

The next morning, Chase took his weekly walk to the ridgetop to pay his respects to the spot where he'd spread some of JoAnn's ashes. Brilliant rays of sun shone through stalks of grass, bathing the field in a ground mist. The dew had evaporated near the guest house where April was working. He'd have to get his clothes in the wash before she saw them in a heap at the main house.

He strolled to the guest house and interrupted April as she swept a tiny cobweb from the ceiling. "Could you please put the broom down for a moment?" he asked.

"Sure, Chase. Something wrong?"

He twirled a yellow balsamroot flower in his hands and put the blossom to his nose. After taking a long whiff, he said, "I just finished taking a walk to the ridge where we scattered some of JoAnn's ashes last spring. I noticed shoots of arrowleaf balsamroot, lupine, and phlox growing there. There weren't wildflowers growing in that spot that I can remember."

April swiveled toward him, her face as soft as the flower petals. Her gray-streaked, waist-length braid whipped around as she turned. She gasped at the flower, tilted her head to the sky, and hesitated, biting her lower lip before answering.

"I confess. Last fall, when I was in the hardware store, I noticed they still had wildflower seeds you could sow before the first frost. I guess they sprouted." She stared at the yellow flower and then looked directly at Chase. "It will be nice to have wildflowers bloom there every spring."

Chase linked his hand with April's and gave it a squeeze. "You've honored her life with living flowers. Thank you."

He wanted to say more to express appreciation for her thoughtfulness and generosity, but he couldn't control his emotions. He turned away, recalling the small amount of JoAnn's ashes in a silver urn in his bedroom. Those were meant to be scattered in the Swiss Alps.

"JoAnn would be happy," he sniffled, "that you chose UC Berkley's official school colors of blue and gold for the flowers."

. . .

Chase retreated to the comforting confines of his tongue-and-groove pine-paneled office, blocking out the sounds of Jed hammering new shakes on the roof. His office had once been business-oriented, but now it served as a healing space for him to retreat and meditate, searching for the meaning of life as a widower. A staircase rose to the left, and two American Indian art paintings hung on the wall above his recliner.

The painting by Crow artist Kevin Red Star, called *Mountain Top Medicine Man*, featured the eyes of the healer of his tribe as narrow slits beneath a buffalo-horn headdress. Chase relied on that stoic face as a source of renewed energy more potent than any energy drink. He lit a sage bundle to cleanse the space of stale, negative forces and welcome fresh, positive energy to generate wisdom and clarity.

He smudged sage with the proper understanding of it as a healing ritual practiced by America's indigenous cultures. He sucked in the smoke and flexed his left bicep and then the right, letting the power of the smoke cleanse him. *Medicine Man* gave him the eerie feeling that his life was being measured, but he was also comforted by the sense of being watched over. He made a mental note to keep himself open to a new world and a spiritual rebirth.

The second was an oil painting by the young Montana artist Colt Idol. Titled *River Walkers*, that painting hung a foot below and to the right of the *Medicine Man*. The artist featured five American Indian scouts riding along a Montana riverside. The piece made Chase realize his smallness in comparison to nature. The diminutive scale of man retreated in proper proportion to the boundless beauty of nature. He'd taken the painting as a personal message, which he used as a screen saver: *All of my wealth can't compare to the natural money in the world.*

He and JoAnn had viewed thousands of paintings at the Western Art Shows in Great Falls. He'd found buried treasures there and had the money to buy them. For now, these pieces were sources of comfort. But he wasn't getting any younger and wondered who else might find solace under their gazes after he died.

Chase had committed to a plan, half-made in jest, without thinking of the repercussions that raised his body temperature and irritability. He'd lost count of how many times he had struggled in the past year to accept her death. That struggle had launched him into the outer limits of isolation. JoAnn had filled his world, but now there were days when he could barely hang on.

One morning, after a restless night of tossing and turning, a midnight pee, and overwhelmingly vivid dreams about JoAnn, he'd grabbed her pillow and sniffed it. He'd never washed her pillowcase and buried his face in it, frantic for a lingering remembrance of his Queen of the Night. There wasn't one.

He'd risen at dawn, absorbed in his thoughts, and expelled a weary sigh as his bare feet touched the cold floor. A sense of being torn in half had ripped through him, one half ruled by his heart, and the other ruled by his head. Staying loyal to JoAnn's wishes was a constant pull on his surgically repaired heart.

Tekla, the unknown younger woman, created an emotional upheaval in his thinking. He couldn't let a possible travel partner slip away, especially if she could help him find peace by casting JoAnn's ashes into the wind as she had wanted. He didn't know if peace might be possible, but he was on the road to find out.

Tekla's email sounded too good to be true, and he believed in the axiom that if something seemed too good, it probably was. He was anxious to find a compatible traveling companion, but Tekla was a generation younger. From what he knew, all they had in common were working out and John Mayall. Potential challenges drifted through his mind. *Is she a late sleeper? Is she a vegan? Does she drink too much wine and talk too much—or too little? Can I travel with a total stranger and not have her drive me nuts?*

As he finger-pecked an answer to Tekla's email, Chase wondered if he was making a mistake. He kept it brief, thanking her for her interest and asking for a phone number and a time to call for further follow-up. He was done with emails and wanted to hear the voice of that young woman.

Chapter 9

Half an hour later, Jed's sixteen-ounce hammer stopped pounding on the roof. Chase's hearing aids picked up the garbled words of men talking and a horse whinnying outside. He ambled out and found Jed near the bottom rung of the ladder while his son, Nate, steadied it.

Once both feet were on the ground, Jed took off his hat and wiped the sweat from his brow with the red bandana he carried in his hip pocket. He pointed to the southwest corner of the fenceline, the hammer still in his hand.

"Chase," he said, "I reckon I'll have Nate ride that section and give me the skinny on what needs to be done." He reached into his shirt pocket and pulled out a can of Cope, popped the tab, and put a fresh pinch between his cheek and gum. "I think we better check the southwest gate to the Grimble land. It sagged last year, and the elk may have caused more havoc."

"Good thinking, Jed." Chase nodded his approval, especially pleased to see Jed's face clear and as bright as the morning sun. "Nate, always great to see you." Chase extended his right hand to the young man.

"My dad said he would be here," Nate replied, "so I made time to saddle up Santiago. Great day to ride fence. Hey, your hair gets any longer you'll have a ponytail like my horse."

Chase ignored the jibe and said, "I'd love to ride along." He rubbed his butt and laughed. "But I need something for the pain after any saddle time." Memories of the persistent ache after his last ride were still fresh.

Nate turned to saddle the horse and Jed grabbed the ladder to carry it back to the work shed. Before either could get too far, Chase said, "Hey, Nate, Jed, wait a second. While you both are here, I've someone for you to watch for."

"Whatcha got?" Jed asked. He rubbed his face with his fist, and his eyes narrowed as he spat.

"I want you guys to be on the lookout for a middle-aged man about six feet tall, dark hair, maybe graying," he said. "Not much to go on except he has this unmistakable habit of touching his eye and grunting while talking. Even more curious, he tends to take a hop when he walks. Keep me posted and document any fishermen or tourists wandering onto the ranch that I didn't clear. But don't confront this guy."

"Not a problem," Nate said, laughing. "Easter bunnies stick out in Montana."

Chase had watched Nate grow up to be a son he'd have given his eye teeth for. He was taller than Jed, who stood six feet on tiptoes. Nate was also more handsome and more aggressive. Rugged, with a jutting jaw, he kept his beard groomed to the fashionable five-day scruff. Long-legged, he looked as natural on a horse as Clint Eastwood. Chase had watched Jed school Nate in the forgotten ways of the West as urbanity encroached upon timeworn values of loyalty, humility, and hard work.

As the young man walked away, Jed said, "You know, Chase, I sometimes wonder if Nate got kicked in the noggin too many times when he lived the life of a modern-day drifter, uncorkin' those broncs by day and chasing honky-tonk angels at night."

Chase placed a hand on his trusted friend's shoulder and watched Nate swing into the saddle. "A penny for your real feelings, partner?"

Jed took a breath, his hands coming to rest, prayer-like, on a fence rail. "When Nate was in his twenties, his head was full of numbers that didn't add up. You know, I wet my whistle and take a nip now and then." Jed paused and spat out a worn wad of chew. He looked Chase in the eye. "I could've sworn that he'd got roostered enough to have tequila amnesia. These days he seems to have come around, though. He tells me he wants to find somebody and settle down."

Chase noticed the shadow that came over Jed's face and said, "I wouldn't worry. It appears he has solved many of life's equations." Chase gently stroked Jed's neck and shoulders, as only old friends do. He grinned then and continued. "You once told me there was a time Nate was drawn to one-night internal rub-down sessions and never wanted to leave that damned old rodeo life."

Jed wiped a drop of sweat off his forehead with the edge of his fist. "I hope you're right, boss."

. . .

By the time everyone had left for the day, Chase felt more exhausted than usual. He hadn't dealt with so many people at once for a long time. He got undressed and cast a glance at the urn. Then he fixated on the last photo of him and JoAnn, the one she'd wanted taken before she lost her hair to chemo. His wife had accepted what fate delivered to her with patient resignation. It brought her contentment, which was good, but her expression in the photo looked like she was forcing herself to appear normal and happy. She couldn't hide the depth of sadness in her face, knowing there would be few tomorrows.

Nighttime was the loneliest part of his day, and Chase dreaded going to sleep in his king bed, the one his missing queen had shared.

Chapter 10

Two days later, Chase received a short, cordial reply from Tekla. *Any Sunday after 6 p.m. is a good time to call*, she'd written. He had advanced another step on the road to finding a travel companion.

Sunday arrived, and he got in his workout first thing. *Beep!* His cell phone app warned him his hearing aid batteries were at half-strength. Now where had he put his pack of fresh ones? He found his office supply depleted and walked outside for the spare packs in his truck. The new wireless technology sucked battery power, and the last thing he wanted was to be in the middle of a conversation with Tekla and hear the *beep beep beep* of a dying battery.

The antique grandfather's clock in the hallway chimed as the hands lined up on twelve and six. He would've preferred to make the call from the deck, but the sound quality would be better in his office. Maybe it was nerves, or maybe it was his enlarged (but benign) prostate, but he made one last stop in the bathroom as a precaution.

She answered on the third ring. "Hello, this is Tekla."

A lump rose in his throat. She sounded young and out of breath.

"Hello, Tekla. Chase DeMers here. How are you today?"

"I'm fine," she said. "I just finished my run. It's Tekla, with a long *e*, like honey*bee*. It's my Polish great-grandmother's name, which means 'God's glory.'"

Her words came out in a rush, as if she'd not stopped running. He wondered if she was trying to impress him with her knowledge. Pushing his chair back from the desk, he propped up his feet, relieved that the introductions were over. He liked information, the more factual the better. With his digitally processed hearing, he would describe Tekla's voice as smooth and confident, just what he was hoping for.

"Very good information. Your Uncle Sean thought we should talk about a trip I'm planning. I see you've been to the Middle East. Ever been out West?"

"One time to attend Army language school in California." She paused and then asked, "Are there any real cowboys left in Montana? Do you have any horses?"

"Good questions, Tekla. There are a few cowboys. And some who just found the hat. No, I don't have horses, but I've access to them." He continued in his polished lawyerly manner. "Let's move on. I'd like to ask a little about how travel goes for you."

"Sure." Her voice brimmed with self-confidence. "I had a smooth trip visiting my sister in Peru last year. She works for the Peace Corps. I get a little uneasy in large crowds. For food, I eat mostly organic and sustainably grown. I keep carbs to a minimum, but sometimes I cheat a bit.

"So no real challenges?" He sensed she was framing her answers.

"No," she said. "No big challenges. People miss so much when they are in a hurry, so I like to set my own pace while walking and spend time with myself."

There was an awkward pause as he processed her response. Walking slower to observe more was a minor concern, but the question about large crowds needed clarification.

"Paris never has small crowds. What brings on your anxiety in large crowds?" he asked with the steady calm of his questioning voice.

"In the Army, I was stationed at or spent time in cities in the middle of conflict, like Baghdad or Kabul." She sniffed loudly. "War was all around me. My training left me living life like . . ." She hesitated. "Like I was on a twenty-four-hour neighborhood watch program. We were taught to heighten awareness of our surroundings. Large crowds, bright lights, and loud noises required hypervigilance and triggered the need to be on guard. It was exhausting." She sighed. "I knew I could be killed at any time. Army training didn't disappear when I retired."

Chase had a sense that her answer was so well-timed and aptly delivered that it might have been rehearsed.

"Understandable. Ah. Excuse me for a minute; just stay on the line, please." Chase growled after streaming was lost in one hearing aid. It happened randomly during phone calls. His audiologist told him streaming could be interrupted despite having the best instruments. He took time to reboot the unit and compose himself.

"Sorry for the interruption. On this trip, I could use a little support at times because of age-related conditions. My low vision and poor hearing are small hurdles. Can you relate?"

"Absolutely. You have low vision. I have 20/15. Uncle Sean mentioned hearing aid batteries run away from you."

"Well, that's true," he said with a chuckle. It was a fact of life. "May I ask what else he briefed you on?"

"Not much, except that you've been a widower for a year and now want to take some kind of farewell tour."

"Why would you consider taking this trip?" Chase asked. He frowned, realizing he should have taken time to rethink what he'd just said. The heady combination of her vibrancy and youth was intoxicating. "I've a few gray hairs on you, and we'd be working from my itinerary. Finding a suitable travel partner has worn me out."

"My uncle told me not to be fooled by your age, and he explained your history together. I believe I can help you."

"Here's the deal." Chase paused, unsure if he should commit further to Tekla. "Maybe ten to twelve days in Europe. Expenses paid. Separate rooms. I've an itinerary in mind that includes scattering my late wife's ashes in the Swiss Alps. If you're interested, I suggest you visit me here in Montana so we can meet in person. We can review the itinerary then."

Chase needed the timeworn Montana gold standard of a traditional face-to-face meeting with Tekla. Emails couldn't reveal her nature, personality, or behavior when around him. Watching her face could provide him with instant feedback. Then he'd know if he should choose her or continue searching.

"It sounds like you need a chief of staff, but there is no staff, right?" she said. "I'm comfortable with the needs of seniors, so I don't see a problem accompanying you on your travels."

He harrumphed. "I recall being a *senior* in college, Tekla, and I didn't need any help. But your concern is well taken."

"I won't thumb wrestle you over that. I got your message," she said by way of apology.

"Good, we're on the same page then. Any questions?"

"None right now. Thank you."

"I'll have Dawn, my travel agent, contact you about reservations for the trip to Montana. Pick any date that works for you. I've a guest house here at the ranch that you are welcome to stay in." His spirit soared after months of empty leads.

"Great! I want to extend my stay in Montana and drive through Yellowstone Park. I would love to try Montana beef while I'm there."

"The thought of Montana grass-fed beef makes my mouth water," he said. "Great choice! It's the beginning of tourist season in Yellowstone, when the invasion of wingnuts who want to feed the bears and bathe in the acidic, body-dissolving hot springs arrive."

"Not a problem, sir," she answered in a that's-a-fact voice. "I've handled tougher situations than wingnut tourists."

They said their goodbyes, and Chase hung up. He rode a dizzying physical high from the rejuvenation of spirit he'd received from the young woman's voice. Tekla had promise as a travel companion.

Day-tripping to Yellowstone or riding a horse were everyday adventures for anyone living in the West, but the prospect of a rare ribeye captured his attention after a year of makeshift dinners from a box.

After making a note to contact Dawn to set up Tekla's travel arrangements, Chase grabbed his fly rod and fishing vest for the evening hatch. The pain in his arthritic back had mysteriously disappeared. For the first time in three years, he experienced a lightness in his step.

Chapter 11

On the Saturday Tekla was to arrive, Chase worked out early, loaded charcoal into his egg-shaped ceramic grill, and seasoned the certified Angus ribeyes. He had the basic techniques of a chef, especially when it came to knife skills, but mishaps occurred. When the lid came off the bottle of granulated garlic, turning his intended smidge into a pour coating on one steak, he growled a "Good gravy!" that bounced off the kitchen walls.

From his somewhat depleted wine cellar, he retrieved a bottle of 1995 Chateau Mouton Rothschild, a bottle he'd been saving for JoAnn's seventieth birthday. She'd been too sick to drink it when the event arrived. It would serve as a great Bordeaux to go with the steak, or it would become a good vinegar. Go big or go home, he'd concluded.

After a cold shower and a close shave, he explored the closet April had organized for him over his protestations. He pulled his favorite white shirt from the hanger, a Wyatt Earp-styled Henley. Forgoing his custom orthotic walking shoes, he struggled to get his feet into his favorite pair of boots. He hoped he could make it to bedtime before they cramped his circulation and numbed his toes.

The sun had passed its zenith when he retreated to his rocker, sank into its seat, and groaned from the combination of pain and relief. He lost himself in memories of JoAnn rocking beside him. Some memories just wouldn't die, and he was comforted by those that stayed.

Laughing to himself, he realized that he had his shit together. He hadn't felt that way for far too long. Per her text, Tekla would be arriving in less than two hours, and his thoughts were waltzing on air.

Chase had barely set a good rhythm to his rocking when he saw a cloud of dust rising in the distance. He bolted upright in his rocker and rubbed his eyes.

What the . . . ? No. No! He'd not logged even five minutes of rocking time, and the intrusion was a gross violation of his widowed rights.

Daisy Grimble's battered white luxury sedan appeared through the rising dust, her late husband's hideous Texas-longhorns hood ornament clearing the way. Chase wished transplanted Texans would stay in Texas. They ticked him off. Clayton and Daisy were at the top of his list.

Clayton had boasted that Texas had been a republic before gaining statehood and was treated like a pair of cheap earrings by Mexico, which didn't recognize its sovereignty. That viewpoint explained the Texan mindset and the toughness that Chase admired. What irked him was that Clayton claimed he loved Montana but talked incessantly about Texas, his mama's vittles, and his daddy's old truck.

"Montana is what Texas used to be," Clayton would say. He once swiped at the air with his tall Stetson in an attempt to raise Chase's ire. His blood boiled and his lips set to twitching that day, but Clayton was all hat and no cattle.

Chase had always countered Clayton's jabs by saying, "Montana is what it always was." He'd make a fist and punch the air before making his ultimate point: "Montana is the Last Best Place."

. . .

"Afternoon, Chase," Daisy called out in her shrillest voice. "I was thinking of you today at the church's bake sale."

"Why, Daisy? I'm not a bake-sale kind of guy, you know." His tone was neither harsh nor kindhearted.

Chase had listened with a tin ear for years when JoAnn told him Daisy was so smitten by his looks, charm, and humanitarian work that she figured the woman had daydreams about doing night things with her husband.

Unfazed by his response, Daisy continued. "Well, I remember you mentioned you didn't like sweets, but I bought a tart rhubarb pie made by Jenny Watkins." She balanced the pie in one hand and swiped away a fly with the other. "You know Jenny wins all the blue ribbons at the fair for her pies, don't you? I thought you might like it, and it's my way of saying thanks for having Jed and Nate fix that swinging gate." Never satisfied with minding her own business, she put her nose in the air and said, "Oh, I smell smoke. Is something burning?"

"It's just lump charcoal in the grill. Mesquite."

"Oh, are you grilling? Why are you so gussied up? I was hoping that maybe we could cut a slice of pie and talk some about your global roaming with JoAnn." Daisy rolled out of the front car seat with the plastic-wrapped pie in her hands.

"Thanks for thinking about me, but I've a business meeting with a fly-in associate. Sorry. Maybe another time." He turned away to hide the grimace forming on his face and said, "Daisy, I gotta run. Have to adjust my grill vents."

Her voice reverted to a deeper Texas twang. "I reckon I'll be moseying along then. Almost forgot. Lexi says hi. Some kind of legal question she needed help on. Maybe next time you're in town you can stop by and see her. Keep the pie. We can chat another time."

"Yeah." He turned back out of courtesy. "Maybe another time. Thanks for the pie." His reply came out colder than he'd intended, about a notch away from sounding like a complete asshole. He regretted that.

He waited until Daisy's horned vehicle moved out of sight before he carried the pie into his kitchen. Daisy had fractured his meditative trance, and he found it hard to return to memories of life with his wife. His twenty-year-old Western boots were cramping his feet and had already started numbing his toes.

Chapter 12

Time slowed to a crawl as Chase awaited Tekla's arrival. The temperature on his grill stayed at a good idle, and he returned to his rocker. As soon as he got settled, dust again rose in his driveway. This time it was a black SUV. All new cars appeared the same to him, but he knew it had to be Tekla, fifteen minutes ahead of schedule.

It was time to call the meeting to order. He struggled with a knife-like back spasm while getting up from the rocker but squared his appearance and pulled both pant legs level.

The black Highlander rolled to a stop, the driver courteous enough not to kick up as much dust as Daisy had. Chase sucked in a hearty breath.

Using the manners his mother had drummed into him from birth, Chase walked down the deck steps to open the car door for his guest, but she beat him to the punch.

Chase called out as he approached the open door. "Tekla?"

"Yes . . . Chase?" she answered. There was a husky softness in her voice. She shook her head to loosen her hair, revealing a faint, jagged scar along her forehead that disturbed the portrait of her face. "Kick-ass ranch you have here. Now I understand the meaning of Big Sky Country. I rode with the windows open and smelled all the blooming grasses and flowers. Wow!"

"Yes, yes. Welcome to Montana. What you just experienced is what I call a prairie high."

She appeared exactly as the pictures she'd sent portrayed her. Her auburn hair hung loose and free just below her shoulders. Her face, bold and distinguished as well as pretty, was offset by her striking lips. She looked so bright. But her conflicted brown eyes hinted at a tale of emotional upheaval and physical pain lodged deep in her soul.

Chase reached for her hand, and she swung her left foot out of the car. That movement caused her black slacks to rise on her right leg. He froze. Her pant leg had risen just high enough to expose a prosthetic leg.

Tekla was an amputee.

His heart skipped a beat. He pulled on one ear and then the other as if to balance the shock. Tekla hadn't mentioned that she had a prosthetic leg. His mouth opened, but no words came out. He didn't flinch or stare. He managed to maintain the you're-lucky-when-you-live-in-the-West smile with which he had greeted hundreds of visitors to his ranch.

The revelation that Tekla was an amputee reinforced the difficulty he had understanding the younger generation. Was that what was happening here? He'd lived long enough to emerge into a new age, an age where people put the "able" back into "disabled" and thought of themselves as possessing special abilities.

Gone were the memories of war veterans with wooden legs who had limited movement and were prohibited from placing full weight on their prostheses. Each new conflict in the world had created its new crop of hero-amputees, along with cutting-edge technology to replace lost limbs.

She'd said she traveled to Peru with no difficulties, and Chase, to JoAnn's vexation, always tended to believe in a person until they showed him otherwise. Tekla and her Uncle Sean did not consider her prosthetic leg a disqualifier, so neither would he. Still, her choice not to put all the cards on the table about her injury annoyed him.

She pulled something from her clutch and palmed it. "I would like a few minutes to freshen up and get off my feet. You know that grungy feeling," she said. An edge of weariness crept into her voice. "Airports can wear you down."

He wondered if she had expected him to be frail, with a thinning crop of white hair.

"Yes, I know the feeling," he replied. "The guest house is that first building on the right."

"Thanks. I can handle it from here. I'll be back in half an hour."

"Perfect." A half-hour should be more than enough time for him to get those damned boots off.

Did her leg hurt as much from a day of navigating airports as his feet did in those old boots? He hadn't noticed any signs of distress, other than a trace of weariness. He had no knowledge of amputees or prosthetics, but he would Google it later. He had time to text Nate and alert him that his partner for tomorrow's horseback ride would be an Army veteran with a prosthetic leg.

. . .

"Would you like the specialty of the house, a DeMers special?" Chase asked. He held a chilled Collins glass in his hand.

"That sounds exciting. What's in it?"

"Sorry, but that's a family secret." He winked.

"Thanks, but I'd better stick with the iced tea."

"Shall we take our drinks to the living room? I'm afraid the late afternoon spring sun is beginning to cloud over, and the smell of rain is in the air."

As he gazed out the large picture window, a soft sideways rain fell from the north. They took seats on opposite ends of his leather couch but were close enough to share the warm glow of the elk-antler chandelier overhead.

"Can I get you something to snack on after a day of pretzels?"

"I did eat pretzels. On both flights." She accompanied her response with a megawatt smile and a twist of her head that flicked her hair to one side.

"I turned the grill up, and I've opened what I hope to be an exquisite bottle of well-aged Bordeaux."

Tekla put her hands to her face in a gesture of surprise. "I'm so sorry, but I'm allergic to the histamines in red wine."

He held his tongue, torqued that she hadn't alerted him to any food allergies. He never drank alone, but this bottle would be history before the night ended.

After years of facing juries, he'd developed a poker face. He put it to good use, waving off his disappointment as he quickly composed his opening statement. "Why don't I tell you a little about my Montana roots?" He pointed to a wall of heirloom photographs and tintypes dating back to 1895.

"I'd love to hear it." She put her hands on her thighs and leaned forward into a comfortable listening position as her eyes darted to individual photos.

Trying for a good stretch to relax his aching back, Chase clasped his hands behind his head and leaned against the couch. He was proud of his family's heritage, so he spoke from his heart.

"Let's start with my surname, DeMers. It's French and translates to English as 'from the sea.'" Pointing to a photo, he said, "My great-grandfather left Nova Scotia at the end of the 1800s and opened a saloon north of Butte. It nestled along the base of the Absaroka Mountains near what is now the small town of Boulder."

"Mm-hmm," she said, nodding. "Your ancestors had a sea history before they moved to the prairies and forests of Montana and opened a saloon?" As she talked, her expressions ranged from a puzzled grimace to a gleaming grin.

"I wonder about that myself at times," he said. "My grandfather was born in 1900. After returning home from World War I, he continued to manage the saloon. Everything changed one day when a stranger, who was a boxing scout, walked into the bar and saw my grandfather duking it out with a belligerent drunk."

Chase had inherited his grandfather's large hands, attached to wrists as thick as fence posts. He raised them for Tekla to see.

"The college scout told him he would train with accomplished sparring partners and get all the contact he wanted if he went to the University of Montana." Chase stopped, releasing the belly laugh that ran through generations of the DeMers family. "He didn't know the difference between a boxing glove and a horse apple. It seems my grandfather hadn't gotten enough physical contact in the war, so he took the offer. He wound up winning the M Club's best-boxer award his senior year."

Chase noticed when Tekla covered her mouth for a small cough and attempted to stifle a yawn. "I think that's a good place to stop, don't you?

Let's eat," he said. He stood and waited for her before moving to the dining room.

"Caesar salad," she said, nodding. She licked her lips, and her eyes grew wide as she gazed at the fresh romaine.

"Local farmer's market. And organic," Chase said with a smile.

Tekla sat in the chair closest to Chase and went to work on her salad.

Chase sipped his second glass of wine, his face relaxing as he breathed in the floral notes in the glass. He caught whiffs of prairie grass from the steak, subdued by his heavy-handed application of garlic. Relief that Tekla was not a vegan washed over him.

"Chase, any chance to ride a horse this trip?" She wiped a smudge of salad dressing off her lips with a white cloth napkin.

Chase developed a coughing fit but recovered quickly. Within five minutes, his long-awaited dinner conversation had him feeling he was having a meal with a jackrabbit. Histamines. Horseback rides. He was glad the wine had settled him.

"Yes. Yes." He paused for effect. "I've arranged a ride for you. You'll go out with Nate, a local friend I call on to take clients on rides. It's short notice, but he's a cowboy and loves his horses."

She dropped her fork in surprise.

"So," Chase said, "am I correct that California was your sole Western experience?"

"I have a hard time counting Army language school as a Western experience," she said. "But I grew up with friends who had horses."

Chase had always been a two-glass man, and he groaned inwardly at his old mental calculus of staying within that limit. He weighed the risks of getting tipsy, but the magnificent wine won over wisdom. He poured a third and raised his glass to an invisible JoAnn. Woozy with wine, the disjointed dinner dialogue, and the unknowns of her prosthetic leg, his mind descended to what was becoming all too familiar to him: a scattered state of confusion.

"Oh, Chase," she said. "I see you spilled wine on that awesome shirt. Change it, and I'll work on the wine stain. Where do you keep your hydrogen peroxide and dish detergent?" She headed to the kitchen, where her hands went into overdrive, opening and closing the cabinet doors.

"Peroxide is in the bathroom," he replied. Embarrassed and feeling every one of his seventy-two years compounded by three glasses of wine, he managed a nonchalant smile and excused himself from the table.

His walk to the bedroom was that of a punch-drunk boxer, his feet wobbling and body swaying. When he emerged, he saw that she'd gathered the dirty plates for the dishwasher and removed the plastic wrap from the pie. "Would you like me to warm up the pie while you sit?" she asked.

"Yes, that will be fine. The grill should be warm enough. No need to turn on the oven."

His mind cleared as a sobering thought came to him, overcoming the triple dosing of the Mouton Rothschild. He realized he would stop searching. There would be no perfect choice. His other interviews hadn't panned out, but in the short time Tekla had been at the ranch, he'd realized his intuition was spot on. She wasn't the most perfect person to take with him, but she was the right one to ask.

Chapter 13

Chase finished dozing in the morning sun and resumed his rocking. Sipping from his favorite canned beverage, eyes throbbing, he realized he should have downed more water after all the wine. His mouth felt like it was stuffed with cotton balls, and his head hung low, thumping like a boxer's in round fifteen. He heard Tekla call out as she neared the deck.

"Let me fix breakfast," she said. "You look a little hungover." With a chuckle, she pulled her hair into a ponytail and went to wash her hands.

Chase couldn't remember the last time someone made breakfast for him. Though it sounded appealing, he was apprehensive about letting a relative stranger root through his cupboards.

"I'll set the table," he said, "and get the pans out for you."

It seemed important to prevent Tekla from disturbing the private world of JoAnn's orderliness. The knives, forks, spoons, and kitchen towels (always folded lengthwise first) remained just as they were when his wife was there.

"There's a honeydew melon in the fridge," he said, "and fresh morel mushrooms that I picked yesterday. You'll find a loaf of sourdough in the pantry."

"Get ready for Tekla's grand-slam breakfast," she said in reply.

Chase covered his ears with his hands and rolled his throbbing head. "That sounds like I'm at Denny's." He filled a glass with water and downed it. "Talking about your prosthesis would be a good place to start the interview for my mission."

"Could we maybe use the word *adventure* instead of *mission*?" she asked.

Chase noticed the forlorn look of a woman soldier who had gone through hell. "So advised," he replied. He nodded slightly and stroked his unshaved chin as if he was back in the courtroom getting instructions from a judge and stood corrected.

. . .

Chase dragged the two rocking chairs to face the morning sun. The heat had started to dry the fresh, dewy smells of the grass and trees around his home. His blissful musing came to an abrupt halt when he heard the screen door slam as Tekla exited the kitchen. He offered her a seat.

"We began yesterday with my family history. Let's say turnabout is fair play. Tell me about you. That's why I invited you here."

A low-flying Forest Service aerial tanker passed overhead on its way to a fire he heard was near Yellowstone. He tracked the plane until it was clean out of sight and then looked at Tekla, waiting for her to begin.

She held closed fists in front of her. "I see my life as two separate parts. There was before the military and after. Which would you like to hear first?"

"Tell me about your military career. I'm more interested in the young woman sitting next to me than the little girl on a bicycle."

"That's logical. Were you in the military?"

"No. Afraid not. I missed the draft by a year. Can't say I craved a senior field trip to Vietnam. What a waste of lives."

"I enlisted for what I believed was a noble cause," she said. "I wanted to use my language skills to help our country, but now it's hard to believe I made a difference."

"You may see that differently in the years ahead."

She took a deep breath and clenched her fists, one over her heart.

"My father fought in Vietnam and retired as a lieutenant colonel. I wanted to carry on a family tradition, damn it."

He was negligent in not having a basic understanding or working knowledge of the military, but he knew it had a rising influence in the world. She explained the lack of sensitivity in the military. Some recruits rejected the warrior mentality, considering it foolish. They believed being trained to run toward bullets and bombs rather than away from them bordered on stupidity.

He took a moment to reflect before replying. "There are many ways people can serve their country besides wearing a uniform."

She gave a thumbs up and said, "You bet. My sister joined the Peace Corps. I was recruited in college for my language skills and received a large signing bonus if I reported thirty days after graduation. That paid my student loans."

Chase hesitated, uncertain how to respond. Money was never an issue in his life. There was little he couldn't afford, and Tekla's pay incentive didn't seem like a lot of money. However, money could never buy the camaraderie of a "band of brothers," which was something he could've used right about then. Most days, but not all, he succumbed to the hollow ache of loneliness. His life had fallen to pieces without JoAnn. All the millions in his portfolio could not fill the void left by his wife's death.

In the end, Chase asked, "Did you make your father proud?"

"Yes, but since leaving Vietnam, he's spent his life never feeling clean, even after a shower."

"How so?"

"He believes he has never washed off all the Agent Orange."

Chase crossed his arms and got lost in his head, trying to remember how he missed the draft, thankful then for his college deferment. He'd been a fortunate son who was able to enjoy a rich college experience and surf Malibu, while men like Tekla's father paid for their service every day of their lives, never feeling clean.

He shook his head to clear it. Her last statement had ushered in disturbing images of war, borrowed from scenes he'd viewed from the safety of a television screen.

She reached down and picked a flower from a pot and rubbed it between her fingers. She put her nose to it to smell the fragrance and smiled. "Hand-to-hand combat and handling weapons were different from kicking soccer balls." She put the flower behind one ear, and her face brightened.

"You strike me as being tough enough," Chase said. He offered her his best praising-his-student smile to show how impressed he was. "I did a little boxing in my younger days." Striking a pose, he pounded his right fist into his left palm and then his left into the right.

"What do you mean by a little boxing?"

"Just enough to win a Golden Glove," he said with a laugh. He continued his boxing simulation, flicking a quick left jab into the air and bobbing his head as if to slip a punch. "How did you do?"

"I kicked some butt," she said while throwing a right jab toward Chase.

"And you were just one month removed from campus life?"

"Yes," she said, "and four years from reducing the number of land mines in Afghanistan by one."

She delivered her comment with the power of a Mike Tyson right uppercut. He gazed into the distant fields and fences, pondering the heartbreaking reality of a young woman who went to war and lost a leg.

"Hey," she said, "it appears we have company."

Dust gathered like a cloud rising off the road.

"Grab your hat. Nate's pulling up with the horses."

Chapter 14

Chase had honored Tekla's wish to ride a horse with a real cowboy. After he plopped his well-creased, turkey-feathered Stetson on her head, she gave a nervous shake of her hair. Butterflies took flight in her stomach. When a long-legged young man swung his legs out of the cab of his black pickup, the butterflies stopped flying, but her heart fluttered like the wings of the hummingbirds that flew around Chase's deck.

"Howdy, Chase," the young man said, tipping his Western hat.

"Nate, I'd like you to meet Tekla, a potential associate of mine from New York."

"Howdy, Tekla." Nate squared his shoulders and removed his hat. "I'm Nate. Chase told me you're ready to get Western. Ah-wright. I like that."

Chase said, "I've some office work, so excuse me. Have fun, Tekla." He headed for the ranch house.

Nate struck a cowboy pose, hitching both thumbs in his belt. He wore sunglasses, so Tekla couldn't tell if he was checking her out.

"Hi, Nate. Thanks for taking me," she said. "I've done some riding back home on my friend's farm, but this . . . ?"

Her face turned pale as she gestured toward the truck-and-trailer combo. "Geez. I'm a bit overwhelmed by all of this."

"I hear ya. You'll be fine."

Two horses pounded their hooves on the floor of the trailer. One let out a long whinny, and then both whinnied together. Nate jerked his thumb over his shoulder toward the trailer. "They're ready when you are."

"Ah . . . um . . . okay. Let's do it." She shuddered with barely suppressed fright when the horse trailer rocked a little from side to side.

"Let me unload them," he drawled. "The sun's broken through, and the trailer will heat up quick."

He led a chestnut-colored gelding to the hitching rail. The horse kicked backward with one leg. "This here's Santiago," he said. He grabbed the reins of his quarter horse and said, "Watch. I'll use a simple bank robber's knot to tie him to the rail. I'll take care of all that, so no need to remember it. You just enjoy yourself."

"Santiago." She pronounced the name with an unmistakably Spanish inflection.

He smiled and said, "Cortez had a dark chestnut stallion with a warrior spirit and plenty of speed. Some say he called the horse Santiago. It seemed a good fit for this guy when I bought him as a colt."

She rubbed the horse's flanks and gained confidence when his muscles quivered at her touch. "He sure is a handsome horse. All those muscles, and his coat shines."

"I condition it," he said, "like what you might do with your hair."

Watching a true cowboy work with his horse impressed her, but she was mystified by the way he kept dragging a saddle blanket across Santiago's back.

"I've never seen anyone saddle a horse like you do. What's with those blanket maneuvers?"

"That's how I roll. I drag the blanket across his back to smooth all his hair in one direction. That way, when I put the saddle on, he doesn't have any potential hot spots that could irritate him. Not my first rodeo."

She backed away when he threw his Western saddle on Santiago's back and made sure the girth was cinched tight and secure. Santiago had tossed his head once and then stood stock still while Nate saddled him.

"You'll ride Cinder, my mother's horse. Hear her pawing the trailer floor? She's anxious to get going."

He unloaded a frisky, well-groomed blue roan. "She'll calm down in a minute. Just a little rambunctious right out of the trailer."

"She is such a pretty horse with that black mane and tail." Tekla's voice dropped to a confessional tone. "I've never ridden on a Western saddle. Just English ones."

Nate dismissed the mention of an English saddle with a wave of his hand. "Western is better. The larger saddle will give you a more secure seat, and it has a horn. You'll never want to ride English again."

"Never rode a quarter horse either. Only Tennessee Walkers."

Tipping his hat higher, he looked her in the eye. "You're in Montana now. Santiago and Cinder go at a slower gait than what you're used to. Quarter horses may not be as flashy, and they don't have that funky four-beat walk about them, but you won't be bounced around in the saddle. I wouldn't put you on Cinder if she'd give you trouble. I don't keep any horses that do."

He wiped beads of perspiration from his forehead. When a horsefly landed on his knuckles, he used his other hand to smack it dead with lightning speed.

Santiago and Cinder flicked their ears and pawed the ground. Tekla assumed they were both restless to get going.

Nate turned back to the trailer to get Cinder's saddle and blanket. Tekla watched him walk away, taking in his rugged cowboy style. Faded straight-legged jeans with a wide leather belt and well-broken-in boots, topped off with a Stetson straw hat, suited him. He wore the cowboy mantle well, and her mind drifted to cozy possibilities.

When her cell phone rang, she jumped as her daydream disappeared, along with her relaxed state of mind. She let it ring three times before she walked away, out of earshot, to answer.

She had little control over the anger that rose within her. Her brown eyebrows turned up in rage like question marks, and her face reddened. A tiny quiver appeared at the base of her throat, and she walked a few paces farther for privacy and to gain self-control.

In a voice loud enough to make the horses' ears flick, she said, "I'm through talking about it, Eric! Stay in your own fucking lane and out of mine. You got it? No. No second chance, you creep. Get some help."

She slid the phone into her vest pocket and turned back to Nate with an I-just-won-the-lotto smile on her face. "I'm sorry," she said. "We were ready to saddle Cinder, yes?"

"No worries. Come over to Cinder from this side and rub her so she can get to know you."

"Like this?" She stroked Cinder's neck in a rhythmic back-and-forth motion. Cinder stomped her foot and nuzzled her head along Tekla's shoulder.

Nate nodded. "One last thing. Before we mount up, I need you to give up Chase's hat for this."

"A freaking helmet? Come on, Nate."

"Don't feel like the Lone Ranger," he said as he switched his own Western headwear for a helmet. "Chase's ranch rules for visitors. Not my rule. I've spare liners in the truck if you need a better fit. Buckle up."

"It fits fine," she replied. "I know how a helmet should fit. If you could just give me a boost, I'm ready to get Western. Is that proper cowboy lingo?"

"Not so fast, greenhorn. I don't know who taught you to mount a horse back East, but I'm going to show you the Montana way, which is how I want you to do it. Savvy?"

"You're the professional. I'm what, a greenhorn? Speak English."

"That's a good answer. Mind if I ask you a personal question before we mount up?"

Tekla stood straighter at Cinder's side and answered with a passable John Wayne imitation. "Speak your mind, cowboy."

Nate hesitated and cleared his throat. "I've never been around . . . well . . . a . . . a . . . person with an artificial limb. Will it hurt to ride?"

"Nate," she said, "it's very kind of you to ask. No, it won't hurt to ride. The truth is that I live in a constant state of discomfort. Imagine yourself wearing a pair of extra-small briefs all day. Savvy?"

He gulped long and hard at the thought. "Oh," he said with a slight shudder. "Not good. We can walk the horses down to Chase's picnic table if you need a step up, or I can give you a boost up right here. Your pick."

"A boost." She did not hesitate.

"I want you to hold on tight when you are in the saddle," he said.

Remember that if you're in discomfort and mount Cinder wrong, it can be painful for her."

"Got it."

"When I boost you up, keep the reins loose so Cinder can rebalance her body. Tight reins restrict her ability to balance. Come a little closer to her body."

"Close enough?"

"Yeah. I'll take hold of your ankle and knee. You grab the reins and a hunk of her mane with your left hand. Hold the pommel with your right hand. When you spring up with the boost, swing your right leg over the saddle. Savvy?"

"Let's do it. I'm ready to savvy!"

He leaned down and ran his hand along her calf before getting a firm grip on her left ankle. All the training she'd done to develop a toned, muscular body made it easy to vault up with his help. She sat tall in the saddle.

"Good job. Let me check you out. Stirrups seem to be at the right length. Wait, one thing. Let your weight fall down into your heels in the stirrup. Like a bike pedal. More relaxing ride."

. . .

They rode in comfortable silence, and Tekla relaxed, free of any intense anxiety. The summer breeze dancing through the high grass blended with the snorting of two horses to lull her into a state of well-being she hadn't felt for a long time.

Without turning his head, Nate called back to her. "I hear Cinder munching grass. Don't let her graze while we ride. Keep her head up so you maintain control. She can graze when we stop for lunch over that ridge."

Topping the ridge, Tekla pulled Cinder's reins to gaze at the creek, which connected a series of long willow-choked bends, the leaves a robust mix of reds and golds. The afternoon sun applied a shiny polish to the surface of the water. A planetary moment of Zen embraced her.

"I want to stop here and take it all in. Let me snap this scene." She loosened her grip on the reins and shot a pano group of pictures. "I hope this is our lunch stop."

"This is it." He turned in his saddle. "Do you need help?"

She surveyed the uneven ground. "I think so, this being my first time on a Western saddle."

After Nate helped Tekla dismount, he said, "This is Chase's holy grail for fishing because the creek is over your head in some places. There are plenty of honey holes, so he can always catch fish. Move back." He took her hand and guided her out of the shadows. "Your shadow spooks the fish. See the glimmer off their bellies?"

"Oh, wow." She raised her hands to her face in amazement. "I wish my father could see this."

"Look where that flowing artesian spring kind of bubbles up and flows along that corner bend. See how the willows overhang? The water there is cold and deep."

Nate's outstretched hands opened like a priest reading from a sermon, and Tekla felt captivated by his knowledge of the land. His good looks didn't hurt either.

He continued. "Trout love to hang out and feed there. Bugs can drop off the willows, and other insects wind up in the swirling water. Take your first gander at a Montana blue-ribbon trout stream."

He tethered the horses to a downed cottonwood tree where they could graze. An insulated pouch from his saddle bag held two sandwich bags packed with double-decker sandwiches of ham and hot pepper cheese, stacked between day-old slices of thick-crusted sourdough bread. Another contained two fudge brownies. Two pints of iced tea completed the spread, which he arranged on a small plaid cloth.

Tekla was patting Cinder's forehead to chase the flies away when Nate shouted, "Chow time!"

"I'm coming." She gave a final pat and strode toward his chosen lunch spot. "Are there any snakes in the grass?"

"None that will bite you."

She'd taken three steps off the traveled path, intending to pick a clump of wild iris to decorate their lunch spread, when she heard the snap of a large twig under her boot.

"Ah, shit!" she yelled. She tripped and face-planted in the tall grass. The fall knocked the wind out of her.

He threw down his sandwich and ran to her.

"Tekla, are you okay?" He pulled the hair away from her face and saw that her eyes were watering.

"Ooh," she moaned. "I think so. I've learned how to fall. Lately, I seem to run into trouble when I walk off the beaten path."

She reached for his hand, and he eased her into a sitting position. She signaled with a tilt of her head that she wanted help to stand. While she recovered, Nate held her hand, and they stood together by the creek's sparkling water.

• • •

While chomping on his sandwich, Nate tossed small breadcrumbs out to the center ring of a new rise from one trout. The big brown snatched the bait, his mouth making a dimple in the water as the bread disappeared.

"Does Chase allow you to feed his fish?" She tossed a few crumbs of her own into the swirling pool. "Have you ever wet a fly of your own here?"

"Oh, yeah, more than once. When I was a kid, Chase sent me here to report back on the fishing conditions." He paused to toss another crumb. "Does your father fish?"

"He taught me to fish at the pond at the county fairgrounds. I fished at the county fair each summer. Does that count? Did you know that Seneca Falls is the home of the *It's a Wonderful Life Museum?*"

"I'll put that on my bucket list," he said. "The best thing my mother and father ever did for me was to have me in Montana. Five years in California was enough for me. How do you like our state so far?"

"I've seen more of Chase than Montana."

"Then how do you like Chase? He told me you were a business client, but you're not like any of the other clients I've taken out."

She shrugged. "What makes you say that?"

"You're not the typical middle-aged, cigar-chomping, grumpy, over-weight venture capitalist from back East."

"Nope," she said. "You're right about that." She pretended to hold a stogie between her fingers. "Do you have a light?"

"You're funnier too. I've been wondering why you don't have a New York accent."

"Army language school cured me of that. Just for you: Can I drink the wah-ter from the rivva?"

He rolled onto his back and howled so hard he kick-started a coughing jag that lasted a minute.

"Wait," she said. "How about this one? If you'd visited me in college, I would've talked like this: 'Let my sistah pahk da cahr.'"

They leaned into each other and laughed like old friends.

"So you had this gift of language and wanted to interpret for the military?"

"Masz to."

"Come on. Give me a break. That's gobbledygook to me."

"That's Polish," she said, smiling. "Means you got it. Polish was the first language I learned from my grandmother. Then came four years of French in high school. Languages came easy for me." She snapped her fingers. "When I entered college, there was a patriotic spike of people learning Arabic that continued after the World Trade Center attacks."

"That's impressive. You do have a way with words. So where'd that lead you?"

"Mostly to hell. Now I'm searching for more peaceful places. Like here. Now tell me about you and your Montana life."

He paused and then laughed heartily, pantomiming riding a bucking bronc.

"Not a problem. Get comfortable in the grass, and I'll play you a song first." He unbuttoned the pearl snap on his vest pocket and pulled out a mini harmonica. Creating a spontaneous jam session for one, he wiped his lips and made it ring with the easiest song to learn: "Folsom Prison Blues."

She covered her mouth in astonishment. "Now I'm impressed! That's so small I would've guessed it was a toy."

"It's better than feeling like you're holed up in a jail cell." He threw his head back and began tapping his foot to set the beat.

He stumbled with the opening chords, but she filled in with the lyrics she knew, and hummed over the parts she didn't. She applauded his performance and asked, "Anything else on your playlist?"

"Sorry, but I'm a one-hit wonder and play by ear. People say any cowboy can carry a tune, but he has trouble unloading it." He gave the harmonica a shake, patted it against his palm, and wiped it clean with his silk bandana. "It makes me happy."

Tekla giggled. "I've heard that when cowboys tell a story, they always begin it with 'Shit, there I was.' Tell me one."

"Shit, there I was, a boy with his pony, dreaming about being a cowboy. Wait. I gotta stop for a second and get into character."

He tilted his head down and let his laughter run its course before digging his thumbs into his belt. He spat an imaginary wad of snoose juice.

Tekla said, "Cameras are rolling for the singing cowboy."

Nate cleared his throat and began his tale. "I rode my hoss to this here spot where we're sittin' and built a big far to keep warm. No fancy grub. Hardtack and bacon. Brought my bed roll to this here hideout of mine and slept 'neath the stars. High-class spread, I always reckoned. My ma and pa partnered with Chase 'n JoAnn fer a spell, and my pa always pondered about when this ranch ran cattle. Diamond Bar S was the brand, I reckon. Chase always held me ace-high and treated me as kin. He's one to ride the river with. Me, I ride fer the brand."

To signify the end, he let go another imaginary spit of chewing tobacco.

"That's so good! You got that spit down perfect." She imitated his technique. "You talk about Chase with such high regard. What's so special about him besides money?" She wanted to know more about the man she might accompany to Europe. "That's pretty impressive for him to consider you like kin." She pulled a blade of grass and ran it through her bottom teeth, a cowboy flossing. "My Uncle Sean said he's childless."

"We're both only children."

She noticed the melancholy air when he mentioned being an only child.

"I bonded with Chase when I was a kid. He always carried this aura of power. I knew I was in elite company when I was with him. He reminds me of a bronc that never bucked, but you knew he could break you."

"I guess that could've been hard on your dad at times."

"Maybe. My dad never said so. He preached I needed to broaden my perspective of the world beyond the Paradise Valley. Chase provided that."

"Wow. That's pretty evolved." She stopped and took a whiff of the air. She smiled and closed her eyes. She took another whiff. "What's that smell?"

"You're sitting on a clump of sweetgrass," he said. "It's sacred to indigenous people. They braid it to use as a smudge for happiness and harmony."

"I need to plant a yard full of it." The notion made her laugh. She pulled several blades and ran them under her nose. "I love the way nature is interwoven through Western indigenous cultures. And you dreamed of being a cowboy, something else woven into the West. How did that dream work out?"

Nate watched the creek and snickered.

"It wasn't long before my cowboy dreams led to weekend rodeos. Rodeos aren't just competition. They can be a painful way of life when you deal with broncs and bulls. It busted me up real good."

"So can the military," she said. Tekla stared at her prosthesis, knowing it would never transform back to the real leg she had on her last normal day.

Nate continued. "I went to Montana State University on a rodeo scholarship, but there weren't many cowboys who scored 735 in math on the SAT."

"Wow," she said. "I was happy with a 625."

"I see we were graced with different intellectual abilities. You have languages, and I can solve equations."

This revelation caused her to halt the lazy tossing of crumbs into the water and face him.

"Were you not recruited by big engineering schools?"

"Yeah, some. Montana State has fantastic engineering programs. I had no need to look anywhere else." He paused to flick a fly off his face. "But I wanted the life of a cowboy. I went to California and got a job breaking horses on a ranch outside Petaluma for five years. I did a little rodeoing on the side." He turned away to see why Santiago kept snorting. Seeing nothing alarming, he went on. "After a few years of gettin' busted up, I realized how much I missed Montana, quit the rodeo circuit, and came home." He brought his knees to his chest and vaulted to his feet.

"Now I teach high school math during the school year. In the summer, I do SAT prep. It's a better life." He pulled out his phone and checked the time. "We should mount up and head out. I told Chase I'd have you back by four."

The gentleman in Nate offered Tekla a hand up, but that time she declined.

"Thanks, but this greenhorn can handle it. I enjoyed our time." She rose on her own and said with a frown, "I'll ache in the morning. Will I see you again before I leave?"

He nodded and untied Cinder, handing the reins to Tekla. With a smooth boost, she was mounted and ready to ride.

"When we get back to the ranch," he said, "I'll groom and load the horses. You better check in with Chase. I gotta bounce to my parents' house for dinner, but I'll stop and say goodbye."

"Nate, if there is one word I should know about Chase, what would it be?"

He scratched his head and then turned in the saddle. "Butte."

"Butte?"

"Remember that. It will all be revealed to you." He pointed to the snowcapped peaks in the distance and said, "You may even shout it out from mountaintops as high as those."

"That's not fair," she said. "If you know something that would help me, I think you should share it instead of making him sound like a soap product to try. Butte doesn't tell me much."

"You're not from Montana. That's why." He thumped his chest. "Maybe it's just me, but I know Butte men are loyal to the core and true models of grit. They'll always have your back. They're also tough—tough in a way that's handed down to each generation."

She spread her hands open in supplication. "How did that come about?"

He shrugged and held it for a three count. "Could be from all the mining disasters and hard winters. They seem to possess a strand of DNA that twists between whupping your ass, Montana style, to buying a stranger a beer. They'd never kick you when you're down. All you need to know I just told you. Does that help?"

"Yes. You do know him well."

"Yep, I do," he said. "And as a bonus, you'll find out Chase tops them all with his weapons-grade charisma."

Chapter 15

Chase was in the kitchen fileting a large brown trout for dinner. He wrapped it in foil with lemon, garlic, and a pat of butter. Tekla interrupted his culinary magic when she waddled through the door with her back hunched. Her moans made him put down his knife and check her out.

"How was your ride? I see you've used muscles you never knew you had. Need something for the pain?"

Standing akimbo, she tried to straighten. "Thanks, but I carry my own. I haven't ridden in ten years, and now my back needs a chiropractor, acupuncture, and physical therapy."

He laughed so hard he needed a kitchen towel to wipe his eyes. "Horseback riding is not all that complicated," he said, "but people get sore, so Nate keeps those rides kind of short. Let me get you a cool glass of water."

"I'll get cleaned up first. I should be back in plenty of time to say goodbye to Nate."

She limped away and returned twenty minutes later with her back a little straighter and wearing a glad-I'm-out-of-the-saddle smile.

Not content to wait for what appeared to be a delayed dinner, she turned to the door. "Think I'll go say thanks to Nate before he walks up here."

Cinder had been loaded and was stomping the floor of the trailer. Santiago had planted his feet, refusing to move. Nate walked him in a slow loop around the truck. She guessed the change of scenery changed the horse's attitude, since all it took the next time around was a tap on Santiago's hind leg to keep him moving up the ramp.

"Nate," she called. "Dinner's late, so I told Chase I'd come out to say goodbye."

He said, "It looks like I got you good and lathered and sore from the saddle." He grabbed a broom and shovel from the trailer to clean up the horse droppings in Chase's driveway.

"Don't worry about me," she said. "I'm good. Thank you for a freaking outrageous Montana experience."

He rested his chin on the broom handle. "You're welcome to come again." Looking into the cloudless sky, he wiped sweat from his brow with a bandana. "It was a good time, but, um, I want to say I'm sorry."

She tipped her head to the side and stared at him. "Sorry for what? I'm still standing. You gave me a great horse."

"I think I called you a greenhorn, but you rode pretty well."

"No worries. I've been called worse than a greenhorn. You never went to basic training." She pointed to the time on her phone and showed it to Nate. "You better hurry, or you'll be late for dinner. Chase has my number. Send me a text and tell me how your summer's going." She intentionally prolonged her goodbye. Nate was the first person who had inspired her to release the openness and laughter she'd wrapped tight within her since Afghanistan.

He replied, "I think I can manage that."

Her heart sped up when he tipped his hat in true cowboy fashion. Tekla stood in the shade of the house and waved as he drove away. She felt her lower lip quiver as she held back tears of joy.

. . .

Chase sat in his rocker with his feet propped on the deck railing. The aroma of fish baking in the oven drifted out from the kitchen. He focused his vision on a distant peak, a peak beyond life itself. It was a very Montana thing to do.

"There's tea and a glass of ice on the table for you," he said when he heard Tekla approach.

He never moved his eyes from the view, which gave her the impression he'd become hypnotized by watching the mountains.

She breathed a deep sigh, hoping she was the answer to his prayer of finding a travel companion. Chase's life needed to be decluttered and refreshed.

. . .

It had taken so much of Chase's energy to reach the point of moving on with his life. Part of him was ready; part would never be. His gut told him that anyone who had battled back from Tekla's combat history was someone he could count on. She injected vitality into his days. It was what he needed most to overcome the dullness of life without his wife.

Was he acting in haste? He owned a disciplined mind and wondered if JoAnn would tell him to slow down and rethink Tekla as his choice. It took only a minute to come to a decision.

"I'm comfortable extending an invitation for you to accompany me to scatter JoAnn's ashes. Have you considered it further since we talked?" His fingers tapped out the time like a drum roll. "How about it?"

"Well, wait a minute," she said, a combination of surprise and wariness on her face. "I need more information. I would love to have the chance to help you fulfill JoAnn's last request, but everything has moved so fast."

He revealed his empathic and intuitive side by asking how he could help. Grief had overshadowed those qualities, and they needed to be awakened. "I'm sorry." He walked his offer back a step with his tone. "Didn't mean to rush you. I've this rooted fear that something will happen to keep me from fulfilling her wish."

"I get it," she said, "but remember when I told you that I travel well with good planning?" He didn't know what she required, like folding crutches. He wasn't aware of the special attention her stump required to keep from breaking down. Managing luggage was another concern, and she would require minor tweaks in her accommodations.

Chase watched her look out the window at the lingering dust kicked up from Nate's truck and trailer. Was she stalling? He couldn't tell.

Tekla hesitated a moment longer and then raised her pant leg. Her fingers hit the release button on her prosthesis, and she slowly removed the smooth black lisle stocking that covered her stump.

His mouth gaped open as he stared blankly at her.

"I invested years of serious physical training to achieve the level I've reached," she said. "My stump needs daily inspection for chafing or blisters."

He recovered his composure and said, "I'm asking you to go with me, and we will make whatever accommodations you need. I'll never mind what you tell me as long as you won't mind what I tell you. I've much to learn about amputees. But remember this," he said. "I had no heads-up about you being an amputee."

"You're right."

"I also have something to admit." He hesitated before saying, "I've not started any travel schedule. I'll have to email it to you later."

Silence fell over them as she reattached her prosthesis. She straightened her pant leg and swiped the hair that had fallen across her face when she bent over.

"Are we good?" he asked.

Tekla nodded. "Yes, we're good. We're not leaving tomorrow, so no problem."

The worry he'd felt lifted.

"Let's move on," she suggested. "Tell me about JoAnn. I don't have a very good picture of her in my mind, and I don't know any details about your younger days together."

Chase's demeanor transformed instantly. Profound joy replaced frustration, and his eyes lit up like headlights at the mention of her name. He uncrossed his legs, relaxed, and got ready to revive memories of his beloved JoAnn.

Chapter 16

"Telling you about JoAnn is important," he said. At the mention of her name, he rubbed his hands together briskly enough to start a fire. "Where should I begin?"

"How about where you met? Was she a Montana girl?"

"Just here," he said, placing his right hand over his heart as if he planned to recite the Pledge of Allegiance. "We met in the depravity and hipness of the sixties. I'd finished law school at the University of Montana and decided to celebrate by seeing some of the world." He spread his hands wide. "Classmates had told me Montana was ten years behind California, and the happening scene was at Malibu. Have you listened to any music by the Beach Boys?" He began snapping his fingers to a rhythm in his head.

"Good Vibrations?" she guessed.

"Yes, those guys." His face glowed like the California sun. "They made you feel that catching a wave was the ultimate experience. How could I not explore that feeling? I packed my Corvair and headed to Malibu. A few days later, shit. There I was, the guy with the most untanned body and shortest hair on the beach, not knowing the first thing about surfing."

He stood up and imitated a surfer's stance, his right foot back. "I never got the hang of getting up on the board. Surf and saltwater were new to me. I didn't catch a wave, but I did several nasty face plants in the sand."

"Sorry, but it's hard for me to picture you as a boxing lawyer from Butte trying to surf at Malibu. You *were* the happening scene!" They both broke into side-splitting laughter.

As joviality faded away, he closed his eyes and let out a low moan. His head sagged, nearly collapsing under the emotional weight of JoAnn's memory, but Tekla forced him back to the present by shaking his knee.

"Yes, we were," he said. "One morning I was sitting on the beach all dejected, and I was ambushed by a wave of love. A tanned, raven-haired girl in a black bikini stopped to talk." His moans echoed once more. "I could've sworn her brown eyes were bright enough to reach into infinity. My first impression was what a beautiful, exotic, and unattainable woman she was."

While he raved on and on about JoAnn's beauty, Tekla ran a finger from the corner of her eye to the bridge of her nose. He saw the distress on her face and realized he'd struck an emotion in her. Tekla's natural looks were stunning, and her demeanor boasted of hopefulness, but her heart outshone them both. He wanted to tell her that but not now. He decided to move on.

"I was out of place and out of time with that culture, but she was very kind to me. I hear JoAnn's first words to me still today. She said, 'I can tell you've never had any instructions on surfing. Grab your board, and I'll show you some tips on the beach first.'"

"So did you pay any attention to the board?" Tekla's voice had the ability to turn seductive without warning. "Or did you just stare at her bikini?"

"As a matter of fact, I believe it was the latter." He howled as if he'd just taken a blast of laughing gas. "After lessons in the sand, we paddled to the breakpoint, resting in the small currents. As we bobbed on the water, she said, 'Wait for an unbroken wave because they're easier to ride. It's like riding a bicycle. You need speed to keep moving and not fall over. The same goes for surfing.'

"I didn't know when an unbroken wave would come, so I waited for her to yell and let me know when one rolled in. It was somewhat mystical for me to catch a wave and become one with a force of nature.

"Yelling to be heard above the crash of the waves, she called out, 'When the wave comes, you have to paddle hard and fast so the wave launches you. Pop up with both feet at once.'

"Many waves rolled in before I heard her yell, 'This one!'

"I turned my board around, paddled like hell, and gulped a gallon of salt water. 'Faster!' she shouted.

"My arms felt like rubber, but I caught the wave and lifted my body to a crouching position. My hands waved in wild circles as I struggled to stay balanced. I stayed in a crouch, afraid to stand, but I made it to shore without wiping out. I stood like a conqueror on the beach waiting for JoAnn.

"'Nice ride,' she said. 'However, you're riding with your feet together. Scoot forward on the board and try to pop up quick. Have you ever seen the way a boxer stands in the ring? You need to stand like that, in an athletic stance. And stop waving at everybody on the beach.'"

Tekla cocked her head to one side, a wistful smile on her face. "That's hilarious, telling you to stand more like a boxer. A beautiful beginning to a romance. But she was attainable."

"Yes, she was." The words rolled off his tongue like they were on the edge of the surf. The catch-a-wave glow on his face faded. Rekindling memories of his days of dancing with the ocean had worn him out.

Chapter 17

The last full moon before Cowboy Christmas, known by Westerners as the Fourth of July, found Chase on his deck sipping a cold Big Hole lager. Merle Haggard streamed through his wireless ears, and his head swam with vexing details. The curled edges of a *National Geographic* map of Switzerland lay on the table among a collection of travel information, creating a giant origami puzzle in need of completion. He hoped to finish before it rained.

His persistent focus prevented him from hearing the rumble of a truck as it approached. He looked up when the sound stopped. Nate swung the door open, strode to the deck, and asked, "You got some chat time?"

"Always. Go grab a cold one and take a seat." Chase cleared space for him at the table.

Nate, beer in hand, turned a chair around and rested his hands on its back. He downed a long gulp and belched before saying, "Still loyal, drinking a Butte brew, I see." He tipped the chair in for a closer look at the paperwork. "By the look of this mess, it appears you have a lot of irons in the fire."

"I do, and they're all hot." Chase pointed to one stack and said, "This pile includes hotels I checked out to accommodate Tekla's prosthesis. That was a curveball I didn't see coming. And that pile is the new research I'm doing on land mines in the world."

Nate whistled like a teakettle, removed his hat, and nodded. "Good deal."

"I'm beginning to feel more like the exuberant man I used to be," Chase said. "Complex details don't bother me as much. I'm on a mission now. I mean an *adventure*."

"I believe you. You always told me not to let moss grow under my feet, and here you are, moss-free."

"Hot damn!" Chase threw both hands up. "I have a new sense of vitality."

"Does this new vitality have a name that begins with the letter T?" Nate slouched over the back of his chair and kicked his legs straight out, waiting for an answer.

Chase replied with a one-eyed scowl. "Did you know there are at least 110 million land mines in the world in 108 countries?" Chase jabbed a finger at the map of the world with numbers printed over several of those countries. "Egypt, twenty-three million land mines; Angola, fifteen million; Afghanistan, ten million. It's the moral responsibility of these countries to clean them up, yet eight million more mines are made each year. This is insane." He shook his head as if to clear his mind, reluctant to believe the demoralizing data." It would take one hundred years to clean them up."

Nate felt he was back at college, captivated by a brilliant professor. He cocked his head to one side, sipping from his bottle as he listened to Chase deliver his lecture.

"The world," Chase said, "should be outraged, damn it! I'm writing our congressmen in the morning."

Nate snorted in frustration. "Do you think most people would care? Kids in my class couldn't find Afghanistan on a map if I pointed to it."

"Not unless a loved one was a victim. Okay, enough preaching." Chase took a swig from his bottle and pushed his paperwork to the side. "You wanted to talk?"

An awkward moment of silence followed. Chase suspected Nate had something sensitive to say, so he said, "Go ahead. I'm done. What's on your mind?"

Nate licked his lips. "Tekla sent me a text, asking how my summer was going."

Chase took off his glasses and leaned back in his chair. He reached for his beer and said, "So she can type. That's fantastic, but surely that's not why you're here." He suspected Nate had the hots for her.

"No, it's not. A couple of days after I replied, Tekla sent another text. She invited me to Seneca Falls for their county fair."

Chase coughed up his last sip of beer, sending a bit of foam through his nose. He pulled a red handkerchief from his back pocket and wiped his nose. "Good gravy! When do you leave?"

"I haven't answered her yet. I wanted to run it by you."

Chase rolled his eyes before saying, "It sounds fantastic. You need a little spontaneity in your life. Get out of town. Live large. You sure don't need my permission."

"Before Tekla and I headed out on horseback, she received a call from some guy named Eric. She's sparky enough and lit him up like yesterday's fireworks. Then she just turned to me like nothing was wrong. It was weird."

Chase's eyes narrowed to slits, like those of the *Medicine Man* in the painting on his wall. He murmured a low "Mm-hmm."

"She changed her behavior, her persona just like that." Nate snapped his fingers to demonstrate the suddenness of the change. "What do you think about that?"

Chase tapped his fingers in beat. "I never noticed anything like that, so I can't comment on it. Are you asking my opinion?"

"Yeah, what do you think?"

Chase paused, intentionally, giving himself a moment to process. "I would venture a guess that she could be dealing with issues from the war. I read of the alarming number of soldiers returning from the Middle East with PTSD."

"How's that?"

Chase spread out his fingers and opened his palms skyward. "Anger and intense anxiety are common symptoms of PTSD. That's what I think. But I could be wrong."

"I hope this info about Tekla's invitation doesn't screw up your plans."

"How in the world are you going to screw things up for me by going to a county fair with a dynamic, beautiful young woman?" Chase pushed himself up from the table and pointed a finger at Nate. "I'd be on the next plane. Good gravy, Nate, she didn't ask you to get married. What could go wrong in two days?"

Chase knew he got wound up when he was making a point, but would Nate listen? "You have apprehensions. That's a natural reaction. But here's a clue: Question your assumptions. Assume shit." Chase picked up his pen and wrote one word on a sheet of notepaper. He turned it around for Nate to read. "Dissect the word *assume*, and you'll see that it makes an ass out of you and me. The point is that the greatest danger in assuming is that you think you know more about her than you really know."

Nate knew Chase had delivered the hard punch of real-world living.

"When appropriate," Chase said, "ask Tekla about her war experience. She'll let you know if she doesn't want to go there. There's no magical wizardry in asking questions."

"You would know."

"You're funny, wise guy." Chase relaxed his face and allowed a smile to form.

"So I need to learn to deal with the facts and proceed with caution."

Chase shrugged, feeling as lost as he usually did when trying to figure out the younger generation. "You're assuming this Eric is a current or past lover. Maybe you're 99.9 percent right. Or maybe he's a persistent car salesman. Or it's a sign of PTSD. I'm not a psychologist. Find out."

Nate sighed and said, "Yeah, yeah. I know. My relations with women have always been like walking in a minefield."

The wrinkles on Chase's forehead deepened and his jaw dropped. "Minefield? An abysmally poor choice of words considering what I was telling you about the land mines in Egypt, Angola, and Afghanistan—not to mention what happened to Tekla."

Nate made the connection and realized he had just put his foot in his mouth big time. "Oh, sorry. My bad, Chase. That was not cool. I'm just confused and concerned."

"Listen, a man's thinking about love needs to evolve above infatuation."

Nate slapped the table as he laughed. "You sure got me by the short hairs on that one."

Chase leaned forward and said, "I believe men sometimes have the propensity to see what we want to see rather than what is truly there. How does accepting an invitation from a new acquaintance mean you're expecting a romantic relationship to develop?"

"I'm hoping for something better than fifteen minutes at the Star Lite Motel," Nate commented. A loud guffaw escaped from his belly, hoping his attempt at humor might reduce the tension at the table.

"Good gravy, I hope so too. You'll be off your home turf, so be easy on yourself. I'm sure Tekla will show you a good time."

"I'm excited to see her again—and see a new part of the country too."

"So when are you leaving?"

Nate checked the calendar on his phone.

"Fair begins the third week of July. I figure two days plus travel. I'll leave late afternoon of the third day."

Chase laughed and reached across the table to give Nate a fist bump. "Benjamin Franklin said fish and visitors smell in three days. Good choice. And good luck."

Chapter 18

Nate buckled his seat belt before landing in Syracuse. He gave it an extra tug, as easy as cinching his saddle. He liked both a little snug. Was it fear, anxiety, or lack of confidence about seeing Tekla again that gave him goosebumps? He decided it was all three.

The day he'd boosted Tekla into the saddle, all his conflicted emotions about being with an amputee vanished. He would take Chase's words to heart and have a good time.

The aircraft's reversers roared as they helped the plane come to a complete stop. Nate was one of the first to unbuckle his seat belt. He leaped to his feet, opened the carry-on compartment, and pulled out his bag. Then he adjusted the brim of his Western straw hat, rolling it just right.

Once inside the airport, he texted Tekla. Overhead signage pointed him to the nearest men's room, where he pumped the last drops of soap from two dispensers. He grabbed the last paper towel and dampened it to refresh his face, leaving him to dry his hands on his jeans.

New York's hot, humid air, fouled by the smell of jet fuel and filled with pollen and other allergens native to the area, swelled his sinuses shut. In seconds, rivulets of perspiration trickled down his face and soaked his hair. Minutes later, his long-sleeved Western shirt was drenched. Wearing jeans had been a bad choice.

While searching the short-term parking lot, he heard his name shouted over the din of buses idling along the curb and the jet engines on the tarmac.

"Over here, Nate!" Tekla called out, waving both hands over her head.

"Phew!" he exclaimed. "I made it. Good to see you. Kind of sultry here." He high-fived her. Sweat trickled down his spine, and his Western garb threatened to suffocate him.

"Happy you're here. It's hot and sticky, but we have clear skies."

He couldn't help but snicker. "Your sky has no color."

"Our sky is hazy," she said. "It's not the Big Sky, but at least we're not under the lapis skies of . . . of Afghanistan. There's ice water in the cooler on the back seat."

"Great." He fished out a bottle and held it to his face before opening it. "It's an hour to your home?"

"A little less, depending on traffic and how heavy my foot is."

She pulled up to pay her parking fee and opened the hatch on the center console.

"Here, let me," Nate said.

"I got it." She shooed his hand away.

When she opened the lid to retrieve the ticket and her wallet, he caught sight of a holstered Beretta M9 pistol with customized grips and a box of 115 gr Remington UMC ammunition. He and his friends always packed Ruger 357s when riding in the wilderness. The weapon could down an attacking grizzly, but seeing Tekla's Beretta in a pickup truck in New York heightened his anxiety.

He drew a deep breath in an effort to slow his heartbeat. He was so far from home and already missed the wide-open vistas.

Tekla had noticed his reaction to her sidearm. She broke the silence as soon as she pulled away from the parking booth. "Hey, it's cool. I have a New York pistol license and qualified as a marksman with the Army. I'm legal. I carry one in my purse too."

Nate was unsure what to say, so he just smiled.

Tekla filled in the awkward moment. "I stay in my lane, so relax. I'll put on some traveling music. Ever hear *White Line Fever* by John Mayall? It's so kick-ass."

He felt uncomfortable and squirmed in his seat. The pistol reminded him of the personality change he'd seen in Montana. Tekla had transformed within an instant into a well armed Bondlike character, curvy and salacious, someone who had led a life filled with danger. His hands twitched and he turned his head to check his side mirror. All clear. No SPECTRE agents were on their tail . . . yet.

"Nice, uh, truck," he mumbled. "I expected a Prius."

She glanced at him, briefly taking her eyes off the road.

"Cars are too tough to get into and out of. I installed this overhead grip on the driver's side and added handicap gas and brake controls."

"Great."

"You're hungry, I'll bet."

"I'm starving. I could also use a quick shower if it's all right with you." He hoped a cold shower would wash away the fear so he could shift into feeling warmer toward her.

"Perfect." She looked in the rearview mirror and swung her truck into the passing lane, turning up the radio in the process. "You shower, and I'll get dinner ready. I'm fixing tofu turkey burgers."

"Can't wait to try 'em." Nate assured himself it was an innocent fib.

She slowed as they entered the tiny hamlet of Seneca Falls and drove past the post office. She hung a right before turning onto Sackett Street.

"Well," she said, "here we are, cowboy. This is home." She pointed with her cell phone, and gave the command: "Alexa, open garage door."

"Nice house," he said. "And I love the maple and oak trees." He swung long legs out of the truck. "Funny how I feel I'm still flying."

"Just land inside," she quipped. "On the couch."

The house was an older split-level home with a winding staircase to the upper rooms. Her house was bare of knickknacks and elaborate furnishings, but the air carried a faint fragrance of lavender that smelled familiar. The absence of rugs allowed the oak to dazzle with its luster.

Above the bricked-off fireplace and its antique cherry mantle hung a framed Purple Heart and battlefield citation, the central photo in a collection that included Tekla's diploma from Boston College (summa cum laude), along with a photo of her in a Boston College soccer uniform, holding a trophy and surrounded by her team.

In a photo with Machu Picchu in the background, Tekla posed with a woman who strongly resembled her. He squinted at the small inscription on the photo: *Great memories, sis. Love you, Erin.*

The remaining photos included Tekla in uniform with her platoon at the Kabul air base in Afghanistan and an older black-and-white photo of a young, robust Army officer. The photo had faded with age, but Nate could make out the name on the uniform: O'Neill.

The last photo on display grabbed his attention the most. *What was the backstory?* he wondered. The scrawled inscription read: *For Tekla. It is always possible to practice kindness. Wishing you many blessings in your recovery.*

Nate spun around in disbelief. Tekla had an autographed portrait of the Dalai Lama. "An autographed photo?" he asked with awe in his voice and wonder on his face.

"I sent him an email." Her statement held an unusual self-mocking tone. She shrugged and said, "Not all that hard to Google his address. You're different from most first-time visitors."

"How's that?"

"Most people stare at my Purple Heart. The Purple Heart is what I did for my country."

His gaze swept over her, slowly, from her loosely tied bun of hair, down the length of her denim cropped pants, to linger on her prosthetic leg.

She smirked. "I'm screwed up from Afghanistan, so I practice the optimism and faithfulness of the Dalai Lama. That I do for myself."

"Maybe," he said, "you should center the Dalai Lama in the display if he's central to your life."

She extended both arms as if to frame her photos after his suggestion and then shook her head. "It's important to me to rebalance my life, not my photos."

"Makes sense."

"Your bedroom," she said, pointing toward the stairway, "is upstairs on the right. I opened the window to let the breeze in."

"Is your bedroom upstairs?"

"No." She pointed her chin down the hall. "My bedroom was added on so I wouldn't have to climb stairs. The hall leads outdoors to my garden." She walked to the kitchen and opened the refrigerator, revealing a twelve-pack of beer. "Would you like a cold one? Something Western for you. Need a glass?"

"Heck, no," he said. "I'll drink it cowboy style."

"After your shower, come out to the garden, and I'll join you with a glass of white wine while I grill the burgers."

He vaulted up the stairs two at a time to reach the top of the paneled hallway leading to his room. He chugged the cold brew, removed his sweat-soaked clothes, and stepped into an icy shower.

. . .

Nate scrutinized the beginning phase of Tekla's garden, a truckload of rocks of varying sizes and a collection of large container plants, each with a drip hose coiled in several loops. He scratched his head, unconvinced that Tekla could have moved all that rock.

She sprayed a mist of canola oil on the end of her spatula before flipping the burgers. "I hope to make a peace garden, a quiet place for mindful meditation. It's supposed to help with my PTSD."

The doorbell chimed twice, disrupting their happy hour.

"I have these burgers to flip. Could you get the door, please? I'm not expecting anyone."

He answered the door to see a teenaged delivery boy holding three cartons of Chinese food and a small bag of fortune cookies.

"Hey, Tekla!" Nate hollered. "Your order for Chinese food is here. Smells good."

"What Chinese food?" she asked from the garden, sounding more irate than annoyed. She made her way to the door, her hand waving the spatula in the air.

"I'm sorry," she said to the young man, "but I didn't order any take-out from you. Perhaps you have the wrong house."

He checked his order and showed Tekla the address. It was hers.

She shook her head slowly. "I didn't order any Chinese. Tell your boss there was a mistake." She tipped him a buck on his way out, the smell of stir fry remaining behind him.

"That was very strange. Let's eat." She walked back to the garden, clutching her spatula.

"I wanted to tell you that I admire your wall of photos. You've had a big life."

"My thirty-three years on the planet have had their moments."

A sharp smell leaked from the grill lid. She peeked underneath it. "Fuck! The burgers are burned from leaving them to deal with the delivery mistake."

Heat rose from the grill to combine with her ire, bringing a tinge of red to her face. She raised her fists in anger, and the spatula clattered to the ground.

"Flame broiled is fine with me." Nate's voice tempered the heat in her demeanor, but he remained warm inside from her outburst.

She took several deep breaths before pulling the charred bean-curd patties off the grill. "Could you please bring the bowl of tabbouleh out from the kitchen? I would like to sit."

"You got it. Tabbouleh?"

The refreshing mint in the tabbouleh detonated the taste buds in his mouth, overriding the burnt tofu.

"You nailed the fresh herbs. What's happening tomorrow?" He coughed once, and then again. A charred bit of burger had stuck in his throat. He swigged a gulp of water, but it wouldn't dislodge, leaving him hacking. After another sip, his throat finally cleared.

"Are you okay?"

He nodded.

"We'll get up early to head to the wildlife refuge by dawn. Then breakfast." She smacked her lips at the thought of eggs benedict. "Then I'll have to check on my parents."

"What about work?" He grabbed the pitcher and refilled his water glass. Something was still stuck in his throat.

"I've had a hard time adjusting to work in the civilian sector. It is better for me to avoid any commitment right now."

"How come, with your high IQ and military experience?"

"It's not about brains. I'm more comfortable with how the military sets expectations about time and discipline." In a fit of rage, she pounded her fist into her hand. "There's no lollygagging in the Army." She karate-chopped the air between them. "There are no repercussions for being late or screwing up in the civilian world. It fucking pisses me off. In the Army, I screamed 'fuck' all the time. The f-bomb is the biggest crutch word we used; it binds us like verbal duct tape."

He took a step back to make room for her wildly swinging arm. Her wrath filled the house, which was still permeated with the smell of burnt tofu.

"Hey, I'm cool with that." He held his hands up, palms flat. "How sweet do you think I talk to a bronc that bucks me off a second out of the gate?"

He relaxed when she laughed and leaned toward him. "Sorry. I got wound up."

"All good."

"The military is not so much about rules as it is a state of mind you acquire after training. I still have that mindset. It's awkward to hear people say, 'Thank you for your service.' I just did my job."

"You don't seem like the type of woman who would shout out, 'Oh fiddlesticks,' when under enemy fire. I don't think less of you for exposing a part of yourself. It's the real you."

She went on, holding his attention captive while she spoke of her moral code and the band-of-brothers mentality of not leaving anybody behind. He was riveted by her admission that she lacked attachments in her work and personal life. She had said she avoided commitment because it could cause intense anxiety. He learned that she had lost her little-girl smile, along with the ability to give affection or ask for help.

He sat, arms crossed over his chest, feeling inspired by her honest revelations. "So," he said, "these attachment issues involve both work and play."

"Yeah," she winced. "You could color that circle mostly true. My biggest fear is that I'll go to the mailbox one day and find a letter ordering me back to Afghanistan. Weird, huh?"

"Help me out here. That attachment issue. Was it caused by your duty in Afghanistan?"

"Frequently it is. That's part of the PTSD that I mentioned. I ache to feel whole and secure again."

She turned away, tucked loose strands of hair behind her ear, and reached into the cupboard below the sink for a dishwasher soap tablet.

He sensed she was done talking about all things PTSD-related. He feared he might have crossed a boundary by digging too far into her private life. Chase had told him to ask questions, but he believed it was best to back off for the moment. So he dropped that discussion.

In three hours, he had peeled away Tekla's outer layers, and not all were as thin as onion skins. With each layer, he understood more of the woman's fears, wants, and desires. He still lacked clarity about what had triggered the instantaneous, intense magnetism he'd felt when he first met her.

He was almost certain the attraction was mutual, but she claimed to have problems with attachment. He wanted to attach longer than fifteen minutes.

He'd become infatuated with her beauty and her honest and simple demeanor. She had shown him strength, complemented by complexity, and he found the combination intoxicating. In New York, his attraction was growing even stronger. Was it because the differences between them were more obvious?

Opposites attract, they say. Maybe that's true. Maybe it's not. A busted-up rodeo star and a blown-up Army officer shared one common denominator: tragedy. But he needed to break it down further. Math made sense to him because it offered solutions. With Tekla, there were no solutions. Not just yet. He could extrapolate the unknowns. Chase once preached that some things were not meant to be and others were not meant to be understood.

Chapter 19

Nate often struggled to fall asleep in new surroundings, whether in a motel or sleeping under the stars in the Bob Marshall Wilderness. Thanks to the creaking of old wood in Tekla's house and the unfamiliar traffic sounds outside, he was too wound up to fall asleep.

Sleeplessness could drag on to 4:00 a.m. before he drifted off. In the Bob, Nate might get out of his sleeping bag to go outside, sip a cold beer, and gaze at the Milky Way. He would then check on Santiago before returning to his tent. Since he wasn't planning to take a stroll around Tekla's neighborhood, he decided to go downstairs and grab another beer from the fridge.

Groggy and fatigued, he reached for his cell phone. His eyes winced at the brightness when he turned on the phone's flashlight feature. In his bare feet, he trod down the oak stairs, which groaned in protest. The house was immersed in darkness except for a dim night light above the kitchen sink and another near Tekla's bedroom. Her door was closed.

Nate tiptoed to the refrigerator and pulled open the door. When the interior light illuminated the kitchen, he froze, overcome with shock by the sight of a hooded man staring at him through the window.

It had to be a prowler. He blinked several times in case his eyes were playing tricks on him. When Nate glanced at the window again, the man had vanished. Nervousness was not his nature, but the episode freaked him out a little. Should he wake Tekla? Should he call the police? Maybe he had imagined it. If he was seeing things that weren't there, he didn't need to interrupt her sleep.

He decided to tell her about it in the morning. After checking all the locks, Nate headed back to bed, beer in hand.

. . .

Morning had broken, and scattered gray clouds filled the sky. Nate opened his eyes to see slivers of sunlight as daylight parted the clouds. The digital sound of a horse whinnying alerted him to an incoming text message. He grabbed the phone off the nightstand and saw Tekla's text on the screen.

"Good morning," he read. "Roll call."

"In five," he texted, adding a pumped-bicep emoticon.

The overlapping layers of birds singing floated through the open window, calming him for a moment. Then he saw the empty beer can on the nightstand and knew last night's fright was no dream. There had been somebody at that kitchen window!

He jumped into clean briefs, pulled on a pair of tan cargo pants, and added a maroon T-shirt with the number 406 imprinted on the front. He stuffed his wallet into a pocket. Before heading out the door, he grabbed his cell phone and Montana State Bobcat ball cap.

Tekla was stuffing two bottles of chilled water into her Army-issued go bag. The oversized pair of aviator sunglasses pushed up on her head left several strands of hair hanging loose. She stood, coming face to face with him. His shirt caught her attention.

"What's with the 406? Is it from running a race?"

"Are you kidding? It's Montana's only area code. Fourth largest state." He thumped his chest, proud of his homeland.

"You should work for the Montana state tourism office. How'd you sleep? I heard you in the kitchen. The tofu leave you hungry?"

"I've got to tell you something," he said. "It's about last night." He turned to look out the kitchen window.

"Hey, are you feeling okay? You look a little pale."

Pistols, prostheses, and prowlers. The three couldn't begin to explain his visit so far. He didn't know where to begin.

"Yesterday was a big day, and I had trouble winding down. I came downstairs to grab another beer."

She laughed. "Who would've guessed that?"

"There's something else. I thought about waking you last night to tell you but decided to wait until this morning." His voice was firm and direct. "When I was in the kitchen, I saw the silhouette of a man in the window. He was wearing a hoodie."

She grabbed her hair by the roots. "That son of a bitch!" she shouted. "Now he's peeping in my windows!" She threw a water bottle against the wall. "It was Eric. He's the one who ordered that Chinese food, just to fuck with my head. He must have seen me pull up with you."

Exasperated, Nate sat in the nearest chair and sank back. Worry crept into his mind, but he could not gauge the implications. "Are you saying you have a stalker, you know who he is, and you haven't told the police?" His normally unruffled demeanor flared into outrage.

After wiping her nose with her sleeve, she sighed and started talking. "Do you remember that phone call I received the morning we went riding at Chase's?"

"I remember a call while I was unloading the horses. That's about it." He thought it best to keep fragments of the truth from her.

"It was Eric," she said, "an old boyfriend. He has some serious issues."

Nate watched her expressions dance between terrified and furious. He hesitated, not sure whether he should encourage her to continue.

She sat with her head in her hands and began to talk about her relationship with Eric. Nate needed to know. She closed her eyes and squeezed her hands into fists.

She had a hard time getting started. "Alyssa, an old friend from high school, called me one night." She stared out the kitchen window, and a tremor moved through her body. "Alyssa works at a sports bar in town. She told me the Bills had been on Monday Night Football. Eric, my boyfriend at the time, was there with a bunch of his beer-drinking buddies. Alyssa overheard one of the guys ask Eric what it was like to have sex with his new amputee girlfriend."

"Whoa, way not cool." His face twitched and trembled from the anger he struggled to contain. He glared at the window.

"According to Alyssa, Eric said he was turned on by my stump. His friends laughed and asked him if he was going to paint a smiley face on it. She said everyone in the bar heard it. Eric told them I was the best piece he'd ever had." Tekla screamed with fury and threw another water bottle at the wall. "And get this. He said he fantasized every day about my stump. He told them it was sexy. Not me—my stump."

Nate felt the vessels in his brain throbbing and put his hand up to signal for a time-out.

Tekla's face had turned pale, her lips purple. She put her hands to her face to muffle the sounds of wailing. A few moments later, she hoped he would hold her till she regained self-control.

"I sought advice from Megan," she said. "She's my civilian counselor. She works with vets. I asked if this was what a woman amputee should expect, and she claimed it wasn't. She helped me understand that while I'd seen Eric as a possible love interest, I couldn't have known about his intentions or fetishes."

Nate's mind and body swirled with emotions as he wondered how he could help. She was not finished.

"Megan helped me understand that fetishes can be offensive, especially those of an ethnic or religious nature, because it's not about the other person as much as it is about a small part of them as devotees." She turned to a bookcase and pulled two books off the top shelf. She handed them to him and said, "These books detail people who are sexually aroused by disabilities or missing limbs. There's a name for this—it's called acrotomophilia."

He flinched in response. "I've never heard of anything like that. I'm just a Montana country boy, but when my horse is sick, I get him help. It seems Eric needs help."

"I think he does need professional help. I perceived goodness in him. That's what drew me to him, but I also sensed an air of uncertainty about him."

"Woman's intuition?"

"Right on," she said, nodding. "He was too clingy. At first, Eric told me my scars didn't bother him, that he liked me for who I was. He gave me that proud-of-my-sacrifice bull and said he would always be there for me. I foolishly believed I maintained control of my heart."

She took a breath and cleared her throat and then resumed. "Then it turned weird." She trembled. "I realized his attraction to me was kinky. He had admitted to his friends that he had a fetish for my stump, even if he didn't use that word. It was like he saw it as some kind of phallic symbol. I knew then that I wanted out."

"Don't short-circuit your life by living in fear." He picked up her phone and handed it to her. "Call the police. You need to protect yourself."

"I know, but he haunts me like the smell of rotten fish. I was nothing more than a novelty for his sick fetish. After discussing this with Megan, I found the strength to tell him how I felt, but I didn't heed her instructions to be cautious, protect myself, and break up slowly."

"I'm sorry this is happening to you. But what's with the break-up-slowly part? Never happened to me." He finished his comment with a resounding "harrumph."

"He couldn't handle my sudden rejection, and now he fixates on me." She wailed, her voice reaching an unbearable pitch. She shook her head so violently that it left her with a badass hairdo. "He cruises down my street at all hours, follows me to the store, sends me flowers, and leaves notes on my truck."

"That sounds threatening." He was trying to console her, but he wondered if he was making things worse.

"He's the reason I carry a pistol in my purse and keep one in my truck and under my pillow."

"Listen up. This shit always gets worse. What have you done to stop him?" He was slouched over, his back against the wall, and he struggled with wanting to hold her.

"I know, I know. I should have ended my relationship in a series of steps. I didn't. Flat-out rejecting him made him angry. And all because I didn't handle his feelings with kid gloves on. No one was gentle with me the day the fucking terrorists blew my leg off." She stopped, exhausted, and then kicked her prosthetic out as if intending to kick someone's ass. "I thought he could take it. He couldn't. Now he stalks me."

"No police, no restraining order?"

"I've called several times, and they told me to notify them if he comes onto my property." She dabbed her nose with her sleeve again and then shifted her gaze to the kitchen window. "I'll call the police about last night for the record. After you leave, I'll go to the courthouse and file for an order of protection."

"Good. I doubt the court will deny your request."

"Thanks. I've stopped shaking. Let's skip the refuge and go to breakfast. I'll bet you're starving."

Chapter 20

Tekla drove three blocks from the diner where they'd eaten breakfast and said, "This is where I grew up. Our family home is the next street over."

Nate sipped his take-out coffee while his eyes swept over the area like a pair of searchlights. Her hometown seemed so different from the Western towns he knew. The working-class neighborhood was checkerboarded with homes that had undergone high-end remodels. The homes still held tightly to prized values: manicured lawns, random toys and bicycles, birdhouses hung from trees. A concrete statue of Jesus with a water feature won top honors among the lawn ornaments. Plenty of American flags hung limp in the sultry, windless morning.

The leafy canopy over the street blocked out the morning's sun. He took his last sip as she slowed and pulled to a stop along a maple-shaded street.

"Here we are. My family home." Her chin came to rest on her hands at the top of the steering wheel, taking a timeout to think about the past.

Nate locked his eyes on the house. Ivy climbed to the Spanish-tiled roof of the brick house. A pair of American flags, one at each end, ruffled in a sudden breeze. "So this is where you grew up?"

"This is it." She exhaled, with both frustration and relief in her voice. "It won't be long before I will need to move my parents into assisted living.

It will be hard on all of us. Their home is their safe haven, filled with rich memories I don't want to take from them."

His gaze softened with empathy as he put his hand on her forearm. "When the time comes, you'll do the right thing."

She gave her head a shake and said, "My father's Pat. He used to like being called Colonel until it got him confused after the onset of dementia. My mother's Natasha, but she prefers Gnat."

"Gnat? Like the bug?"

"When they were first married, my father often told her she bugged him, so he called her Gnat. Don't worry; it's a term of endearment. My mother can't hear the doorbell if she's in the kitchen, so I just knock and go in."

"Pat and Gnat. Got it." Nate smiled and formed the okay sign with his thumb and forefinger.

"Mom. Mom, I'm here," Tekla called from the doorway as she led Nate inside.

Her mother, a stylish, late-sixtyish woman, appeared in a doorway, wearing a garden-green apron covered with flour dust. She removed her hairnet, releasing pewter-gray strands of hair that fell to their full length just above her shoulders. Nate noticed that Tekla's habit of giving her hair a flick to the left came from her mother. He wondered if she felt nervous, as she struggled to untie her apron strings.

"Mom, this is Nate," Tekla said as she hugged her mother. "He is my friend from Montana. A real cowboy. Nate, this is my mother, Gnat. We caught her making the best pierogis in Seneca Falls." She finished by giving her mother a kiss on the cheek.

Gnat gave Nate a military-grade inspection and nodded to her daughter. Wiping her hands on the apron prompted a sneeze from the loose flour dust. "Tekla has told me all about you. So nice to have you here in Seneca Falls." Gnat sneezed again and wiped her nose with a tissue she pulled from under her blouse.

"Nice to meet you. Can I help with that knot on your apron? I'm good with knots."

"Yes, you may."

As Nate freed Gnat from her apron, Tekla asked, "Where's Dad, Mom?"

"Resting in the den, dear." She dabbed at her nose. "I told him you were coming."

Gnat and Tekla led Nate to the den where they found Pat in his recliner. He was no longer the war horse Nate had seen in the portrait. Pat pulled a blanket off his lap and struggled to his feet. When he'd shuffled a step toward Tekla, recognition lit up his face like a one-hundred-watt bulb.

His greeting was so quiet that Nate wondered how he'd ever led troops, but he figured that might be part of aging. Or dementia. Closing the distance between them, Nate held out his hand. A bright raspberry-hued bruise above Pat's right eye caught his attention.

Tekla saw it too, and her face turned the color of the bruise. "Dad, this is Nate, my friend from Montana I told you about. Say hello, Dad."

"Nate?" he responded a few decibels above a whisper. "Where's Eric? Is this Eric?" It was clear that the neurons in Pat's brain were not connecting. His hands trembled. Anxiety furrowed his forehead. His eyes darted to Tekla, then Gnat, and then to Nate.

"No, Dad. This is not Eric. This is my friend Nate from Montana. We're going to the fair. Nate, could you please chat with Dad for a few minutes?"

"Mom. Can I see what's going on in your kitchen?" Tekla's voice sounded off like a drill sergeant's.

"Oh, my," Gnat said. "I need to fix a place for Nate to sit. I'm sorry. There are clothes and magazines everywhere in here. Let me get him some coffee."

Tekla's voice rose higher. "Leave it, Mom. Nate can handle it." She turned and left the room, her mother following.

Nate tried to engage Pat in conversation, which required him to lean in close to Pat's face. He still couldn't discern the whispered words, but occasionally answered, "Yes, that's right," or "I know, sir."

Nate cringed when he heard a mother-daughter shouting match erupt in the kitchen. They had slipped into another language. Polish? Whatever it was, Tekla outshouted her mother fiercely. Nate stood, feeling drawn to the conflict in the kitchen, but he stopped himself and remained with Pat.

Pat's faded green eyes paled further, and Nate pulled the old soldier's blanket over his legs.

A few minutes later, Tekla strode into the room with a smile on her face, smoothing her hair like nothing had happened. Her mother followed as if in a hypnotic trance, her eyes on the floor. Tekla moved to the corner of the den and placed Pat's walker so it would be within his reach.

She returned to the spot where her mother appeared to be rooted, and said sternly, "Mom, keep the walker where Dad can get to it without having to walk across the room."

Gnat's shoulders sagged. "I'll try to remember, dear."

Tekla helped her father get comfortable in his recliner, fluffing his pillow. She used her ministrations to get a closer look at the bruise.

"Mom, a little antibiotic cream on Dad's bruise would be good, but no bandage."

"I was going to do that after I finished in the kitchen."

Tekla bent and gave her father a smooch on both cheeks and gently squeezed his hand. All tension eased from his face at Tekla's touch.

"I'll call you later, Mom, to see how he's doing."

Gnat coughed twice and wiped her nose again. "Yes, dear. Enjoy yourselves."

"We have a lot to see. Bye, Mom. I'll call later. Love you, Dad. Let's hit the road, Nate."

Chapter 21

Nate's chest heaved, craving air, as he walked out of the house. He counted his pulse with his thumb and forefinger. He could've blamed the coffee for his rapid heartbeat, but it was Tekla's tirade that had gotten his heart racing. He slowed his breathing to chill out a bit.

Nate's head was full of mental clamor, which exhausted him. He assessed what brought him joy when he was with Tekla—and what aspects of her personality made him uncomfortable.

Tekla had scratched his heart in a passionate way, but he made a note to raise his shield for his own protection. He should talk to Chase about her inconsistent character traits and her erratic emotions. Would Chase be comfortable taking her to Switzerland once he learned what Nate had experienced? His romantic dreams of cuddling with Tekla had fizzled after the morning's confusing roller coaster of events.

First, Tekla had exploded in an emotional frazzle after learning of Eric's peeping, and then she went ballistic in a double dip of anger toward her mother. Worse, Nate couldn't forget that Pat had thought he was Eric.

Mathematics had to provide the answer. He needed a method for finding a life partner, something that could improve his odds beyond rolling the dice with Tekla. His disastrous relationships had never gotten solved because he never knew why they'd gone wrong. Was it him? Was it them?

His calamitous affairs had all caught fire innocently, as did those of most men. They all started with the sweetness of the first kiss. The night would be fragrant with the scent of a woman as fresh as evening rain, a rain that could nurture the pleasures of intimacy.

But Nate needed more. More attention. More admiration. More comfort when he got bucked off. The addictive fix of new beginnings dimmed with time and eventually created panic and anxiety. Then the process began again with the surefire remedy of another communion involving locked bodies, baptized in tequila. There were so many forgotten names, but he remembered the faces from his loose nights at the Star Lite Motel. Tekla, however—she was a horse of a different color.

Tekla's voice interrupted the downward spiral of Nate's thoughts. "Good! I just got an updated weather advisory." Tekla had become energized by a new spirit, free from tension. She pointed to the screen on her truck's dashboard. "It might be a good day to drive around Seneca Lake. The wind is up, so there will be lots of whitecaps. Not good for swimming. But I can show you the town along the way."

The first stop was a museum where he learned the history of *It's a Wonderful Life*. The museum bored him. His lack of knowledge about local history made it difficult to connect with anything he saw in the displays. Tekla's high school visit triggered his emotions as he watched her assume a goalie's stance in front of the goal on the school's soccer field.

Since the choppy lake made swimming unappealing, they nibbled on pretzels at the Rooster Fish Brew Pub and toasted the day's adventures by blowing foam off their bottled microbrews at one another.

. . .

Back at Tekla's house, she ordered a half mega meat and half veggie pizza from the local pizzeria, which featured cauliflower crusts. They munched the red pie together, sitting once again in her unfinished garden and listening to a diverse mix of country rock tunes.

Later in the evening, Nate lounged in her leather recliner and mentally rehashed the events of the day, the soaring highs and discouraging lows. It felt like he was trying to catch butterflies with a case of hiccups.

Tekla had settled on the couch in quiet contemplation. She twirled the tips of her hair while collecting pictures of Japanese gardens on her tablet.

Nate sensed an opening to bring up the fiery topic of Eric. "Hey, can we talk for a moment?"

"No problem." She turned off the tablet and gave him her undivided attention. "I've just been pricing different plans and options for my garden. What's up? Ready to watch the movie?"

"Not yet. Hear me out, please. I want to tell you why I came to Seneca Falls."

She shot him a look he couldn't decipher. "Is there something I don't know about? I invited you, remember?" She hooked her hair behind her ears. "I felt a connection with you the first time we met at the ranch. I hope I left you with a great experience, because you sure left me with one."

Her raving review of their time together calmed him, and his insecurity about having a relationship with her decreased. He said, "The past month, you were on my mind every day, and I wondered what you were doing. Now I need to know something."

Tekla held up her hand like the town cop directing traffic. "Before you ask, let me say that my trip to Montana changed me. Opening up to you took a massive weight off my shoulders. I didn't meet just a cowboy but a handsome, genuine, caring man. I've missed having someone like you in my life. Now, what's your question?"

"I do remember hearing Eric's name in Montana that morning." He crossed his fingers that she would stay calm. "I've since learned that Eric was stalking you and why. Then your father thought I was Eric. It's a no-brainer that when you hear his name, it invokes a holy reign of shit."

A cloud seemed to pass over her face, and her eyes lost focus, almost as if she was no longer there.

"And what about the fight with your mother? I didn't say much when you lit her up, but it bothered me. That just made it harder on your dad."

Tekla said nothing, but the cloud passed, and the focus and fighting mettle of a proven warrior emerged. His masculinity contracted. She stood and faced him.

"That's a fair question. And, yes, it's time you knew more about me and Eric," she admitted. "But first, about my mother. It's a little bit of both of us. Since losing my leg, I've needed her for emotional support, and I don't get it. She gives it all to my father. I understand. It makes sense, but when I see him not getting the care and support he needs, well . . . you saw what happens. I'm sorry about that."

"No judgment. I see how hard it is for all of you. No worries."

"That means a lot." She clasped and gently squeezed his hand. "And now about Eric."

"Please, enlighten me."

She took his hand, and they walked together past the wall of photos, through the kitchen, and into Tekla's bedroom, where she whispered to him, "My confessional."

. . .

It was in her bedroom, her realm of privacy, where Tekla could speak a language of openness, commitment, and vulnerability—the unknown world of an amputee that she was now prepared to share. She closed the sheer drape where the tiniest slivers of sunlight seeped through to reflect off the polished floor.

"Why don't you sit right here. No, a little more that way, closer to the floor lamp." She pointed, noticing his confusion.

She straightened the duvet on her queen bed, disturbing several odd-shaped pillows at the foot in the process. She turned the diffuser on the nightstand up a notch, misting the room with the scent of lavender.

As she moved around the bed, Nate took in his surroundings. A high-tech exercise bike sat near the window with a view into her backyard. Near the head of the bed was a walker, and a set of folding crutches leaned into the corner. She glanced toward a tattered paperback book on surviving and thriving with PTSD that lay open on her nightstand.

"Are you comfortable?" she asked. "Can you hear me from here?"

"Yeah, sure."

Tekla moved closer to the window and turned her back to him. She crossed one arm across her breast, her thumb and forefinger cradling her chin.

"In Afghanistan, everyone in my platoon called me Shamrock. I'm half Irish, and they were superstitious, thinking I would bring them good luck in the field." She pulled her blouse over her head in one smooth motion and tossed it onto her bed. "I hope you're not offended by my lack of modesty. Are you uncomfortable?"

"Hey, I don't see anything inappropriate."

"I lived with modesty and almost died with it. Land mines and combat hospitals have a way of removing such notions. But Eric's comments and his fetishes hurt me emotionally. I want you to see why I received a Purple Heart."

She undid the clasps on her black bra and pitched it on the bed next to her blouse. With a familiar swoosh of hair off her left shoulder, she revealed withered, scarred skin that extended from the end of her scapula to her elbow. Her movements were deliberate, softened by an artsy flair she incorporated to help lessen the shock.

"This scar was from shrapnel. The bulletproof vest protected my torso, but you can see where my vest ended. The shrapnel chewed everything else. Shrapnel also hit my forehead just below my helmet." She paused. "Are you good with this?"

He inched his chair closer, staring at what her clothing hid. "I'm good."

She unbuttoned her denim crop pants and let them fall to the floor. With her right hand, she pulled the right side of her black panties down to her right mid-buttocks.

"This area was below my vest and received some of the blast." She gestured to her backside at a point two inches above her waist. She spoke with emotion, touching scars she could not feel, scars that were embedded within her soul.

"Why didn't the explosion do more damage?" he asked.

"When we went outside the wire, we were also required to wear blast-proof diapers. That's what saved me. Without it, I probably would've died. I'm one hundred percent woman. The diaper protected all my organs."

He remained motionless and said nothing in response.

"Look at my right leg. The mine blew my lower leg completely off. I'm lucky to be a below-the-knee amputee. I still have my knee."

She stopped and adjusted the flow of the lavender mist again.

"Lavender," she said, "was once considered a holy herb for its positive effects on mood, stress, and anxiety." The aroma hung like a fragrant cloud in her bedroom.

Tekla's left leg was covered with crepe-paper skin and featured the carved gouges of shrapnel wounds, but the muscles beneath were toned and firm like the rest of her body.

"I almost lost this leg too. A hundred pieces of shrapnel were dug out. Eleven surgeries on it. The doctors fought like hell to avoid infection."

A second ticked off. Then a few more. The bedroom had become as quiet as death. Then the wounded warrior came face-to-face with Nate. Her shoulders trembled with tension.

"Nate, are you a man who would view me as some novelty or the star of a romantic comedy? Would you treat my stump as a sacred religious artifact?" She drew in a long breath, her body ravaged by war but unwavering as she stood, unashamed of her nakedness and filled with a spirit of undeterred courage.

He rose from his chair, opened his arms, and wrapped her close to him. He squeezed her lightly at first and then a little harder. She had known her story would rattle him and the new terms might confuse him. She hoped that in some way he would find honor in her personal account of war, in seeing her scars, in knowing her pain. She hoped he would respect all of it because she had more to tell.

"No," he whispered. "I would never see your amputation as some fetish." He held her in stillness. "You need to be honored and not mocked. You deserve the best."

"Do you think you could lie next to me until I fall asleep tonight?"

He took a deep breath and reached for her right hand. Rubbing it across his scruffy beard, Nate said, "You don't have to ask."

Chapter 22

A thin blanket was not enough to warm Tekla, even on a sticky, humid night in Seneca Falls. She'd killed the ghost of a man, a lover turned stalker who thought of her as his novelty sex toy. The ghosts of fallen soldiers and land mines continued to haunt her. Body parts filling trash cans were something she couldn't block out.

She slid a hand under her pillow and felt the chill steel of the pistol. Those bullets were powerless against the surging fear of apparitions coming to life in another flashback. Surgeries, more surgeries, a prosthesis, counseling, and physical therapy had taken their toll.

An inner fire had smoldered since the day she was blown up, but Eric had doused that flame. Tonight she craved Nate, a fire starter, a man who fanned the dying embers of love. He had rekindled the fire down below, a feeling she'd thought to be buried in the past.

She pretended to fall asleep as his hand glided along her shoulder the way she'd seen him stroke Cinder. What a tough but tender man he was. She wanted him to fulfill her horizontal desires but not that night. Revealing her scars had been difficult, bringing back everything that led to them. Sleep would not be easy.

Lying motionless, she faked it. After a few minutes, he slipped out of bed and left the room, closing the door behind him.

. . .

A real-deal cowboy like Nate felt every bit of the strain the day had provided. Tekla needed to sleep; he didn't. He grabbed another beer and sat in the chair she'd occupied the day before. Her tablet sat on a yellow legal pad. The top sheet appeared to be a handwritten letter.

He was torn. Should he respect her privacy and not read the letter? Or should he read it as a way to gain insight into a most intriguing woman? It had been less than an hour since she bared all in front of him, admitting that her sense of modesty disappeared in combat hospitals. Did the letter fall under the same abdication of privacy? Did she want him to read it?

He could not make the decision lightly. In the end, he decided it was the right thing to do to advance their relationship. He'd read it.

The letter began with "Dear Megan." The letter carried a certain mystique as the handwriting was printed, rather than in longhand, and the style was neither feminine nor masculine.

As instructed, I'm writing this letter to record my last normal day. Fuck, I didn't want to go outside the wire. Shit always happened outside the wire. It was Veterans Day back home, and I was six days away from completing my 180-day deployment. I wanted to go home. Temps were so hot the rubber around the vehicle's windshield was melting.

Nate shook his head. He'd never experienced heat like that, and the only wire he knew was barbed.

The dirt was filthy from centuries of people shitting and pissing anywhere. We called the dirt moon dust. It cracked my skin. My butt crack was chafed raw. I was just another soldier with monkey butt, and my vision was always blurred.

Tekla had blacked out the next line, her pen almost tearing the paper. He closed his eyes, thinking of what the woman sleeping down the hall had gone through. Her writing was not restrained, but the printing deteriorated to a scribble. Three wrinkled spots blurred the ink as if tears had fallen and dried. His eyes fixated on the photo of her at Kabul, smiling with her platoon. He sniffed twice and swallowed hard before continuing.

Fuck all terrorists; shoot them all. Let God sort them out. In Afghan, there is no word for forgiveness. The letter ended with two sentences: *It was another day in the hospital, translating. Did you know children scream in the same language?* Another blacked-out line followed, and she'd written three words in the left margin: *Jesus huts*, *pizza*, and *grapes*. The letter ended with an exploding star, the word BLAST written over it in oversized print.

He sat stunned, oblivious even to his own breathing. Clearly, she'd suffered while composing the letter. He replaced everything as he'd found it and moved to stand directly in front of her Afghan photo. He traced her with a finger, as she stood among other soldiers. He wondered how many of them had been or would be "blown up," as Tekla had described what happened to her.

Nate admitted to himself that he craved her, ached for her, was proud of her. In that moment, he needed to attach, to have an emotional charge. He kissed his forefinger and dabbed it over her, as her image stood behind the glass.

. . .

A soft knock awakened Tekla. She rose to a sitting position, the edge of her blanket raised to her chin. Nate opened the door a crack and said, "Hey, it's eight o'clock." The words fell from his mouth in a hushed tone.

"Where am I?" The bedroom air was dense with remnants of her dream-shattered sleep.

"In your bedroom, in your own bed. Are you okay?"

She gave a slight nod.

"I've been up since six. I walked to Starbucks. Brought you back a chai, extra hot."

"Thanks. I tossed and turned all night. Maybe the chai will clear my head."

"Bad dream?"

She clutched her hair in both fists, as if she wanted to pull the night's flashback out of her consciousness.

"No, it wasn't exactly a dream. My counselor calls them post-traumatic flashbacks." She coughed once to clear her throat and pulled the blanket higher, not ready to ease away from its warmth. "Explaining Eric's actions and reviewing how I got my scars set off some triggers. It makes me fear that I'm losing it. I wish the flashbacks would go away. And stay away."

He sat beside her on the bed. "I'm sorry. Are flashbacks part of PTSD? Do you suffer a lot from them? Is there anything I can do to help?"

"No, I don't suffer from them. It's more accurate to say I'm bothered by them sometimes." Her lips curved into a smile. "The chai was pretty considerate of you."

She sank back with her eyes open, breathing slow, cleansing breaths to quiet her overactive mind. She did not want to lose control of her mind. After retrieving the small bottle of lavender essential oil from the bedside table, she inhaled its soothing aroma to clear her head. As soon as she felt steady, Tekla reached for her walker and headed to the shower. On the way, she called to him. "I have eggs and some mushrooms to use up. In the bottom drawer, you'll find sausage."

"I'm on it."

He pulled out the makings for breakfast and read the sausage label: This sausage is plant-based and smells, sizzles, and tastes like real pork.

• • •

Tekla sat at her kitchen table holding a paper-cup chalice of her favorite Afghan tea. She inhaled the aromatics and submerged her muddled mind in the chai before taking the first sip.

The chai soon refreshed her enough to think about the day's activities. "I hope you're ready to go fishing for the big one tonight."

"I left my rod and tackle box at home."

She found his answer funny and laughed. "You're in luck. The kiddie pond provides everything you need. I like it more in the evening when the air is cooler, and the twinkling lights give it an aura of enchantment. I could use some time to get it together."

"After the night you had, taking it slow is a good idea."

She sipped her tea and searched his face for clues of what he might be thinking about her night. "Seneca Lake will be calmer and warmer. We'll have plenty of time to make both the fair and the rodeo."

"Rodeo?" he asked, frowning with one eye closed. His wagging head said, "No way."

"Whoa, cowboy! Why so upset? Did I say that wrong? Ro-*day*-o maybe?"

"I heard you the first time. Have you ever been to one?"

She was taken aback by the change in his tone, which had gone from one of anticipation to dread and hostility.

"Yes," she said. "Several. What's got you worked up?"

"I don't need to see any more rodeos."

She couldn't fathom what had caused his sudden shift in attitude.

"All right, no rodeo. I planned it for you. You've never been to one in the East, and I thought . . ."

"I've had enough of them. I'll enjoy the Ferris wheel more."

She pressed the palms of her hands together as an apology. "I'm sorry for planning the rodeo. At least promise me you'll ride the carousel so I can take your picture on a painted pony."

"That's a better idea."

Chapter 23

As the morning wore on, Nate and Tekla became restless. She had developed an itch to hit the road and thought he was ready to let her scratch it. Her heavy foot pressed the gas pedal more than halfway, sending them flying down the highway. Speed had a strange effect on her. It brought serenity. She felt ready to complete her war story.

"I think I told you about the doctors saving my leg."

"It's not easy to forget."

"I didn't tell you everything. I was medevacked to Kandahar, where they stabilized me. I had cleanout surgeries there once or twice a day. From Kandahar, I was flown to Bagram, where I received my Purple Heart."

"What about when you got home?"

"My sister dropped out of college for a semester, and my father never left my side. He wound up needing help from the VA because he developed flashbacks from Nam. It all sucked." A hint of anger tinged her voice. "The cards and letters that flowed in from family and friends helped, especially a wonderful card with a quote from the Dalai Lama."

"What was the message?"

"When we meet real tragedy in life, we can react in two ways—either by losing hope and falling into self-destructive habits, or by using the challenge to find our inner strength."

"I guarantee you've not lost hope for the future."

She glanced at her prosthesis and smirked. "Thanks. I've come too far to lose hope. I had the mental toughness to endure temporary pain. Maybe that's a gift too."

"But won't you be in pain forever?"

"Come on, Nate. No pain, no glory, right? I wrote a letter to the Dalai Lama, thanking him for the words that inspired me. Three months later, I received his signed photo."

"Chase said something about you working in the Middle East. Didn't you have enough of camels, whirling clouds of sand, and combat the first time? Why go back?"

"My language skills could command a good salary in the private sector," she said with a flick of an eye. "I had a position with a defense contractor who was involved with the Iraq Administrative Reform Project. Baghdad was no longer the cultural center of the Arab Islamic civilization, not like it was in the ninth century."

"Taco John's on every block?" he mused.

"No. Just little shops selling spices and jewelry along the Tigris River. Bombings were nearly a daily—"

"Holy shit! Tekla—no-o-o!" Nate collapsed in his seat, head in his hands. As soon as he could catch his breath, he exploded. "You just blew that four-way. Didn't you see the semi?" His chest continued to heave from the fright.

"What semi?"

"I'm taking the wheel," he said in a tone that defied opposition. "You need to get it together."

"I'm sorry." Tekla was breathing fast, her face frozen with dread. Talking about Iraq had tripped a switch in her brain.

Within an hour, they reached the shores of Seneca Lake. Nate slowed at the entrance to one of the marinas. She pointed out the window, signaling him to stop. "There's my family's favorite beach."

"I don't see many people swimming."

"Don't be a pansy." She cackled, questioning his toughness. "The fact that this glacial lake is over 600 feet deep and around 50 degrees shouldn't be a problem, right?"

He mimicked a shiver. "That's cold, even compared to our Flathead Lake."

Despite his protests about the chilly condition of the lake, Nate slung a beach blanket over his shoulder and carried the chairs and cooler to the water's edge.

Tekla settled into one of the chairs, pulled off her sunglasses, and wiped them down with a lens cleaner. After smearing sunscreen on her face, she let the morning sun warm it for a few minutes. Then she pulled her tablet from the bag at her feet and shaded the screen with both hands.

"I need to rest my leg," she said. This will be a long day." She wanted to review Chase's plan and check the list of ornamental exhibits she wished to see at the fair. She pointed into the distance and said, "The changing shack is over there. Go swim. I'm fine right here."

He snickered, gave a thumbs up, and broke into a jog toward the shack.

When Nate returned, he placed his shoes and neatly folded cargo shorts on the chair next to Tekla's. After peeling off his T-shirt, he made a mad dash for the water, but not before she saw a menacing scar on his back.

He blasted into the water with a running sprint and let out a war whoop, followed by a girlish scream when the chill took hold. She laughed out loud. *So much for manly toughness.*

Refocusing her thoughts, she dug into Chase's plans. He had her scheduled to fly to Montana three days prior to the beginning of the trip. They would leave together on September 28th. Other than her hospital stay in Germany, she'd never been to Europe. It thrilled her that the trip would include France, Austria, and Switzerland. Chase closed his email with a statement in all caps: I WILL CONDUCT JOANN'S CEREMONY ON THE GLACIER PRIVATELY.

Nothing in his agenda seemed out of her comfort zone, so she sent him a confirmation message and slid her tablet back into the bag. Nate returned at that moment, dripping wet and trembling. She tossed him the sun-warmed beach towel.

"*Numbing* is a good description for that swim," he said through chattering teeth. The water had been so cold that his lips were blue. She quietly reassessed his manliness. He had stayed in the water longer than most would have.

Tekla didn't know what level of privacy he expected, but she was mindful of her own disclosure. She jumped in and asked the question on her mind. "I noticed the scar on your back when you ran to the water. May I ask what happened?"

He reached behind his back with his right hand. It rested on a long, ragged, purplish scar that ran five inches above his waist to mid-back. "I don't talk about it much," he said. Using the dry end of the towel, he rubbed his hair and slipped on his T-shirt. "It was at the Pendleton Roundup five years ago. A prayer is always offered before the rodeo for the cowboys' safety and for the preservation of the cowboy way of life." He paused to reverse his shirt, which he'd just realized was inside out. "Maybe I experienced an unanswered prayer that night, but I'm not sure if I believe in a simple prayer changing someone's life."

"Have you ever revisited that feeling?"

"No, I try not to think about it. I was a champion saddle bronc rider. Broncs are the hardest rodeo event because it's all about timing and technique. Bull riding is harder on the body, and your mind has to be right before you climb on one. I had an old college rodeo friend convince me to try riding bulls for a change 'If you're tough enough,' he said. I took his challenge as a dare. I'd trained a little and had the physical strength. But that night my mind wasn't set. Wasn't smart."

He pointed a twirling finger at his temple to indicate he'd been a little cuckoo. A cheesy smile spread across his lips when he said, "Only good thing about bull riding is that I got to meet a lot of pretty nurses."

"That doesn't surprise me," she said with a chuckle.

He grabbed a bottle of water from the cooler and took two long sips. "I drew a rank ol' bull called, Livin' Lightning. He was full of high spirits and high kicks and had thrown forty-five straight riders. My two seconds on his back seemed like an eternity." He rubbed the stubble on his strong chin, and the sun's rays highlighted the first gray whiskers on his face. He formed a V with two fingers and flashed them in her face. "A two-second ride. That bull tossed me right over his head. His horn hooked me on the way down.

Spent two weeks in a hospital with a lacerated kidney, ruptured spleen, five cracked ribs, a fractured wrist, and a concussion."

"Wow. That's really an extreme sport!" she said.

"I was headstrong and curious." He let out a long deep breath.

She sensed the misery and remorse he'd felt.

"It was a wakeup call to quit the rodeo circuit, quit tequila, quit chewing tobacco, and quit dead-end dating. I left with a saddlebag full of wisdom to show off."

"Oh, how our lives change," she said, "when unthinkable tragedy comes to visit." She leaned back. "You know something? It feels as if the sun's rays are piercing layers of my war memories. Maybe you're feeling it too."

They sat and watched the small waves that lapped the shore.

He broke the silence. "Chasing glory in the dust and rain of rodeo arenas had gotten old. I wasn't proud of who I was. That ride on the bull almost knocked the life out of me. Literally."

"Maybe revisit that bull ride sometime. Consider why you did it. Knowing your mind wasn't right, you climbed on anyway. Did you believe you could stay on?"

He had never wanted to relive that awful night in Pendleton, especially the moment when he thought he was dying in the dust, a ragged remnant of the saddle bronc champion he'd once been.

"I knew the price of being a champion." He looked at her, one eye squinting from the sun and giving him an unusually cocky appearance.

She stroked her forehead in deep contemplation. She hesitated to dive deep by sharing spiritual thoughts she had freely borrowed from multiple practices. Then she decided.

"I believe the vast majority of champions are humble. An unanswered prayer might not happen because God, or whatever higher power you sub-scribe to, does not want you to have a safe ride. Maybe it would have been unfair to answer the prayer if you had no faith or humility. You knew the risks," she said, "and you came out all right. Was that not an answer to the cowboys' prayer?"

He picked up a thin rock and skipped it across the water. "I never saw it that way."

"We were both meant to live while doing the things that were important to us," she said. "You'll never get a nasty scar like that teaching math."

"I hope not," he muttered.

"It's not about the boy you were." She laid her hand on his shoulder, squeezed it, and then massaged it lightly. "It's about the changed man sitting beside me."

He cast his eyes at the cloud-filled sky and gazed at the seagulls gliding on the wind. "When I moved back to Montana, I was a different man. Teaching math matters more to me than any belt buckle I ever won."

"The scars tell the story of our lives," she added.

She looked down and fixated on her prosthetic limb. She felt awe when it was framed by an everyday object like her Nike running shoe.

. . .

Nate assessed the Seneca County Fair based on the hundred fairs he'd attended, all of them examples of unrelenting boredom. Without a rodeo, what was there? Pedigreed pigs? Demolition derby? Pink cotton candy and funnel cakes? Boot-scootin' tunes played by an aging country singer?

Tekla interrupted his inner diatribe. "I'd like to visit the ornamental horticulture exhibit," she said, "and get some ideas for my peace garden."

"Sounds great." He grinned when he saw the sign for the tractor pull. "Fair trade?" He pointed to the sign, his idea of a good time.

"I guess I can handle that. I carry a set of earplugs in my purse for concerts."

He endured the horticulture exhibit as effectively as she suffered through the tractor pull. The final featured two tractors, bellowing with the strain as they pulled a huge concrete block. She lost a quarter bet when she wagered on the losing tractor.

"I guess I know tractors better than you do." A degree of smugness accompanied his reply as he accepted the quarter from her with one hand and flipped it into the other.

Tekla said, "It's time for the main event. Carnival fishing is always good, and everyone goes home with a winning catch."

Her grand plan of showing him how to fish for the big ones backfired when he snagged Fish #42, which gave him the prize of a stuffed three-foot-tall white rabbit. She caught Fish #17, which won her a pair of Chinese handcuffs.

"Be on the watch for the first kid in need of an oversized white rabbit. I feel like a nerd carrying this." He hoped she could contain her giggling until then.

"Sure thing," she replied. "So far, you've taken me on home turf in two events. Let's make it interesting. Double or nothing on the air rifles."

Puffing himself up, Nate said, "Why don't I just take your quarters now and save you the embarrassment of losing?"

The group of fairgoers in the area retreated, giving the two contestants space to shoot it out. They squared off to a 25-25 dead heat in the first round, when each balloon popped. Her timing was smoother, true to her training. He continued to joke and ham it up with the audience.

With the score 24-24 in the second round, she turned to him and said, "It's all in your mind." She fooled with a pesky eyelash, sighted the balloon, and squeezed the trigger in one slow motion." *Pop!* Her fiftieth shot nailed the red balloon. "Fifty out of fifty, cowboy."

"Not a problem," he replied. "Prepare for the knockout round."

He missed his shot when the white rabbit fell against his leg. The damage to his pride was the sole injury sustained in the great Seneca shootout. "Throw a flag!" he shouted. "That was interference on the rabbit. I want to throw my challenge flag."

She faced the crowd and gave a thumbs up. "Tell it to the rabbit, Nate. The call on the field stands."

Losing the air rifle match didn't deflate his attitude. In fact, he chuckled to himself all the way to the Ferris wheel. There was no way he'd missed that shot. Maybe the air rifle had malfunctioned. Maybe Tekla had psyched him out by telling him a good shot was all in his head.

While they stood in line, waiting for their turn on the wheel, he offered the rabbit to a little girl whose mother shook her head with a wry smile. They were three rides away from getting on when the heavily tattooed carny operator noticed that Tekla was an amputee. He motioned her to the front of the line, but she waved him off.

Nate said, "I think it's fair. These kids won't be upset if we cut the line."

"It's not fair to them. I'm okay with waiting. When I was a kid, I had a fear of falling out of the chair if it rocked while at the top." She reached for his hand. "Promise me, Nate Hutchens, that you won't do that to me."

"You take all the fun out of it."

They climbed in when their turn came. The wheel came to a stop at the apogee of its great circle, and Nate released his hold on the bar to whip out his cell phone. "This is a moment to remember." He snapped a selfie of Tekla's worried face next to his. The chair rocked at that moment, swinging and swaying in the summer breeze.

"Nate! Stop it, or I'll puke." She clapped her hand across her mouth and drove her shoulder into his.

He put his arm around her for the rest of the ride, all twenty revolutions of the big wheel. When it came to a stop at the bottom, he said, "See, you didn't fall out."

She maintained a choke hold on the safety bar. "Any dipshit can take a picture. I'm still shaking."

"I'm sorry. I was having fun. I didn't mean to scare you."

She released her hands from the bar to climb out and turned to him. "Gotcha, cowboy. We're good." With a toss of her hair, she grabbed his hand and swung it high in the air before leading him to the parking lot.

Chapter 24

While trying to sleep in the guest bed at Tekla's home, Nate heard the wind howling and the sirens of the local police. He threw back the covers and struggled to close the window in its warped frame. After hopping back into bed, he interlocked his fingers behind his head and yawned.

It had been late when he and Tekla returned from the fair. The evening ended when she thanked him for a fun day and headed to bed after a somewhat formal goodnight handshake. His thoughts tangled in overlapping knots. What were her intentions? What had he expected?

Nate was awake before his cell phone alarm went off at six, still baffled about how to interpret Tekla's behavior the night before. He jumped into the shower, hoping the water might wash away his doubts about any prospect of a romantic connection with Tekla. Pulsing jets of water worked out the kinks in his neck from the insanely plush pillows he'd sunk into each night.

He heard a horse's whinny and then another. Wrapping the towel around his waist, he grabbed his phone and read the incoming text: "If you are up and showered, I'd like to see you, please." A rising-sun emoji accompanied the message from Tekla. He texted a thumbs-up in reply.

He dried off, brushed his teeth, and slipped on a T-shirt. Freeballing it, he slid into his cargo shorts. He'd dress for the trip home later.

Downstairs, the aroma of fresh chai tickled his nose, but Tekla was not in the kitchen or living room. "Tekla, where are you?" he called out, lost for the moment in her game of hide-and-seek.

"I'm in my bedroom. You can come in."

He found her sitting on the edge of her bed, covered in a summery linen bathrobe. The cut of the robe detailed the curves of her muscular, well-defined body. Her hair tumbled off her shoulders in a way that he'd never seen, loose and wavy. Unmasked, her true feminine nature glowed in the morning light. He noted the mischievous gleam that danced across her eyes.

"Wow," he said, "is this how you wake up every day?"

She patted the edge of the bed. "Come sit beside me." She spoke softly and scooted over to make room.

"You texted. Are you okay?"

"About last night," she said. "I wanted to let you know I was not playing some cruel game with your emotions. If we'd had sex, I would have given all of myself to you in that moment."

He remembered Tekla's admission that she had attachment issues. Was she now speaking the language of love? Could it be a safe moment for her to attempt to pick up the pieces of love that had been shattered by war? Ever since he'd first met her, Nate had dreamed of the possibility. Was what he saw in her face a desire for understanding and validation?

"Does that make sense?" she asked. "I don't mean to confuse you."

"It's all good. I understand about last night."

"You handled it well. You're special. Let me explain."

"Sure, go ahead." He gave her a half-hearted shrug. *What was she suggesting?*

"Last night, it was dark, it was late, and my leg throbbed. I wanted to do things right, to help acquaint you with my blown-up body." She pulled her robe high enough to show her thigh and prosthesis. "In daylight, I can take the time to help you feel comfortable. You haven't seen me without my leg on. I know it's not a real leg, but when I take it off, there will be nothing. Just a stump. I want you to be relaxed about that."

"I hadn't thought about any of that. I'm sorry." He looked toward the ceiling, shaking his head.

Tekla continued. "After what I just said, would you like to pick up where we left off last night, with no promises of anything more?"

His eyebrows lifted in two perfect arches. He was fully aroused and not just physically. The choice was his. Given what he'd been through with her so far, how could he remain vigilant? Was the pistol still under her pillow? All he said was "Now?"

"Do you like it more in the evening than in the morning?"

"Um, no . . ." He panicked, gritting his teeth and trying to remember if he'd put a new condom in his wallet. After assuring himself that the wallet was in his pocket, and it did contain a condom, he said, "Now would be fine."

"Before we go any further, do you have me covered?"

"You're covered."

"Thank goodness. First, would you like to remove my leg?"

He looked at his large, hardened hands, more adept at saddling a horse than removing a prosthesis. "I'd like to try after you show me how." A slight tremor in his voice revealed how unsure he felt.

"Don't be scared." Her words were as tender as her touch. "I'll release it and show you first. It is held on by an augmented vacuum suspension. When I take it off, I first roll down the silicone suspension sleeve."

"I don't want to hurt you."

"Trust me, you won't," she said. "Pull the prosthetic off the stump, like this. Then I roll off the silicone liner, which protects my skin." She paused, giving him a chance to see, understand, and get comfortable. "There is a protective sock over my stump. You'll pull that off too. I'll put it back on, and then you do it."

"I can't believe it's that simple."

"It is."

He followed her instructions and pulled off her prosthesis without issue or complaint.

"Rub my thigh, and you'll see that everything above my knee is like touching any other woman."

The intensity in her voice drove him wild with passion.

"Sometimes my stump will be touchy and sore, but I'll warn you if that's the case. Then you'll never have to ask me if I'm good to go. Got it?"

"I got it." His blood was running so hot it felt like fire coursing through his veins.

"One more thing. See my walker over there? I always have it at my bedside, so make sure it's not moved after we take my prosthesis off."

He held the cold metal of her prosthetic limb, unforgiving in its reality. The attached Nike running shoe seemed lost without her stump. No warmth, no life. The only life it had was when it was attached to her.

He set the prosthesis aside and caressed both legs with tender strokes, his callused hands running along her silky thighs.

"I like that." She spoke in a whisper, bringing him to his knees. "Could you help me take off my robe?"

He dropped his cargo shorts and tore off his T-shirt. In one smooth pull, he removed her robe as she rolled sideways to help free it. No bra. No panties. No leg.

It was not an optical illusion. He gently traced the lines of a woman. The tantalizing curve of her hips and her silky skin hardened him. He moved slowly, exploring everywhere. He skimmed every fold, nook, and cranny of her body while his lips ran up and over her flat belly with small, staccato kisses.

She arched her back and writhed with pleasure as he fondled her breasts. She let out an animalistic moan, a throaty growl, as he initiated more pleasure. She was aroused. She spread out her arms. Her firm breasts, nipples erect, grabbed all his attention. Her hair fanned out like an eagle in flight. How he longed to get tangled in it.

She motioned for him to climb on top of her, to love her and attach. He kneeled between her leg and stump. He stroked her inner thighs and spread her legs. Then he cupped his hands over her breasts and came face-to-face with her, sweeping away the few strands of hair that covered her eyelids.

"You're beautiful, Tekla," he whispered into her ear. His eyes remained wide open.

She drew his face to hers, kissed his forehead, and then kissed his mouth. Her lips burned his like hot wax from a dripping candle. Their mouths connected them like two celestial bodies linking in space. Her breath tasted of cinnamon, cardamom, and allspice from her morning chai.

"Let me hear your voice again," Tekla whispered.

"I can feel your heartbeat," Nate murmured. He experienced more than sexual pleasure as he found his way inside her. On the threshold of a new pleasure, intimacy, Nate trembled. He was experiencing the ferocity of a lion and the gentleness of a dove, both part of the woman below him.

"I like that. Ah . . . slow . . . slow. Oh, my God . . ."

A lavender mist floated over them.

Chapter 25

*"M*y Life-Stretching Wire." *Yep, that could be the name of my memoir,* Jed thought, chuckling as if he'd just shared a good joke with himself. He downed a short pull of Kentucky's finest from the small flask he kept zipped inside his vest. The buttery, caramel-tinged elixir warmed his mouth before he swallowed its sweet heat. When the first pull didn't satisfy, he swallowed another.

No, no. "Tight Wire," he mused. *Yeah, that's better.* He wondered if the final snort had guided and enlightened him through the holy spirit that dwelled in distilled corn.

Jed scowled at the black Angus cows across the fence on Grimble property. They paid him no mind when he bawled back at a stray calf. Jed didn't like being tight, nor did he enjoy fibbing to Chase. He'd promised to watch his drinking at work that year. Most days he did; some days he didn't. Today was one of the latter, and he blamed his aching back.

Jed drained the last slosh from the flask for good measure and promised himself it would be the last he'd take on the job that day. However, the evening was full of possibilities.

Barbed wire, chicken wire, electrical wire—Jed had stretched it all. Now he worked with smooth wire. Jed sometimes wondered why Chase paid him and April full-time wages for part-time work. The ranch had no livestock to water or feed. No branding, vaccinations, or calving either. No wheel lines to move. *Not like the old days,* he thought.

Now his days were locked up with one activity, replacing the perfectly good bottom strand of barbed wire with smooth wire. Chase had agreed to modify certain sections of his fence line to be "wildlife friendly," in line with recommendations from Montana conservation groups.

In Jed's time, he had seen the valley become half privately owned ground. He watched Chase's property turn from a working ranch to an "amenity ranch," bought as an investment and a place for solitude. The focus had turned to improving the ecological health of the land, creating more biodiversity, forming conservation easements, and concentrating on wildlife over cattle. That ramped up his respect for Chase, a true Montana man.

"The antelope need easier access to roam north," Chase had told him. Jed, who sometimes had more knowledge about ranching, understood his boss's views on stopping the antelope from tearing up the fences. "Now they can crawl under the fence without scraping their hides. Antelope don't make a habit of jumping fences, because they have not evolved like deer in their jumping ability," Chase had said.

Jed knew well the habits and patterns of antelope, but he had listened without commenting. The fencing master cranked the slack out of a new strand and pulled a fencing tool from his leather work pouch to staple the wire. Satisfied that the wire was at the proper tension, Jed let out a satisfied grunt and wiped his gloved hand over the bottom of his chin.

Chase had been busy with medical appointments, laying out clothes for his trip and finalizing his itinerary, so he hadn't been around much. Jed knew Chase would rather fight off the ropes than ask for help. He'd never figured out that character quirk, and it confused him even more after JoAnn's death.

Jed, April, Nate, and Chase were closer than most families. It boggled his mind that Chase had asked strangers for help. Why would he search worldwide when suitable choices were just a shout away?

. . .

Stress led Chase to a new obsession, nonstop checking of his phone for new emails from Tekla. He'd sent her critical documents for carrying JoAnn's ashes abroad, but he hadn't heard anything in return. After he'd bounced around his ranch like a shit-house mouse, so much anxiety had piled up that he assigned the blame to her.

Darn it, Tekla needs to contact me more often. The words echoed in his head daily.

The wide Montana sky, a panacea for taxing times, called him outside. Maybe a blast of cool autumnal air would shake off his recent compulsions. Taking a ride was the perfect prescription for what ailed him, and Chase would swing by the spot where Jed was fencing. He needed to give him a to-do list to tackle in his absence.

Chase fired up his ATV and strapped on his brain bucket. He'd packed a dented thermos of steaming black coffee and a frosty can of his energy boost, and he was ready to head out. The engine coughed once and then fired. He roared over the ridge, taking in the splendor of a less-traveled section of his ranch as he headed to a spot east of Antelope Ridge.

"Break time!" Chase called out as he dismounted and unscrewed the cup from the thermos.

Jed removed his leather gloves and said, "Morning, boss. Sure could use some coffee about now."

"What's behind that fish-eating grin?" Chase asked. He topped off Jed's cup, holding his tongue about Jed's slurred speech.

"Oh, just seeing you. April traded my coffee grounds for tea leaves today, thinking it would relax me more."

"She might have been right, but now you need something unleaded." He gave Jed a closer inspection and noticed a thin line of egg yolk that Mr. Jimmy had not washed off Jed's upper lip. "You have enough lead in your tank already." Chase took a swig from his can.

Jed let the lead comment slide. "How are things shaping up for the trip?" He spat out a wad of well-worked chewing tobacco.

"Not good as of this morning." Chase wrinkled his nose at the smell of whiskey floating in the air. Tensing, he ground his molars, more upset about the lack of communication from Tekla than Jed's morning elixir.

"Ow! This is hot." Jed had burned his lip with the first sip of coffee. "I'm sure there's plenty of paperwork. Nothing's easy anymore, not after 9/11."

Chase figured the tea Jed had for breakfast might have calmed him but hoped the coffee would sober him. "Very true," he said as he blew on his chilled fingers. "My travel agent is out on sick leave. The whole trip hinges on whether Tekla can get permission from the consulates of France, Austria, and Switzerland in time." Chase walked ten steps away from Jed, turned, and took a leak.

"Watch the wind, boss," Jed said, howling.

Chase gave a defiant shrug, zipped up, and turned back to Jed.

"Half the stuff was in French. I was clueless, just like the government."

"That sounds stressful," Jed said, "but from what I hear, your chief of staff should be able to handle it. Those documents all sound like a lot of bullshit to me, but who knows?"

Chase shook his head at the mention of bullshit. "It's hard. I believed a death certificate and cremation document would be good enough. The letter from the health department stating JoAnn's remains pose no threat meant nothing. Now I need an apostille from our secretary of state."

He crumpled the beverage can with a squeeze from his powerful hand as rage and helplessness overwhelmed him. "I've failed her again."

The sense of being played like a broken record had worn out his brain. He felt hobbled with worries about failing to fulfill JoAnn's last wish. "If I just hadn't left her side to go for a gawddamn pork-chop sandwich, Jed . . ."

"Be forgiving, boss. Don't be so hard on yourself." Jed didn't hesitate to put a hand on Chase's shoulder. "You have Tekla, and she'll get those documents done."

Chase had become utterly disconnected from all things not related to JoAnn. He couldn't shake the eerie feeling that Tekla was slighting him. He'd welcomed her into his life as a new rising sun, and now she seemed as cold and distant as a star in a far-off galaxy. It was out of character for Chase to jump to such a conclusion, but that's how he felt.

He shook his head to clear his mind. "Tekla told me not to worry. Then she said her father had further complications she had to tend to. If only she'd contact me."

"She never told you to worry, did she? Her father's taking up her time too. Cut her some slack, Chase."

Jed's words didn't give him any relief. It stuck in his craw that Tekla had let her father steal time she had promised to Chase. Her father was in the way. Chase found himself in a mental brawl, but he could not limit himself by narrowing life down to his needs alone.

Moments passed. Just as the sun burst through the clouds, Chase's phone vibrated. He fiddled with the zipper on his vest pocket, finally freeing the phone. The message was from Tekla. *It had better be good news*, he thought. He removed his glasses from the other pocket. With the world in better focus, he shared Tekla's text with Jed.

"She says here, *Chase, please stay calm. We are transporting JoAnn's ashes, not her body. You will need to declare her ashes in customs and make sure they are in a nonmetallic container. Or you can send them by express mail to the hotel in Zurich. Hope this helps. Be well. Tekla.*"

Chase squeezed his eyes together to stop the watering caused by Tekla's report. He squinted at the text again and said, "All the angst I put myself through over such an oversight. I should have double-checked my facts: ashes, not a body."

Jed reached out to pat Chase on the shoulder, but Chase turned away, not wanting to be touched. He needed a moment to rebound from the unnecessary anxiety he'd blamed on Tekla.

Jed reached out again, this time verbally. "There's your good news, so relax. Say, April and I wanted to have you and Tekla and Nate over for dinner one night before you leave. We'd love to meet her."

Chase nodded. "Thanks for the invite and for your support. By the way, how's your boy doing?"

Jed looked away, shaking his head. "He's busy at the beginning of a new school year, but lately he seems a bit introverted . . . isolating himself."

That's typical Jed, Chase thought. Jed would rather fixate on and stress over Nate's behavior than just ask him what was going on in his life.

Jed crossed his arms across his worn denim shirt, a signal Chase considered a cry for help, so he listened intently. "I think he's confused," Jed said.

"Confused about what?" Chase asked, wondering what had sent Jed into a tizzy.

"Hell, I don't know. He was on cloud nine after New York, but now he walks around with this hangdog face."

Perplexed about Jed's concern, Chase stated the obvious: "Ask him."

"I try to stay out of his kitchen," Jed moaned. "A few days ago, April and I went to the Main Street Diner for the clam chowder special. Nate was inside having a heated discussion with a pretty, dark-haired woman we didn't know." Jed paused in that Western way of reaching for his can of Cope to refresh his chew, only to find the can near empty. "We opted for the Paradise Cafe instead. Yesterday, I saw him leaving the Merc with a children's book in his hand, looking dazed. He hasn't been the same the past few days. I thought he might have talked with you."

Chase hesitated before answering. "No, we haven't talked, but let me give you my opinion. I think Nate experienced a little Eastern religion back in Seneca Falls that left him in the clouds. I don't know about the woman in the café, but I'll say it again. Ask him."

"Nuts!" Jed threw his hat to the ground. "He hasn't dated anyone here that I know of. Think that's it, a woman?"

Chase shrugged and rolled his head back to stare at the empty sky.

Jed continued. "If it is a woman, Chase, I could advise him about my three marriages."

"Good gravy, Jed! It usually is a woman. If not that, then it's money. You think his truck's low tire pressure indicator is troubling him?"

Jed had no answer.

"Wait until you meet Tekla, and then take a read of Nate's face. You'll have a ringside seat." Chase hoped his attempts at counseling might help Jed cope with the inner turmoil that stemmed from seeing Nate with a children's book.

Chase believed that politics could never split his and Jed's relationship. Neither could religion, Jed's friend Jim Beam, or whether to be a Montana State Bobcat or a Montana Grizzly fan. But Chase had a problem with Jed's hands-off approach to parenting adult children.

After Nate turned eighteen, Jed and April left him to learn from his mistakes. They felt they had taught him right from wrong and the time had come for Nate to make decisions on his own. Chase, though not a parent, was steadfast in his belief that parents retained the right to counsel their children, no matter the age. "Tell 'em once and walk away," he'd once told Jed.

Chase glanced at his watch. It was eleven, and he'd spent enough time shooting the shit with Jed. He said adios and was on his way before he remembered he hadn't gone over Jed's work assignments. Doubling back, he gave Jed his work list.

Already behind schedule, Chase took an unfamiliar, albeit shorter route across Antelope Ridge back to the ranch. Busting a hole in the morning breeze had revitalized him, and he was in a giddy-up state of mind after Tekla's report. He opened the throttle another quarter turn. The ATV responded with a surge of power and speed, and its engine replied by roaring far into the hills.

The morning sun blazed in Chase's face, reflecting off the fresh snow that had fallen on the peaks of the rugged Absaroka Range to the east. Without sunglasses or a tinted visor, he squinted. His gaze hooked onto the distant peaks, and he forgot the cardinal rule of reading the trail ahead. *Thump!*

He failed to see the ribbed patch of exposed bedrock before his left front wheel slammed into it. The impact threw him up and forward and then back before ejecting him from the seat. As he launched backward, his wrist strap yanked the kill-engine switch, and the ATV came to a dead stop. Chase continued his topsy-turvy, twisting dismount and failed to stick the landing. His neck thrashed like a cracked whip.

When he landed several feet away, his buttocks absorbed the full force of the impact. His spine rattled, and shock waves traveled to the base of his skull when his shoulders slammed into the ground after his butt. His helmet kissed the ground just hard enough to jar a memory from the deep recesses of his mind. An image of Frank Oglesby, who had been a faded memory, appeared as a jarring apparition that mouthed, "I'm innocent," in rapid fire bursts.

Chase shook his head to clear the image and whatever cobwebs had become dislodged in his brain. Seeing a ghost of Oglesby affirmed the nagging doubts in his mind. He had not provided the man with effective assistance of counsel. He had failed to produce evidence, which then remained undiscovered. Oglesby may have been innocent.

Chase returned to the ranch with the ATV in low gear, nursing a headache. The throbbing was compounded by his fear that the crash might be a premonition of how his trip would unfold.

When the headache hadn't let up by the following day, he consulted with his doctor over the phone. The doc ordered a CT scan, which indicated he'd not suffered a concussion. The final diagnosis was whiplash. Chase dutifully dedicated the next ten days to rest, as ordered, and scheduled physical therapy.

Chapter 26

In the moonlit midnight hour, Tekla walked into the guest house at the ranch. A large bouquet of fresh flowers sat on the table in a tall vase, and the slow spin of the ceiling fan carried the scent to all corners of the room. It was a thoughtful gesture, but it did little to relax her.

She'd crashed through her sleep zone, and the hydrocodone had given her a throbbing headache. Sitting on the edge of the bed, she gazed through the window at the bright waning gibbous moon—three days past full—illuminating the mountain range on the Western horizon.

Yawning, she unfolded her travel crutches and placed them at the head of the bed. Then, with a long exhalation, she removed her prosthesis, finding comfort in the pleasure of its release.

Tekla tossed and turned, but sleep wouldn't come. Being back in Montana, her kind of place, a place of peace where she could live with less stress, made her wish Nate was with her. Misery hung over her shoulders like a shroud.

One New York father. One New York stalker. Two Montana men. One was pulling away from her; one was obsessed with her. One needed her, and one wanted her. Four men were tearing her apart like taffy in an old-fashioned pull.

Her father, a bulldog of a man in fighting spirit, had deteriorated to the point of drooling. She had to have a tissue handy when she talked to him.

While he could still live at home, her mother needed help, so her sister would arrive to lend a hand as soon as she finished in Peru.

Eric, she hoped, would abide by the restraining order she'd been granted.

But Chase's recent bout of anxiety had come out of the dark. She'd secured the needed documents, which were simple exercises he could've handled. He told her it made him feel lost in a wilderness of mirrors, and she knew her language skills had expedited the process.

For a week, Chase had sent her a text or email two or three times a day, asking if she had any updates. There were days that she didn't answer every message. When busy with her father, she would switch her cell phone setting to *Do Not Disturb*.

Nate was the hardest pull, a stretching pressure on her heart muscles that left her overwhelmed by a sense of futility. She needed to talk to Megan and learn if reattachment could help heal her emotional battle wounds. Could a breakout from emotional hibernation to bonding and loving more deeply than in the moment be possible? The question nagged her.

Nate wanted more from her, even though she didn't have it to give. She knew it would be hard to maintain personal growth while falling in love. Was she falling in love . . . or was she just attracted to him?

His most recent text confused her because of its lack of clarity about his plans. Then he'd sent her a dozen roses, thanking her for their time together. Tekla felt overwhelmed by life and confused by love. Falling in love was invariably temporary.

Nate had accepted her, from her scars to her f-bombs to her PTSD. He didn't just accept her but believed in her. She viewed her PTSD as a minor hiccup on the road of life, nothing more. But was he withdrawing after his visit to Seneca Falls? Was the thrill gone? Had she again painted herself as a victim or as a novelty for predatory men?

. . .

By the time Tekla ambled into the ranch house before nine the next morning, Chase had hot water and the chai he'd ordered online ready. His energy perked up when she walked into the kitchen. The effect was greater than anything a drink could deliver.

"Sorry I didn't wait up last night. My neck stiffened, so I hit the bed. How are you this morning?" He rummaged through his cupboard to find one of his favorite Montana mugs for her.

"I'm pretty good after such a long day yesterday." She breathed deeply. Just inhaling the chai's aroma gave her enough energy to stretch her arms above her head. "How's your neck feel today?"

"A little creaky." He rotated his head to the left and then right, holding each stretch for five seconds. "My physical therapist told me to keep up with my stretching." He folded his hands behind his head and leaned back in the chair. "You told me there were complications with your father." Tekla seemed to be in a relaxed state, and that was a good sign.

"The doctors adjusted his meds, and that helped. I set up home health nurse visits, which will relieve the strain on my mother." She bobbed the tea bag up and down in the hot water.

Chase moved his hands to the table as if in prayer. He loved it when a plan came together. While he felt relieved to hear about her father's improved situation, a little black cloud hovered over his mind. He feared that something would go wrong, and she would have to leave him.

Tekla's voice broke through his thoughts. "I'm so glad we got those clearances for JoAnn's ashes. Maybe the first thing we should do is check your meds and download your passport to your phone." She turned her phone to show Chase her passport.

Chase read the name on the screen. "Tekla Kathleen O'Neill. Your middle name is Kathleen?"

"Another family name. Why?"

After a pregnant pause, Chase doubled his hands across his ribs to restrain himself. "I just realized your initials are TKO. I knew you were a knockout, a KO. I just didn't know you were a *technical* knockout. That's all."

"I'm no lightweight fighter." She tapped him gently on the arm, and her face broke into a grin. "I also brought my packing list. It's the Army way, all routine. Now, let me see your passport."

"Here you go." He handed her his heavily stamped document.

She opened his passport to the first page. "Your hair was so much shorter eight years ago." She looked at Chase, laughed, and shook her head at the change. A split-second later, she said, "Oh, no!"

He froze. Her stunned, wide-eyed look meant something.

She closed the passport and shook her head again. This time he saw irritation in her expression.

"Chase, did you know your passport will expire close to our return date?" She slid it across the table. "What if we're delayed?"

"Good gravy, that can't be. It expires next year." He wondered if she'd misread the date but was afraid to look in case she hadn't.

Tekla took the last sip of chai and sunk back into her chair. "This *is* next year. It will only be a problem if we have a delay of a few weeks."

"All right. It's all right. We'll make it home in plenty of time." Chase knew he often walked the tightrope between embarrassingly forgetful and highly organized. That morning, he was so sure of himself that his voice never wavered. "What's that thing you say? No worries? Let's make breakfast."

"Let me," she said. "I know my way around your kitchen. What are your plans this morning?" She grabbed eggs, butter, and strawberries from the refrigerator.

"Think I'll go to town and put a hold order on my mail. Phyllis never answers the darn phone."

Tekla was ready to crack the first egg but stopped halfway. "What? It's not the seventies. Just log onto usps.com. Click *hold mail*. Real simple. You just plug in the dates."

"I remember JoAnn doing that." Being forgetful annoyed him. It reminded him how much JoAnn's death had affected his memory and ability to focus. Grief had taken root in his brain. He felt he'd taken on the persona of a man missing in action for the past year. "I should be more with it. Oh, I almost forgot to tell you. I accepted a dinner invitation for both of us at the Hutchens' tonight."

"Sounds great," she said, pouring whipped eggs into Chase's well-seasoned cast-iron skillet. "One more thing," she added. "Immune system support tablets are in my purse for you. Take three tablets three times a day."

He sat, shaking his head, unconvinced. He hated taking pills for anything when he wasn't sick.

Chapter 27

April had been in a dither all morning, flipping through gravy-stained pages of all-time favorite family recipes.

Nate told her not to worry about it. "Just try using tofu, and she'll be happy."

She had surfed the Internet and found that her signature dish, beef stroganoff, could be modified to use extra-firm tofu instead of beef. Her well-stocked pantry had everything for the dish except tofu. She was sure that City Market carried tofu in its new Asian section, so she settled on stroganoff as the main course.

She'd never eaten tofu and doubted it would ever rival Angus beef in the agricultural-output tables of Montana. After a quick trip to the market, she spent the day on cloud nine, floating through the kitchen with a wooden spoon in each hand.

At six o'clock on the dot, the doorbell chimed. Jed rose from his recliner to answer, making one last adjustment to his bolo tie and hitching up his jeans on the way. April hurried to his side as he opened the door.

"Evening, Chase. And my, my, my . . . you must be . . ."

"I'm Tekla, and these are for you and April. I picked them from Chase's flower patch."

April was quite taken with Tekla. The young woman's voice was so warm, and her face lit up the room. "Whose flower patch?" April winked at Chase, and he shrugged.

"Come in. Come in." Jed stepped away from the door and ushered them inside. "Let me put these flowers in some water. Nate's in the kitchen. Nate," he called, "our guests have arrived."

"At long last, I get to meet you, Tekla." Jed tilted his head, looked her over, and gave a short whistle. "I swear you're just as Nate described."

April's stomach tightened with Jed's whistle. She knew he could be a cad sometimes, and that was one of those times. She watched Tekla's cheeks blush a pale rose hue before she lowered her face and murmured, "Thank you."

April whispered something in Tekla's ear that caused them both to laugh. Nate came into the room and reached out to shake Tekla's hand. Then he dropped it, hesitated, and pulled her into a tight hug.

"Hey," he said, "you're looking good. I'm sorry for not keeping in touch. Some life things came up that kept me busy."

Tekla grinned and said, "Thanks for explaining that." She tossed her hair, which made the newly added streak of blonde shimmer. "I thought you might still be sore about losing the air rifle match."

"I want a rematch with real rifles." Nate's voice carried a cool tinge that irritated April.

"You're talking jive, cowboy," Tekla replied. A robust laugh followed. "It'll end the same."

April noticed that when Nate released Tekla from his hug, something was missing, something a mother could sense. In a moment, it came to her. The hug had lacked happiness.

Chase, Jed, and Nate fell into a discussion about Daisy Grimble's plan to subdivide one hundred acres of her ranch. Tekla stared at the massive set of elk antlers that hung over the fireplace.

April said, "Excuse me, Nate. I need you in the kitchen for a moment. Tekla, you're a guest, so get comfortable. Dinner will be ready in five. Chase, you relax too."

In the kitchen, April sensed that Nate's emotions were as tossed as the salad he was plating. His embrace with Tekla had been awkward, and she suspected something other than a general lack of happiness was involved.

When his brooding melancholy had surfaced that week, she was unsure if her instincts were right, but not now. He paled in comparison to the man who had ridden Santiago like the wind, bareback, through the fields one day after returning from Seneca Falls.

A mother's instinct, combined with Jed's comment after talking with Chase, told her that Nate and Tekla most likely tussled between the sheets. The vision she had imagined, Tekla's tangled hair around him, the touch of his fingers fondling her, was hard to imagine now. She would be delighted for them if they clicked, but his mood told a different story.

When everyone was seated at the table, April said, "This was a spur-of-the-moment creation. When Nate told me Tekla likes tofu, I surfed the Internet for a recipe." She hoped the woodsy smell of mushrooms and fried tofu that wafted over the table carried a fragrance befitting the great out-doors of Montana. "The guys love my stroganoff, so I found a version that substituted tofu for the beef."

"What in the devil is this tofu stuff?" Jed asked. He forked up a bite of the mystery meat, strange sponge-like cubes of April's new version of an old standard. He hesitated before tasting. "I never imagined I'd see this on my table in cattle country. What happened to 'Eat More Beef?'"

"Tofu is so down-home Montana." Nate mustered a smile and plunged a fork into his food. "You rocked it, Mom."

April believed Nate's compliment, but she did not believe he was pleased about Tekla's presence. The usually warm, welcoming, friendly Western ambiance of the Hutchens' home had shifted into a cool and distant atmo-sphere. April had no idea what burr had gotten under Nate's saddle.

· · ·

The next morning, Tekla rolled Chase's shirts into the packing cubes. Her heart felt frayed around the edges, her mood mixed. She disguised her pain with a cheery mask as she tried to reason out Nate's behavior at dinner. The look on his face, the way he'd stared at her, open-mouthed, kept popping into her mind.

It wasn't the affectionate cowboy greeting she'd gotten when they first met at the ranch. And it was far from the rapturous face of a tender lover whispering, 'I can hear your heartbeat.' Tekla would've been more com-fortable in a Jesus hut in Afghanistan than sitting next to the shrunken and withdrawn version of Nate at the table.

The methodical movements of rolling and packing one shirt after another did nothing to still the noise that roared through her head.

Chase was in his office across the hall, handling last-minute preparations for the trip. Both worked in silence until Tekla came to his door, holding an unrolled shirt. "Why do you think Nate was so distant last night? I was afraid to trip on the elephant in the room."

"Wish I knew." He dropped his pen on the desk and flung his arms out. "After all the years JoAnn and I sat at that table, I was as comfortable as a chicken in a church last night."

She wished Chase would swivel his chair around to face her and acknowledge her frustration. What was up with these guys? She believed Chase was experiencing the same sense of disillusionment and disappointment with Nate that she was.

He pushed away from his desk, turned, and shrugged his shoulders in what she recognized as resignation. "We can't worry about that now. Whatever it is, I believe it is his to deal with, and I don't think it involves you."

"I'll trust you on that. It kind of hurts, but let's move on. Okay, I'll finish packing, but can I ask you a question first?"

"Shoot."

"Why are we driving an hour and a half west to Butte to fly east to Minneapolis?" The plan had been troubling her. Was it another manifestation of Chase's confusion? "Leaving from Bozeman gets us to Minneapolis at the same time."

"That's right. But for me, it is the beginning and the end. Butte is something of the alpha and omega in our adventure." He locked his fingers and aligned his thumbs like an altar boy.

Tekla puckered her lips and twirled a loose strand of hair around her finger, trying to decipher Chase's cryptic statement. *Alpha . . . omega . . . beginning . . . end.* "I've got it!" She threw her hands up and exclaimed, "You were born in Butte. JoAnn died in Butte. We are leaving Montana from Butte to scatter her ashes where she felt close to heaven. The beginning and the end. Right?"

She watched him turn away to gaze through the open window at the solitary rocker on his porch.

"Something like that," he said with a deep and mournful tone.

Chapter 28

In the silence of the main cabin, eight miles above the earth, Chase imagined he heard JoAnn whisper. He pinched himself, and he wasn't dreaming.

He and JoAnn always held hands during takeoffs and landings, and she would lay her head on his shoulder. He could almost see her sitting next to him, but there would be no handholding on this trip. Her ashes rested just above him, packed carefully in his carry-on bag.

The smell of fresh-brewed French roast coffee stirred his senses, so Chase asked a passing flight attendant for the can of choice for his morning jolt. He needed something to help the four Advil kick in and ease his barking back.

Outside, the darkness fractured into slivers of sunlight as it lit the cabin through the raised shades. When the main cabin lights flashed on, other passengers removed their black sleep masks. The cabin speakers buzzed with a message from the captain. It sounded like digitized gibberish to him.

"Tekla, what's he saying?" The lack of closed captioning on the screen annoyed him.

"It's just the weather forecast in Paris and our updated ETA. We've been placed into a holding pattern for at least an hour."

He groaned and noticed she was unbuckling her seat belt. He descended back into dreamland.

. . .

In the lavatory, Tekla washed her face, touched up her mascara, and applied a thin coat of raspberry-hued lipstick. She fidgeted with her hair, shaking it from the loose bun and pulling it back into a ponytail. After retrieving a red beret from her bag, she fiddled with it to attain the proper angle, the right side no lower than mid-ear, a practice learned while wearing a beret in the military.

Satisfied it would pass inspection, she nodded to her reflection, repacked her toiletries, and returned to her seat.

"Achoo! Achoo!" Chase's double sneeze startled him awake.

"You're not catching a cold, are you?" Tekla asked.

Chase remained in a reclined position, his head supported on the headrest. He coughed and blew his nose with the tissue a flight attendant offered just as he needed it.

"No," he said. "I'm not catching a cold. I think I'm having a full-blown allergy attack, probably triggered from that cheap perfume I'm smelling." He rubbed his watery eyes and wiped his runny nose. When his eyes cleared, he saw her headwear. "What's with the beret?"

"This will help you find me in a crowd. If we get separated, just look for the red beret."

Chase smiled and raised his eyebrows. "Couldn't there be more than one red beret in Paris? This could develop into a scene from a *Pink Panther* movie."

She didn't know what to make of his devilish grin, but she felt relieved that a degree of silliness had replaced his earlier grouchiness.

"Don't worry about it. There's no way you're leaving my sight." She used two fingers to point to her eyes and then his. "You fell asleep while we were talking about initiating our travels in Paris."

"Paris," he mumbled. "I've told you about my spiritual path, and it was quite different from JoAnn's."

"Should I take notes?"

Chase dismissed her question with a wave of his hand and blew his nose again. "JoAnn was a devout Catholic and insisted we visit Notre Dame. That cathedral had long been a symbol of the transcendent human spirit, as well as her own faith journey." He felt out of place and out of sorts and took a moment to reflect. "I was born a Butte Catholic but was not churchy as a boy. I grew up trying to do the right thing. Nothing more."

Tekla realized traveling the world might have provided much insight, making him cautious about discussing unpopular or differing religious views and customs.

"I'm not sure if I'm prepared to brace my skepticism against JoAnn's unwavering beliefs." Despair and doubt intermingled in his voice. "She believed her cancer and pain were part of a heavenly plan to punish her."

"Punish her for what?" Tekla's voice escalated, and her face reddened. "Building hospitals and orphanages? Famine relief for children in Sudan? Are you serious?"

Their talk was interrupted by a flight attendant collecting waste. Chase contributed his used tissues. His head drooped, and he mumbled his response. "No, she thought she was being punished for not bringing me closer to her God. She never understood that Montana's my holy land."

Static from the cabin speakers interrupted his thoughts. "What's the captain yakking about now?"

"We're about to begin our descent into Paris. Current time is nine-eleven, with light rain falling."

Outside her window, the sun shone until the plane entered the gun-smoke-colored clouds that appeared to soften their descent into Paris. The welcome rumble of the landing gears sent small vibrations through her seat.

"Never fails," he growled. "Rain in Paris. How are you doing? Any problems?"

"I'm good. Sure beats flying in a military C-17 Globemaster, banking hard to avoid missile fire. And you?"

"I'm hoping we don't have to take off the gloves at passport control while declaring JoAnn's ashes. Ah, my ears." He pinched his nostrils and blew gently, popping his ears.

"Relax." She pinched her thumb and index finger on his thumb joint and massaged it, focusing on the pressure point. Then she did the same to the other hand.

"Thanks. That helped."

"Look out the window," she said. "We're out of the clouds now, and there's Paris."

. . .

The cabin doors opened, and Chase led Tekla down the jetway to the terminal. He froze when the noise and physical intensity crashed into him. A sea of humanity flooded around him, all speaking in different tongues. His head thumped. His back ached. Toddlers screamed while parents talked on cell phones, bumping elbows with him.

The plastic wheels of suitcases grinding across the floor added to the din. His hearing aids became more of a nuisance than an aid because digital technology was not fast enough to process the sheer number of sounds. Chase used his phone app to lower the ambient sound by half, but it did not lessen his anxiety.

His low vision, combined with the shifting conglomeration of color and motion, heightened his unease. He almost stumbled when a man zipped past him with a load of luggage. Then he lost sight of Tekla.

Chase missed Montana already. Those sweet memories of arriving in Paris, holding JoAnn's hand while surrounded by people who were excited to be there, were just that: memories. The diversity of cultures remained, but instead of being surrounded by happy people, he found himself between two Middle Eastern men, one wearing a roughly tied turban and the other in a black kufi skull cap. They shoved one another and argued in a language he didn't understand, their voices rising to shout in his face.

Two women stood nearby, hands clenched. Chase was unsure if they were going to swing at him, at one another, or at their men. His boxing genes flamed to life with the motto *Protect yourself at all times*. His muscle memory formed a fist as he automatically prepared to defend himself. Losing track of Tekla and her red beret pushed Chase to fear-induced paranoia.

. . .

Despite every treatment she'd had for PTSD, including her recent counseling session with Megan, Tekla was unprepared for Charles de Gaulle Airport. In a blink, she'd lost sight of Chase. Confusion erupted into overwhelm. The sheer number of sights and sounds sent her into a terrifying spiral. Hearing the plaited sounds of Arabic sent her into anxious tears and spun her into what Megan had termed a dissociative state. The firewall that guarded her reserves had been breached. Nothing around her seemed real.

"*Ya kalb!*" one man screamed near her ear.

"*Tozz feek!*" the other yelled in reply, shaking his fist. Was he directing the insult at her?

She head-tripped back to Afghanistan, every sense on high alert for terrorists who might be hiding in the crowd. Sirens wailed nonstop. Uniformed police agents cradled Beretta PMX submachine guns and scanned the crowds. Frantic, Tekla tried a grounding exercise, recalling three things she liked to eat. Nothing came to mind. She then tried three favorite places. Again her mind was blank. She needed Chase. Where was he?

The terminal filled with PTSD triggers, all being squeezed at once. Her heart raced as her brain fought to hang onto what was real. She looked at her hands, cold and white, almost plastic to the touch. The running dialogue in her head checked off possible threats in her vicinity: *That woman carrying her burka. Check her out. May be a bomb. That guy on the escalator wearing the shemagh. Check him out too.*

As the room began to spin, she yelled, "Chase, help!" The din of the crowd muffled her plea.

$$\cdot \ \cdot \ \cdot$$

Chase searched left and right, picking apart the crowd for a red beret. Then he heard his name. Turning toward the sound, he saw Tekla standing less than ten feet away. Her eyes darted from one person in the crowd to another.

"Tekla, what's going on?" A cold fear rushed over him. He clutched her by the shoulders and buried his face into her hair, steadying her wobbling body. When he pulled away to check her out, her pupils had the thousand-yard stare he'd heard about. She looked like a zombie. This woman was not the Tekla he thought he knew.

She said, "We need to get out of here quick. We're in a nest with some bad birds."

He would always remember the sound of her voice in that moment, filled with terror. He realized the trip had become more difficult for her than he'd imagined.

Airport security agents swarmed the area, handcuffing the two men who'd been arguing and taking them into custody. Another agent blew a shrill whistle in three rapid bursts. Agents surrounded Tekla and Chase.

"Keep away! Keep away!" she yelled. "It's a trap. They want to take us all out. All of you stay in your own lane." She threw a flying elbow at an imaginary opponent. "Fuck off. Don't touch me!"

Chase locked her hands in his and spoke calmly. "Tekla, this is Chase. Can you hear me? Tell me you know who I am." He hoped to enter what appeared to be a flashback and rescue her from the chaos that had overtaken her mind.

Gradually, the tension and terror on her face disappeared. She flung her ponytail off her shoulder, and the beret fell to the floor. Throwing her arms around him, she said, "Chase, thank you, thank you." She clung to him, her fingernails digging into his arms.

He squeezed her hand and gently massaged her shoulder, praying his comforting touch would calm her. Tekla's attention had turned inward, her mouth moving as if talking to herself.

Chase's bad hearing had forced him to learn the rudiments of lipreading, and he realized she was counting backward.

Suddenly, she spoke to him. "Do you think I'm a wack job?" A runaway tear trickled down her cheek.

Rescuing her had brought emotions to the surface. He felt energized by the closeness that had occurred between them. "Absolutely not! You were confused, but you're okay now."

The stomp of heavy boots directed his attention to the approach of a French security detail. He was in no mood to play twenty questions with them about an American veteran with PTSD. His main worry was whether the trip had exceeded her emotional limits. Chase whispered in Tekla's ear, "Let me handle this."

Chase gave his account to the burly senior-ranking official, who sported a jagged scar from his right ear to the bottom of his chin. Half his ear was missing as well. The man nodded, glanced at Tekla, and returned his attention to Chase.

"I'm Henri, Chief of Security. What is wrong with your travel partner? She is maybe a little high? Drugs perhaps?"

Chase's past legal partners hadn't hidden their respect for his ability to shred opposing counsel with surgical precision. In an instant, Chase constructed a strategy to end the investigation quickly. Tired and on edge, Chase admitted to himself that he did have a cold. He wanted to wrap up the fiasco and get to the hotel. He had one way to redirect Monsieur Henri's attention without throwing Tekla under the bus.

Chase utilized an eye roll to maximum effect, which caused Henri to stare straight at him and not Tekla. The legal eagle spread his arms wide in a plea for understanding and nodded toward Tekla's feet. He spoke one word in a bone-chilling monotone: "War."

Henri's gaze focused on Tekla's cropped black slacks, which exposed the shiny metal prosthesis below the hemline. The security guard's stance relaxed. He bowed his head and placed his right hand over his heart. "Ah, *je comprends*. I too have seen war and know of these things. You two come with me. I will escort you to the front of the passport line."

Chapter 29

"They didn't ask twice," Chase muttered, "about declaring JoAnn's ashes." He zipped his passport into his pants pocket, shaking his head.

"No worries. That's why I signed on, to make it easier for you." She knew she'd let him down and that he was about to question her.

"Easy for me?" His voice was a growl from deep in his gut. "We almost created an international scene at the airport. Let's take a cab rather than wait for the hotel's shuttle."

They headed for ground transportation. Tekla hailed the first cab, a black Mercedes Benz with two radio antennae whipping above the roof and tinted windows that gave it the appearance of a tank. The driver was a black-bearded man about five feet four, dressed in a black polo shirt. The fact that he wore aviator sunglasses with black lenses, even though the skies were gray and gloomy, made her tense. Her nerves remained on edge. She knew she was over-compensating in her efforts to maintain self-control.

The driver tossed their luggage into the open trunk and then popped open a hi-vis green umbrella to shield her from the sudden cloudburst.

"*Est-ce que vous parlez français?*" he asked from his seat behind the wheel.

Though the horrific flashback had cleared, Tekla examined every detail of the driver's appearance, stereotyping. She knew she shouldn't make snap judgments but couldn't shut down well-honed survival tools easily, not after the episode in the terminal.

She identified him as Algerian. There was something about the jawline of an Algerian man. His preference for French over Arabic confirmed her impression. She determined he was not a threat.

"*Bonjour. Voudriez-vous s'il vous plaît nous emmener à l'Hôtel du Mont Blanc, Vingt-huit Rue de Harpe?*" The driver acknowledged her instructions with a nod.

As they pulled up to the hotel, Chase said, "I think you'll like the place. It's old Paris, with small bedrooms. It smells four hundred years old, but it'll be good for us. Only a ten-minute walk to the cathedral."

"It's lovely," she cooed, "and definitely old." Through the drizzle, she gave the hotel a once-over from top to bottom, her head moving like sand through an hourglass. "American tourists," she commented, "expect every part of foreign travel to be like home. Let them spend a night in the US Army Hotel Plywood Kandahar with eighteen-foot T-walls and sandbags. No views, but great blast protection."

"There's an elevator that stops at each floor, and our suite on the seventh floor has adjoining bedrooms," he said.

The bellhop dodged raindrops as he hustled from the hotel and secured their luggage.

To delay any questions he might have about her airport meltdown and the state of her mental health, Tekla sat on a lounge chair in the lobby while he checked them in.

When Chase returned, he looked at her, cocked his head, and ran his fingers through his tousled hair. She assumed he was analyzing her, possibly doubting her stability.

She'd read that Paris smells the sweetest after a rain, and she was ready to open a window, start anew, and breathe out all the tension bottled inside her. She would inhale those sweet smells and believe they might give her freedom from fear and lessen any anxiety. But first, she needed to eat.

"I spotted my fantasy lunch in the window of the café next door. French Brie baked in a snug wrapper of flaky puff pastry." When she stumbled on the word *flaky*, she became self-conscious, thinking it could further incriminate her with Chase. But he looked fatigued and pale and didn't seem to notice.

"I've a weakness for pizza but maybe soup for now. I think a cold is coming on." He drew out two long sniffs. "After we eat, I'll call it a day. If I need anything, I'll call room service."

During lunch, she proposed they skip the hotel breakfast the next morning and eat outside the nearby bakery, Boulangerie Saint Michel.

. . .

"Everything boils down to the Paris vibe," she said with a jubilant smile. She used both hands to pull her hair back and tuck it behind her ears. She leaned in a little closer. "The lights through my window last night, this café, the fountains and statues, mimes, people drinking and singing. Aromas from the food blending with the smells of the Seine. What a sensory explosion!" She arched back to kiss the sky and embrace the morning, flooded with sunshine. "No wonder Parisians seem so happy. So contented."

He nodded in agreement. "JoAnn and I shared a similar opinion. We were charmed by the elegance of Paris." He made his breakfast choice and set the menu aside. "But I would not trade the beauty of Montana for it."

The waiter arrived to announce the breakfast special, a spinach and feta cheese croissant. Tekla chose the special and a cup of chai. Chase ordered his favorite French breakfast, *Croque monsieur*.

The waiter winked as he wrote the order. "Good choices."

Chase handed the menus back and surveyed Tekla's appearance. "How did you sleep last night?"

"A few pillow adjustments for my leg. That's all. And how are you? You sound better."

He hesitated, unsure whether to take his own advice on how to proceed. Should he bring up the airport scene? If so, how best to do it? His fingers drummed the table with a forceful and ominous beat.

"Tekla?"

"Chase?"

"I don't want to greet the morning with a Mexican standoff."

"I know," she said. "I know. The airport, right? It wasn't fair to dump my PTSD fruitcake on you like that." She folded her hands as if petitioning for a pardon.

He searched for hints to help him assess her mental state. He'd never let his face reveal his emotions. After a few minutes, he said, "I'll admit I planned for you to be my rock. I anticipated some accommodations because of your leg and my own challenges, but I'm not clear about why that incident happened yesterday."

He grabbed his handkerchief to stifle a sneeze. "I believe a little insight would help. Can you tell me about this so-called fruitcake you served up at the airport?"

Breakfast arrived, and she reached for her cup of chai, cradling it in her hands. Calmness came with her chai, he noticed. Her breathing had regained its usual rhythm, rolling in and out like a tumbleweed in the wind across his beloved Montana fields.

"I know it can be alarming. I know you are concerned, but you need not be." She closed her eyes and remained silent for a few minutes, rocking back and forth in her chair. "The fruitcake," she said in a sad, sorrowful voice. "That was a full-scale PTSD panic attack."

"How is that a fruitcake?"

"I see the confusion on your face. Let me explain. Sometimes I'll slip and call it the loonies; sometimes I say wacky or crazy when referring to my condition." Her words sounded more apologetic than angry. "My counselor wants me to move on from considering PTSD a life sentence. She told me not to demean myself by referring to it as some chronic disorder. So I call it whatever comes to mind. It's my way of coping with something I don't like but can't always control."

"It is your mental health, and you should do what works for you." His kind response did not overshadow the growing concern he had about her stability. He blamed himself for not parsing Nate's evaluation of her mental health issues. He believed she might be getting better, but he doubted any significant improvement would happen during the two weeks they would be together. Like a good lawyer, he asked her if she had more to say.

"Yesterday was just a textbook case of PTSD, brought on by the emotional triggers of combat: the machine guns, uniforms, armored vests." She answered like she had an excuse slip from Megan.

Chase had reached the end of his rope in dealing with Tekla's proclivity to hoard information. First her prosthesis, then her allergy to red wine, and now her PTSD. He believed she could gain understanding and find comfort by sharing information about her condition. It appeared she wanted to live life on a level field with everyone else, but she was not like everyone else. The life she wanted was not congruent with the life she was living. Her symptoms made that impossible.

In his frustration, his next statement came out as an accusation. "You should have alerted me to this, Tekla! I've heard about PTSD, but not from you!"

"I'm sorry," she said, looking down.

"Really?" He felt embarrassed he had used such a confrontational tone and tried to walk it back. "I'm sorry too."

She looked up and said in a soft voice, "An overload of triggers can cause my mind to flash back to the day I was blown up. My care team gave me exercises to help manage an attack by staying in the present time."

"I'm sorry. Although I don't have children, Nate's presence in my life makes it easy for me to slip into a parental role." He clenched his fingers and shook them like a preacher at a Chautauqua meeting. "I need you, Tekla. I've grown dependent on you. But you must learn to tell me things, especially about these fruitcake episodes or loonies or whatever you call them." He stopped, realizing what he'd said. "Excuse me. Your panic attacks. Even if they are less frequent than they used to be."

After a long, silent pause, Chase opened his hands as a beggar asks for alms. Thanks to his low vision, he knocked over a half-full glass of water. He signaled for their waiter to bring a dry napkin.

"This situation tells me that we are not on the same page emotionally. You have repeatedly withheld information I feel I should know." Tekla's face flushed, and he feared he'd embarrassed her. "I understand you don't heal from PTSD overnight, but I have doubts about whether I can rely on you."

"I'll try harder to remember my coping skills. Last night I emailed Megan, my counselor, and told her what happened." Tekla felt emotionally drained and let her chai go unfinished. "She reminded me of the exercises I need to do when I feel panic coming on."

"So Megan helped you?"

"Yes, she did. I understand that you need me."

Her words and the sincerity in her voice helped restore the emotional balance and trust between them.

"Let's drink up then." He waved to the waiter for the check. "It's a short walk to the cathedral."

. . .

They had walked two blocks when he halted and gazed at the gothic spires of the Notre Dame Cathedral in the distance.

"Because of the recent fire, access to Paris Point Zero is not available. We'll have to settle for getting as close as we can." He looked around as if to triangulate a location. "This spot is close enough." He glanced at the cathedral again and toe-tapped a large cobblestone on the street to mark the spot.

"Why here?" she asked. "I know from my French studies that Point Zero is the spot from which all distances in France are measured, but why did you want to come here?"

"JoAnn and I stood on that circle nearly twenty-five years ago, and I received a gift."

"Great. Knowing you and hearing about JoAnn, I bet you two shared a kiss to affirm your eternal devotion." She snapped a picture of him silhouetted against the backdrop of the cathedral.

Her sarcasm left him unnerved and unamused. He cast an eye toward heaven before shooting her a look that could've soured milk. JoAnn's gift was not to be taken lightly. "No, I received something more than eternal devotion. I received forgiveness, the highest form of love." He coughed, more from emotion than sickness, clearing his throat to coax his confession along.

"Oh, no," she said. "I'm sorry. I'm so sorry." Her tone implored forgiveness. "I didn't mean to be so smug. I can see this means a lot to you. How can I help?"

"How far along are you in forgiving the terrorists who blew your leg off? I despise terrorist acts." He thrust a finger to the sky. "But JoAnn reminded me that everyone in this world needs and is worthy of forgiveness. In forgiving someone, you achieve a certain freedom."

Tekla's face grew pale, and she became as still as a Parisian statue. Almost whispering, she said, "I'm sorry to have pricked an emotional nerve. I hope I haven't failed you again."

"You haven't failed me, but you need to understand that the greatest strength is knowing when you need support."

"I can interpret hidden messages too. You've just called me out on my own path to forgiveness."

He folded his arms across his chest and nodded, validating her assumption.

"The terrorists. My leg." She paused to regain her composure. "I'm aware that being angry and resentful aren't helping me, but forgiving them is a work in progress." She cleared her throat. "What did JoAnn forgive you for? Was it another woman?"

He scowled, his eyes burning with disgust, as he searched for the words to tell her how wrong she was and how low she'd stooped to assume he would be unfaithful to JoAnn.

Unable to restrain his outrage, he erupted in a full-throttle rave. "No, of course not!" He paused to calm himself and continued. "JoAnn brought her great-grandmother's rosary to the cathedral." He pointed over his shoulder to the spires. "The rosary had been in her family for more than 150 years, and it was her great-grandmother's final wish to have it blessed at Notre Dame. She hoped to have it blessed during evening vespers." Like a magnet, the mention of the cathedral pulled him around to stare at it once again.

Tentatively, Tekla said, "Why don't we sit on that bench? You look a little shaky."

He'd felt the blood pounding through his veins, followed by the sensation he was about to faint. He grabbed Tekla's hand to steady himself as he followed her suggestion to sit. Head in hands, Chase noticed that a pigeon had landed at his feet and started to nibble breadcrumbs. The memory of laughing at the pigeons with JoAnn made him laugh again.

His anger spent, he continued. "We did have the rosary blessed and then left the church. JoAnn put it in a jewelry box and stashed the box in her purse. She wanted to buy a watercolor print of the cathedral, and we found one in a nearby shop."

He looked off in the distance, trying to pinpoint which direction they'd gone or what had happened next. Then he remembered. "She emptied her purse on the counter to find her credit card and handed the jewelry box to me. It wasn't until we were back in Montana that she realized the rosary was not in her purse."

Tekla put her hands to her face and mouthed, "Oh, my God! Her rosary? You freakin' lost her rosary?"

He felt the need to speak in his defense. "I didn't exactly lose it. I just forgot what I did with it. We returned to Paris ten years later and stood on Point Zero. She told me she'd forgiven me and that it helped the loss hurt less."

Tekla said, "Let me think." She stood motionless, her right hand shading her eyes. She affirmed her decision. "Chase, that rosary is not lost. It's here in Paris. I feel it. Listen to yourself; you're a believer in karma."

He wanted to believe her, so he'd listen. It was the only way he could create his own path to forgiveness.

"What's your point?" he asked. He watched her appeal, praying with her clasped fingers, her body rocking back and forth to the rhythm of the tolling bells.

"We have to find that store. We're here, so why not try?"

She had the same energy as an Army recruiting commercial.

"Good gravy," he said, raising one eyebrow. "You really think after forty years that we can find that rosary?"

"Yep." She nodded and bumped fists with him. "Let's just do it. I feel I was meant to be here, to help you. Maybe this is one way I can help." She moved closer to him. "Can you describe the rosary?"

"It was a five-decade rosary." He used his left hand to pinch his eyebrows together as he tried to recall the image. "It had a crucifix with fifty-three green glass beads. Six beads were different from the rest. Her great-grandparents were from Murano, Italy, where the beads were made."

"I think you would've likely turned right from here because of the way the traffic flows."

He had a strong sense of the direction he and JoAnn had taken that day, but after forty years it was difficult to recall the exact street. "Yes, maybe that way. Possibly a ten-minute walk from here. The store was on the right side of the street, and it was owned by an older Jewish man who wore a black beret. A young couple was helping him. That's all I remember."

"Your ten minutes forty years ago with JoAnn would be fifteen minutes today, given your age and my prosthesis-related pace." She pointed to the street closest to Chase's memory of the direction. "Let's roll."

He fell in step alongside her. Although she'd been handling all the walking and standing without complaint, searching the Paris streets for a rosary missing for forty years was something above and beyond. But that seemed to be part of her essence. He was learning that Tekla was a woman who always went above and beyond, distinguishing herself by encouraging others. She was also stubborn. He'd stand a better chance of counting all the fountains in Paris than changing her mind.

Chase went along with her plan to stop at each store and ask if anyone remembered a Jewish man forty years ago who sold watercolor prints. He was amazed that not only had many of the store owners not been around for forty years, but they knew nothing about the stores directly adjacent to them.

"Pit stop," he announced. "I'm hungry, and I just got pinged for a battery change."

"I'm ready to sit." She sighed and took a seat at the outdoor café. Her leg needed to rest. She removed her prosthesis and placed it safely out of the way. "You need help with those batteries?"

"Thanks. My fingers are a little stiff today. Blame the rain yesterday."

The plastic caps on the batteries were a struggle to open, and she chipped a fingernail. "Crap," she said. After a shake of her head, she glanced down the street and groaned: "I'm good for one more street after lunch."

. . .

Her stump ached, and her back felt stiff. She needed relief and reached for her pill pack of hydrocodone and swallowed her max dose of two tablets with a sip of water. She asked him to wait a minute while she checked her stump. It was okay, so they set out again.

They had walked halfway down the next street. She was up for the challenge, setting the pace, with Chase following alongside. "This could be it," she'd say, only to be disappointed again.

Her energy faded after the fourth shop. Instead of walking on her prosthesis, she believed she was dragging it over the cobblestones. Dodging motor scooters and bumping elbows were all part of a walk on Parisian streets. At one point, she took a moment to rest against a white statue of Caesar. The statue let out an audible grunt of protest. That's when she realized the statue was a mime.

"I refuse to accept failure, but my leg has had enough for today." The pain in her voice was softened by the meds.

. . .

That night she borrowed the large-scale walking map of Paris that he'd used on previous visits. It was waterproof but dog-eared from constant use. He'd used a red marker to highlight areas he and JoAnn had visited. She knew Chase was a detail-oriented man, and the area they walked that afternoon had been heavily starred.

She turned the map over and saw the names of cafes and stores in his bold printing. One that stood out was the brasserie, le Musset, where he and JoAnn had lunched. He'd noted an order of *croque monsieur* and French onion soup, both of which received four stars.

A single "woo-hoo" left her lips. The next star on the list, its name worn from wear, read *Notre Dame Watercolor*. She folded the map and tucked it away in her shoulder bag. A rush of adrenaline coursed through her, and it was all she could do to remove her prosthesis and hit the rack.

Chapter 30

The next morning, she led Chase on a singularly focused trek to one address.

"Remember," he reminded her, "we have time for one street."

At the beginning of the next block, map in hand, she came to an abrupt halt at a small art shop with prints of the Notre Dame cathedral in the window. She double-checked the map and the address. The address starred on the map was a women's boutique two doors down. Could he have been wrong? She doubted it. She had a gut feeling the print store was the one he and JoAnn visited.

"Oh, yeah," she said, "We may have found something here." She waved the map over her head.

He asked, "What's going on?"

Without a response, Tekla entered the store. Parisian watercolors and refrigerator magnets featuring Notre Dame were stacked ceiling to floor. A kaleidoscope of colored ball caps and T-shirts filled the remaining space. A tall, skull-shaved man wearing a black beret was finalizing a credit card sale for a customer. Around the man's neck was a small gold necklace featuring the Star of David.

She approached an empty bronze chair in a corner of the store. In the nick of time, she noticed the *No Sitting* sign and realized the chair was a piece of art and not a piece of furniture.

Several minutes passed before the sales transaction was completed and the store owner turned to her. "How may I help you?"

Tekla's response was interrupted by an attractive, small-boned, gray-haired woman who emerged from the back of the store. She conversed with the bald man in French as if Tekla weren't there.

"*Excusez-moi. Gabe, est-ce que cette commande de cartes postales est arrivée? Il y a une femme à l'arrière, mais qui est vide.*"

"*Laleh, trop occupé pour ouvrir la boîte,*" he answered. "*Cartes encore en fonction.*"

Tekla turned to Chase and said, "She asked him whether the postcards arrived, and he said he's been too busy to open the box."

The woman turned to Tekla and nodded, as if to pardon her interruption, and left the room.

"Now, how may I help you? You need postcards too?" He turned a display rack showing his new postcards and flashed a meltdown smile at Tekla. "They just arrived. You like?"

"No postcards. My friend and I are trying to locate a store that was here about forty years ago. The owner was an older gentleman and maybe wore a black beret. A younger couple might have worked with him."

"Yes, yes, my father, Achim. My wife and I manage the store since he passed twenty years ago. I'm Gabe."

"I'm Tekla," she replied, "and this is my friend Chase." She turned to Chase. "It's your story now."

. . .

Chase shook Gabe's hand and hesitated to let go. He drew in a wispy breath of anticipation. He glanced around, feeling rather disoriented. "I'm not sure if this was the same store that my wife and I visited forty years ago."

"Ah. We move from two doors away twenty years ago. This store has more room," Gabe said. He spread his arms open, his face radiating happiness as he surveyed his inventory.

"Then my wife and I visited your old store. I believe I may have left my wife's rosary in your store. We're searching for it."

Gabe frowned. "Maybe we can find it. I don't know. This some silly treasure hunt maybe?"

"Absolutely not." Chase straightened, annoyed with the inference. "No. No game. A green glass beaded rosary is what I'm searching for."

Chase had hoped for the unexpected, something miraculous, even though the years the rosary had been lost predicted otherwise. He saw Tekla crossing her fingers on both hands.

Gabe nodded. "We are Polish Jews, and my father was a Krakow ghetto fighter during war. Fought many skirmishes with Nazis. He wasn't attached to material goods because he lost much. He opened Paris store. Many people forget things in his store."

He raised his hands as if making an offering, unable to express the sadness of collecting forgotten items in his store. He let out a sorrowful groan and shook his head twice. "My father believed lost articles are not lost. They have a life of their own. He meant to keep that life alive until they were found. You see that chair in the corner?"

"Does that empty chair have any special meaning?" Tekla asked.

"Yes, I tell you. We always keep an empty chair in the store in respect of 68,000 Kraków Jews killed. Empty Chair Monument in Kraków. Sixty-eight chairs."

Chase was profoundly moved by the impact the war had on the Polish people. How else could he explain the sudden sadness that swept over Gabe at the mention of the killing of Jews? Chase was proud of Gabe for not permitting the memory of the executed Jews to be lost.

The hush that had fallen over the room collapsed when Tekla spoke to Gabe in Polish, a language that was second to her.

"*Jestem w połowie Polakiem i byłem amerykańskim żołnierzem nikiem. Jak dumny musisz być*," she said, summing up her Polish heritage and experience as an American soldier.

Gabe's face lit up like one big flashlight. "*Dawno nie słyszałem, jak mówi się po polsku. Twój polski lepszy niż mój. Dziękuję za miłe słowa o ojcu.*"

Tekla translated for Chase. "He said he hasn't heard Polish spoken for a long time and that my pronunciation is better than his."

Gabe turned to Chase. "So what year you visit my store?"

"1975."

"I'll go to cellar and bring box up. After my father passed, Laleh and I combined items by decade. I bring up box for 1970."

Laleh came to Chase, who was standing by the register. "I hope you find wife's rosary. Rosary very religious, yes?"

Chase could not explain that this particular rosary was more than a string of beads to count devotions. They were not part of his belief system, but it didn't stop his profound respect for them.

"Yes, they are very religious."

Chase's nerves tingled when he heard the creaking steps of Gabe's climb from the basement. The mildewed box he carried saturated the air with a musty scent.

"You take box to back office and try to find rosary. I need to work the store," Gabe said with a sneeze.

The reality of the moment struck Chase like a blow to the chin. His knees wobbled. He clutched the soggy-bottomed box and hoped the decade of lost items would not break through to spill across the floor. It was bigger than three shoeboxes. Inside were people's treasures. Would his be included?

"Holy smokes! Can you believe this?" Tekla asked as she stretched out her arms like a magician who had conjured a white dove out of a hat. Then she went to work, sorting the items while Chase watched.

Car keys . . . more car keys . . . hotel keys . . . an Italian leather wallet . . . nylon wallets . . . a tiny pocket camera . . . a transistor radio . . . a small comb with strands of hair . . . credit cards . . . a woman's vanity mirror still smudged with fingerprints . . . lip gloss.

He sighed at the inventory of lost items.

She was just halfway through the box when her fingers came upon a small case. A gray jeweler's case. Could it be the rosary? "Unbelievable! You open it."

He held his breath for a moment and then sucked in a gulp of air. As he took the box from her hands, he said, "I remember it being a black case."

He had traveled through decades of remorse and guilt to reach that moment. The opening of that box of *alive items*, as Gabe had called them, provided him a momentary relief from anxiety and the guilt that fed it. His large hands shook. If he found the rosary, his tranquility and peace of mind would be restored.

If not . . . His anxiety spiked with that thought. His heart pounded as it had when he flattened an opponent in the ring. His legs felt sapped of all energy. His fingers trembled with hope and adrenaline.

Chase easily pried the box open, and there they were: the green-glass Italian beads of JoAnn's rosary.

His chest expanded, his heart thumped, and his shoulders and neck swayed in a trance-like state as he clasped the tiny box between his hands. From his throat a low "ooohm" resonated, reminiscent of a meditative chant he knew.

"They were never lost, Tekla. They were never lost. What were the odds we'd ever find them?" He praised her persistence and backed up his joy with a hug.

"No, they weren't lost." Her face glowed with equal parts astonishment and thrill. "I think Gabe and his wife deserve a hug too."

It was an incredible moment when all four shook hands and hugged. Tekla preserved the moment with a selfie. Chase blinked away his emotions and reached for her hand. Together, they walked in silence to the bench outside.

A quarter-hour passed while tour boats cruised the Seine, their boisterous passengers sipping champagne. Chase's fingers remained locked on the box, his knuckles white with tension. And then, in a measured moment, he flipped the box open again. That time he held the rosary up into the late afternoon sun. The beads sparkled, and tiny prisms of light danced on his face.

"Tekla, would you open your hands, please?"

"No, no. Please, I can't." She backed away.

With one last glimpse of the rosary shining in the sky, he reached forward and placed it in her hands, wrapping his fingers over hers.

"Tekla, these are yours now. The pain I experienced after losing them is over. May they help you find the power of forgiveness, as I received it. That's all I ask and all that I wish."

Tekla, a wounded warrior, a woman of kindness, courage, positivity, and passion, clenched the rosary. The Seine gurgled in the background. Church bells pealed as if to mark the discovery. She wept for the first time since that day outside a village in the mountains of Afghanistan—the day her leg was blasted from her boot and the luscious grapes that bordered an Afghan village went unpicked.

Chapter 31

Rocking from his toes to his heels to burn off anxiety, Nate scanned the town park for a spot to think. He located a splinter-free picnic table and sat, brooding, elbows on his knees and chin in his hands.

The soft, chattering call of a robin broke through his thoughts about the upcoming meeting with a woman from his past. His unexpected relationship with Tekla had the makings of a cosmic bond. Maybe she was his soulmate. Tekla sure tugged at his heartstrings. He wondered (and then worried) if she would ever let go.

He could not isolate a single source of his emotions but sensed his connection to Tekla was driven by the character and moral substance she displayed despite her PTSD, physical pain, and attachment issues. Tekla was light years beyond the women he'd encountered in his rodeo days, which put her outside his comfort zone. He struggled to balance so many conflicting emotions.

His evaluation process had already been complex, and now an outside variable threatened to make the dilemma harder to resolve. Someone from his almost-forgotten past rode into town from California. Carli, a black-haired beauty from his rodeo days had arrived unannounced. The news she brought could derail his budding relationship with Tekla. Carli claimed that Nate was the father of her four-year-old daughter.

Nate vaguely remembered her as a careless and naive lover. He frowned, recalling that she'd been a perfect fit for trysts in cheap hotel rooms after a night of rodeo. He mostly remembered the herbal scent of her shampoo. That, and the way her hair parted in the center, covering most of her right eye. The more he pondered, the more he remembered—*the ambulance ride after his goring—Carli at his bedside when he woke from surgery—his anger driving her away.* Time and tequila had blurred any other memories of her.

After delivering the shocking revelation, Carli had given him a day to process it all before telling him more of her story. Motherhood had changed her. She displayed kindness and a generosity of spirit that seemed genuine.

Nate had also matured beyond the days of his rough-and-tough cowboy lifestyle, but could he envision himself as a father? Being bucked off a bronc had never jarred him as much. Carli's announcement ushered Nate into a world of denial. He longed for a degree of predictability that had not been part of his past love affairs.

He tossed the faint memories of Carli aside and let the robin's song convince him to keep calm. He let the lilting sounds carry him back to the diversions of his youth. He'd loved bailing off the tall, timbered swing, landing solidly on his feet. Working the monkey bars displayed his uncanny ability to twist, bend, and balance, all traits of a future rodeo cowboy.

Nate tilted his ball cap off his forehead and tried to lock Carli in a little box in the back of his mind. He wished he could escape the dark cave of despair where he'd lived since Carli's arrival. If only he could rub Aladdin's lamp and ask the genie to revive the larger-than-life sensation of Tekla's embrace and the sweetness of her lips.

What did Carli want? Why now? How did she know it was his child? He wanted answers and hoped she would make good on her promise to provide them. Nate had squandered the time she'd given him to think, creating his own hell on earth.

He had acted like a petulant child, embarrassing himself in front of Tekla at dinner. Chase would say he'd reaped what he sowed. His father would say he'd behaved like a horse's ass. Both would be right. Did his neglect to use protection make this turn of events all his fault? Every story has two sides.

Tekla had just come into his life, but he was drawn to her. Did their relationship have to end because of one error in judgment years ago? It was a tough question. Perhaps the answer was hiding in the deep recesses of his psyche. He needed to search harder.

First, he needed to hear what Carli had to say, to hear the whole story. He aimed to speak his mind too and make the case for how unlikely it was that he had fathered her child. He would insist that she prove her claim. That wasn't likely to go over well.

His quickie flings during the rodeo days had always ended on the rocks. Back then, he'd feared the future as much as he dreaded being bucked sky-ward by the next bronc he rode. Years of being battered in the arena in front of 20,000 fans had left him with one fear that scared him the most, the fear of losing control.

Now he might be losing control. He wasn't going to let a foolish fling from his past ruin his future. However, the troubling possibility that she might be right lingered in the recesses of his mind. Maybe she wasn't the tight-jeaned body with a pretty face and an unstable mind that he recalled from his rodeo days. Besides, who was he to call someone from those days *unstable*? He might have overlooked something special about her.

Carli's maroon SUV pulled to a stop near his picnic table. *Show time.* After an acrobatic dismount, Nate stood tall and cinched his concho belt one notch tighter.

. . .

Carli's mind had returned to the welcoming beauty of Montana, fol-lowed by the hostility when she confronted Nate at the café. As she pulled up to the park, she practiced yoga breathing techniques to calm her mind. One deep breath cleared all apprehension, and her shoulders relaxed.

She hesitated and then checked her appearance one more time. After retouching her lipstick, she climbed out of the vehicle, swung her purse over one shoulder, and grabbed two iced teas off the seat. The Montana sun was warmer than she'd expected, but the breeze blew in at the perfect temperature.

Long strands of silky black hair kept falling across her eyes, so she curled them behind her ears. To make sure the strands didn't escape, she pushed her sunglasses to the top of her forehead.

Carli remembered Nate as a decent man, so she hadn't been afraid to discuss the paternity of her daughter, Olivia, with him. Still, she hoped she wasn't making a mistake by bringing Nate into her and Olivia's life. She couldn't have been a wife five years ago, nor Nate a husband. As Carli came face-to-face with Nate, she wondered if there was ever a right time to become a spouse—or a parent.

"I didn't know if you were going to show, but I brought two iced teas anyway. Consider it a peace offering. Would you like one?" The tea was her olive branch, and she hoped this meeting would fare better than the shock-and-awe version she'd delivered at the café.

"Sure."

"I kept up with your rodeoing on the internet but read you were no longer competing and now teach high school math. You seem to have healed nicely."

"So much for a private life, even here in Montana. But, yeah, I have the scars to remind me of my rodeo days."

She had no idea what had ignited the bitterness in his voice.

"Our last meeting was, well, tense. I have more to tell you, so I'll just jump in. I had an interview with the local school board last night. I like my chances for the English teacher opening." She squeezed the wedge of lemon into her tea and took a long draw through the straw. "I'd been searching for positions close to here, and I finally lucked out when a teacher at your school took medical leave."

"What are you talking about?" Nate jumped to his feet so abruptly that he spilled half his tea. "You intend to move here?" His voice rose another register. "The English vacancy at *my* school? You're kidding, right?"

She knew he could be hardnosed when backed into a corner, but she held her ground. "No, I'm not kidding. Olivia is ready to enroll in preschool, and I need to find full-time work." She took another sip of tea and checked her emotions. After draining the cup, she continued. "She's been asking where her daddy was. I told her he was lost. She needs you."

"What did you tell her about me?"

"When Olivia asked, I told her that she had a daddy and we needed to find him." She unzipped her purse and pulled out a legal-sized envelope. She wagged it in his face. "I listed you as the father on her birth certificate."

"You're shitting me." He pivoted to walk away but turned back. "After all these years, you now see me as a father and want me to be in your daughter's life?" The fire in his eyes frightened her. "You don't know me, and I don't know you."

She sensed that they both needed more space and took a step back. "Come on, Nate. Who was at your hospital bed after you had surgery in Pendleton?" She stomped her foot in frustration as well as for emphasis. "Who picked up your saddle from the arena? Who packed up your motel room?"

"All we did was knock boots together a couple of nights five years ago."

Nate was hot with anger. She'd never seen it in him before. Carli gently raised her hands as if surrendering, hoping for peace. It seemed to calm him down.

"My guess is that you've already talked to a lawyer. Right? What's next? Papers to pay four years of back child support when you've never said a word about your daughter, let alone sent me as much as a picture?"

"I would never do that to you. I've talked with a counselor but not a single lawyer."

Carli rubbed her temples to relieve a throbbing headache. Taking a temporary respite from the argument, she watched two squirrels chase each other up a tree. She needed a break from her long-held assumption that life had dealt her a shitty hand.

While she had done her best to control her emotions, Nate could only offer her an ice-cold heart. She struggled with what to do next. Should she describe Olivia to him? She hesitated to show him the three-by-five photo of Olivia but sensed it was the right thing to do. Her purse still open, she reached for the photo.

Olivia was with Carli's mother at the hotel. Carli wasn't ready for them to meet, not until a paternity test proved he was Olivia's father. Without further hesitation, she handed the photo to him.

"This is Olivia. Isn't she just darling?" She looked up from the photo to stare at Nate. "See that chin and her daddy's little grin? Do you see yourself in her?"

He snatched the photo of Olivia from her. His jaw dropped when he saw the resemblance to him.

"What do you think now?" His reaction told her he saw the likeness.

"I'm having trouble talking with this lump in my throat."

"She is beautiful, healthy, and full of innocence, sitting on her pony. She has my hair, but check out her nose, lips, and mouth."

Nate's legs wobbled as if one of Montana's small earthquakes rumbled beneath him.

"If Olivia is my child, I'll be responsible for her safety for all eternity." He swallowed hard against the golf-ball-sized lump still wedged in his throat. "It's a little much to digest right now."

Should she trust her intuition, she wondered? Their past had become ancient history, but Carli was ready for a new chapter. The prologue would open with her taking the first steps toward creating a new relationship with him.

Chapter 32

“Jed,” April groused, “would you look at me? I’m trying to talk to you. Nate’s planning on stopping by. Are you going to talk to him?”

“Hmph.”

“Quit pussy footin’ around,” she said while absently watering the houseplants. “Oh, darn. See what you made me do? I wasn’t concentrating and poured too much water on the spider plant.”

It pissed her off when Jed got into one of his unyielding, unbending moods. She would not let his smoldering stare over the half cup of steaming coffee shut her out. She waited while he picked out an embedded splinter on his forefinger with a safety pin.

“Jed!” she finally shouted.

“What do you want, April?” His head swiveled and his eyes bulged. “I’m busy. Is that all Nate told you? That he’s stopping by?” He finished the last of the coffee and held out his cup for a refill.

“Yes. For a few minutes.” She emptied the last of the pot into his cup.

“Maybe he won’t.” The safety pin was bent, and he couldn’t close it.

April pounded her fist on the table for effect. “You’re gonna have to buck up and talk to him. Chase isn’t his father—you are.”

“Sorry, April. I gotta call *low blow* on that Chase dig.” He waved his coffee mug at her, splashing part of the contents on the table.

"I'm sorry, Jed. It's just that I think he needs you."

"Please don't henpeck me or mother-hen him. I'll take care of it."

. . .

Jed hated to use Mr. Jimmy as a crutch, but he didn't like crawling through life without him either. He'd felt April's wrath the past winter after her gardening club members had found him passed out on the living room couch. Drunk, he'd peed a puddle on the wooden floor. It was an utter disgrace that resulted in April giving him a boot back to the wagon.

He'd been sober for a long spell, but there were times he needed a shot of courage. He wondered if it was to boost his confidence and stand tall next to Chase DeMers. Maybe he thought he could control the drinking. But the sweetness of the corn gave way to warmth on the tongue. And the ensuing jolt to his heart lifted him into euphoria, like being in a cloud that was larger than life. Most of all, the bourbon made him glow, and he liked that.

Later that afternoon, he rambled downstairs, smacking his lips as he walked through the guest bedroom to the adjoining bathroom. April had never discovered his private stash, and he could always count on a new fifth of Jim Beam, sunk halfway in the cool water in the tank, chilled with no need for ice.

Jed caught sight of his face in the mirror and froze. His skin was bronzed from decades of working outdoors, and the Montana sun had baked lines into his face. The lines highlighted how regret had tracked its passage. Regret from not being able to dream anymore. Regret for punishing himself. Regret for refusing self-forgiveness even though April always had his back.

His lupine-colored pupils stared out the window to the distant prairie, thinking about the peaks and valleys from places far back in his life. He was a proud man, gritty from a life roughened by reality. He refused to become red-eyed and numb from the bourbon despite the craving that simmered from throat to belly.

The devil had Jed by the ass, and he struggled to regain control, knowing he needed to be absolutely straight to take on Nate. His body wanted the drink, but his mind ruled in that solitary moment. He slid the tank cover back into place without much noise. He didn't need Chase DeMers—or bourbon—to do his job as a father, at least not that day. Not as long as he didn't get the shakes.

He turned to leave. He intended to leave. But the devil called him back. His need for firewater won over his best intentions. He rationalized that it would be his last drink and drained the bottle in three chugs. Then Jed smiled. The bottle had not let him down.

. . .

Nate rapped the elk antler knocker on the door of his family home. He'd been born in that house, and it peeved him to have to knock to come into his own home, but he bowed to his father's terms and his old-school values.

He loved the atmosphere of his old home, which had been constructed on the edge of town in the late thirties. The house had been in rough enough shape when his father bought it, and some thought the structure should have been pushed over with a bulldozer. Jed had paid twenty thousand dollars for ten acres of land and a million-dollar view. He fixed the place up. Nate was always proud of what his father could do with a hammer and nail.

His mother kept the photographs; he kept the memories.

When his mother opened the door, Nate said, "Hi, Mom. Sorry I couldn't make supper. Dad around?"

"He was out in the shop refinishing that walnut gun stock from his Browning, so I'll text him you're here."

Nate shuttled between standing, sitting, and checking his phone. His mom said, "You seem a little stressed. I'll bring you a slice of apple pie just out of the oven."

Nate knew what he had to say, but the offer of pie delayed it a bit. By the time he'd finished his piece of pie, his parents would've come to grips with the possibility they might be grandparents, with no wedding and no daughter-in-law.

The real world had arrived. He'd decided to take a paternity test, but the date of Olivia's birth and the facial likeness left little doubt in his mind that he was Olivia's father.

"What's up, son?" Jed kicked off his boots and hung his hat on the peg in the hallway.

Nate had to get it out, had to let them know. "Um, Dad. Mom. I had an old friend come to town." His voice dwindled with each word. "I haven't seen her since my California days."

"How wonderful," April said. "Do you know her from the ranch in Petaluma? Montana has a lure for attracting Californians these days." She dropped a dollop of crème fraiche on Nate's slice of pie. "Was she on vacation?"

Nate's body grew stiffer with each passing moment. He felt like a Western clothing store mannequin with a head slouched at an awkward angle. He fought for the right words. "No, business is more like it."

His mother held his leathery hands and rubbed warmth into them. She looked at Jed and rolled her eyes. He stood, swirling a water glass, the melting ice cubes rattling against the sides. "Go on," Jed said. "Seems important."

"Her name is Carli Castellano, and we dated for a short time about five years ago. Her father's ranch supplied a lot of the rodeo stock. I hadn't seen or heard from her since. Until she showed up here."

His mother smiled, indicating her happiness that he reconnected with an old flame. Her words were honey smooth. "Well, it's nice you two are still friends and staying in touch. I've never known too many couples who remained friends after going their separate ways."

"We were more than friends, if you get what I'm saying." Nate took a moment to scrutinize his mother's and dad's reactions.

"Nate," Jed howled, "we don't need a show-and-tell right now. What business brought Carli to town?"

Nate looked away, not wanting to see his father's cock-eyed stare. He fidgeted with his leather bracelet, twisting it in half circles before looking at his mother to gain confidence. "Um, family business. Yeah, family business."

"Does she have family here? My, what a small world. Don't you think so, Jed?"

"Castellanos? Never heard of that clan in these parts. What's their line of business?"

Nate pursed his lips, knowing that once he said the words out loud, he couldn't take them back.

"*I'm* her business." He rushed his words, speeding through them as if embarrassed by them. "She came here to inform me that I'm the father of her four-year-old daughter, Olivia. There. Now you know, grandma and grandpa."

"What?" Jed and April cried in unison.

Nate felt an awkward stillness sweep over the room. His mother clutched her heart. His father's chin sank to his chest. Nate tried to envision what this news would mean for everyone.

"Mom, I'm sorry."

She used both hands to smooth the cultivated stubble on his face.

"Sorry is not going to raise that child. I must say the news would've frosted your grandmother in her day." She held Nate's hand and also took hold of her husband's. "Four years seems like an awfully long time to wait before telling you. Are you sure you're the father? Are you planning to marry this Carli if you are?"

"Whoa, whoa, whoa!" Jed hollered. "Let's not put the cart before the horse here, April. No need for a shotgun wedding." He huffed in disgust. "Nate needs a lawyer and to have paternity established first. This is California wing-nut behavior." He turned his back and uttered a string of expletives under his breath. Calmness finally returned. "Chase will be back in ten days, and we can ask him for counsel."

"That seems wise," April said, nodding.

A hush fell over the Hutchens family parley. It took a minute for Jed to speak again. "When will we be able to meet Olivia? I need to be prepared not to let her see my disappointment in you."

"Jed!" April shouted. "What the hell!" To Nate, her voice sounded as loud as a thundering herd of buffalo.

Jed didn't respond but stared at Nate.

"That's a cheap shot, Dad. There's never been a lack of disappointment on my part about your attachment to the bottle," Nate shot back. "But I respected you enough to keep it to myself."

"Knock it off! Both of you." April had had enough. "Jed, fill your glass with some ice water and chill out. Nate, finish up with what you wanted to tell us about Carli."

The atmosphere quieted, but the emotional temperature rose as Nate continued.

"Carli wants to introduce Olivia to me after the results of the paternity test. I called a lab in Bozeman, and they informed me it would take two to three days for the test to be completed."

Jed put his hand on his son's shoulder and gave it a squeeze. Nate flinched at the touch.

"I'm sorry, Nate. That's a lot of earth-shaking news you laid on us. That's all I got to say right now. I've had a tough day, so I reckon I'll turn in and let you two chat some more."

His father's words had stung like salt in a wound, but it was best to let it go. "Thanks for coming around, Dad."

"We're family. We'll deal with it. Good night."

Nate hugged his mother, and she walked him out to his truck. She stood in the glow of the porchlight, clutching her arms to her chest as he drove off. Misty-eyed, she headed inside.

. . .

Jed had endured more than enough stress for one night. The news of being a grandfather created an immediate need to loosen up, unwind, and take the edge off with Mr. Jimmy. The devil was calling again. He licked his lips as each squeaky step took him closer to his elixir of comfort. One more stride, and he would be able to lift the cover off the toilet tank. He needed to be quiet. After a cautionary glance over his shoulder, he licked his upper lip one last time and removed the tank cover.

"Oh, sweet Jesus!" The sanctity of his hiding place had been breached.

His new bottle of Mr. Jimmy bobbed near the surface, drained to a two-ounce nip in the bottom of the bottle. Floating on the water was a sealed note kept dry in a sandwich bag. He fished out the baggie.

"Well, I'll be a son of a bitch." He read the note and then tossed it into the trash can. As a final act, he gave the can a swift kick across the room.

The neatly folded note had been written in April's flowing handwriting. *Jed. AA meetings Monday, Wednesday, and Friday at 9:00 a.m. at the Methodist church. Tuesday and Thursdays at 7:00 p.m. downstairs in the community hall. I love you, cowboy. April.*

Chapter 33

In Tekla's opinion, Paris Est Train Station could have been a combination mini-mall/museum. She sensed the history and admired the architecture. An assortment of hair salons and chic designer stores added a modern touch. The tantalizing baked goods in the windows made her salivate and displays of the newest perfume by Nina Ricci explained the scent emanating from women everywhere in Paris.

An elderly gentleman tickled the ivories on a piano, playing a soulful rendition of "Respect." The song reverberated with attitude, which was not out of sync with the unique ambiance of the Paris train station.

Tekla inhaled the aroma of fresh-baked bread and pastries. It rose above the scent of perfumed executives rushing by and the musty odor of well-worn travelers dragging their squeaky-wheeled luggage along the platform.

She remembered her duty to Chase and made sure he was still nearby. Checking the ever-changing electronic board, she waited for their assigned platform for Salzburg to appear and wondered how she would get her luggage onto the train. Tekla appealed to Chase for help, but he was having his own luggage issue, wrestling with the telescoping handle on his bag.

"Another case of luggage lunacy," she heard him say.

"I don't have much train experience," she admitted. "Do we have to schlep our own bags off the platform and into the car?"

Chase laughed. "Only in Hollywood movies do you see a porter help train passengers with luggage. We have to get our own bags to the proper car and then hustle them on board. But I've seen people help older folks and pregnant women."

"Hey, I'm not that old, and I'm not pregnant!"

He let out a hearty hoot. With a twinkle in his eye, he said, "Thanks for sharing that information. I'll tip someone to help, if necessary. Your job is to make sure we are on the right train and in the right car."

She pointed at the board above their heads. "Our train just appeared. We need to get to Platform 4. We have twelve minutes."

"Plenty of time."

Chase offered 20 € to a bulked-up French student whose baggage consisted of a small day pack. He made short work of hustling their bags aboard. They found their reserved section and collapsed into the plump leather seats.

Tekla was primed to start her railway escapade. She pulled out her tablet and charted the train's route east. "I'd hoped we would travel through Provence. The olive groves and fields of lavender and sunflowers must be as vibrant as an artist's palette."

"JoAnn loved Provence, which she said reminded her of the post-impressionist artist van Gogh. June is the best time."

Tekla spotted the complimentary buffet toward the front of their car. The selection of fruit and cheeses made her stomach rumble with anticipation. "Before the wheels roll, I think I'll get a wedge of brie. Maybe a few strawberries too."

Chase placed his hand on her shoulder. "Let me," he said.

He stood too quickly and felt lightheaded. Legs wobbling, he managed to fill two small plates. As he carried them to their seats, three toots alerted passengers that the train was reversing.

Chase stopped moving and flexed his knees to stabilize himself, but they buckled under him. He shot his arms out to each side, holding the plates as if he were balancing on a tightrope. A second later, his arms flailed.

Tekla failed to connect when she reached out to grab him. Chase's head bobbed at a rhythmic pace. The thought passed through his mind that he'd created a new dance. He added a move when he crumpled to the floor and landed facedown. One hand still clung to an empty plate while the other covered his face.

Pulling himself into a kneeling position, he saw the strawberries scattered on the floor around him, the wedge of brie nearby.

"Are you okay?" she cried out, offering him her hand.

"I'm fine. I'm fine," he growled, cursing his loss of balance. He brushed her hand aside, grabbed the armrest of the nearest seat, and stood.

"No damage done," he said, easing himself into his seat.

A railroad service agent made sure he wasn't injured and insisted he leave the cleanup to her. She returned a few minutes later with fresh plates of fruit and cheese.

The whistle blew two long and lonesome toots in an *au revoir* to Paris as the train rolled east. Tekla opened her tablet and began typing. The wheels made a clicking sound that coordinated with her keystrokes.

"Writing home?" Chase asked. "What's the news on your father?"

She leaned back, rolling her shoulders. "My mother's morning email informed me he's declining. I try to hold out hope that he'll get better, but I'm afraid my hope is waning. I think I'll send Nate an email."

"Good gravy, aren't your fingers cramped from all that typing?" It upset Chase that Tekla was missing the glorious views of the French countryside. He moaned in disbelief. "Your generation has a compulsion to post everything while seeing nothing. Take a look at the view outside the window. This is champagne country!"

"I know, I know. It's just my practice to follow up."

"I'm curious. It was only days ago that you didn't want anything to do with Nate. Now you're writing him."

"I've taken your lecture on forgiveness to heart." She let out a long sigh, a throwback to the way she began confessions as a young girl. "I've developed feelings for him that I can't explain. It's more than infatuation. There was this attraction between us, and I thought it could be the start of something good."

She saw Chase arch his eyebrows and wanted to get the tweezers from her bag and pluck the hairs between them.

"After his visit, I believed he was different from other men." She continued in a dreamy voice. "He was a man who excited me. He stole my breath away. He wanted me despite all my troublesome baggage. But I'm not capable of getting serious right now."

"I'll say it again. Nate is still the man you believed he was. We all have baggage."

Chase knew he wasn't exempt. He carried a heavy load of JoAnn baggage. "Don't resist it. Learn from it." She did not respond, but he was not done. "I don't know how heavy Nate's load is, but you don't need to carry his baggage."

"I'm pretty strong."

Chase needed Tekla to be his support on the trip and wished she could leave Nate behind while she was traveling with him. His next words carried an edge of annoyance. "His burden is not yours to carry. Something happened that turned his world upside down, and it coincided with our departure."

She put her tablet away and said, "I lost the fire for him. I'm not angry, but this may be tough for you to hear."

"I wasn't aware that you downed a double dose of cowboy love potion. Now you're dealing with the side effects."

She clutched her breasts and pretended to swoon. "Oh, wise one. Do you know of an antidote?"

"You'll have to look on your phone for a YouTube video for that information." His face fluctuated between a hard stare and a wide grin. "Sometimes the ideal path never opens. Focus on what matters. Right now, that's helping me fulfill JoAnn's wishes. Not everything needs a response."

"Understood."

She heard a piercing noise, followed by a whistle blowing and passengers shouting. She pitched forward when the train came to a grinding stop. A bottle of water rolled off her lap. Her tablet followed.

"What's happening?" Her head swiveled as she looked for the source of the confusion.

"Nothing to worry about. Could just be cows on the track." He returned to reading a day-old copy of *USA Today*.

"Are you sure?" She tilted her head for a view out the window. Lights flashed from police cars parked near the tracks. Civilians clashed with the police. "Oh, God! A tear gas canister just went off. Fucking terrorist attack! No-o-o." She clutched her throat, fighting for air while she struggled to talk. "I'm fucking losing it," she cried. "Help me, help me!"

His chest tightened and his breath shortened, but he reached for her and clutched her shoulder. "Stay with me, Tekla. It's going to be fine. Stay on the train. I've got you."

He pulled her into his arms and rocked her. His voice became a soothing balm that calmed the confusion in her head.

"Protests are quite common in France. We may be held up for a while. They just want to disrupt service, that's all. They're not terrorists."

He continued to rock the imperfect, complex woman who was filled with anxiety and fear. Her duty to her country had left her fighting off another flashback, this time in France. PTSD had no boundaries.

"Try to calm yourself. Think of your father's face. What does he look like? Here, take a sip of water."

Color returned to her face, and her breathing normalized. "I'm okay," she said. Her voice sounded puny, not yet catching up to her body. "I feel so lonely, so desolate after an attack. Thanks for being here."

Chase sighed, and his shoulders and head slumped. He too was drained emotionally and physically.

Tekla had rebounded enough to softly massage his temples and neck muscles. They loosened, and he drifted into a sleep interrupted only by one low moan.

• • •

Tekla wished she had the combination to the safe in Chase's brain, the one that held his treasure trove of memories about JoAnn. Fulfilling JoAnn's last wish, having him dust the Alps with her ashes, would become the final entry for Chase. She needed to make it happen.

During the journey by train, seeing the Alps and how they cradled Salzburg filled her with excitement. The mountains resembled fists, with fingers poking the sky. She found wonderment in the pristine blue-green lakes that bordered them. It seemed like a heavenly place to visit, and she understood how Mozart might have found inspiration by spending his childhood there.

When she stepped off the train at the Salzburg Hauptbahnhof main station, she was welcomed not by the ancient, baroque city but by a raw wind in her face. She hated the wind when it pressed against her. It had a way of interrupting her personal peace. At times, tranquility blew away with it.

Wind reminded her of Afghanistan, where gusts could blow for four months straight. "The Wind of 120 Days," is what the Afghans called it. Anxiety rose when the wind reminded her of the last normal day in Afghanistan before her bloody boot lay in the shadow of succulent grapes.

The specter of death, which haunted and tainted the simplest pleasures in her daily life, like riding a Ferris wheel, was linked to her PTSD. Wind had been the first phobia she vanquished, but a wind that blew forty miles an hour was hard to forget, so any gust of wind could deliver fresh anxieties.

Chapter 34

"Let's grab that taxi." Tekla waved her hand in a circle over her head and caught the eye of a driver who had been playing with his phone while his taxi idled. "Hotel Schloss Mönchstein," she said to him. The instructions brought a smile to the cabbie's face.

When the driver opened the door after they arrived at their destination, she sensed it was the hotel of her dreams. Built in the style of a castle, it sat on the well-manicured grounds of Mönchsberg Hill at the foot of the Salzach River in central Salzburg. A large park surrounded the hotel and offered panoramic views of the small city. The restorative pealing of the city's bells prompted a desire to experience the lasting impression of a Mozart concerto one day.

Chase broke into her reverie. "This hotel," he said, "was once a castle. JoAnn and I were treated like royalty when we stayed here." His plan was neatly falling into place. At last, he felt the stars had aligned themselves. A thin grin spread from ear to ear.

Tekla created a mental picture of Chase and JoAnn as king and queen and squeezed her eyes shut to lock in that image. Chase was already royalty in her book, a real king of hearts.

Running her fingers through her messy hair, she tried to immerse herself in the idyllic surroundings of the hotel and wondered why Salzburg had altered him.

He was no longer the hearty young pugilist from Butte or the learned, logical lawyer from Los Angeles. He had transformed into a shrunken septuagenarian who existed on a low-calorie diet of memories braised in guilt.

"She sipped a brilliant bone-dry Riesling from the Dachau Valley," Chase said, "and I enjoyed an Austrian lager brewed by monks." He pointed directly behind him. "See that terrace? We sat there and marveled at the views of the Alps you see to the east. Oh, those were the days."

She watched him drift off to another world and time. He'd closed his eyes, and she thought she heard something. Listening closely, she realized he was humming a tune she didn't recognize.

The cloud-covered Alps made her wish she could hire a helicopter to drop them off on one of the peaks. She wanted Chase to see the beauty of life that he was missing. Then she saw the contented look on his face and knew there was no difference between the life he was living and the life he was dreaming. JoAnn was the main event in both.

"Shall we check in?" she asked. His head jerked as her voice broke him from his captivated state.

. . .

In her room, Tekla reveled in the polished marble, bathed in transcendent golden sunshine from the glass ceiling and walls. After freshening up in their separate rooms, they met in the hotel lounge.

"I had hoped to relax outdoors," he said. Looking through the window, he shook his head and took a seat. "The wind and rain don't hold much promise for spending time outside."

"I don't like the wind," she said emphatically. One persistent memory formed when she helped unload a dead soldier from a Humvee in a howling windstorm in Afghanistan. The wind had whipped sand across her face, blurring her vision of the distant mountains, but it couldn't erase the image of the soldier's mask of death. Wind had a way of blowing that image back into her mind. She shook away the memory and returned her attention to the present.

"I looked up events in Salzburg for this evening. There's an Oktoberfest being held under a large tent just minutes from here. You up for that?" She secretly crossed her fingers that he was.

He rubbed the bridge of his nose where his glasses had rested earlier. She could tell what he was thinking before he voiced it. "I believe that is something you'd like, but there'll be a crowd and lots of beer, food, and music. Crowds give you trouble, and there was that incident at the airport."

Thanks for reminding me, she thought. She wished he would forget that incident and never bring it up again.

"I think it'll be fine. I'll take my chances with a beer stein over a machine gun." She embraced confidence and tucked her fears away.

A uniformed employee brought two glasses of chilled water with lemon wedges, along with a menu. Chase put his glasses back on and squinted at the back of the menu through his smudged lenses.

Tekla focused on her tablet, lost in thought while reviewing their itinerary. It prompted her to ask a question. "For a man who lives his life more in tune with theosophy, why are we visiting another Catholic cathedral tomorrow?" She'd spoken with a touch of humor that went unnoticed.

"You can't leave without visiting Dom zu Salzburg. Unbelievable construction for the 700s. Forty years ago, JoAnn set eyes upon that church and heard the pealing of the seven bells in the tower." Choked with emotion, he struggled to continue. "She claimed the bell-ringing was a symbol of the beginning and the end. The beginning for her. The end for me."

Tekla shuddered at his maudlin interpretation and withered from her own expectations of growing old. She saw herself as a lonely, one-legged woman, becoming less attractive and less healthy with each trip around the sun. Her face revealed the uneasiness creeping into her mind as she said, "I'm fine hearing your story, but it seems to be getting intensely personal."

"Let me get this out, please," he replied. "That same afternoon, we listened to the musical feast of bells upstairs in our room." His voice carried the longing for a love from the distant past. "Windows open, the Bavarian breeze in her hair, the pleasure we created under the covers—"

"I'm sorry," she said, interrupting. "But are you sure you want me to hear this?"

He either wasn't listening or didn't hear her. With her eyes squeezed shut, Tekla tried to block out his voice by covering her ears. It didn't work.

"JoAnn knew she became pregnant that autumn day. Mozart was born and baptized in that cathedral, but we never got to baptize our child any-where. We lost him two months later in Montana."

She relented and let him continue. It hurt her to know that his retelling left him without relief and only added another layer to his burden of guilt. Feeling the weight of his confession, she understood that beneath his knowledgeable, larger-than-life Western persona stood a solitary man weighed down by an undigested pork-chop sandwich.

"This is so freaking sad that I'm ready to cry," she said before tears rolled down her cheeks. The smile she had brought to the table had been wiped from her face.

"The bells are now a nuisance to my ears," he confessed. "I was sorry I never had the right words. I'm sorry I didn't hold her all those lonely times. I'm sorry I never forgave her for losing our child, something we created together that we could never buy. I'm still sorry." Out of breath, his face heavy with sorrow, he turned to the mountains. "Life didn't work out the way we planned."

In the relatively brief time she'd known Chase, she'd been a witness to an epic series of memories, musings, and mantras. It was always JoAnn this or JoAnn that. She couldn't turn it off or turn down the volume because she had signed on for it.

"I can't give you penance, advice, or absolution." Her voice, a low monotone, sounded like the voice of a priest in a confessional. "Your feelings are heartbreaking and sincere, but please try to live with some emotional honesty." Words of compassion flowed easily for her. "I'm here to help you. You can't blame yourself for something that was out of your hands, right?"

"I shouldn't have gone—"

"Let it be, Chase."

Her conciliatory voice brought a calmness to him, and that comforted her. "We both have suffered great losses. I'm thirty-three, yet I want to focus on moving forward in a lifetime without my leg. You had a large life with JoAnn. Now you have to find peace." She saw his limbs stiffen when she uttered the word *peace*. It was as if he were in the beginning stages of rigor mortis. A blank stare hardened his face, and it was several moments before he regained focus and composure.

"I'm sorry. I deserved that. It's so hard when I get tangled up in her loss."

"I'm here for you, but just as managing my panic attacks are a work in progress for me, you need to process your grief as well. How about following the lesson of the rosary?"

"To forgive?"

"Yes. Yes. She never hurt you." Her voice resonated with the essence of goodness. "Try to forgive yourself. She didn't have a miscarriage on purpose."

It was clear that his rehashed and recycled memories had worn him down, leaving him with a deep pain he wanted to shuck off. Her plan was to encourage him to live in the present time. Create a world of fresh memories. Somehow, he'd have to get over living with pork-chop guilt.

Just as she finished her thought, his thoughts turned to the present. "I'll call for the shuttle. We've had a big day."

Chapter 35

The shuttle driver apologized for having to let them out a short distance from the main tent. He explained that he was not permitted to drive through the raucous crowd. A fifty-meter walk through the drizzle was the best he could offer.

Tekla stepped out of the shuttle and joined Chase, who was pulling a windbreaker over his head. The wind shifted without warning and rose in intensity. It didn't bring the usual torrent of dark memories with it. Instead, she perceived a fresh, slow-moving stream of consciousness. *Did I tumble into grace?* she wondered.

When the sound of boughs snapping from an ancient beech tree reminded her of cannon fire, the polka tune bellowing from the main beer tent helped dispel her fears. Bending with the wind, she saw plastic bags, napkins, and paper plates snagged on the branches of ornamental trees. Chase said they reminded him of Tibetan prayer flags flapping in a breeze. Overhead, festival banners blew and frayed in the wind. When the folds of the beer tent opened, she tailed him inside. No one was manning the pay booth.

"I see an open chair right there." He pointed to an empty chair near the entrance.

Hundreds of beer-drenched revelers filled the tent. Most men were dressed in traditional Lederhosen leather shorts, and some women accentuated their female curves with tight bodices and high-waisted dirndls. The crowd danced to the polka medley, which ruffled the walls of the tent.

The foam-soaked hands of a buxom barmaid, her long blond pigtails tied with red ribbon, delivered an armload of ten frothy steins and plunked them down near their table. Tekla looked at Chase and pointed to her ears. "Can you hear me?" she shouted above the noise. The beer swillers all talking, singing, or chomping on large pretzels while keeping time with the loud polka beat drowned out conversation.

He pointed to his ears and gave a thumbs-up signal. "Have fun," he mouthed.

Something wasn't right. Her sense of the heebie-jeebies surged, and the need to scope out her surroundings rose to high alert. Anxiety ruled the moment. Her eyes flicked left to the buffet line. She turned right and saw the barmaids filling steins. All normal. Then she tilted her head back and was shaken to see how the wind pressure had puffed out the ceiling canvas like a deployed parachute. She sucked in large gulps of air, then small ones. Her heart quieted.

Just then, the stitching along the tent's wall tore from the floor and gave way to a slit that ran from the floor to the ceiling. The tent's loose flapping parts ripped. She peered through the gap. Darkness had not yet fallen, and a frantic scene erupted outside, with tables and chairs flying sideways and the smaller tent for smokers taking flight. The band played on.

When she whipped her head back toward the inside of the tent, her keen vision detected what a hundred revelers could not. One of the corner support poles near her was bending but holding. The center beams swung from side to side.

"Chase!" she screamed. "Get out! Get out now!" Her hands pawed the air to get his attention.

He couldn't hear. He didn't see. She charged toward him.

The big beams lifted up. She still had the lightning-quick reflexes that made her a top collegiate goalie. Lowering her shoulder, she wrapped her arms around his lower waist.

"Tekla," he growled. His beer stein went flying. "What the hell?"

In two great steps, she launched them both out the exit flap, using all the power she could muster from her good leg. Her prosthetic leg hooked an uncovered power cord before she tackled him to the ground. She landed on top of him, still clasping his thighs. Chase grunted and then rolled onto his back. His face was the color of chalk, and his eyes were closed. He opened them when she touched his cheek and neck, checking him for injuries.

"I'm fine. See if you can help the others." He gingerly got to his right knee first, as a groggy fighter might have done.

"Oh, no!" she screamed. Their end of the tent collapsed as costumed revelers fought for openings between the fallen poles.

She moved Chase back from the first responders who had arrived on the scene. A bombardment of sirens and flashing blue lights from local police vehicles blended with the shrieks of those exiting the chaos inside the tent.

She watched Chase cradle his right arm and turn his head in gentle rotations.

"Your neck," she said.

"It's nothing," he replied, grumbling. "Just aggravated that ATV accident. How are you?"

"Landing on you helped. I pray no one was critically injured."

He reached for her with both arms and drew her near. His hand cradled the back of her head and brought her closer. He rocked her, moving loose strands of hair away from her eyes.

"Thank you. That was a hell of a move you put on me. You may have saved me from serious injury or worse."

She sniffed twice and moved back from his comforting embrace to wipe her wet face with the back of her hand. She sniffed again and tilted her head skyward. A gust of wind drove the rain into her face, leaving her drenched. "Chase, did I ever tell you how much I hate the wind?"

Chapter 36

Jed sat at the dining room table as the familiar smell of fried hash browns floated from April's kitchen. She carried three plates of crisped bacon, sunny-up eggs, and huckleberry flapjacks into the room and set them on the table. For years, she had made the same Saturday morning cowboy special for the Hutchens men.

Jed swirled the floating coffee grounds in his cup and tried to read them as a gypsy would read tea leaves. Not surprisingly, the random selection of grounds couldn't tell him what he needed to know.

He wolfed down most of his breakfast before bringing up the topic that was on everyone's mind. "Son," he said, looking at the younger man. "You get the results of the paternity test back?" When Nate didn't answer immediately, Jed gulped his second jumbo mug of cowboy coffee and waited, rocking in his chair.

"Yeah," Nate finally replied, without looking up. "Signed, sealed, and delivered yesterday." Jed noticed the heaviness of doubt had left his son, and he was no longer slouching. "There are eleven repeating markers from me and nine from Carli, so legally it's a match. With this notarized finding, I'm a father. Just like that."

He snapped his fingers and then felt embarrassed about it, feeling the pressure and uncertainty of his future. "I'm sorry to lay this on you both."

Jed felt himself sag with the weight of the revelation. "My gut feeling is that you have a moral obligation to live up to the results of that paternity test." He looked at April, knowing he couldn't hide his shock from her no matter how confident he tried to sound. "This affects all of us, Nate. I'm a grandfather now, whether I want to be or not."

April gave him a stern look he knew well. He tried another approach. "How do you like being a grandmother, dear?"

She shrugged and said, "We have no choice, so I say we get on the bus. I, for one, can't wait to meet our granddaughter. If you don't feel the same, you need to change your attitude."

Jed bobbed his head in agreement. He did need to change his attitude. He also needed to get rid of his drinking habit. April made him want to be a better man. A simple nod from him always found a home in her heart and put a smile on her face.

They had been married thirty-six years. Beneath the hardened veneer of an uncompromising man, Jed knew his wife saw in him the spirit of a loving husband and father. Whenever he lost sight of that, she reminded him. He knew her love for him outweighed her irritation that he often sought comfort at the bottom of a glass.

Coffee mug in hand and a new outlook on his mind, Jed's expression changed to that of a doting grandfather. "So when can we meet Olivia?"

"Soon." Nate had trouble finding the words he wanted to say. "I missed out on the diaper years." He hesitated. "I guess I'll have to go straight to teaching her to ride a horse." His parents weren't smiling, so he tried again. "I'll get her Western real quick."

"What about you and Carli?" April asked. "Have you two talked about reconnecting and maybe getting married? It's better to have a father present every day in a child's life, and you've already missed too much of hers."

Nate replied, "Let me dispel any notions you have about me and Carli getting married. It's not going to happen." He looked back and forth between his parents. "A few nights with Carli did not commit me to marriage. I'm committed to accepting my role as Olivia's father, but marrying Carli would be a façade Olivia would see through as she gets older."

"Well, my goodness, Nate." His mother's sarcastic tone was less than helpful. "You don't know Carli that well. There must have been something about her that attracted you." The sarcasm disappeared, replaced with love and a bit of guilt. "Think about giving Olivia a real family." Then she turned to her husband. "Don't you agree, Jed?"

Jed cringed inwardly, but said, "Yes. Surely, under your tequila-soaked brain, son, you sensed something special about this woman." Jed regretted his comment the moment he uttered it.

Nate spread his arms wide for emphasis, something he'd done since childhood. "The years I spent cowboying in California were some of the best times I ever had, but they were also some of the most reckless. I didn't look beyond the surface of anything."

Nate's honesty offered his father a new perspective about his son.

Jed nodded. He remembered what goes on between men and women in their twenties. Nate was no different. Was he prepared to hear Nate's story? He was about to find out.

Nate scowled with the memory of that time. "At first, I worked horses on the ranch." His voice was as flat as one of his mother's pancakes. "It wasn't long before I competed in small-town rodeos."

He noticed that his son had lost the zest of recounting his glory days. The same had happened to Jed as he grew older and more mature.

Nate stared at his empty plate and cracked a knuckle. "I won often enough to get my PRCA card. You don't compete in rodeo; you live to hear the roar of the Sunday crowd."

Jed was familiar with the cheers of the beer-fueled crowd in the stands and how it acted as pure adrenaline for the cowboy in the arena. He also knew the addiction it created.

"The more I competed," Nate said, "the more I wanted. And the more I drank."

That remark caused Jed to bite his lip. He bobbed his head slowly to let Nate know he'd traveled the same road in his own way and knew the feeling. He'd never really left that road. As a result, he lived most days with the devil grabbing his ass. He did not want Nate to take that path.

"I suffered too many rodeo hangovers." Nate dropped his head and stared at his boots. "I wasn't drinking to celebrate but to ease the pain. Smoking a little weed helped me sleep."

Jed closed his eyes, imagining a younger, innocent Nate. He sat back in his chair, adjusted the wad of snuff in his cheek, and shrugged.

A horse's whinny came from Nate's cell phone. He scanned the message and said, "Just a text from Henry Struth, saying he's late but he'll still be here to shoe Santiago."

"So, you kept nipping cactus juice," Jed said, wagging a finger in Nate's face. "And getting stoned during the day."

Nate tipped back in his chair and crossed his arms across his chest. Jed felt the heat from Nate's blooming smirk before he said, "Dad, that's a little like the pot calling the kettle black, isn't it?"

"Jed, knock it off." April waved her hands at him like a two-bladed windmill in a tornado. "I'm leaving the dishes for you. Nate, back off your father or join him doing dishes. You two, get it together. This family could use a fat spliff right now. Maybe we should all should sit on the floor, bang a drum, and sing kumbaya."

Jed laughed out loud. He had always appreciated her use of humor when she was mad. Another laugh erupted when he thought she should ask Nate to learn kumbaya on his harmonica.

Nate ignored the ribbing. "The pain kept me isolated socially. I only found pleasure in one-nighters. I was a relationship junkie, imagining that all the women were giving love to me. I got so I'd rather feel good than compete well." He kept his head low and his voice lower. "After I was gored, a doctor diagnosed me with depression. It scared me. I woke up and left the past in my rearview mirror."

Jed thought Nate was always looking in the rearview mirror. It had concerned him enough to talk to Chase about it. Now he understood that his son saw life differently.

"Carli"—Nate paused—"was part of the past I had left behind. I had forgotten all about her until she showed up in town."

"Carli is here now," April said. "Don't you think it would be wise to explore and repair your relationship with her?"

Nate pushed his chair away from the table, and stood slowly, hitching up his jeans. "That's the point, Mom. You don't get it. There never was a relationship."

Jed's dread meter rose. The stillness that enveloped the room shattered when he experienced an epiphany. He rose straight from his chair, his eyes like cracking blue marbles. He put one hand on his son's shoulder. With the other, he summoned his wife and embraced her with a twist of his arthritic shoulder.

"No harm, son, in calling me out." Jed shifted his eyes to his wife and was warmed by her gentle nod of approval. It gave him more than a shot of courage to wrestle with the devil. "I gotta stay with AA this time. I have a granddaughter. She's here in this Montana valley and not in California. She has our blood, and I'm gonna cowboy up."

Nate and April each gave him a hug, and his heart felt the love where words failed.

"I'm sorry. I love you, son, and will stand behind you, just like your mother. Ain't that right, Mama?" Jed whooped and slapped his thigh to drive home the point.

"I've never seen you so happy!" April exclaimed. "What's happened?"

Jed stood between his wife and son, his face alternately revealing the pain of his past and the newfound joy of becoming a grandfather. "In the past few hours since Nate told us about Olivia, I've felt something I never believed possible in the past ten years. I feel sober and happy—at the same time."

. . .

Nate walked out of the house with a sense of relief. They would welcome Olivia into the family as their granddaughter. That only solved half of his dilemma. His mother wanted him to embrace a relationship with Carli that never existed. He was on his way to meet the woman, and a part of him dreaded it.

Overcome by his feelings, torn between two women, he picked up a pebble and aimed for the telephone pole across the street. His aim was true. What about his feelings?

Tekla had taken residence in his heart but not his life. Carli had inserted herself into his life but not his heart. He'd waited for that one special flame, that one incredible love that burned beyond passion, his own ring of fire.

He wondered if he was being presumptuous. Did either of them have similar feelings for him?

He thought how screwed up his life had become. He had discovered Tekla, only to learn he'd fathered a child with a woman he'd like to forget. The dilemma had turned his world upside down.

Chapter 37

Carli was sitting cross-legged, with a paperback book on her lap, when he arrived at their designated spot in the town park. Nate stared at her face, which was filled with eager curiosity.

"How did it go with your parents?" she asked. She stood smoothly, with the grace and control of a yoga master. Taking a deep breath, she smoothed out the seat of her jeans.

He checked the sky overhead and glanced to the east and then to the west. "It went like a weather forecast in Montana—severe early storm warning, giving way to partly sunny skies by midafternoon. No chance of rain. Sunny tomorrow."

"I remember that cowboy humor." She laughed and pulled her hair back into a loose bun. "Olivia and my mother are waiting for us. I arranged for a counselor to be present to help introduce you to your daughter."

Her voice sounded as if it had been dipped in honey, seeking sweetness.

"You can forget about the counselor. I'll be honest with both of you. A counselor is just one more face for Olivia to sort through. No hotel room either."

"I know this is hard," she said, reaching for his hand. He let her hold it. "Whatever is best for you. Olivia is used to rolling with whatever comes her way."

Nate noted both worry and kindness in Carli's expression. He locked hands with her but thought she sounded slicker than a used-car salesman at closing. He said, "I'll wait for you here, and we can take a drive out to the ranch where my dad works." He jutted his chin to the southeast. "Maybe we can take a four-wheeler for a ride. Olivia can sit up front with me."

"That's too much, Nate. She's only four. Trail riding doesn't sound all that safe. Can't we go for ice cream instead?"

"Four-wheelers are safer than bull-riding." His voice resonated with past pain, the memory of Pendleton stirring deep within. "Does your mother have to come?"

"No," she said. "I don't want her to come. She's too bossy and butts in with her bromides about my new-age parenting skills. In her opinion, I can never do anything right."

Mindful of keeping the peace for Olivia's sake, he said, "I don't want to make it any harder than it has to be. My knees are shaking already."

"Just relax." She pulled the car keys from her purse. "I'll have Olivia here within the hour."

More than half an hour passed, and Nate felt as restless as the falling leaves. He checked the weather on his phone. The forty-percent chance of afternoon showers had been updated to arrive sooner than predicted. But that could change.

The sound of crunching gravel surprised him. Carli's SUV appeared in the parking lot and pulled to a stop. Carli stepped out, and a small girl with well-brushed black hair bolted out of the passenger door, hair blowing in the breeze.

Her small hand latched onto Carli's fingers. Together they walked toward him. Olivia dropped Carli's hand and scoped Nate out, from head to toe. "Are you a real cowboy?" she asked. Olivia's gaze shifted to two small girls playing on a see-saw and back to Nate. "Where's your horse?"

He understood how unsure she must be of her new surroundings and the cowboy in front of her without a horse. He got down on one knee and came face to face with her, speaking in a softer tone than he'd ever used before. "I was a cowboy once, but now I teach school. I know your name is Olivia. Do you know my name?"

"You're Nate. Mommy said you're my daddy."

Her tiny voice made his heart race. "That's right, Olivia. I'm your daddy. I couldn't find you because I was lost." He couldn't see straight for a moment. "Now I've found you, and I won't get lost again. I promise." He raised his right hand so she would believe him.

Carli moved closer, stooped, and ran her fingers along Olivia's face.

"That chin and those eyes. My goodness. Do you see yourself in her?"

He analyzed the genetic likeness. Olivia had Carli's hair, but her lips, nose, and mouth were a spitting image of himself as a boy.

Olivia's gaze never shifted from him. "How come you got lost? Did your horse get lost too? You should come live with Mommy and me. Then you wouldn't get lost again."

He hadn't been around children much, but the truth and power in her little voice rocked him. "Yes, my horse got lost too, but I found him, and he helped me find you. I brought a little present for you." He beamed as if he had the winning Kentucky Derby ticket.

Nate felt as if his heart would tear apart with happiness. Montana wasn't as bright as the edge of the lightning bolt he now stood in. He picked up the wrapped present from the picnic table and handed it to Olivia. The thought that this beautiful child had come from thirty minutes with Carli in a $30.00 motel room blew his mind.

"Can I open it, Mommy?" Olivia asked. Hopping from one foot to the other, she repeated her request. "Can I open it, Mommy, please?"

Carli removed the tape that sealed the present and handed it to Olivia. "Presents are meant to be opened. Go ahead and see what Daddy brought you."

"Mommy, Mommy," Olivia said, giggling as she tore off the wrapping. "A book with funny animals." She pointed to the buffalo on the cover, her eyes wide with astonishment.

Nate flipped to the first page. He drew closer, and she put her hand on his leg. "These animals all live here in Montana. This one is a bobcat." He produced a deep, throaty purr. "That's how they sound, like a big kitty cat."

She lifted her wide eyes to his face. "He sounds hungry."

"Lots of people like bobcats. On this page is the grizzly bear." He pointed, prepared to growl, but her attention span was short.

"Mommy, can we ride in Nate's big truck now?" She hopped from one foot to the other while trying to touch her nose.

"You bet," he said, giving Carli no time to answer. His truck offered him a sense of control, so he was happy to fulfill Olivia's request. He backed off the urge to carry her on his shoulders. "You can ride shotgun. Right next to me."

Leaving the town's pavement behind, Nate turned east on the unpaved County Line Road. He contemplated the potential joy of being a father, but he had zero experience as a parent. The future was unknown, but the moment he met Olivia, he'd resigned himself to the one emotion that felt right: profound happiness.

Lost in thoughts about what being a dad might bring and feeling out of step with his new role, Nate drove too close to the truck ahead. The cab became smothered with road dust. His musings ended when Carli grabbed his ear.

"Hey, cowboy, slow down." She was hacking and wheezing in the back seat from the dust. "I can't breathe or see."

"Yeah, yeah, yeah. I'm sorry."

Olivia seemed oblivious to her mother's distress. She was naming the horses in the field they were passing.

"I think that one should be Spot." She erupted with a giggle, pointing to an Appaloosa trotting next to the fence.

"I always loved this country," Carli said. "The sagebrush hills, the striking gold of the willows, the first splotches of fall on the cottonwoods. Then her attention turned to her daughter. "Olivia, stop being so silly and stop pressing those buttons."

"Relax, Carli. Look there." Nate pointed at Chase's log ranch house and the tall pines ahead of them.

Carli saw the pride on his face. "What goes on at this spread?" she asked as her gaze moved across the sagebrush hills. "There's no livestock. No hay bales."

The crestfallen cowboy realized she failed to see the splendor of the ranch he loved. "Yep, like many other Montana ranches, this one's become a retreat for the rich. The owner is an excellent steward of the land, so that's good." He ended on an upbeat, flattering note that paid homage to a man he worshipped.

Nate slowed his truck as they drove across the first cattle guard at Willow Creek, which marked the northern property boundary of the DeMers ranch. He grabbed his phone and snapped a picture of an older red Ford pickup with Utah plates and a badly cracked windshield. The truck was parked on the edge of the road, and a middle-aged man with a powerful build stood in the shadows of the willows next to the creek. He wore a ball cap and a long-sleeved camo shirt. A short spinning rod leaned against his chest. He touched his eye before raising a pair of mini binoculars, glassing in the direction of Chase's ranch house.

Chase had his property signed to allow fishing and hunting with permission, but Nate did not know the man next to the creek. Chase had told him to look out for a particular man. Seeing the stranger raised a red flag.

Nate glanced back at Carli and took in the worry lines that crept across her face as her smile vanished. "Is something wrong, Nate?"

"These are blue-ribbon trout streams. That guy has a spinning rod. No fly rod, net, vest, or tackle box. It seems odd." He eyed the man in his rearview mirror as he drove on. Maybe it was his imagination, but the man executed one distinct hop in his walk along the creek.

"He's glassing something, and he's definitely not savvy about fishing. Since Olivia's in the truck, I won't stop, but I'll let my father know." He'd done what Chase had asked him to do, so he drove on.

Heavy frost had hit the valley, and his mother's prized lavender clumps had lost their fragrance and purple vibrancy. Still, seeing the lavender triggered a lingering remembrance of its fragrance misting his body on a hot morning in Seneca Falls.

As the truck came to a stop, Carli interrupted his blissful memory. "This is some ranch. What a view!" She was admiring the scenic panorama of the mountains when Nate opened Olivia's door and she trotted off to the corrals where two horses were munching hay.

Olivia had climbed to the second rail before Carli and Nate caught up with her. Her eyes were as big as lollipops.

"You have pretty horses. You're more fun than the other guys Mommy sees. They aren't my dad." After ratting out her mother, Olivia bounced up and down on the rail.

"Olivia!" Carli said, stopping her from climbing to the next rail.

"She's all right," Nate said. He gave Santiago a two-fingered whistle to come closer.

"Maybe we can go—on the four-wheeler—another time. She loves horses as you can tell." Carli pulled an inhaler from her pocket, took one puff, and tucked it away. "Allergies," she said by way of explanation.

"Here's my horse. His name is Santiago," Nate said. The long reach of his arm across the top rail let him rub Santiago behind his ears. "And there's my mother's horse, Cinder. Let me get some McIntosh apples from the shed, and Olivia can feed them."

When he returned, Cinder trotted to the fence, sniffing the sweet aroma of rotting apples in Nate's hand. She whinnied and tossed her head. Santiago snorted, and Olivia laughed loudly in her little-girl way.

"Santiago will grab it with his lips." Nate pantomimed, eliciting a delightful chortle of glee from the small girl. "I chop them into smaller pieces and take the seeds out first." He pulled a small Buck knife from his jeans and started cutting.

"Watch me, and I'll show you how to feed them to the horses." He demonstrated and said, "See how he licked me with his lips? That's his way of saying hi. Now your turn. Call him."

"Here, Saditago." Olivia called, adding a new twist to his name. Santiago rolled his tongue and licked the apple slice from Olivia's tiny hand.

"Mommy, I like Nate's horses. Can we ride his horse?"

Carli avoided being the go-between and said, "You'll have to ask Nate; it's his horse."

Nate said, "I'll make you a deal. How about I give you a piggyback ride to the truck and we go for ice cream. We can ride Santiago another day."

"Ice cream! I like ice cream."

With a whoosh of energy, he lifted Olivia off the ground and sat her squarely on his shoulders. She tapped her heels on his back, spurring him on while saying, "Giddy up, horsey!"

He laughed between the kicks and said, "Look, Carli. My family tree just got taller."

Olivia fell asleep as soon as he put her in the car seat he'd installed after he got the results of the paternity test.

Nate lowered the window to shoo out a horsefly and glanced at Carli in his rearview mirror. "I think she handled the day pretty well. Wouldn't you agree?"

"Olivia's a child. Not all days are going to be sprinkled with pixie dust like today." She wiggled her fingers to imitate dust falling. "I didn't know how it was going to go, but she likes you, Nate. Any mother could see that."

Carli's voice sounded calm, and he sensed her nerves were at rest. He tried to return the compliment.

"Life has given me a great gift, and my father taught me to never refuse one. I can accept that I'm a father now, and my love for Olivia will grow stronger. The years I missed because you kept her from me—that will take some time to forgive. And I'll admit I'm suspicious of your motive for reconnecting after so many years. That's all."

"I don't want to fight, okay?" Her voice was filled with despair and raw emotion. It occurred to him that Carli was trying to make the best of a life-altering event.

She took a deep breath and said, "Let's move on. I haven't heard back on the job yet. I doubt I'll get it."

"What makes you say that?"

"I'm from California, and there are a lot of Montana teachers out of work. Plus I have some master's credits that may price me out."

"It's too bad you don't have a mentor to plead your case." A smug glow of satisfaction tinged his voice. "I might know someone who can help."

"What's your fee for this mutually beneficial arrangement?" she asked.

He took on the personality of a car salesman sealing a transaction. "Here's the deal. I'll put in a good word for you with the president of the school board. I'll help you find a place to move into, and we'll work on splitting Olivia's custody down the middle. Okay?"

Carli crossed her arms, looked at her napping daughter, and said, "Sounds like an offer I shouldn't refuse, but let me think on it."

Chapter 38

On Sunday morning, Tekla and Chase cruised a long, straight stretch of the German autobahn with Chase at the wheel, yearning to fulfill his need for speed. The broad highway was tempting. He'd suffered no ill effects from Tekla's tackle the day before, and his fingers held a loose grip on the speed-sensitive steering of his rental SUV. He'd scored a tricked-out Mercedes with technology that only a rocket scientist could decipher.

He watched the needle crack the 150 kilometers-per-hour mark, but it was not enough. He let the mechanical steed have its head, giving it the entire 500 horsepower to play with. He was in the grips of a giddy-up-and-go state of mind that came upon him when he tried to outrun his memories.

"How is this for German engineering?" he said with a chuckle worthy of a speed-obsessed teenager. "I've only depressed the pedal halfway." A glimpse of his face in the rearview mirror showed him it was lit up brighter than the instrument panel.

"Like, maybe, move over." Tekla said as she double-checked her seat belt and tightened it before it was too late. "We're drifting over the edge of the lane boundary. Feel the rumble strip?"

"Relax."

"Why am I shaking?"

"There's no speed limit on this part of the autobahn, but I could back it off a bit." He peaked the speedometer at 160. At that speed, the lines on the road looked like dots.

"Slow down, Chase!" she shouted. She clapped her hands over her face, covering her eyes. "My life is passing by."

Thanks to his acute hearing loss, he missed out on her quite-sensible concern. He sped on.

"Chase! Your vision is not good enough to handle this terminal velocity." Her voice finally penetrated, and her tone telegraphed a direct and forceful challenge for him to slow down. "Remember your ATV crash? You were driving too fast for the conditions, right?"

"Almost have this sucker up to 110 miles an hour."

She yelled louder. "The last time I was in Germany, I was in a hospital bed! Got it? I don't like going this fast unless I'm doing the driving."

He finally understood her concern. "Sorry," he said. "I forgot that Germany might be an awful warfare memory for you. The power and speed of the autobahn is just such a rush." He kept his eyes focused on the road and replied without turning his head.

"I didn't know we were in a race, Chase. What's that sound? I hear something behind us." She looked out the back window. "Watch out!"

Chase backed off the gas and stole a glance into the side-view mirror. "Good gravy! Where did he come from?"

A high-powered sports car blew by them with a throaty roar. As the cherry red Ferrari rocketed past, the exhaust sounded like the tearing of canvas when the Salzburg tent collapsed.

His hands shook then, disrupting his steering enough that he swerved—a little to the left—a little to the right. He almost lost control of both the car and his bladder.

"They call that color Ferrari red for a reason, and there it goes." The thrill had disappeared from his voice.

"My God, that was fast," Tekla said. "How do you know it was a Ferrari?"

"Even if I hadn't seen it with my eyes, my poor hearing can still identify a Ferrari. Nothing else compares, not even a Porsche."

Tekla folded the roadmap she'd been clutching and slid it above the visor.

"If we don't crash first," she said in a calm tone, "we'll arrive in Zurich in time for lunch."

"Got it." His voice resonated with a delicious cackle. If she only knew how much he wanted to catch that red Ferrari.

. . .

"The Google map says we need to take the next exit for Zurich's Hauptbahnhof." Tekla opened the folder that held all their travel documents. "Here are the train tickets to Uetilberg Station."

"Wonderful," he said. "We'll board at the main station and take a twenty-minute ride to the end of the line at Uetilberg. It's trains only, no cars allowed. We can hike the few minutes to the summit and have lunch at the restaurant."

As they approached the station, they searched for a parking spot.

"There," he said. "That digital billboard is showing an open space: C69. It's all automated now."

"It's C89," she said, correcting him.

Situations like that made him grateful Tekla was with him. He could relax and breathe easier. But what he said was "I see that." His ego wouldn't let him admit that he hadn't seen it at all.

Being in Switzerland rendered him nostalgic, and he longed for spaetzle and beef goulash. The terminal was filled with cheerful-looking people, some carrying small picnic baskets. A few carried children in backpacks. Two paragliders dipped and soared high in the sky over the summit of what was termed a mountain. Chase saw nothing more than a small hill with superb views.

He walked at a brisk pace, the wind in his face, and stopped only to suck in a lungful of crisp Swiss air. Tekla lagged a step behind because she was searching for the prepaid tickets she'd stuffed into her black tote bag.

Relying on memories of his visit a decade earlier, Chase led the way into the main terminal. He came to an abrupt halt when he almost crashed into an accordion player who was pumping out the chords of a rousing folk song. His father had played the accordion at church picnics, and the music transported him back to the happy times of his youth. The music that had brought healing in those days added to his embarrassment after nearly running the man over.

Chase apologized for his clumsiness while taking stock of the musician. His crest of cropped black hair sat over a broad forehead, and his lips curved into a warm smile below a hooked nose. When Chase looked into his mysterious dark almond shaped eyes, he saw both deep pain and fierce strength. Despite his disarming grin, the man emanated the heart of a warrior.

The musician nodded and resumed playing, his hands floating over the yellowed ivory keys of his instrument. He played a heady blend of delightful notes with a hand that was missing its middle, ring, and little finger at the first joint. The surprise he experienced turned to amazement when he saw the musician's right leg was also missing.

The man had fashioned a prosthesis that resembled a long-handled toilet plunger duct-taped to his stump. A small ledge had been attached to give the end of the keyboard something to rest on. The ill-fitting prosthesis caused him to tilt to the left, while he kept the beat with his good leg.

At his feet sat a large wooden bowl containing paper money and coins from countries around the world, but his expression compelled passersby to appreciate the music. There wasn't a trace of shame or self-consciousness in his demeanor. He appeared neither to want nor need sympathy.

While the musician's physical condition shocked Chase, his primary reaction was rage that so many people have to live with such devastating injuries. He was not in the practice of making assumptions, but the man's missing body parts hinted at a gruesome injury in his past. Unsolved, the mystery could haunt Chase, as did learning about disarmed land mines injuring innocent people.

"Tekla, could you ask his name and where he's from?" Chase's head spun with nightmarish visions about how the injuries might have occurred. "Try to get a little background information, if he seems willing to talk."

"Take the glasses off the top of your head and put them on," she said, "and you'll see what I see. It's most likely a blast injury. I've seen plenty like his." She dropped several loose coins into his bowl.

"He has a story, and I'd like to hear it. I need to hear it. Hearing what happened to him might help you too."

The accordion player rested his hands on top of his instrument after finishing a song and gave his attention to the young woman he didn't know was also a tragedy of war. Chase witnessed Tekla's gift, her ability to communicate. Her hands danced through the air as they accompanied words that made the man's face shine like the sun, which had peeked through the clouds.

Slightly annoyed that he did not have Tekla's linguistic skills, Chase asked, "What's going on?"

"Meet Abdullah." She spoke a few words to the musician, who stretched his right hand toward Chase. Chase gripped the stubs of Abdullah's fingers with his hand. He was afraid he'd gripped a little too hard.

"Abdullah." The musician used his thumb to point to himself and then pointed to Chase.

"I'm Chase."

Chase was relieved that Abdullah hadn't flinched during the awkward handshake and that he had some understanding of English.

"What do we know?" Chase asked, a hint of urgency in his voice. Patience had never been easy for him, even when trying legal cases.

"He speaks a little broken English. I think he is Albanian," she said with a shrug. "He left Kosovo when it split from Serbia after the war in 1998."

"You got all that? Anything else?"

"He's a Muslim."

She continued to converse with Abdullah. Chase felt sure that Abdullah wanted to tell his story, and his rapt attention to Tekla proved his assumption. When she pulled her pants leg high enough for Abdullah to see her prosthesis, Chase made out one word: Afghanistan.

Abdullah stared intently at Tekla, transmitting his understanding of their similarities. He pointed to his handmade prosthesis. Abdullah gestured with his hands to simulate an explosion.

"Did you tell him your story?" Chase asked Tekla.

"I told him I was an American soldier. He's overwhelmed by the technology of my prosthetic limb. I'm not a whiz with Balkan dialects, but I understood part of it. He was a partisan who fought the Serbs in their holy war, when they participated in an ethnic cleansing against the Albanians. A land mine in his village took off his leg and fingertips. His youngest son and wife were killed in the same blast. Russian soldiers raped his daughter. I filled in some gaps based on my knowledge of the war."

Something in Abdullah's demeanor revealed a humble spirit infused with courage. It was clear he did not take his life for granted. Chase had never taken for granted his wealth or the privileges that came with it. He'd always been aware that money was a fragile concept, and he handled it with care. And here was Abdullah, smiling and cheerful while living on the coins that were dropped into his basket.

Chase had taken up boxing as a boy in Butte to protect those who were getting their asses kicked or having their lunch money stolen by bullies. He maintained a robust affection for those who fought for noble causes, for the downtrodden of the world. He thought of all the innocents who had suffered the consequences of land mines.

Chase had faced a moral dilemma when he saw the effects on Tekla of losing a limb in service to her country. Then his research revealed that millions of land mines around the world had not been defused or removed and remained a threat.

JoAnn had expressed her desire for their estate to be donated to cancer research upon Chase's death. He now saw it differently. After learning about Abdullah's experience, he wanted to make a significant difference in one man's life.

He tapped Tekla on the shoulder and said, "Excuse me for a minute. I need to use the men's room."

She nodded.

That part was true, but he also wanted to use the ATM adjacent to the men's room. After a minute's walk, he lost his bearings and stood dazed in the crowd. He wandered through the station until he found a service desk. The agent was a pert woman in her sixties, with silver hair and a pair of stylish reading glasses perched on her nose.

"Uh, hello. Could you help me? I'm having trouble finding an ATM."

She asked him a question, and he thought he heard "ATM." Her German accent was thick.

Chase pointed to his ears and then threw his hands up in frustration. He couldn't make heads or tails of what she'd said. The noise of the crowd didn't help either. "I'm sorry," he said. "I'm hearing impaired."

The agent simulated inserting a credit card into an ATM.

"ATM, ja?" she asked.

"Yes, yes. ATM." He then asked his Swiss hero for directions. "Which way?"

She talked briefly in German to her associate and then exited her kiosk to take Chase by the hand and escort him through the crowded terminal. After they walked through an exit door, the agent halted and pointed. "ATM, ja?"

"Thank you, thank you." Chase squeezed her hand gently to express his gratitude.

He was relieved not only to find the ATM but to realize that the kindness of the rail agent was not a dream. He quickly used the restroom and then walked the few step to the ATM. He pulled out his leather wallet and unzipped a separate lining to access his American Express Centurion card. The so-called "black card" was offered only to those who were financially well-off and at times needed a withdrawal with no limit on the amount. He entered his password, the date of his birthday followed by JoAnn's. The ATM responded, dispensing banknotes with Swiss precision. Chase stuffed them into one of the banking envelopes available at the ATM.

He found his way back to Tekla without additional assistance. Abdullah had resumed his playing. Chase said, "He perseveres. What is the lesson?"

She paused, pondering. Then she grinned before shouting it to the heavens and anyone within listening range. "For the love of Mike, he forgave."

Chase patted her on the back and said, "Congratulations. You're learning."

Tekla paused and cleared her throat, searching for the words to continue. "He came to Zurich with his surviving son and his daughter with the help of a missionary outreach program. He has no medical help or assistance, and playing the accordion provides his sole income."

Chase removed the envelope stuffed with Swiss banknotes from his pocket and discretely palmed it to Tekla.

"I want you to give this to Abdullah and tell him to put it in his pocket."

"Treating the family to pizza?"

"For the next three years."

Chase reached for Abdullah's hand, shook it, and slipped away.

At that very moment, on a sun-splashed morning in Zurich, amidst the din of train whistles, idling buses, and chattering children, Chase DeMers stood as tall as he ever had. Shoulders back and head tilted to gaze at the sky, he was overcome with an emotion he could not quench. Eying the faint glimmer of the Alps on the horizon, he imagined he heard the mountains call to him to do his duty. His universe cracked above him to pull the burdensome weight of JoAnn's final wish through it. But it got stuck halfway.

Chase's once-clear directive to follow JoAnn's final wish was in conflict. He experienced a calling, a revelation about how he could help the world in a different way. His new vision was as sharp and clean as a laser's beam. His face warmed as the cold heartache and sense of isolation were replaced with the glow of enlightenment. He knew where he was headed, and he knew who to ask for help. It would change his plans, but JoAnn would understand.

Determination burst into action. He said loudly enough for anyone to hear, "Gawddamn it. A civilian who lost a limb to a land mine deserves more than a toilet plunger for a prosthesis." He then rested his case.

Chapter 39

A northwest wind rattled the slopes of the Bernese Alps and stiffened the Swiss flags planted on the Aletch Glacier. Chase stood alone, his face stinging from the gusts that carried glittering snow crystals. His breathing had become rapid, a common reaction when the body adjusts to a higher altitude.

Chase's response to Tekla's request to accompany him had been a blunt *no*. He required solitude to suppress his fears and focus on the ceremony. He'd practiced it hundreds of times in his head.

Maybe he had been too harsh with Tekla. She was concerned for his well-being, and he regretted his rudeness. He sucked in a lungful of air and regretted that too when it burned his throat and lungs.

A dense crowd of tourists had ruined the idyllic setting he'd imagined. The Aletch Glacier served as a journal entry for people seeking their own mountain glory, whether it involved standing in awe of the ancient mountain peaks, meditating, skiing, or hiking. Diverse cultures were content to huddle in a mass of humanity just beyond the entrance to the glacier.

The mixed bag of tourists represented a myriad of ethnicities, all chattering in their native tongues. Photographers unpacked their cameras and lenses. Mountaineers shouldered their skis, and fathers loaded their children into backpacks for glacier trekking. Narcissists with selfie sticks blocked the best views and the entrances to many trails.

He feared he would not be able to recreate the spiritual haven he and

JoAnn had once enjoyed, an essential part of the ceremony he had planned. Chase viewed the crowd as a threat, poised to interrupt his private ritual and the serenity he hoped to attain.

He leaned into the squall, his hand gripping the guide ropes for support. At times, the wind blew hard enough to knock him head over heels if he became careless. Gloveless, he struggled to snap the high collar of his outer shell, a 3-in-1 cocoon of a coat. After he applied another layer of cherry lip moisturizer and cinched his polarized glasses to fit more tightly, Chase felt ready to move on.

For the fourth time that morning, he patted the coat's side pocket, assuring himself that the sealed baggie of JoAnn's ashes remained safe. A glove dropped from his pocket, and he stooped to pick it up. He hesitated, his posture locked in a deep bend at the waist, and stared at the pair of rental six-point crampons lying at his feet. He wondered how they had fallen out of his backpack.

That morning, Tekla had given him an earful about throwing caution to the wind, but he had won his case. "I'll use the crampons if I need to," he'd promised.

At that, she'd thrown her hands up in frustration, and Chase knew she doubted his sanity.

"I'll be back in an hour," he'd said, hoping his tone conveyed the level of self-confidence he wished he felt. He understood her fears and concerns, as well as her guilt in letting him walk on the glacier alone.

She'd hugged him tight before he walked away, saying, "Please be safe out there. I wish you great peace today."

Once on the glacier, he found the tourist-packed snow was neither polished nor icy, so he stashed the crampons in his day pack. They joined half a liter of water and a stale, half-eaten chocolate protein bar from some previous adventure.

Picking his way through the first group of adventure seekers, he huffed at their manners and came close to screaming loud enough to be heard above the wind.

He repeated "Out of my way, please" and "Excuse me" as he navigated around the mass of tourists. "Get that stick out of my face!" he yelled at one teenager, giving in to frustration.

The tension mounted with every minute he spent surrounded by strangers. In his mind, he heard JoAnn's nurse telling him it was all right to leave his wife's side and go for that sandwich. Now, instead of vanquishing his guilt and memorializing her life, he brooded and fumed. He knew those people were sightseers with as much right to be on the trail as he had. But he craved privacy, even if it was the largest glacier in the Alps.

The serenity he'd experienced there with JoAnn had vanished. The sanctity of his glacial altar had been defiled. The sacred site was being trampled with abandon.

However, the mountain cathedrals remained intact. The Eiger, the Mönch, and the Jungfrau were so dramatic, so immense that they inspired awe. He strained his neck and looked upward to see them in all their glory. Soaring to more than 13,000 feet, rimmed with silver and gray clouds, their diamond-glinted summits transformed them into the holiest church he'd ever visited.

He patted his pocket again, as if to assure JoAnn that she would soon be free to join her angels.

· · ·

He trudged on, uncharacteristically obsessed and unaware of anything that got in his way. Every step took him closer to the trail leading to the Mönchsjoch warming hut. The hut had been built over a snow-covered glacier, which was an astonishing 800 meters thick in places. Though the hut provided a base for ice climbing and mountain-based adventure, it also served as a warm and functional shelter. Was his memory clear about the hut being so close to the observatory? Age had taken its toll when it came to judging time and distance.

He stopped to pull his woolen hat lower over his ears. The crampons were still in his pack, and he would leave them there. Although mindful of his pledge to Tekla, he tramped on, continuing his mad trek to privacy.

The trail was well-marked and relatively flat, and it led him away from the irritating crush of tourists. Solitary snow crystals blew across the glacier, refracting into rainbow colors in the cold, clear sunshine. A few hikers walked alone, while others dawdled and stopped every twenty steps to snap another picture. They had maintained a steady presence in front of and behind him.

Chase was in pursuit of privacy, and he would hike until he found it. In desperation, he moved off the marked trail and walked a step closer to solitude, eager to share his new understanding with the Eiger. He finally comprehended JoAnn's perception of the mountains as a source of divine inspiration. Their majesty connected her to God.

He ambled a few steps more before reaching the ice field. His heart raced with a new fear, a sense of dread that the glacier might no longer be as he remembered it. The extensive Aletch Glacier still dwarfed him. It was the same sense of proportion that had led him to buy the painting *River Walkers*, which portrayed the diminutive scale of man in proper proportion to the boundless beauty of nature.

He continued on, walking like a penguin, waddling on the flat ice that stretched for 100 meters before the terrain angled toward the surrounding ridgeline. It was there that Chase discovered the perfect spot for his glacial altar. At last, he'd found solemnity beyond the wind and tourists.

Chase shook with shock, and then wonderment. The enormity of the glacier, the staggering peaks all around him, and the absolute solitude made it the ideal place to set JoAnn free.

After removing his gloves and unsnapping the pocket that held JoAnn's ashes, he surveyed the expansive ice field. Amid the shades of black, white, and gray, which matched the color of his coat, he saw a patch of brilliant blue. He knew what it was: glacial ice more than 10,000 years old. How much longer would it last?

He had found JoAnn's new home. He was there at last. He'd done it. JoAnn's final wish would be fulfilled.

Windblown snow crystals landed on his hands and melted. The wind left his fingertips numb, but gloved hands would not be able to open the plastic bag.

Then he heard something that didn't fit. The sound rose above the wind, loud enough that his hearing aids processed it. He turned to find the source of the sound. Loose rocks had been kicked free by an ibex high on the rocky ledge in front of him. The quick turn of his head made him dizzy, but the old boxer found his legs.

He squeezed and massaged the bag in his hand, ready to surrender its contents to the alpine wind. He felt an eerie presence of angels watching his every move.

He held the bag in one hand while the cold fingers on the other hand fiddled with the opening. The wind gusted, blowing with a triple fury before ripping the sealed bag of ashes out of his hand.

"No! No! JoAnn!" Chase howled like a banshee, the icy air numbing his throat.

He lunged for the bag but missed it by an inch. It skimmed across the glacier, ruled by the wind, its unbroken seal keeping JoAnn trapped in plastic.

"Her ashes! Her ashes!" he cried to the careless, uncaring wind. No one heard his wailing.

Chase hung his head, consumed by complete grief, a sorrow that had not been sanded down or worn away by time. His grief had returned to the guilt stage, fueled by the memory of that gawddamn pork-chop sandwich. He had made peace with himself outside the Zurich train station, but letting JoAnn down a final time was something he could not accept.

Exhausted and panting, his heart thumping, he watched the bagged ashes fly clean out of sight. All he needed was a miracle. One miracle. Chase pleaded to the mountain spirits to deliver one.

The spirits listened.

A new wind swirled from the north, and the baggie came skimming across the glacier toward him like a yo-yo on a string. He sprang for the baggie, but the return was a tease. He missed the bag when it skipped below his altitudinal vision defect, and he grasped only air. He cursed the wind, even though the wind was not to blame for his poor vision.

JoAnn's ashes continued on their wayward course, her burned, crushed bones trapped in a plastic bag, the very type of bag his blasted sandwich had come in. The plastic could take more than 500 years to decompose and set her free.

He had not only missed the baggie, but he missed seeing a hole covered with a thin layer of snow. His right foot plunged through the snow bridge, and he slid feet first into a crevasse, his butt and backpack bouncing along, the pack absorbing most of the impact to his head. The slide peeled off his woolen hat.

His fall took him along a slanting ice wall five meters deep into the Aletch Glacier. His limp body came to rest on a narrow snow bridge, a precarious perch that saved him from falling into greater depths within the fissure. The sky seemed to turn black. In his woozy state, he saw a million stars float by.

A single shaft of white light from the surface pierced the space and aroused him from his grogginess. He moaned, his body sore and his mind confused by his surroundings. In that stillness, he felt chilled by the melted glacial ice trickling from a seepage directly overhead. The water drenched his head and ran beneath the high collar of his coat.

The icy water initiated an alpine shock treatment. He struggled to a sitting position on the snow bridge, and his heart sank as he comprehended the predicament he faced. His ice prison was formed with walls four meters wide. Next, he evaluated his wounds. He had no open fractures, but he'd sustained a few minor injuries: a goose egg on his head, two aching elbows, a battered butt, and a twisted ankle.

All in all, it was a good place to land, but it was hard to avoid the dripping water without stepping off the snow bridge. The best he could do was turn his head away from the water. If he moved too much, he could lose his balance and plunge into the great unknown.

He still had the crampons in his shouldered pack, but he had no ice screws to keep him from falling off the ledge and no ice axe to chisel some steps. He also had no rope, which all but eliminated any chance of rescuing himself. At seventy-two, he found himself in the most precarious situation of his life. Even if he had a rope anchored on top, he had neither the skills nor the strength to prusik himself out. He thought of praying but worried he was not worthy enough.

Peering over the edge of the snow bridge, Chase called into the depths of the crevasse, "JoAnn!" The return was muddled in the rumbling echoes of the vast chasm of ice. The results confirmed what he feared: the crevasse descended to unknown depths.

He'd landed in a fortunate spot and grasped at the strange possibility that a guardian angel was watching over him. The idea collided with his lifelong doubt about divine intervention and added to his uncertainty. But didn't Willie sing about miracles appearing in the strangest of places?

Perhaps divine intervention could happen in the depths of a crevasse on the Aletch glacier. JoAnn would say there was no place too strange for a miracle.

Majestic in its silence, the crevasse felt like something from a dream. Odd thoughts flitted through Chase's mind, including an assessment that the striking blueness of the ice was the color of his favorite aftershave. Instead of panic, he entered a state of peaceful stillness, reflecting again on how small and insignificant he was in the fundamental relationship between humans and nature. A passing cloud dimmed the sunlight from the hole above.

Reminded of his dilemma, he shrugged off the day pack and explored all the zippered pockets, hoping to find something, anything that could give him hope. Several sheets of toilet paper and two extra-strength pain pills in a tin were all he found, other than the half-eaten energy bar and a small container of water he'd discovered earlier. He swallowed the two gel tabs to ease the pain in his ankle, washing them down with a swig of water.

Grabbing his cell phone, Chase tried to text Tekla, but the message wouldn't go through. In desperation, he dialed 1-1-2, Switzerland's 9-1-1 equivalent. When his distress call failed as well, he suspected the low temperature had drained his phone's battery. He reached inside a zippered inner coat pocket and fingered the emergency rescue whistle that had come with the winter garb.

Without a working phone, he had little hope of being rescued. As the urgency of his situation sunk in, Chase confronted the terror of being frozen alive. The fight-or-flight genes woven into his DNA activated instantly, bringing out the defiant survival instinct within him. His adrenal glands went into overdrive, pumping adrenalin into his bloodstream. The Butte fighter remained standing.

He knew he was in a real fight, and real fights were brutal and ugly. He slapped his hands together to warm them and keep the blood flowing. JoAnn's remains had been subjected to fire, and his might well be frozen. "Fire and ice, fire and ice," he repeated.

The saving grace was knowing he'd been blessed with great endurance and self-control. Fighting off the ropes in his Golden Glove championship bout, Chase had been pounded in a slugfest, battling toe-to-toe in the center of the ring against a bigger and stronger foe. At the bell, his corner told him he would not last the fight unless he changed his mode of attack.

Though bloodied and at the brink of exhaustion, Chase fought off the ropes, his body punches wearing down his opponent. The fighter dropped his hands for a split second, and Chase grasped the opportunity. He used the canvas as a springboard to deliver a crushing uppercut that knocked his opponent off his feet.

More than fifty years later, Chase was again in a desperate struggle, a battle to survive a greater foe than he'd ever faced. The largest glacier in the Alps had captured him. He had no self-rescue tools, no thermal sheet for warmth, and a dead cell phone. Could the tiny orange whistle be his saving grace?

Panic was a word he seldom used. Chase believed that victory against a formidable foe could come only from the one thing he had always trusted: his disciplined mind.

Trickling glacial water continued to find a way inside his waterproof coat, and he was aware that his body was losing the battle for warmth. His survival rested on the rescue whistle latched to his coat. Putting the whistle to his lips, he blew three long blasts. He would blow three more, waiting a minute between them, and hoping for another miracle—like the rosary.

Chapter 40

Bundled in an army-green hooded parka, Tekla stood on the terrace of the observation deck of the Sphinx Observatory. Her lean face was flushed, both from arguing with Chase about joining him on the glacier and from the snow crystals swirling in the air. She removed one glove, stuck it in her coat pocket, fiddled with the rosary, and whispered prayers to ease her mind.

"This is what I want," Chase had said. He had been adamant when he made the blunt statement on the cogwheel train ride that morning. "I can handle it from here."

She'd respectfully disagreed but promised to be a good soldier and heed his orders. She'd have his back. "You ever see the movie, *Top Gun*? 'Never leave your wingman!' Remember that line?"

"No, I don't."

"Well, that's what you're determined to do."

She had watched him turn and begin the longest, loneliest walk of his life. The sun glared off the snow, stealing even his shadow as he wandered among the crowd of sightseers who were unaware of his quest for privacy.

She sipped a cup of velvety hot chocolate beneath crystal-clear, dark-blue skies that faded to almost white on the horizon. She lowered her sunglasses. Between sips, she breathed in a lung-cleansing breath of alpine air and stared at the crowd formed by hundreds of tourist groups below her. She'd lost Chase among the mob, and her concern dial was maxing out.

On the glacier, chaos prevailed as people scrambled in all directions. Others were herded into groups. It all seemed too congested for enjoyment. How had one of the most iconic places in Switzerland turned into a tourist trap? She had, however, rated the train trip from Grindelwald at five stars for its breathtaking views of the rural Swiss villages below, crowned by the icy peaks of the Alps above.

Tekla gazed at the Eiger and then turned toward the Aletch Glacier. She absorbed the beautiful silence, in awe of the majestic spectacle. Above the silence, a strong wind blew. She abhorred the wind and grabbed a railing for support, concerned about the icy floor.

Another sip, another breath, and she turned toward the elevator to take the 100-meter ride down to the overly commercial souvenir shops and restaurants at the Top of Europe.

Not ready for lunch, she checked out the Top of Europe shop. In the Swissness Corner of the shop, she found what she was searching for, a Swiss Army knife for Chase. She considered him a sharp, practical man with multiple talents, a Swiss Army sort of guy.

Red plastic was definitely not Chase, so she chose the Huntsman model for its walnut handles. *Chase is unbreakable*, she thought. At the last second, she added a Top-of-Europe refrigerator magnet for herself so she would always have something to remind her of the trip.

"Fifty-four francs, *s'il vous plait*," the pleasant clerk said. She ran Tekla's Visa card and then wrapped the knife in its box.

"Which restaurant has good soup?" Tekla asked.

"Restaurant Eigerglescher," the clerk replied, pointing out the direction.

Tekla checked her phone, which she'd set to track Chase's time on the glacier. She unzipped her parka, thanked the clerk, and headed for the restaurant.

· · ·

Liam led his best friends, Mattia and Timo, along the trail after they finished a day of skiing high above the valley floor of the Aletch Glacier. All three were young, bearded Swiss ski guides. Their physique shared the qualities of modern male ballet dancers, with their toned upper bodies and muscular thighs.

The guides spent their off day exploring a secret stash of pockets of powder. The sun had splashed the Alps and created shadows of rooster tails that trailed their descents. Energy still flowing, the trio planned to celebrate after making it down the mountain in one piece. They looked forward to a few beers, followed by hot tubbing with a group of pretty Italian women they'd guided the day before.

Accomplished mountaineers, they skied the edges of insanity. They had left the Mönchsjoch warming hut with their alpine touring skis buckled on. On their backs, each carried a light, compact glacier rescue kit and a mini avalanche shovel. Each man wore an avalanche beacon attached to the outerwear on his right arm. Being swept away in an avalanche or falling into crevasses was uncommon, but skiing on a glacier was unpredictable. They accepted responsibility for their own safety and prepared accordingly.

Their skis, without climbing skins, glided smoothly and effortlessly along the edge of the glacier. Blissed out, they poled along in a state of nirvana, knowing they owned the mountain that day. Liam relished the rhythm of smooth, linked skiing turns that carved up trails of champagne powder behind them.

Exhilarated, Liam said, "What a kick-ass day!" He stopped and offered a third of his chocolate bar to his Swiss friends. "It was like skiing on diamond dust."

"Nah, thanks," Mattia replied. "It'll ruin my taste for beer."

Timo also waved the offering away.

Then Liam held his hand up, signaling all to remain still. His teeth clamped down on a piece of chocolate as he shielded his eyes from the sun. After scanning the ice field, he asked, "You see that?"

He raised his sunglasses above his eyebrows and pointed to a spot below the ridgeline, 200 meters off the trail. "I swear someone just disappeared off the glacier."

"No shit?" Timo raised his shades and wiped his nose with a sleeve. "Maybe a mirage? Or maybe those Italian girls are on your mind?"

"Yes, maybe the sun is playing tricks." Liam poked Timo with his ski pole, payback for his comment about the girls they planned to meet. "But I swear I saw the silhouette of a person on the glacier and then it just freakin' disappeared."

Mattia shook his head and said, "I'm beat, and now you want us to tromp out there and check out a mirage?"

Liam held his ground. "I think we should. What Swiss guide would say no?"

"All right," Mattia said. "Timo, you in?"

"Yeah. Let's do it," Timo said. "Maybe the signorinas will wait for us. Beers are on Liam if it was a mirage." He adjusted the wrist strap on his pole before gliding off.

• • •

Chase hovered near the border of consciousness, as well as the edge of unknown depths. His core body temperature was falling. The icy, dripping water served its own brand of water torture.

He continued to stand, resting his back on the ice wall for support. Lost and alone, half-frozen and wet, Chase struggled with the powerful reality of never being rescued. He shivered, the cold so penetrating it rattled his bones. He realized he had entered the beginning stages of hypothermia. There was no JoAnn beside him to kiss away the shivers.

The haunting prospect of dying brought out the next layer of strength in him. He refused to believe it was his destiny to die there. Fearing the snow bridge could collapse at any time, he blew the whistle again.

• • •

Tekla ordered a bowl of sherried lobster bisque, which featured small nubbins of lobster meat. Although a seafood choice seemed out of sync with her mountain surroundings, she believed the bisque would bolster her morale. She regretted the way the glorious train ride had been marred by her confrontation with Chase.

Glad to be off her feet, she paused to let the steamy chowder offer a dose of uplifting aromatherapy. The first spoonful burned her tongue, so she gave it time to cool. Taking advantage of the soup break, she removed the prosthesis from her throbbing stump, and tucked it below the table. The restaurant offered free Wi-Fi, so she opened her email, something she hadn't done that morning. A new email from her mother alarmed her.

My dearest Tekla,

Hope all is well with your journey with Mr. DeMers. Your father's Parkinson's has worsened since you were here. Yesterday he had a severe stroke, paralyzing his right side. He is resting comfortably in the hospital. His doctor has told me he has maybe three to six months. He will stay here for at least a week, as his rehabilitation plan will be evaluated. This morning, in a moment of clarity, he blurted out your name. I know you are nearing the end of your trip, and it would mean so much to him and me if you came home and spent some time in the few weeks or months he may have left. Your sister will be here soon, and it would be lovely for all of us to be together now.

Your loving mother

Tekla wiped the tears off her cheek, pushed her bowl of bisque to the side, and left a twenty Swiss franc note beneath the bowl. She'd lost her appetite.

"My father needs me," she whispered, clutching her hands to her breast. It sunk in that she'd never told him how much she loved him or how proud she was of him. She'd never spoken of love, written about it, or let the emotion penetrate since her last "normal day."

How she ached for that butterfly feeling of being *in* love. Nate's acceptance of her war wounds and the mental baggage of her PTSD had been heartening. He'd reignited her heart's flame. In that moment, she vowed to love again.

After attaching her prosthesis, she made her way back to the observation deck. Facing the wind, she grasped the rail and shouted to the towering peaks, "Daddy, I love you so much." It was a message she needed to deliver while he was still living, no matter how far away he was. She'd just admitted him into her heart, and screaming her love for him allowed her soul to sing.

Chapter 41

Liam led the way, stopping intermittently to examine the tracks heading onto the glacier.

"I see ski tracings everywhere," Timo said as his eyes scanned the tracks.

"No, right there," Liam shouted. Using his ski pole, he pointed to a separate set of footprints with no evidence of crampons as they left the trail. "I know what I saw was not a mirage. Let's follow the tracks."

"Think they'll lead to your missing person?" Timo asked.

"We'll find out after 200 meters."

Liam, the most experienced alpinist of the trio, kept his dark feelings to himself about where they might end. When he heard a faint sound, he motioned for everyone to stop moving and strained to hear. Was that a whistle blowing beneath the howls of the wind?

Liam cupped his hand to his ear and said, "I hear a whistle. You guys hear that?"

"Yeah, I do," Timo replied, nodding. "Can't be the wind. I heard it and then it stopped. Now I hear it again."

Liam's eyes darted along the shadows on the ice. "Watch your step. Snow's covering these potholes. Crevasses everywhere! These footprints lead to that big crack fifty meters straight ahead." He pointed to the spot.

Twenty meters from the crevasse, Liam turned to face his companions.

"No crystal ball needed now. You two hold up here." He held his hands up like a traffic cop. "I'll check the crevasse."

Inch by inch, Liam crawled forward. Using his ice axe, he checked the snow conditions as he got closer to the lip. He knew that if the snow was unstable near the edge, a chunk could break off and fall on whoever was below. Relief accompanied his discovery that the snow was stable.

Peering into the wide crack on the ice, he yelled, "Hello! Anybody down there?"

. . .

Tekla watched the afternoon sun duck behind slivers of clouds that hung in the vast blue sky. The throngs of tourists on the Aletch glacier had thinned. They were making their way back to civilization for food, alcohol, or the next train down the mountain. She scoured the landscape. Ignoring the groups, which Chase would've shunned, she watched for a solitary man, a man who had just released the burden of fulfilling his wife's final wish.

Tekla had lost track of the time after reading her mother's letter. When she checked her phone, it shocked her to see that it had been two hours since Chase set off. Worry bloomed in her mind. Had she misjudged his ability to navigate the glacier?

Then a massive concern flooded through her. *Fuck me! Tell me he didn't kill himself out there to join JoAnn! Was that why he didn't want me to go along? No, that can't be it. He wouldn't do that.*

Several more minutes ticked by. Then came the moment when she knew something had happened to Chase. She didn't care about blowback from him. She had to report him as missing. Pivoting away from the panoramic window, Tekla made a left turn onto the elevator and bolted straight to Emergency Services.

. . .

Chase's energy had waned, reducing his whistle-blowing to a single blast. His breathing had become slow and shallow, and his eyes closed as he gave in to a deep desire to drift off to sleep. Then he heard a sound that couldn't be water or wind. One hearing aid was dead, and the other crackled. What he heard was a lot of mumbo and not enough jumbo, but it was enough to summon one last burst of adrenaline.

"I need help!" he yelled. Then the old fighter went down, landing squarely on his beaten butt.

. . .

Liam tried again to establish what injuries the man had sustained in his fall. "Are you hurt?"

Liam struggled to comprehend the voice he heard from below, but the crevasse trapped the reply. Immediately, he waved for his two companions to join him. Reaching into a zipped pocket on his pack, he pulled out a Swiss Army knife equipped with an LED flashlight. Aiming the concentrated beam into the crevasse, he lit up the inner sanctum.

Then he saw him, an elderly man sitting on a snow bridge, his back resting on the icy wall. A steady stream of melting ice trickled over his head. Liam directed the flashlight toward the man's face, and a small peep from a whistle sounded from his clenched lips.

"Are you hurt?" Liam shouted.

The stranded man's inability to answer prompted Liam to make a command decision, relying on a natural skill that had been honed to a fine edge as a junior officer in the Swiss Army. The orders rolled off his tongue in slow motion so as not to be confused by the wind.

"Timo, call Air Zermatt. Give our coordinates for helicopter crevasse rescue—one known victim—conscious—elderly—at rest on a snow bridge at five meters—injuries unknown—likely hypothermic—no cloud cover at site—temperature -1.0-degree C—estimated wind speed thirty kilometers an hour out of the northwest. Then report our actions to Dario at the observatory."

Liam scanned the landscape and then called out to Mattia. "Get all the strawberry energy powder packets we have. Sprinkle an X on the snow fifty meters back on our path to help the pilot spot us. I'll build a snow anchor to rappel down and bolt him to the ice. The snow bridge could collapse at any time, and we could lose him."

Liam had his ice axe trenched in and was laying out twenty meters of 6.0 mm glacier cord when Timo and Mattia returned.

"Help is on the way," Timo reported. "An hour out. Shouldn't we wait for them?"

"No. We have unknown medical issues. He's not responding to my questions." Liam's voice had become hoarse from hollering in the cold air. "The rescue will take more time after they arrive." He reached into his pack and pulled out his climbing harness. Next, he tightened a loose crampon. "The bridge could collapse at any minute. Mattia, let me have your harness. I'll stay down with him until the rescue team arrives."

After checking the snow anchor, Liam attached to the belay line and walked to the edge of the crevasse above the injured man. He moved five meters to the right and sat at the edge of the crevasse, kicking at the lip as a final check on the snow's stability. He padded the lip of the crevasse by burying Mattia's ice axe so the rope wouldn't cut into the edge. After one last inspection of his setup and a quick glance at the sky, he turned and issued his last instruction.

"Timo, Mattia, I will shout out after we're both secured. Here we go."

Without hesitation, Liam stepped over the edge and into the icy blue domain of the crevasse, Mattia's climbing harness attached to his.

It was Liam's seventh crevasse rescue, but he never relaxed on the descent. Descending into the unknown, the eerie silence could be punctuated by the heart-stopping noise of glacial ice cracking. Aside from the crunch as the tips of his crampons dug into the ice, all he heard was the sound of melting water running out of a crack. That heightened his anxiety. He would need to get the injured man away from the water—but not before he bolted him to the ice wall.

Dangling on a rope inside the fissure and using his crampons to stop the swaying, Liam pulled one ice screw off his harness and held the light in his teeth. He found a patch of clear, unclouded ice and bolted himself to the wall away from the falling water.

He turned to the man and said, "Sir, are you hurt?"

The older man was pale but shook his head no. Liam assumed he might be deaf when he saw one hearing aid hanging by the wire from his left ear. He was also aware of the possibility of shock.

Liam demonstrated how he would need to step into the harness and indicated that the rescue line would be attached to pull him up. The shivering man gave Liam a nod.

Liam untwisted the harness and made a few small adjustments. After taking the kinks out of the harness and making sure the buckles were loose, Liam helped him put it on. It was as easy as putting on a pair of pants, but the old man was nearly frozen stiff.

As Liam prepared the webbing to attach it to the ice screw, the man wheezed and whispered inches from Liam's face, "I prayed for a miracle. Or a quick death. Can't hear. My partner—"

"Yes, yes, your partner. Where? Below you?" He aimed his flashlight deep into the depths.

"No—ah, her name—*what was her name*? Um—Tekla." Chase spoke so softly that Liam could barely hear him.

"What's your name?"

"What? Huh?"

"Your name," Liam asked. He directed the light to his face and repeated the words.

"Ch—Ch—Chase."

"Where is Tekla?" Liam questioned Chase not only for information but to keep him from drifting off.

"Ob—ser—va—tory."

"Good, good."

With the help of the dim light from above the crevasse, Liam gauged Chase's facial expression. It had improved from cold and blank to a mixture of relief and calm. Liam cinched the leg loops tight and then bolted Chase to the wall, providing safety from falling but leaving enough slack for him to step away from the falling water.

When a sharp crack in the ice reverberated from the glacier, a lump the size of the glacier rose in Liam's throat. Then he remembered his training. Hypothermic patients needed fluids.

"Drink," he said, handing over a half-filled bottle, which contained water mixed with strawberry-flavored energy powder.

Chase chugged it down in three gulps.

Pointing to his own head, Liam asked, "Where's your hat? You're losing heat from your head."

Chase touched his head absently.

Liam removed his helmet, pulled out the wool liner, and handed it to Chase. "It'll keep your head warm. Hang in there. You with me?"

"Uh-huh."

"I hear the helicopter now." Liam pointed upward, his fingers spinning like helicopter rotor blades. He knew the red-and-white-starred Air Zermatt was ready to touch down.

. . .

Timo felt pride as he watched the paramedic and the Air Zermatt team go into action, men who had trained ten years for moments like this. One day he hoped to be part of the team, but that day his job was laying coils of multicolored rope with surgical precision, clipping and tying special knots and carabiners with gloved hands.

Once all the ropes and the tripod winch were in place, the rescue appeared to be nothing more than a well-orchestrated ritual. The paramedic dropped over the edge.

"Our paramedic," the pilot said, "will secure himself. Then we'll rig up the victim to the rescue line and winch him out."

One rescue team member opened battery packs for the portable drill that would turn the gears. He inserted the first pack and then turned to Timo.

"Hold on. Getting a call from the paramedic. Roger that. Victim's body temp is 35 degrees Celsius. That's four degrees too low. In his seventies. Roger that. I'm radioing the hospital in Interlaken. We're coming. What? 10-4. I'll tell them."

The pilot swiveled the microphone away from his face and updated Timo and Mattia. "We have the guy on the rescue line. It seems the snow bridge let go, but the bolt saved him. He's on his way up. Your man's ascending and wants you to help him at the ledge. He said you both need to be ready to make tracks to the Sphinx Observatory. We're flying the patient to Interlaken Hospital."

"So maybe those signorinas will just be a dream tonight," Timo moaned while Mattia coiled rope.

. . .

Tekla's worry intensified the longer she sat in the waiting area of Ski Patrol and Emergency Services. It seemed like yesterday when she'd filled out the missing-person report. Thirty minutes . . . forty minutes . . . now an hour. Worrying about Chase had been replaced with another mind demon she had worked to manage in therapy: anxiety.

"It's all my fault," she muttered. Dario, the rescue coordinator, listened and offered words of hope.

"Tekla, nothing's your fault. We get many calls that are false alarms. Our best men are searching for your partner. Try to have faith."

"I shouldn't have let him go out there by himself. He can't hear. He can't see. But no. I was a good soldier and followed orders."

Tekla slouched in the chair, hands to her forehead, elbows on her knees. Her counselor had drilled into her that too much anxiety could lead to panic and possibly a meltdown. She needed to breathe slowly and stay grounded. She'd have to keep it together and trust in faith.

Tekla tried to assume her military posture, needing the structure it delivered. She straightened her back and squared her shoulders. Her mind went back to Montana, the smell of the wild grass, horses whinnying, and the gurgle of a trout stream. Strains of "Folsom Prison" floated through her mind and kept her hanging on.

Suddenly, the cackling of a radio commanded Dario's attention, and he turned and adjusted his headphones. He pulled out a swivel chair and sat, holding up his hand to signal Tekla not to talk. After a minute, he pushed his chair back and turned to her.

"I got a message from Timo, a guide stationed here. He just called Air Zermatt, a helicopter rescue service we use. They were called by him and not by our ski patrol. The helicopter is en route to a crevasse rescue near here."

"A crevasse rescue! Oh, my God," she yelled. There was no mistaking the sense of blood draining from her face.

"This is good news, Tekla. They say it's a rescue, not a recovery."

The next hour was a blur of confusion and frustration. She grimaced as her neck and shoulder muscles tightened. Still no word. *Is it Chase? Is he alive? What's happening? My father needs me.*

. . .

Beads of sweat rolled down Liam's face. His nose snorted steam into the cold air. His body was that of a highly conditioned athlete, and he was used to having it respond to what he needed to do. His breathing was steady despite having redlined his heart rate during the sprint ski back to the Top of Europe. Sucking in gulps of frigid air had dried his throat. He doffed his pack and skis at the entrance to the station a minute ahead of his two comrades.

"Here, take my gear and head for the terminal," Liam told Timo and Mattia. "We have little time to make the last train down, but I want to see if Dario knows where that guy's wife is." Liam feared she might be thinking the worst and was probably shaken up. He could brief her on her partner's condition. She might need a ride into Interlaken.

"Got it," Timo said. "There may still be hope for getting cozy with those Italian girls."

Liam pulled off his outer shell down to the black hi-tech base layer that displayed his well-defined arm, shoulder, and back muscles. Two decades of double poling on skis did that.

"Move it, Timo," Liam yelled. He shook his head, grumbling, trying to keep his friend's mind from wandering according to its usual pattern. He then bounded up the ten steps, two at a time. When he reached the ski patrol office, he found Dario scanning weather updates on his computer.

"*Hoi*, Dario." Liam announced his entrance with a rich, raspy voice. His thick Swiss-German accent could strip paint off the walls.

Dario spun in his chair and threw a fist bump to his friend.

"*Hoi*, yourself. Another day of high adventure? I got Timo's call about sending Air Zermatt for a crevasse rescue."

"Yeah," Liam said. He was still sucking air.

"The chopper radioed the old guy is stable. They confirmed they were flying him to Interlaken."

"Sort of a miracle we found him. He may have a wife back here." Liam paused and scratched his head, hoping he could remember her name. "Tekla, I believe. She here?"

"She was," Dario said. "She came in to report her partner missing. Not her husband. I'd just gathered enough info to send a patrol out when we got the call about the crevasse. Description fit her partner. She just left for the station. Why?"

"I feel oddly connected after rescuing him." His face was blank, absent the intensity he'd spent rescuing the old man.

"You can't miss her. Tekla's not that old. Maybe early thirties. Athletic. Very long reddish-brown hair in a ponytail. Prosthetic leg."

"Prosthetic leg? Thanks."

"Later, Liam." Dario pointed to the clock on the wall and waved his friend off. Liam swore it seemed to be moving faster than usual.

. . .

The last train of the day was so packed with tourists that Liam had difficulty finding Timo, Mattia, and the young woman with a ponytail. Scanning the crowd, he hoped Tekla hadn't boarded yet. He didn't want to have to catch up to her later when the trains switched at the Kleine Scheidegg station.

That ponytail should make her stand out in the crowd, he thought. Liam, the trained Army captain, checked his six, and there she was, directly behind him, wearing a woolen hat and with a ponytail draped off her left shoulder. Her head was bowed, and her thumbs were a blur as she tapped out a text message. Finished, she slipped the device into a zippered pocket and climbed aboard the cogwheel train, leaving the towering Alps at her back.

Liam boarded, nudging ahead of a younger man and his girlfriend, which allowed him to follow Tekla to the last empty seat. He held to his recollection of the hypothermic man in the crevasse who had been vaguely coherent. He couldn't know for sure if the old guy was going to make it. If not, she should know that his last words were about her.

Her face told the story of a life filled with worry and anxiety. One hand fidgeted with her phone as if it were a lifeline, while the other hand ruffled something in her coat pocket. She removed her left hand from the pocket, plopped something into her mouth, and swigged a gulp of bottled water.

Her eyes shifted, and her expression tightened when Liam slid next to her.

"*Hoi*," Liam said. He felt uncomfortable, fearing he would come across as if delivering a comedic pickup line. "English?"

Tekla nodded and uncrossed her legs.

"I'm trying to find a woman by the name of Tekla. Is that you?"

"Yes. I don't know how you know me. You're probably a great guy, but I'm not interested in small talk." He saw suspicion in her eyes. "I need to get to Interlaken," she said.

"Yes, I know. I'm Liam. Not here to chat you up. I know all about your friend's fall because my friends and I heard him whistling from a crevasse."

"It was you who found him in that crevasse?" She relaxed upon hearing his comment.

"It's what I trained to do. I spent time in the Swiss Army and taught and trained foreign troops on mountain skills. Your friend was very lucky. I was with him until the helo came."

Her voice barely a whisper, she said, "He's a tough man. Is he going to make it?"

"Our doctors are tremendous in treating hypothermia, so try not to worry." Did he care put his hands on her to help calm her? He didn't. "I caught up to you because I wanted you to know that while we were waiting for rescue, he mumbled your name. That's something you should know, I think."

She turned away and crossed her legs. Her face burned a rosy red. "Fuck it all. I failed him. I failed him." She spun away to look out the window.

"Hey, no problem. Lots of stress, I know. We're about ready to change trains in Kleine Scheidegg. Would you like me to hang with you to Grindelwald?" This time he rested his hand on her thigh as he spoke. Her face plainly showed the stress and exhaustion she'd dealt with that day. "Do you need a ride to Interlaken?"

"Yes. I'll take you up on the ride. I'm not up to driving right now."

Chapter 42

Tina relished her morning power walk to work. She would spend the next twelve hours on her feet while pouring shots and drawing tap beer and do it all over again the following day.

Her home bordered the edge of the little town, and she high-stepped along Main Street, which was just three blocks long. Four blocks, if you included skirting around the Montana Highway Department's workshop, road graders, and gravel pile. Passing her favorite coffee wagon, which had recently closed due to lack of help, she kicked a loose rock down the maple-lined street as she'd done as a little girl. She missed one kick and almost fell. Starting the week without a coffee and cruller did not bode well.

The post office sat on one corner, with City Bakery next door. Flo was busy baking bread, bagels, and buns, so she hadn't opened yet. Tina's last chance to grab a coffee was a bust. She wondered how she would make it through the rest of the morning without it. Buying her own coffee maker might solve the problem, but it was a hassle she didn't need.

As she passed Paradise Mercantile, purchased by Daisy Grimble after she'd subdivided a hundred acres of her ranch, Tina considered sticking her head inside to say good morning to the manager. Lexi was Daisy's over-educated, trail-running, fly-fishing, ski-addict niece. She had visited Daisy one summer and never returned to Texas. An anthropologist by education but an adventuress by choice, Montana suited her.

It amused Tina to hear Lexi greet customers by name, her syrupy Southern drawl pulling three syllables out of the word "yeah." Her lively spirit and natural charm encouraged tourists to pour money into the town, something everyone could appreciate. Tina admired Lexi's creative redesign of the original storefront façade, which rocked with Old West sentimentality.

Her business acumen included meticulous merchandising. In one corner near the entrance sat a revolving carousel of made-in-Montana products. On a nearby shelf was a small assortment of maps and fishing supplies. Eva Gates' huckleberry products took up the remaining space.

Tina walked on, ending her trek at the Mint Bar, the communication hub and central nervous system of the town. She served as the owner, bartender, plumber, bouncer, and swamper, along with tackling a host of other jobs that allowed her to work more hours for less money. Despite the challenges, she felt lucky to live in the West.

Her only respite from the never-ending toil came on Saturday nights when Lexi pulled on a pair of skinny jeans and bartended for her. When Tina looked in the mirror the progression of the years showed in her eyes. She was getting older. Although she hated to admit it, Lexi had the looks and charm for a Saturday night crowd of young cowboys thirsty for tequila and eager to impress hot young women.

The Mint Bar kept no secrets. A decade earlier, while repainting the exterior, the owner had cracked the neon tube that formed the letter M in Mint. Tina refused to replace it because the townspeople considered the "int" bar sign as the most hilarious misnomer among Montana's watering holes.

That afternoon, Tina stepped outside to light her third cigarette of the day and blew smoke rings from the corner of her mouth. Her blond hair echoed the hues of local native grasses in the fall. Standing next to the green walls of the bar, she coordinated with Paradise Valley's color scheme.

The Montana afternoon lived up to its surrealistic moniker: Big Sky Country. She stared into the distant mountains, exhaled her last drag, and twirled back into the bar, ready for much-needed business. Afternoon trade had been slow, and the swing time between tourist season and hunting season grew close. She was in a sad state when she realized that she'd spent money she didn't have, and income was at a trickle.

While Tina was inventorying her liquor supply, the first customer of the day ambled in, a rough-looking middle-aged guy who carried himself like a man who had been beaten down by life. He wasn't too clean or too dirty, and facial scars hinted of past battles. He viewed the world through a pair of wrap-around drugstore sunglasses, with an orange hunting cap pulled low on his forehead. Overall, he was as rough-textured as the Montana country. But it was the random caveman grunting coming from him that made her uncomfortable.

Twenty years of owning a bar had taught her to be wary of strangers when she was by herself. For security, she kept a snub-nosed .38 revolver out of sight near the cash register and had a shortened blackjack tucked into her high Western boots.

"Howdy, partner, what'll you have?" she said by way of welcome. She toweled the bar top where he sat and offered the shake-a-day cup to him. He declined to play.

Seconds ticked off as the man watched the minute hand sweep to the even hour on the wall clock. Satisfied, he thumbed his gray-streaked stubble and then raised his glasses to his forehead.

"Tall tonic." His voice sounded as scratchy as sandpaper.

"No gin?" she asked.

"Just a dash of Rose's, please."

He pulled a Lincoln from a thin wallet and laid it on the bar. After sneaking a peek at the door, he spun on his heels, hopped once, and headed for the men's room.

Tina watched the red *Occupied* light come on. Because the jukebox wasn't playing, she heard the urinal flush, followed by the rumble of hot water in the sink. The water ran long enough that experience suggested the guy was too cheap to buy a shower at the truck stop. He'd probably use a tank of hot water and half a roll of paper towels to bathe.

She felt irked enough to ask him for a buck or two for all the water he'd used, but she changed her mind when she saw a cleaner man walk out, a flush spread over his hollow cheeks, and his chest expanded.

She relaxed a bit.

He returned to his seat on the stool and slid a fiver her way. "Appreciate it." She fed her empty tip jar with the wrinkled Lincoln.

Reconsidering her previous assessment of the man, she decided to give him the benefit of the doubt, summing up his off-putting entrance as the need for relief.

"You know this country?" he asked while fondling his scrub beard, which he'd shaved into a fine line along the contours of a narrow jaw. Then he took a second to touch his eyeball.

Her thinking had altered when she saw the change in his posture. He seemed more at ease and teased her, but she'd been thrice married and was no longer interested in flirting. The small tattoos of crosses on his knuckles made her take one step closer to the cash register. Her antenna went up before replying.

"Sure do. My ex was an outfitter, and I was the camp cook for years. Shot a few myself."

"I always hunkered to get into trophy elk like—*grunt*—those here in the Paradise Valley. I see on my map a heck of a lot of checkerboard ownership. I hunted early morning on public land and chased some elk onto posted ground. Are there any ranches—*grunt*—that allow hunting elk without draining my bank account?"

Tina drew a fine line about giving strangers information on her neighbors, but he'd asked a common question, so she wasn't overly alarmed. The man intrigued her. How could he hunt elk while grunting like a bull elk in the rut?

"I'll give you the names of a few of my regulars who have given me the green light to refer hunters."

Her business depended on discretion, and this guy wasn't from Montana. She could tell that after years behind the bar. A camo shirt didn't make an elk hunter. She exhaled, craving another smoke and hesitant to break confidence with landowners who trusted her to make good choices.

"Most private ranches have booked their hunters a year or two in advance. You're a little late." She pointed to a wall calendar that featured a bull elk bugling on a frosty morning. "Times have changed here. Lots of out-of-state landowners are making it hard to access public land. Some will allow only friends to hunt."

The man was not put off.

"How about—*grunt*—giving me a few names? Help me out here. It's hard on a guy when he doesn't know his way around."

"I'll give you a couple of names you can try. No promises. You gotta do the rest. Go next door to the Merc and ask Lexi to show you some good maps of the valley. You could also ask her. Her aunt's ranch has some of the finest elk country around. I shot that big-balled six-point there." She aimed her forefinger toward the massive set of antlers hanging on the wall. "He came from the Grimble ranch."

"Any others?"

"Might try Double Diamond Land and Cattle. Ask for Cal. The DeMers spread is another possibility. He allows hunting by permission only. No fees, but I hear he's picky about who he lets in."

"I'll remember that. The DeMers spread. Thanks. How do I find his ranch?" Tina responds with: "Take County Line Road to the end."

He drained the tonic, worked a few ice cubes around in his mouth, and dabbed his lips dry on a cocktail napkin. With a final nod to Tina, the stranger strolled out of the Mint with a hop and a grunt.

Chapter 43

Jed swirled his coffee and hacked on the last swallow. Clearing his throat, he came face-to-face with April, who stared at him with a question behind her eyes.

She set a small tray of homemade chocolate chip cookies on the table and smacked his hand away when he reached for one. "Nate and Carli are due to arrive soon with Olivia. Are you ready, Jed? What's your gut feeling?"

"Ya know I usually go with my hunch, but sometimes I mind you. Once in a while, I listen to others. In this case, I think Olivia is the hope for our family's future." He sipped his coffee, his eyes locked on the cookies. "She's going to carry on the Hutchens' family heritage. Carli named Nate on Olivia's birth certificate as the little girl's father, so I reckon we're off to a good start there. But when it comes to Nate and Carli, I just don't know."

April shook her head ruefully and said, "I wish he would at least explore a life with Carli, but he seems dead set against it."

Jed looked around the room, seeming lost in his own kitchen. Recent developments fogged his brain, and everything seemed different. His voice was tinged with confusion when he said, "All that boy told me was he'd have to finagle a bigger horse trailer."

"What? He just bought one last year." April refilled her husband's half-empty cup.

Jed scratched his head and said, "I reckon it's because the first item on his agenda is buying Olivia a horse."

April glanced at the clock. "They'll be here in a few minutes." Taking a seat beside him, she laid a hand on his leg and looked him in the eye. "Are you happy with a granddaughter instead of a grandson?"

He crossed his arms and gave her a one-eyed glance. *Should I tell her what she wants to hear?* he wondered. He crafted his words delicately.

"If I had my choice," he said, "I'd have preferred a boy to be our first grandchild. Nate's an only child, and I always wished for a grandson to carry on the family name. Not many Hutchens left." He shook his head in quiet resignation. "I worried that Nate would be the last twig on our family tree. Mind you, that was before I knew about Olivia. Now it's the way it is."

"I don't think you're all that disappointed, Jed. I've nagged you for years to get rid of the junk in Nate's old bedroom, but you blew me off. All it took was Olivia working her little-girl magic on you."

Jed stood up and sauntered toward the room. "I wanted Olivia to have a place where she can paint, read, or work on puzzles when she visits. We need to get a bed in there so she can spend the night now and again."

He opened the bedroom door and pointed to the trophy mule-deer head mounts that still hung on the wall. "Hope Nate will take those to his house."

"Lord, I hope so too. The way those glass eyes stare at you might scare Olivia half to death."

"Maybe you can invite Carli to go to Bozeman and help you pick out some furnishings. It'll give you two some mother-daughter bonding time." He ducked just in time to miss the wet dish rag April aimed at his face.

"Knock it off, Jed. Nate just pulled up. How do I look? Just fine or pretty good?" She took off her apron and loosened her braid, letting the still-thick gray hair fall to her waist.

"Too young to be a grandmother." He slicked his hair back and pecked a kiss on her cheek.

. . .

Nate opened the truck door for Carli, who had styled her hair in a French braid, a way of acknowledging a transformation in her life. She reached for Nate's hand, and he took it, but Olivia ignored her father's outstretched hand and broke for the lead.

230

Carli tried to rein her in. "Olivia, please quit bouncing ahead of us. This is a big day for all of us. We're meeting your daddy's parents. They are your grandparents, so mind your manners."

"Do grandparents have ice cream, Mommy?"

"Olivia, please. Take your daddy's hand."

Nate and Carli ambled, Olivia bounced, and all three stumbled into Jed's and April's welcoming arms.

"Mom, Dad, I'd like you to meet Carli and Olivia. Carli, this is my mom, April, and my dad, Jed.

"Welcome to Montana and to our little family," April said, almost vibrating with joy.

"I feel at home already," Carli replied, accepting her new life with outstretched arms. Jed and April had just given her a new lens with which to view the world, and she was contented in a way she'd never experienced.

"Happy to have you and Olivia as family," Jed said. He and April took turns giving polite hugs to Carli. Then Jed shaded his eyes with a hand as if he were an American Indian scout seeking a trail. Rotating his head in a half circle, he said, "I want to find Olivia. Has anyone seen Olivia?" Then he called in a sing-song voice, "Oh-liv-ee-uh."

The little girl tugged on Jed's free arm. "That's me, that's me. I'm Olivia."

"Oh, I see. You're Olivia. My, my, what a surprise. April, see who has come to visit?"

"Come here, precious," April said. She got down on one knee and motioned Olivia into her arms. "We're your daddy's mother and father, so that makes us your grandparents. Nate," she asked, tilting her head, "have you and Carli talked about what Olivia should call us?"

"No, Mom, we haven't. Your call."

April looked at Jed, and he gave her a nod of approval, having already decided on his preference.

"Olivia, from now on, you can call me Nana." She grabbed Jed's hand and said, "And you can call this man Pop-Pop."

"Pop-Pop?" Nate slapped his thigh and laughed and laughed. "Sounds like a honey-coated breakfast cereal for kids."

Jed winked at Carli before giving Nate a crooked smile.

April said, "Olivia, why don't we go inside, and you can have one of Nana's chocolate chip cookies. Would you like that?"

"Yes, please. And ice cream too?"

Carli twitched her lips at the mention of more sweets. The last thing she needed that day was Olivia on a sugar high. But she didn't want to put a damper on April's enthusiasm. "It's a special day. It'll be fine, April."

. . .

April headed for the basement to root through her freezer for chocolate ice cream while the rest of the group gathered around the dining room table.

Olivia whispered in her mother's ear. Carli leaned toward Jed and whispered, "We need to use the potty."

"Down the hall on your left," he said, pointing the way.

When Nate heard the bathroom door close, he turned to his father. "Dad, thanks for making this easier for me." He put a hand on his father's shoulder. "It would be darned hard without your support and Mom's. And I'm proud of you for going to AA. How's that going?"

"Day at a time. I'm not as strong as I used to be, but I need to put the family first." He took a seat at the table and folded his hands, prayer-like.

Nate sensed the importance of the moment. His father said, "You're my only son, and Olivia may be my only grandchild. I can't lose either to liquor."

"Why now? It didn't seem all that important to you when I was a boy."

"I believed that I could teach myself to drink responsibly as I got older. Everyone drinks around here, which makes it hard." His father's words consumed Nate's attention.

"I think of my father and how his strict, antisocial, nonconformist views about alcohol use shaped my life." Jed paused to gain traction as an emotional memory washed over him. "You know that my twin brother died from boozing. I don't want the past to pull me toward the very thing I'm trying to avoid. Having a granddaughter gives me another reason to stay on the wagon. I'm sorry I let you down." He reached across the table for Nate's hands. "Asking for forgiveness is not easy for an ol' cowboy like me."

"I won't let you think you let me down." Nate gripped his father's hands and squeezed tight. "You're my dad and always did right by me."

Jed warmed to the meaning of his son's touch, that he would never let him go. Father and son were on solid ground at last. "Dad, there's no need to ask me for forgiveness. Just forgive yourself."

"I'm rarin' to do that."

"I believe you, but let me know if I can help. I want to support you too."

"Thanks, son."

Jed knew he approached life with a hard veneer of crustiness, but he believed the goodness in him outweighed the bad. He sniffed twice and wiped the corner of his eye on his handkerchief. He'd lost wives, a brother, and money to liquor. But he'd never lost his son's love. Now he needed to change for his granddaughter. He just had to. Not wanting to dig up any more old bones, he moved the conversation along.

"How is it going for Carli?"

"Things are happening. She got the job, which means I don't have to consider moving back to California. Thank God. I can't wait for Chase to meet Olivia."

Jed said, "Speaking of the big guy, have you heard from him or Tekla? I hope Chase comes home with a lot less mental anguish."

They heard the sound of a door opening, followed by Carli's voice. "Nate, could you go to the truck and bring my purse, please?"

"I'm on my way," Nate yelled down the hallway. He turned to his father and said, "Excuse me. I've been summoned." The wooden legs of the chair scraped across the wooden floor as Nate got up.

. . .

Once outside, Nate realized his father's mention of Tekla had made him jittery and confused. Lately, life felt easier if he didn't think about her. When she came to mind, he was reminded that his fervent fever for her had not broken but spiked.

He viewed Carli as an aesthetic wonder, a woman able to suck all the oxygen from a room. Having both women on his mind created a maelstrom of confusion, two pathways competing for his attention. Should he pursue an exciting, passionate, challenging life with Tekla and deal with prowlers and pistols under pillows? Or should he further explore the unexpected kindness and ease that Carli brought to his days?

And then there was Olivia. The love he felt for his daughter was deep, genuine, and bound for eternity.

While the scales of romantic love easily tipped in favor of Tekla, he was wise enough to remember that when previous relationships ignited on an emotional high, they always ended with the weight of loss. It was a simple math problem. Carli tempted him with her beauty and compassion. And she was the mother of his newfound daughter.

But would any attempt to rekindle a relationship with Carli be doomed before it bloomed? The passion he'd experienced with Tekla had tapped into something deep in him, and he wanted more. With Carli, intimacy had never gotten beyond a quickie at the Star Lite, but that didn't mean it couldn't grow.

No memory of his past with Carli touched his heart, but Olivia filled it with joy. That joy overrode his internal tug of war: Tekla. Carli. Tekla. Carli. Nate grabbed Carli's purse, concluding that his attraction to Tekla had distorted his perception of the mother of his child. He needed to find clarity.

. . .

After Nate handed off Carli's purse to her, Jed returned to the topic of Chase. "About those messages. Any from Chase or Tekla?"

Nate checked his phone. "Nothing yet. Soon, I hope. They're due to leave Switzerland in two days." He glanced toward the hallway. "I'll check on Carli and Olivia."

Jed's head turned when he heard the basement stairs creak. April returned empty-handed. "I swear, Jed, we had a quart of chocolate ice cream, but I can't find it. Unless you buried it under all that elk meat. Where'd everybody go?"

"It seems Olivia may have had a small medical emergency." He noticed the sudden concern on April's face and held out his hands to her. They sat in silence until they heard the sound of boots shuffling along the oak floor. Nate made his way down the hall with Olivia in his arms. The little girl clung to him and nestled her face in the crook of his neck. Carli followed behind, her purse bouncing on her back.

"I'm sorry, April, but Olivia's not feeling well," she said. "I think it's best if we leave."

Jed's head sank. The reverie of the day had just been lost.

"Oh, my. You just got here," April said.

Jed chimed in. "Don't worry. You do what's best. This has been a big day for her. Nate, let me know if you hear from Chase, you hear?"

"I will. You ready, Carli?"

"Yes, and thanks. I'm sorry to have to leave so soon after we got here. We'll have better visits, I'm sure."

. . .

Jed and April stood on their porch and watched Nate drive off under a light drizzle.

Jed chuckled. "Well, that was quick. I forgot how it goes with kids sometimes." He paused for a dip of chew since Olivia wasn't there. "We have an afternoon to ourselves, and I've a little work out in the shop. But, first, why don't you take a day off from kitchen duty? Maybe we can head to the Paradise Cafe for the Sunday special."

"You got yourself a deal, cowboy." April hung her apron on the kitchen hanger. "I'm not in the mood to cook, and maybe we can walk to the cafe like we did in the old days?"

"The wild old days," Jed said grinning.

Chapter 44

Nate sat in his truck in the City Motel parking lot, thinking it best to allow Carli to deal with Olivia without him. Olivia's sudden illness mystified him. He was no child expert but hoped she was all right. He'd never had a normal relationship, and he was clueless about how to handle one, especially when it involved a sick child.

When Carli climbed into his truck, Nate asked, "How is she? I'm better at doctoring horses than children."

"That's real funny." Her cold stare and narrowed eyes chilled him. "Maybe you should have become a vet. Little kids get these bugs all the time. Her tummy was hurting, but I don't think it's anything serious. She's fallen asleep. My mother will watch her for a bit."

Nate tipped his hat back, relieved to hear the prognosis. "That's good." He turned to face her. "My mom and dad are hoping Olivia won't have to live in a motel much longer. I told them you have two more weeks of motel living before that rental house is available."

"I need to dash back," she said with a groan. "I'll have to return to California, load up a U-Haul, and point it back to Montana."

His mind ran through a mental balance sheet of the expenses that remained until payday. A Montana high school teacher's salary didn't go far. Now that he was facing child support, he would have to resume horseback riding lessons along with the SAT prep to stay ahead.

There was also the possibility of getting a casting call to play a non-speaking cowboy role in a movie being filmed near Yellowstone. He had no idea where that could lead, or if they would ever call back.

"I didn't have Olivia in this month's budget. What if I give you a couple hundred bucks to help with gas for the trip back to Montana?"

"No, save it until I get back. Maybe you could put it toward tuition for a private preschool I'm checking out."

"Then let me treat you to dinner. I think being seen together in public and letting me introduce you to townsfolk could help you at school."

She countered with another suggestion. "Let's pick up a few things from the grocery store and go to your place. I'll fix something quick and simple and bring the leftovers back to the motel."

"Um." He cleared his throat. "That's an idea, but why don't we make it easy and go to the Paradise Cafe for their Sunday special? You can order takeout for your mom and Olivia. And you'll get to see one of this town's two yippy-ki-yay weekly events."

"Wow," she said. "What could be more rip-roaring than that?"

"Saturday night at the Mint Bar."

. . .

Jed loved the Paradise Cafe. For decades, the cafe had served the local community and offered the area's premier culinary experience.

The cafe's success came from sticking with the Montana gold standards, which could be found in diners from Two Dot to Wisdom, three separate cheeseburger plate offerings served with a mountain of golden fries. By Jed's account, the cafe served the best chicken fried steak in the West. The he-man-sized helping came with a side of velvety smooth mashed potatoes made the old-fashioned way. The gravy, however, came from a box, and the corn from a can. On Sundays, Montana wild game and local greens took center stage on the menu.

The cafe featured the kitchen magic of Fergie "Fingers" Calhoun, a sixtyish ex card shark from Vegas who found an alternative career in his thirties as a short-order chef. He'd stopped at the diner while hightailing it away from a bad situation with bad men in Vegas and fell in love with his waitress at first sight. He discovered he was better at flipping hash browns than cards.

"I see the regular crowd is shuffling in," Jed announced. He removed his hat and wiped his boots, more out of habit than need. His nostrils flared. "Sure smells good in here."

"Too bad Chase isn't with us. Check out the back corner," April said, pointing with her chin. "I believe that's Daisy Grimble." She kept her voice low. "She's chatting with her niece and Phyllis."

"You're right. Let's sit here." He pulled out two chairs at a table far from Daisy's, not wanting to play the woman's question game about Chase.

April arranged her chair to avoid Daisy's gaze. "This is nice, but I hope maybe someday we can have Nate, Carli, and Olivia over for Sunday dinner."

"Everything changes when a child enters the picture. Remember how we wanted to go out when Nate was a baby?"

"Oh, Jed," she said, "lighten up."

The waitress took their order for two specials after bringing their customary iced teas. Jed had just squeezed lemon into both glasses when April poked him in the ribs. "Check out who the wind blew in."

"Who?" Twisting around, Jed saw Nate and Carli enter the diner. He stood and rubbed his eyes to clear them because he was stunned to see them both at the diner. "You two slide that empty table over here and join us. Where's Olivia? Is anything wrong?"

"She's fine, Pop-Pop. Carli's mother's watching her. I didn't see your truck outside," Nate said.

"Your dad and I walked, even though the mist had turned to a light drizzle."

"Excuse me," Carli said. "What's good here?" As she looked around the café, a man washing dishes caught her attention. He had a funny way of hopping as he worked, and he kept touching his eye.

Jed's voice returned her attention to the table. "I recommend the special. Our chef prepares elk that is tender and not too gamey." He closed his eyes and inhaled a deep whiff as the scent of elk drifted from the kitchen. It solved all his present concerns.

"Do you think they could fix a peanut butter and jelly sandwich for Olivia?" Carli asked.

"That shouldn't be a problem," Nate said. He was about to order when his phone whinnied with a text alert.

"I'm sorry. Let me get this. It could be Chase."

Small talk resumed around the table, but Jed's heart skipped a beat when he saw Nate give his phone a pop-eyed stare.

"Oh, no." Nate pinched the top of his nose and reread the message. "I can't believe this."

"What is it?" April asked. "What's wrong?"

"I just got a text from Tekla. Chase has been in a serious accident."

"What kind of accident?" Jed's voice boomed off the walls. "Read it so we can all hear."

"Who's Tekla?" Carli asked.

"Read it, Nate." Jed spoke in his best basso profundo voice, sounding like the roar of his truck's V-8. Carli's question was cast aside.

"Here's what she wrote: *Dear Nate, Jed, and April. A few hours ago, Chase went out on the glacier to say goodbye to JoAnn. I'm sorry to report that he had a serious fall into a crevasse, was rescued, and was flown by helicopter to a hospital in Interlaken. I have no further details except that the guide who rescued him said he was conscious at the time of rescue but had hypothermia. Other injuries were minor. I'm told the hospital has excellent care for hypothermic patients. I'm on my way to the hospital now and will keep you all updated . . . Tekla.*"

Jed jumped up and waved his hands in the air like a rodeo clown redirecting the charge of a bull from a fallen cowboy. Nervous diners sat stony-faced as he ranted at top volume. "That's it? Two weeks and this is the news we get from Tekla? Damn her anyhow! What a bunch of bullshit. She was supposed to keep an eye out for his safety. I knew it!"

"Jed, sit down and shut your big mouth. Right now." April's fiery expression and direct order stopped him in mid-rant. His hands were shaking. Was it from the embarrassment of making a scene, or was he getting the shakes from his recent alcohol withdrawal?

"We don't know the whole story yet, and Tekla seems to be on top of the situation." April's tone calmed them all.

"It's after midnight there. I'll text her," Nate said.

"Yes, yes," Jed said, nodding.

All the diners had returned to their meals except Daisy Grimble, who continued to watch the goings-on at the Hutchens' table from the corner of her eye.

"It's been delivered," Nate said, "so I guess we'll have to wait for an answer."

"Excuse me," Carli interjected, "but I don't know what's going on. Who is Tekla? And who is this Chase who fell into a crevasse?"

"Jed, let's see if they can put a rush on our order and make it to go. Carli, can you eat with us at our home?" April reached again for Jed's hand as he reached for hers, one half of him craving Mr. Jimmy and the other half praying for Chase.

"I'm sorry," Carli said. She scooted her chair in and grabbed her purse. "I want to take my food back to the motel. I've other mouths to feed, and you all have a lot going on."

Nate said, "I'll drop you guys off, take Carli back to the motel, and then swing by. Maybe we'll have a response by then."

"You'd damn well better hope so, or I'm on the next flight to Switzerland," Jed roared. "And that's a fact."

. . .

When Nate walked into the kitchen, his mother pulled open the oven door, hoping she'd not dried out his dinner. She and Jed had already eaten.

"Thanks, Mom. I was parking my truck when another text arrived from Tekla."

"Let's hear it." Jed sat at the table, his half-eaten dinner pushed to the side. "She'd better tell us he's okay."

"Here it is." Nate began to read aloud. *Dear Nate, I'm at the hospital, and it is three a.m. I'll spend the night here. Chase's doctors told me his prognosis is excellent. That's a relief. They have him on a heated blanket, and they have also given him warm IV infusions. He is off the dehumidified oxygen, and the doctors were shocked when he asked if he could leave just after the oxygen tubes came out. He's been sedated and is sleeping now. Because of his age, his doctor told me he is facing five days minimum here in the Interlaken hospital. Since I've time to write,*

I want to let you know that I will accompany Chase to JFK and then fly home to Seneca Falls. My father is failing, and I need to be with him now. Please don't worry, as I'm in the process of finding a replacement to travel back to Montana with Chase. I will confirm this later."

The news from Tekla left Jed somewhere between numb and shell-shocked. He was slowly simmering toward the boiling point. Chase had become the brother he'd lost. They had shared so much that he felt they were fused together. "I don't know what to say." Jed's expression revealed as much distress as his voice.

"Tekla gave us all the information she had. Chase's prognosis is excellent," April said. "That's a good thing. Nate, what are your thoughts?"

"I'm with Mom. There's not much we can do here."

"You're going to call her, son. Right?" Jed asked. The lines in his face had grown deeper since hearing about Chase. He found temporary relief from a hefty pinch of snuff in his cheek.

"I'll call her in the morning. It'll be afternoon for her, and she should have an update on Chase by then."

. . .

Monday morning had not yet broken in the Paradise Valley. Usually up with the birds, Nate had spent the night in the liminal state between sleeping and waking, wrapped in an anxious mist that clung to him. He needed to roll out and call Tekla. Clasping his hands behind his head, he retreated to vivid memories of lying with her. He recalled the sweet, spicy scent of chai on her breath, and the luxury of wrapping himself in her hair. Nate couldn't get her out of his head. He was still crazy about her.

His fear of calling Tekla came from concerns about Chase combined with the recent additions to his life. He shook his head to clear the lingering scent of Carli's herbal shampoo from his nose, hoping it would simplify his call to Tekla.

He rolled over and scratched his elbows raw. Patches of eczema had reappeared, a result of the stress he'd been feeling. The memory of Tekla's voice floated in his head. "Do you like it better in the evening than in the morning?" He groaned as his mind fell into a chaotic synch with his heart.

At that moment, learning more about Chase's condition was

paramount. He separated himself from memories of the Seneca Falls tryst and stuffed his dreams of Tekla back into the small treasure chest he kept in his mind. Carli couldn't fit in that box.

It was time. Six-thirty in Montana meant it was two-thirty in Interlaken. He took a breath and dialed Tekla's number. She answered on the third ring.

"Nate, I was waiting for your call." She sounded calm and upbeat, even reasonable. "I'm at the motel. How are you?"

She was not alone, as he heard a man's voice in the room. *Who is that*, he wondered? The bedroom mirror reflected a muddled-brained man who wasn't happy being excluded from Tekla's life. That night after dinner with his parents, how he had wanted to take Tekla home, light some candles, wrap himself in her hair, and forget everything else. They could share his big Montana world. But was he man enough to tell her about the child who called him Daddy?

"Hey," he said. "We were a little shaken up when we got your message last night about Chase. What's going on? Is he going to be all right?"

"I met with the doctors this morning when they made their rounds." It sounded like she sipped something and then a small cough delayed her response. "He responded to treatment and is out of the danger zone. They may have to tie him up to evaluate his liver and kidneys. He will be here for a couple of days." She coughed again. "Sorry," she said, sniffing. "It may take a week because of his age."

Nate kept hearing a man's voice in the room, and it annoyed him. He heard her say, "I'll just be a minute."

His anxiety increased, but he said, "We're grateful you're there. How are you doing?"

"This trip was very emotional for Chase, even before his fall on the glacier. I've had a little help," she said, hesitating a moment, "from Liam, one of his rescuers. What a hero. He's here now to take me to lunch before I head back to the hospital."

Hearing Tekla talk about a man who was helping her, a hero no less, sent Nate spiraling into a bottomless well of anguish for the woman he craved. That woman was now receiving comfort and aid from another man. In his mind, he still heard her voice purring in pleasure as he lay on top of her. Instead of hearing her heartbeat, he now heard his own. Thump . . . thump . . . thump. It was beating faster and heavier than ever before.

He forced himself back to the conversation. "I'm sorry to hear your dad has taken a turn. You're planning to take Chase only as far as JFK?"

"I haven't confirmed it yet, but I asked my Uncle Sean to meet us at JFK. He will probably be the one to accompany Chase back to Montana."

Nate heard the tiredness in her voice, balanced by her optimism that all would be well. He needed to raise the level of his response.

"And you?"

"I'll head to Seneca Falls."

Nate said, "I was hoping to see you again back here in Montana." He knew he was waffling. It was a stall tactic, but he knew he couldn't prolong the announcement. "I've some big news to tell you. I have . . ."

"Come on, Nate . . ."

He wished she would drop that damned seductive nuance in her voice. Or was he just wishing that's what it was?

"I hope you're going to tell me you took some beautiful girl out on horseback and serenaded her by a creek."

"No, not since you. But I've had a big change in my life."

"Oh, sorry. Liam has an appointment, and I need to leave for lunch now. We'll finish talking later. I've got Chase covered."

"Sure. Goodbye."

Nate stared into space. He'd never been to Switzerland. If it hadn't been for Olivia, he would have been on the next plane. Wild horses wouldn't have been able to hold him back.

Chapter 45

Tekla held her breath and closed her eyes tightly as if squeezing a lemon inside her head. What if Chase falls again? She avoided thinking about it but was unable to hide her anxiety. Breathing exercises usually helped, but her fingernails dug into the armrest when Chase unbuckled his seat belt and struggled to his feet.

"Your elbow should be slightly bent when you hold your cane," she told him for the third time on the flight home. "And don't forget to step forward using your good leg."

Raising his cane, he said, "Good gravy! I'll be fine once I get off this plane, even with this darned walking cast." He punctuated his declaration by tapping the cast with the cane. "I've already had practice falls on this trip. I just need to stretch my legs. Is it time for my muscle relaxer?"

"Yes, here it is. Uncle Sean will help you take the next dose." She feigned an evasive maneuver, having heard from her uncle how he and Chase liked to rib one another.

"Make my day," he said with humor that faded to fondness. Swallowing the medication with too little water made the pill stick in his throat, prompting him to cough it up and try again. Once the pill went down, he settled back into his seat.

Tekla let her head roll back against the headrest, and exhaustion pressed her deeper into the seat. Homecomings drained her, but life was not always magical away from home. College had been brutal academically, while Afghanistan had been physically grueling and emotionally cruel. Everything felt different when she returned home from the Middle East. This time she was returning to care for her ailing father. His needs would drain her further. Should she hide her dread and fear of failure from Chase?

He must have heard her thoughts, because he asked, "How are you doing?"

"I'm holding up," she said. "Now my prayers are that my father won't suffer."

"I'm so proud to have had you with me." He reached for her hand. "Your father is a blessed man to have you as a daughter. I mean it." A warm smile accompanied his soothing words.

"When I was a confused teen," Tekla said, "I tried to emulate his kindness, but at times I considered it a weakness rather than a strength."

"Sharing your challenges makes you vulnerable," Chase said, "but it also gives you courage."

She felt changed in a deep and meaningful way and wondered what had brought it about. As Tekla pondered the transformation, fatigue made it easy to slip into a trance. She automatically switched to yoga breathing, which connected her mind to her heart. Soon she slipped into a dream-filled sleep that took her on a meditative review of recent life events.

She felt the healing of her broken heart, and a small flame began to flicker there. It was clear that kindness and forgiveness could spread only if her heart shone brightly. Had it all begun with the words from the Dalai Lama that showed her how kindness can be infectious and carry her great distances?

She saw that the trip with Chase had opened new doors of understanding. When panic surged, she recommitted to staying grounded, relying on a resilient faith she'd never known she possessed. She learned that she was a fighter, the kind of fighter that made Chase proud. At last, Tekla realized she would never give up. Staying in the fight was everything.

She understood how Gabe had absorbed his father's belief that nothing was ever lost in this world—it just hadn't been found. Her leg had been blown off, and she sometimes felt phantom aches and pains. Although that leg was no longer a part of her, a prosthetic limb had taken its place. Her leg had been transformed. Thus, it was never lost.

She accepted the necessity of forgiveness through her encounter with Abdullah, a man living out the lesson JoAnn had given Chase. Abdullah was a man who had freed himself from anger and the desire for revenge. Forgiving his enemies enabled him to live a purposeful life after suffering remarkable losses.

She had opened herself to a new kind of love when she met Liam. His first touch was electric. It grounded her, initiating an abiding sense of peace in the short time she was with him. Could it grow into more? His life was stable and structured, maybe due to his time in the military. She longed to return to that level of predictability. Had she fallen in love for the first time? Would it last? Liam and she would be an ocean apart. Could she have both distance and closeness?

Before Liam, there had been Nate. He'd offered what she needed at the time. The intersection of fate and coincidence during their brief connection reminded her of the desire to love and be loved in return. It was a random moment of recklessness, but she felt no regret.

Love was a mighty challenger that might conquer all her fears and every ghost that had followed her from the war. However, love and fear could not coexist, no more than hot and cold or black and white could occur at the same time. She finally accepted the truth that she could not hide her inner conflicts from any man.

"Hey, wake up over there." Chase nudged her arm, returning her to reality. "You've been asleep for an hour. We're beginning our descent to JFK."

. . .

A uniformed Delta agent waited at the aircraft's exit, standing in front of a motorized cart. In his hand was an electronic tablet, its screen facing the exiting passengers. *Chase DeMers* was displayed in yellow letters against a black background.

"Ah, no. I don't think so, Tekla. Was this your idea?" He swung his cane to dismiss the cart.

"Consider this an order. There is no way we both can hop on the AirTrain and navigate border control and customs with only two good legs between us." Then she winked and said, "A wise man once told me that kindness is a strength. So sit."

He did as Tekla ordered and gave her a thumbs up. The agent navigated them through the crowds and confusion as if it were an art form.

At Chase's departure gate, Tekla checked her text alert and groaned at the news that her flight to Syracuse had been delayed by three hours. Then she realized it would give her more time with Chase before she had to say goodbye. Undoubtedly, she would be brokenhearted no matter when she left. She loved Chase too much. He had taken her from f-bombs to forgiveness. "Now I can stay with you and see my uncle. I wasn't ready to say goodbye anyway."

"Tekla," he said, looking up from his chair. She was overcome by the wisdom that resided in his now-sad eyes. "Goodbyes will make our journeys harder. You need to be strong." A barrage of sniffs followed. "Focus on your father. Later, when the time is right, I have much to talk to you about. When that time comes, I'd like you to return to the ranch."

"Really?" Her voice throbbed with emotion. She thought of her panic attacks, her nondisclosures, the lessons she'd learned along the way, and what waited for her at home. For the first time since she lost her leg, she knew she would live a wonderful life.

. . .

Tekla stole a glance at the departure sign and then sank into a chair opposite Chase. Weariness clung to her, and she sighed before saying, "We made your passport deadline by days."

"No worries," he said with a laugh.

She said, "I'm going to use those USB ports. If you'll give me your phone, I can charge them both."

"My phone? You have it," Chase commented while checking his pockets just to make sure.

"I don't have your phone. You had it when we cleared TSA. I downloaded your boarding pass on it."

His face flushed with panic while he quickly unzipped every pocket on his pants and vest. Then he sighed with relief and said, "Oh, here it is. Stuck in the corner of my chair. Thought I'd checked there."

She took note of his confusion, and then it came to her. She grabbed the Swiss prescription from her purse and read the back of the label. *Warning. This medication may cause short-term memory loss for some users.*

She'd just finished reading the label when Chase said, "Oh, I need to use the men's room." He stood, arthritically bent and rocking on his legs, clearly in a hurry-up state of mind.

Everything hit her at once: her post-flight exhaustion, the delay of her flight, Chase's sudden memory lapse, and his urgent need to pee. She also had to pee, but she had to keep an eye on their personal items. Looking left, she saw signs for the nearby men's restroom.

At that instant, her phone pinged with another text alert, this one from her uncle Sean. *Tekla, I see your plane has landed. Bad wreck has traffic backed up, but I should be there with slight delay. US*

After tucking her phone away, she realized Chase was nowhere to be seen. Had he made it to the men's room while she was reading her uncle's text? Should she go in? Her mind shifted to the text. She'd forgotten to reply, so she took out her phone and texted a thumbs-up emoticon.

Again, she scanned for any sign of Chase, craning her neck left and then right. Should she call security? Then she heard the sound of women shouting. Chase, cane in hand, had just hobbled out of the ladies' rest room. His face was red with embarrassment.

Tekla covered her face with her hands and sank deeper into her seat. To avoid adding to his humiliation, she said, "Now that we've found your phone, I'm going to recharge both phones and then use the restroom. Be right back."

After plugging in the phones, she took a deep breath, closed her eyes, and indulged in a fleeting moment of Zen. It didn't last long. There was no mistaking her uncle Sean's voice.

He had found it humorous to point out Chase's cane. "Well, looky here. If it's not Crash DeMers, sitting with his hands folded like some worn-out sacristan. How are you, you ornery old cuss?" Tekla heard a note of affection in his verbal jab.

"You want the short answer or the long version, Sean?" Chase asked, prodding the tip of his cane into Sean's thigh.

Sean had left his executive suit in the closet and wore high-end, made-to-measure denim jeans. His shaved and bronzed head could have been confused for that of a monk.

"Should I bow or light some incense?" Chase asked, hooting and pounding the tip of his cane on the floor. "Doesn't Goldman Sachs have fashion police?"

Sean shook his head in response. "I spend your money wisely on good clothes and a clean shave, dear man," he replied with a grin.

Seeing her uncle had given Tekla a burst of energy. Sean was always a good sport, and she noticed how the two men's camaraderie lit up the waiting area.

Chase said, "You can spend more of my money and take Tekla and me to lunch." He stood, clutching his cane between his knees while he blew his nose.

Sean slid off his light coat and opened his arms to hug Tekla. The embrace was more paternal than genial, and he ran his fingers through her magnificent head of hair.

"Few nieces are as beautiful as you," Sean said as he reached to give her another hug. "I'm glad you're home safe. I want to hear all about it, but we'd better do as Chase said and have lunch first."

Chase pointed to the charging area before heading to lunch and said, "Don't forget our phones."

"I'll meet you two in the restaurant in a minute," she said. She'd let them catch up while she retrieved the phones and revisited the restroom.

Chapter 46

Chase believed that tears were meant for small sorrows, and his goodbye to Tekla did not involve a trivial sadness. He doubted the human body could produce enough tears to purge the bone-deep grief he felt. Instead, he delivered a bear hug that had the amazing effect of quieting Tekla's racing heart. His gratitude for her commitment to him was immense, but if he dallied a moment longer, he might become dewy-eyed after all.

Chase and Sean had settled into their assigned seats on the plane when Chase said, "Your niece is remarkable."

"There's no denying she's a survivor." Sean opened the overhead compartment to stash their coats. "She embodies extraordinary qualities. Wouldn't you agree?" Sean laid his hand on Chase's shoulder. Chase flinched and turned his face to the window.

"Yes," Chase replied without turning back. "I agree."

As the jet climbed higher, Chase sank lower. Without Tekla beside him, he felt unsettled, his mind in a fog as thick as the cloud bank they were flying through.

Chase had hidden his feelings about Sean's failure to share crucial facts about Tekla, including her combat casualty, PTSD, and prosthesis. He considered asking Sean about it right then, but the timing didn't feel right. Maybe there would never be a good time. Tekla had confessed her inclination to hoard information. She said it was a way to avoid thinking about her PTSD. Perhaps Sean had never been aware of her struggles with it. Maybe none of that mattered anymore.

Instead of asking about Sean's awareness of Tekla's PTSD, Chase said, "You know, I could've handled these flights back to Montana without help." His tone conveyed the gilded edges of toughness and independence that had cemented his enduring friendship with Sean.

"Yes, partner, I'm sure you could have," Sean replied, "but having me do this was a great relief for Tekla."

"I appreciate that." Chase's smile was both knowing and heartfelt. "My ordeal on the glacier put her through hell. She cared for me, and she now needs to turn her attention to her ailing father." He unbuckled his seatbelt and reclined the seat before changing the subject. "May I ask how your brother is doing?"

"He's slip-sliding away. I plan to spend a day in Montana and then head back to support the family if that's good with you."

"You do what you have to do. I'm under orders to rest and check in with my doctor."

"Any concerns?"

Chase wiped his mouth with his handkerchief. He hesitated to elaborate further, but he knew he could trust Sean. "Not a word to Tekla, you hear?"

"You got it."

"I had a CAT scan done while at the Swiss hospital. The fall banged me up. Nothing serious. But the doctors found a shadow behind one of my lungs and told me to follow up immediately when I got home."

"You scared?"

"Of what?" Chase said with irritation. "A shadow? You're asking a man from Butte if he's scared of a shadow? Get real."

"Come on, man. Let's be honest here. Was there ever a moment in your life when you were scared?"

Chase bit his lip. "Sorry I snapped. Yeah, when JoAnn died."

"Wow! Chase DeMers is mortal. He just admitted to being scared one time."

"Hmph. Here's the deal. The docs said the shadow could be old scar tissue from boxing, or it could be . . ."

"I know," Sean said. "JoAnn died from cancer. It's hard not to have your mind go there."

Chase felt weary. Psychological exhaustion pressed down on him. Jet lag, sleep deprivation, and arthritic pain challenged him. Bumps, bruises, and a busted leg reminded him of his fall into a crevasse. It could've killed him.

Chase missed Tekla. Remembering the swish of her hair and the sweet touch of her hand left him wearier. Her scent lingered in his mind and was the hardest memory to set aside. Thinking about her made him miss her even more.

He was no longer the agile fighter who could bob, weave, and slip punches. He wasn't knocked out, and he certainly was not scared, but any boxing referee would've given him a standing eight count.

Chase made a gear-shifting movement with his arm to indicate that he wanted to change topics.

Sean acknowledged it with a wave of his hand, and said, "Let's hear it. Get it out. I think they're ready to offer coffee and snacks."

"It's just a notion," Chase said, feeling revived just by thinking about his plan. "You're familiar with JoAnn's will and her wish that our estate be dedicated to cancer research."

"That was the plan."

"But she included a clause that left me with a little wiggle room."

Sean shrugged. "You've always been a critical thinker. I imagine you're on solid ground. What's your wiggle room?"

"A moral dilemma." Chase's answer reflected the ability to reason that had made him a capable attorney. "Most cancer research is funded by the feds. While I want to fulfill her wish, I've discovered a great need that is underfunded. I want to divert a large portion of our portfolio to it."

"I'm listening. What's the dilemma clause?"

Chase pulled out several pages of notes, ready to reveal the plan he'd sketched out during the trip. "It takes $30," he said, "to build a land mine. Just thirty gawddamn dollars! There are global treaties to ban them, but casualties from those weapons, as well as from unexploded munitions hiding in war-torn countries, continue to climb. Financial contributions have plummeted."

He folded his notes with more fury than finesse and laid them on his tray table. He covered his eyes with his hands, struggling to keep from breaking down. When he continued, he spoke from his heart. "I want to reverse that trend." He dangled his pause for effect and then pointed to his notes. I want to support continued removal of the land mines, but the need to get prostheses to amputees in undeveloped countries is equally important. Our mission will be to recycle used prosthetic components from this country and get them to those who can't afford them."

Sean considered what his friend had revealed before he spoke. "Recycle them?"

Chase folded his notes in half and slid them into his pocket. His next words were tinged with anger. "Yes. It's crazy how this country wastes medical supplies and materials. Just think of the innocent civilians, especially the children, all of those who are maimed and torn apart without access to the kind of medical help Tekla got. How can I not help that cause?"

"I don't see a moral conflict, Chase. You have a better answer. What would JoAnn say? She was a pragmatist, and she gave you the green light to use your discretion."

Chase DeMers had spent much time deliberating that exact question. What was he to do? He had contemplated his own mortality from the vantage point of a bottomless crevasse. Small pieces of the solemn state of humanity hinged on his decision. In the end, he waved off the standing eight count. He rallied in his own fight against the guilt he felt about going out for a gawddamn pork sandwich and missing his wife's final moments.

What had his boxing coach preached? *To triumph without risk is to win without glory*. He'd risk it all if it meant saving one child's life or limb. He had no kids of his own, but his heart and soul dictated that innocent children must be protected. Let others be held accountable for their failure to defend them. But don't blame him.

JoAnn would understand.

Chapter 47

At the first bounce of the jet's wheels on Montana ground, a new feeling wrapped around Chase. The rubber striking Bozeman's tarmac grounded him with a sense of relief and accomplishment. He'd paid his fare and deposited every bit of guilt and sorrow in an icy blue crevasse. No longer was grief a vocation. No longer did he wish to live in solitary confinement.

He gazed out the window. New snow topped the serrated mountain peaks. Ever since being trapped in the crevasse, the thought of feeling cold again freaked him out. He pivoted his head south to the Gallatin Range and then east to the Bridger Range, all jutting from the Gallatin Valley of southwestern Montana. This view had always been more welcoming than anywhere he and JoAnn had traveled. He was back on Montana sod, in a state that boasted more cattle than people, and he believed that was something to moo about.

Chase's body calmed, his pulse slowed, and his emotions followed suit. Fight-or-flight mode was in the past. His mind cleared, released from the memory of JoAnn's remains skimming across a glacier, trapped in a plastic bag. There were no security agents with machine guns, as he'd seen in Paris, and Montana had no icy crevasses to fall into.

Tekla's absence changed his psychological landscape the most. Instinctively—or from muscle memory—he reached for JoAnn's hand.

"I'll give you my hand after we come to a complete stop," Sean said. "Just hold on, partner. Must feel good to be on the tarmac after spending a day on a plane."

Chase muttered, "Good gravy," and withdrew his hand. He slouched into the seat. The need for a pain pill to soothe his throbbing ankle battled with embarrassment for grasping Sean's fingers.

Groggy, red-eyed, and sporting extra stubble, he craved rest, recuperation, and ranch time. Most of all, he needed to put his near-death fall into the crevasse far behind him. The last thing he wanted was to share the details of his odyssey with the Hutchens and all the inquiring minds of those he met while doing his weekly errands.

A *ping* signaled the flight crew to prepare for passengers to exit the plane. "I made it home," Chase said, pumping his fist in the air. He stood and immediately shouted, "Ow, ow, ow! My ankle. I need a minute, Sean."

When the pain eased enough for Chase to leave the plane, he relied on his cane for support. Sean handled the carry-on baggage.

A shotgun blast of fresh Montana air welcomed Chase as he stepped onto the jetway.

Jed was waiting for him inside the terminal, a man as tough as nails and as loyal a friend as he could ever hope for. With one hand, Jed tipped his cowboy hat. The other hand held an eight-ounce can of vigor in Chase's favorite flavor.

They stood huddled, three amigos, each sizing up the others. Chase detected new energy in Jed. There was less puffiness around the eyes, and his face was leaner and had more color. Chase wondered if Jed had started some sort of rejuvenation diet, maybe eating more tofu and drinking raw vegetable juices instead of distilled spirits from corn mash. The wide-open face before him bore little resemblance to the guarded countenance he remembered.

Once more, the realization that he was home washed over him. Montana reverberated in Chase's soul. He recognized the distinctive pulse that he felt only when he was within its borders. He reveled in the shifting of gorgeous landscapes under a big sky, a place sparsely populated with friendly, independent people.

His trip overseas had ended his desire ever to leave it again. While he had grown grayer during the trip, he'd also outgrown the agitated state of mind that had developed from his grief over the gawddamn pork-chop sandwich.

The transformation had been hard and gritty, almost as if he were reborn. The indelible spirit of a wounded warrior with her army 'all in' attitude had helped him make the transition. Humbled by Tekla's sense of duty and sacrifice to her country, as well as her enduring loyalty to him, Chase could not resist feeling eager to experience the future.

He no longer felt preoccupied with the merciless burden of guilt that once had him wrapped in a cocoon. He had become as free as one of the Monarch butterflies that flitted around his lilac bushes.

"Welcome home, boss," Jed said, pulling him from his reverie. "From what I heard, it was one tough trip, especially on the glacier. Glad you're back safe. How's the leg?"

"It's a miracle is all I can say." Chase flipped his hand above his head, indicating that was about all he wanted to say about the trip. "Angels," he mumbled. "Angels." He looked out the huge airport window, lifted his eyes to the mountains, and shook his head. "Angels."

Jed turned to Chase's companion. "Sean, haven't seen you since JoAnn's service. Glad you could help out." His eyes scanned Sean's attire, and he whistled softly when he noticed the flashy jeans. "Whoo-ee. Aren't you the fancy dresser?"

Sean ignored the jab. "Great to see you, Jed. You're a good man for Chase to lean on now that he's back in Montana. Let's get the big guy home."

Chase said, "I'm more than ready."

"Wait here, and I'll pull the truck around," Jed said. "I'll call April and tell her we're on our way."

Chase felt the chill of the can in his hand more than the fatigue in his bones. With a flick of his wrist, he tipped the can and drained the much needed pick-me-up in four swallows.

Chapter 48

Tears started to roll down April's cheeks as she tacked the last corner of her "Welcome Home Chase" banner across the deck's railing. She'd decorated the outside and inside of his home with dried Montana wheat, Indian corn, gourds, and pumpkins. Halloween had just passed, but the theme would hold through Thanksgiving, one of Chase's favorite holidays.

Her heart felt so full it might burst. She could hardly wait for Chase to arrive home safe, if slightly dinged-up, from his tumble into the glacial crevasse. As soon as he was rested, she'd tell him about Olivia. *No,* she thought. *I'll leave it all for Nate to tell.*

The peaceful quiet was broken by the unmistakable rumble of Jed's truck. It was a most welcome noise. She gave the house one last lip-smack of approval, unwringing her hands so as not to look like an anxious maid. She turned off the reggae and adjusted the flowers on the table one last time.

The truck sat too high for Chase to step down without Jed's help. Sean gathered the luggage. On the stone path to the house, April welcomed Chase with a look of endearment that reflected the affection they felt for each other. April started to extend her arms to hug him, but he propped his cane against the deck and laid a tight hug on her first.

He walked into the house like a stranger in his own home, the look on his face a million miles from the present. He appeared changed, more peaceful and gentle. He had shed the bankrupt spirit, weighed down by grief. Even with his cane, he walked with confidence, his chest forward like a boxer entering the ring.

"Oh, Chase," she said. "You're a wondrous sight to see." She patted his shoulders and face as if to assure herself he was real. "We've missed you. Now you just rest," she ordered, "and get that leg healed up." She turned to her husband. "Jed, let's give Chase some time to relax while you get Sean squared away in the guest house. I'll have soup and sandwiches ready for all of us around six this evening. Will that work?"

"April, that sounds wonderful," Sean replied. "I remember your cooking with great fondness. Ready, Jed?"

"Let's roll." He gave his wife a peck on the cheek and grabbed the keys to the guesthouse from a hook on the wall.

After Jed and Sean left, April walked behind Chase while he did a homecoming tour, first passing his bedroom. "Nothing like sleeping in your own bed," she said.

"The saying 'No place like home' never gets old," he replied. "You outdid yourself with those fall decorations."

She nodded and gave Chase her you're-darn-tootin' smile.

He stopped in front of his family's heirloom grandfather clock, which stood as a sentinel in the hallway. April was relieved that she'd remembered to wind and set it before he arrived home. She wondered how his calamity on the crevasse might interrupt the ongoing tick-tock of his life.

Trailing him to his office, she saw him lock his gaze on the frame of the *Medicine Man* before giving it a small nudge to the left. He did the same with *River Walkers*. He nodded, satisfied they were level, and headed for the couch. April had already arranged the pillows before he sat.

He smiled with satisfaction when the grandfather clock chimed five times. "Before I lie down, what's new?" he asked. "How have things been here with you and Jed? I hadn't planned on such a lengthy trip." He removed his walking boot and propped his cane against the sofa.

She noticed how the light from the antler chandelier silvered Chase's hair and detailed the shadows in his handsome face. She sat at one end of the sofa and squirmed on the leather cushion, longing to shout out the news that she was a grandmother.

"So, what's new in paradise?" Chase asked.

She struggled to find the right words and finally said, "We've kept busy."

"That's it? You and Jed kept busy?"

She let out a breath and offered the first thing that crossed her mind. "Jed got his elk."

"Good for him. And how about Nate? Did he keep busy?"

"He got his elk too."

"Guess it's good the wolves left a few." He revealed his bewilderment about April's lack of news with a raised eyebrow and a lopsided shoulder shrug.

"Can I get you anything before you take a nap?" April asked as she laid his slippers next to the walking boot. "I'll prepare some meals for a few days so you can rest properly. Daisy Grimble dropped by earlier with an elk meatloaf and a fresh loaf of Flo's sourdough. That was nice of her."

"Yes," he said with a smirk. "Yes, it was thoughtful of her. Montana elk defiled with her Texas barbecue sauce, I imagine." Chase's comment seemed to suggest a smidge of acceptance toward Daisy that he'd never shown.

He said, "Fix it tomorrow when Sean's here for supper. If you'll excuse me, I need to get flat. But first I've medicine to take."

"I'll be in the kitchen if you need me," she said, breathing a sigh of relief that he hadn't pressed for more information about Nate. Her son planned to visit Chase the next day. He could break his fatherly news then.

Chapter 49

Chase stopped taking his muscle relaxants the next morning. They made him spacey, and he had a lot on his agenda. He was sitting at the breakfast table organizing a stockpile of notes when the clock chimed seven. Sean should arrive at any minute. He'd complete his business with him before April arrived to fix breakfast.

Outlining his new vision to Sean was the first task on his list. He and JoAnn had a philanthropic history of funding and organizing twenty charities but had no involvement with landmine removal. Their landmine knowledge had been limited to an awareness of Princess Diana's walk through an Angolan minefield to bring global attention to their use in war-torn countries. That had been more than twenty years ago. Landmines became personal to him the moment he learned of Tekla's devastating encounter with one. It was time to act.

He had started a pot of coffee for Sean just as his Wall Street wizard knocked on the door.

"Come on in," Chase said by way of greeting his old friend.

"How's your Montana morning?" Sean asked as he wiped his feet. He hung his jacket on a peg near the door.

"Better now that you're here." Chase reached for a mug and handed it to Sean. "Fill it up, and let's head to my office. We'll give April space to make breakfast. I see she and Jed just pulled up."

"How's the leg? Did you get some rest?"

"I'm fine. I'll get plenty of rest after I die."

Sean took a seat in Chase's office and sipped from his cup. His eyes roamed the room and settled on the *Medicine Man.*

Chase was putting his notes in order when Sean interrupted him. "Don't forget to schedule that follow-up medical appointment you told me about."

"Oh, yeah," Chase growled. "Me and my shadow. But I'm interested in a more pressing matter right now. Here's the deal. I've used Tekla as a filter on some thoughts I want to run by you."

"I'm all ears. Oh, before I forget, last night Jed asked me if I wanted to go for an ATV ride this afternoon. He's going to remove the batteries for the winter on Monday."

Chase finished straightening his notes and said, "That's a great idea. Now, let's get started on my proposal with a few spreadsheets." Sean generally frowned on having lawyers talk about budgets. Chase hoped that describing the state of the world's landmines would influence Sean to come around to his way of thinking.

"For the past twenty years, you have served as the foundation director and CEO of the JoAnn DeMers Foundation, and I'd like you to stay on as I transition into a new arena." Chase paused to honor the extent of Sean's service.

"The landmine initiatives you mentioned? You've reconciled JoAnn's wishes, then?"

"Yes," he said. "I'm at peace with my decision. My idea is to start laying some groundwork today by creating a name. That always solidifies my planning. From there, we can develop our mission statement, including purpose, funding, and goals."

"Your cause is more than visionary," Sean said. "You're also a doer." Sean's cell phone rang, interrupting the discussion. He checked it and let the call go to voicemail. "Sorry. It's on silent now. Back to business. You want to help the Teklas in this world," he commented. "You bet I'm in. What do you have so far?"

"I've learned that land mines are ubiquitous, cheap, and brutal. I've prepared a release to that effect for you."

"Go for it."

"Let me read it. *Landmines blow up military personnel and civilians alike. It's morally reprehensible to involve civilians, so the new smart land mines being developed need operators to trigger them and a policy to address the current changes. Our name will be distinctive and focus on hope for landmine victims: Chase and JoAnn Demers Foundation for Prosthetic Restoration.*"

He reread the release, rubbing his eyes.

"I see you've changed your perspective. You no longer wish to be anonymous, huh?"

"A lot has changed, so let's be ready to move ahead after the holidays. One more thing. I'd like to speak with Tekla and offer her a role in this project."

Sean looked Chase in the eye and nodded in acknowledgement and agreement. "Good plan. And what an ambassador she'll make."

Chapter 50

Nate's acceptance of his responsibilities as a father came easier to him than riding saddle broncs. He knew Carli had once doubted he was father material. The fact that she spent four years raising his daughter without telling him he was Olivia's dad rankled him. He found little reason to forgive and forget Carli's decision to keep it from him.

Maybe he hadn't been one hundred percent ready to be a father, but she lacked motherly suitability herself. What Carli hadn't known was that Nate's father, despite his occasional benders, was a good dad. Jed had kept the magic of boyhood adventures alive for his son. He also taught him right from wrong, playing with him and demonstrating what fatherhood stands for. His father had made up for the shortcomings of his own childhood. Jed's dad had made babies but was a father to none of them.

In the weeks after Chase left for his European trip, Nate's world had gotten bigger than just Santiago. How would he explain Carli to Chase? Nate had flourished when he listened to his father and failed when he didn't listen to him enough. He also lived with a nagging fear of being a source of disappointment to Chase. He hoped Olivia would melt Chase's heart.

Chase was standing just off the deck, his cane at his side. He leaned on the hitching post like a sheriff in an old Western movie waiting for his horse to be delivered. A wintry gust ruffled the hair on Chase's uncapped head. When Nate got out of his truck, Chase beamed a smile as wide as the pumpkin at his feet.

"What's happening, Clintwood?" Nate said, reviving a greeting from his boyhood days.

Chase's jaw dropped at the sight of the young man. "You shaved!" he said, staring.

"I did." Nate stroked his chin. "My beard rubbed some people the wrong way."

They hugged like father and son, Nate brimming with questions to ask and a secret to tell.

They sat across from each other, catching up and sipping beers in the glow of the fireplace. Nate listened with fascination to Chase's travel tales, shuddering involuntarily when he heard about his fall into the crevasse. Then it was Nate's turn. He eased into it.

"Mom told me you're using a spare pair of hearing aids. How are they working for you?"

"They're old, but these still do the job. What brought that up?"

"I've some big news to share," Nate said. "I want to make sure you hear it. I had a visit from a woman I knew back in my rodeo days in California."

Chase laughed. "You must have made a lasting impression for her to come and visit after—how long has it been now? Four years?"

Nate paused, the tip of the bottle at his lips. He had the perfect come-back line to answer Chase, yet he waffled on the propriety of it. In the end, he couldn't hold it in. "She gave me a surprise gift that will last a lifetime."

Chase frowned, clearly puzzled. Nate realized that Chase, given his age and still recovering from a near-death experience, wasn't up for a guessing game. "You got me, Nate. What was the gift?"

"My daughter!"

"Your daughter. Hmm. I seem to have missed the punchline."

"I'm serious. I don't know how else to break it to you, but the fact is I'm a dad."

The bottle of beer slipped from Chase's hand.

They both ignored the bottle draining its contents onto the floor. Nate continued. "I got a woman, Carli, pregnant almost five years ago when I was cowboying in California. She came to town right before you left with Tekla. I didn't believe her claim that I was the father, so I had a paternity test done in Bozeman."

"And the results were positive?"

"Yes. I'm the father to a beautiful four-year-old girl named Olivia."

"Whoa. Whoa, whoa, big boy. Let me come up for air."

Nate had just told a story to Chase that didn't involve riding a fast horse. For the next hour, Nate's words stumbled out a few at a time, each cluster separated by a long stretch of silence. The discussion stopped only for another bottle of beer for each of them and a hearing-aid battery change for Chase.

Nate told the story of meeting Carli in California, how she'd delivered the news about Olivia after four years, his anger over the delay, and Carli's move to the valley. Nate did not rein in his expressions of deep love and loyalty toward Olivia. That fire, deep in his gut, had burned away all the bad memories attached to his wild-oat days. However, nothing he said indicated a desire to explore a romantic relationship with Carli.

Chase's phone rang in his vest pocket. Before hitting the green light to accept the call, he turned the screen to show Nate the picture of the caller. Nate's stomach churned. It was Tekla.

Nate wished Chase had excused himself and taken the call in private. Did Chase suspect his feelings for Tekla?

He listened to Chase's side of the conversation. "Yes, yes, I'm doing fine. Yes, I've got my boot on. No, your Uncle Sean has gone for an ATV ride with Jed. Yes, and Nate will be here for supper too. No tofu. Elk meatloaf. Tell me how your father is doing. Uh-huh, I know how the last days can be. That's right. Just appreciate each moment for what it is. Your mother needs you. I understand. And I feel the same about you. Yes, I'll stay in touch."

"How's she doing?" Nate asked. There was genuine concern in his voice. Chase's heartfelt words touched a nerve in him. Could he be as unwavering in his support as Chase was? He shook his head to clear it.

"She's remarkable." Chase spoke calmly but could not hide his enthusiasm and affection for Tekla. "With all that I put her through. With everything that serving our country put her through. And now her father." He sniffed twice. "And she is able to carry such a beautiful vitality through all of it."

Nate noticed that Chase had become emotionally and physically spent from talking to Tekla. His voice was on the edge of fading away, but he had more to say.

"I don't get it." He yawned. "I've listened to you talk about how your past delivered a wonderful gift to you with Olivia. I couldn't be happier for you. Your mother and father must be so excited about becoming grand-parents." He paused and hung his head. "But I'm disappointed too."

"About what?"

Propping his head with his hands, Chase fished for words. Nate had forgotten the one critical quality that he had tried to instill in him since he was a boy. The quality was *others*. How could Nate have forgotten to live it?

Nate attempted to apologize, although he didn't know what he was apologizing for. "I didn't mean to piss you off," he said.

"You can sit here and carry on for an hour about Olivia's beauty and innocence." Chase was almost riled enough to spit out an expletive more pointed than talking about gravy. "But you're thinking of her mother as being no more important than a horse dropping. You really need to reflect on this."

Nate realized he'd just disappointed his most loyal fan, other than his father.

Chase continued. "You owe it to Olivia to try to establish a relationship with her mother. She'll ask you one day why you didn't. Is that the legacy you want to leave?"

Nate had learned not to engage with Chase when he caught him playing with his ball of confusion. Nate wanted to tear apart the wound that the mysteries of love had opened. But the more he tore, the more it unraveled. Chase talked of Carli. He saw only Tekla. What a bewildering jumble of emotions.

Chapter 51

Nate was lost . . . so lost that he couldn't find himself beyond Chase's judgment about his actions. Had it been premature? Was it just?

He could not think clearly. His mother thought he should explore a relationship with Carli because Oprah had said children lose self-esteem without a father in their lives. His mother had Oprah on her side, and he was left standing in weak sauce.

His father blamed Nate and his tequila-soaked brain for misjudging Carli, considering her good enough to knock boots with but not special enough for a relationship. Nate failed to get attached to any woman; it was easier to walk away after their rumble between the sheets. It had been simple, like riding a new bronc in every rodeo.

Being gored by that bull and his bout with depression led to his decision to leave the damned old rodeo. He knew he was getting older, but what scared him was his loss of competitive confidence. He'd lost the no-blink mentality necessary for riding broncs.

Now, four years later, Carli had presented him with a beautiful child. Despite his immediate and overwhelming love for Olivia, Nate still lacked any interest in connecting romantically with her mother.

Chase's words always found ways to land flush. He had managed to punch and counterpunch before delivering the knockout blow to Nate's self-esteem. After he learned that Nate had ignored the keyword men should live by—*others*—Chase landed a haymaker squarely on Nate's chin.

The blow stung because Chase's words were true. It shook Nate to realize how little it took from Chase to make him feel small. He'd told everyone there was no chance of a relationship with Carli. Why should he even try? She hadn't thought of anyone but herself. She had, after all, kept Olivia away from him for four years.

To make the situation more complicated, Tekla had injected him with some sort of magical attraction serum, despite her admission that she wrestled with her own attachment issues. Nate had long ago decided math made more sense than romantic entanglements. His current dilemma convinced him he'd been right to avoid them.

Olivia had become Nate's brave new world. Protecting the innocence of her childhood and shielding her from all the pain in the universe was his mission. He suspected it would absorb his soul for the rest of his life.

. . .

Nate welcomed any opportunity to spend more time with his daughter, so he accepted Carli's invitation for dinner at her place on Friday night without a second thought.

It seemed odd for the three of them to gather around the table as if they were a family. Sensing how awkward he felt, Carli broke the tension by asking, "So how did it go with Chase?" She refilled his water glass while waiting for an answer.

"Great. Always does."

"I'm excited to meet him at your parents' Thanksgiving dinner this week." She turned to Olivia and said, "Ah, no, Olivia. No finger painting at the table right now, please. After dinner, you and Daddy can work on your dinosaur puzzle."

Carli excused herself from the table to check on dinner. She knew Olivia was easy for Nate to figure out. His daughter had become his bullseye, the center of his world. Olivia rode him like a horse, hugging him around the neck, never wanting to let go. *Is there a place in Nate's heart for me as well?* she wondered.

When Carli returned to the table, she sat next to Nate and said, "Where were we? Oh, yeah. Chase. What did he say?"

"He didn't offer much detail, but what he went through, especially at his age, would qualify him as a five-star action movie hero."

"How about Tekla? You've never told me how well you know her." When Nate flinched at the mention of her name, Carli wondered if there was more to their relationship than she'd realized.

Nate scooted his chair closer to Olivia and started tickling her belly, causing her to giggle loud enough that Carli shushed her and told Nate to stop. "Not at the supper table, you two."

She led Olivia away from the table for a brief discussion. When they returned, Carli settled Olivia in her seat and said, "I'm still curious to hear about Tekla."

"Just met her this last summer. Chase's guests sometimes want to get Western and go for horseback rides. He pays me well to do something I love to do. That's how we met."

"That's it?" she asked, peering at him intently and trusting her sixth sense, which had always guided her through life. Without a doubt, there was something he wasn't telling her.

"More or less. I'll take you and Olivia riding this weekend if you'd like."

"I saw your mother yesterday at City Market. She said Chase talks about Tekla all the time." Carli rested her chin on her hands and tilted her head. "You went to visit her soon after her first visit at the ranch. That sounds like fun. What line of work is she in?"

"She's a retired Army officer, looking at a career change."

"An Army officer. That sounds intense," Carli said, wondering if he was feeding her half-truths.

He quickly changed the subject. "How about that family ride? Sunday, maybe?"

"I'm not sure about that yet. I'd prefer to have you and Olivia spend time getting to know each other before going on any adventures. Why did you flinch when I mentioned Tekla?"

She saw the evasion in his eyes just before he looked away. *I've sprung the trap*, she thought. *There's more.*

Chapter 52

Chase rubbed his huge hands together as if to produce sparks. They were numb, and he'd forgotten to grab his gloves. The air was far from still that November morning, with brisk winds and the occasional gust stinging and reddening his cheeks. He'd just covered the row of rhododendron bushes with burlap for the winter.

In the kitchen, April gave her homemade chicken soup another stir and pulled two bowls from the cabinet.

Chase had noticed Jed's truck was still gone and asked, "Jed's not going to join us?"

"He just texted," she said. "He told me we should eat without him. He spotted a big pine snag the day he took Sean for a ride. He didn't want it to fall across the fence, so I figure he went to cut it for firewood."

"Thanksgiving's this week. Is he going to smoke a turkey this year?"

"He was, but he didn't know if Carli and Olivia would like it, so I'm roasting a bird in the oven. Keeping things traditional."

As Chase sipped his soup, he listened while April talked about her favorite topic, her granddaughter. She regaled him with the tale of the little girl fingerpainting a picture of them both and mentioned how Olivia would snitch a cookie from the jar when she wasn't looking.

Just then, Chase's cell phone rang. It was Tekla. He'd spoken with her two days prior, and she had said the nurses revealed that her father didn't have long. He wanted to tell her not to believe what they said. No one knew when the person you love would go. If they had known how soon JoAnn would be gone, he wouldn't have left to get that pork-chop sandwich. Chase had chosen to stay silent on the topic and let it be.

He hesitated, fearing sad news, but picked up on the third ring. "Hello, Tekla."

"Chase," she cried, "my father's gone. God, it's so hard." She let out a wail from a mix of sorrow and relief. Sniffing, she said, "The mortuary just wheeled him away, but his spirit still fills the house. I don't know what to do or what to feel."

"I'm so sorry, Tekla. Your father was a gallant and patriotic soldier. I want you to know you have the love of your Montana family supporting you, and we're all praying for you."

"Up until the very end, he always felt honored to serve his country," she said.

"Like father, like daughter. Is there anything I can do for you? I'm able to travel and would like to attend his service and pay my respects."

"There will be no viewing and no special service here," she said. "He's being buried in Arlington with full military honors. There's a backlog, which we expected, and it could take six to eight months to be scheduled. Our local funeral home will store his body until then as payment in kind for his military service."

Chase slowly shook his head, one hand rubbing his forehead as he talked. "How is your mother coping? I remember that I leaned on Jed pretty hard the first several weeks after losing JoAnn."

"She has several caring friends, some with military connections. She cries in seclusion and suffers in silence, as an officer's wife is expected to do."

"Be strong, dear. I'm here for you."

"I miss you," she said. And then the wails came in a torrent of grief.

Chase could pen a book about grieving and what an individual process it is. He would write that everyone grieves. It is an inescapable part of life, the price we all pay for loving others. There was his word again: *others*. He sucked in the deepest breath possible and blew it out slowly.

After Tekla's emotions settled, she ended the call to check on her mother. Chase tucked his phone back in his pocket, but it wasn't as easy to tuck away the familiar sense of sorrow. It churned beneath his skin and deep in his brain.

April did not have the history he'd shared with Tekla, but after hearing the news, she looked at the floor, fighting back tears and clutching a tissue to her nose. "That girl," she said, "has been through so much loss. My heart aches for her and her family."

"Let me call Nate," he said. "I'll tell him about Tekla's father. I'm working on mending some fences between us."

Chapter 53

April ran her hand over the surface of their antique oak dining table before laying the tablecloth. "You know, Jed," she mused, "I always wished for a big family. Now that ours has grown, I believe we need a new dining table. Even with an added leaf, it will be hard to seat six. Four is already a squeeze. And the few times Olivia was here for dinner, she brought a toy to the table."

"It's only a few hours before Thanksgiving dinner, April. We'll make do. Serve it buffet style." Jed opened the living room curtain. "The snow they predicted is falling. Looks like blizzard conditions."

"You know Montana weather. Last year we had a brown Christmas. This year we'll have a white Thanksgiving. Go figure."

"I gave up predicting weather long ago, but I'll predict that Montana Hutterite turkey will impress everyone."

. . .

"Olivia, what have you done to your hair? Let me work on those tangles." Carli let out a long, weary sigh as she faced taming another bird's nest in her daughter's hair. She grabbed a boar-bristle brush off her vanity and sat Olivia on the floor between her legs. "What a mess. There's fingerpaint in your hair too! We can't go to Thanksgiving dinner with your hair looking like this."

"I like it messy, Mommy."

"If you want your hair long like mine, you can't wear it messy. Now sit."

Carli started brushing, counting out one hundred strokes. She tried to release one haunted memory from her past with each pull of the brush.

When she'd learned that she was pregnant, she felt bitter and filled with resentment, blaming not only Nate but herself for an unplanned, unwanted pregnancy. Finding that she was carrying twins compounded the matter.

Now she feared losing control of the life she'd made for Olivia. She no longer had the luxury of time she'd had while raising an infant. Olivia was old enough to ask questions, and Carli didn't know how to provide some of the answers. How and when would she tell Olivia that her twin brother had died at birth? Should she tell Nate? Would he blame her for his death?

Now living in Montana, she wanted to write a new chapter in her life, an honest chapter that was overdue. It would begin when the rodeo ended and the clowns had gone to wherever rodeo clowns went when the show was over.

Nate had never harmed her, hurt her, abused her, or disrespected her, so why had she not told him? Would it be wrong *not* to tell him about the son he'd lost, the son he never knew existed?

· · ·

Nate shuddered and turned his shoulders against the wind. The snow numbed his bare fingers as he trod the two hundred paces from his kitchen door to the corral. Many locals considered snow an inconvenience, but not Nate. He welcomed it and envisioned taking Olivia on horseback that weekend to look for a Christmas tree on Chase's ranch. The thought of recreating a nostalgic scene from a Christmas card warmed him. He smiled at the image of a cowboy with a child beside him in the saddle, dragging a fir tree behind his horse, with smoke rising from the chimney on the distant ranch house.

Above the wind, he heard a loud snort from Santiago, who stomped his feet and trotted over to him. His eager expression revealed an awareness that grain was coming. He usually fed his horses mixed grains and hay early in the morning and again in the evening, but it was Thanksgiving. Nate would be gone from late morning to early evening for dinner at his parents, so he tossed in an extra ration of alfalfa hay.

His cell phone rang, and he pulled the phone from his coat pocket with stiff fingers. It was Carli's number, but the voice was Olivia's, bubbling with excitement. "Daddy, Daddy! Mommy wants to know when you are leaving for Pop Pop and Nana's house."

"Well, sweetie, you tell Mommy I'm leaving soon. I can't wait to hug you."

"Will Nana have ice cream?"

"It's supposed to be a secret, but I guess I can tell you. Nana told me she has pumpkin ice cream just for you."

"Pumpkin ice cream!"

"You betcha. I saw it in the freezer. Now Daddy has to go and get ready. I'll see you soon."

Hearing Olivia's sweet voice made his heart swell with unfamiliar joy. He tilted his face to the darkened sky, his mind swirling as much as the cold, dry snowflakes that settled on his face. Within a moment of melting, they diluted the salty droplet that dribbled along the bridge of his nose.

Chapter 54

Jed plopped into his recliner, rubbing his hands together as he anticipated the kickoff between the Lions and the Cowboys. He was not a fan of either team but planned to watch the first quarter, a welcome diversion to keep him out of the kitchen. Helping April baste the turkey had been enough.

His viewing plan was interrupted by three perfectly spaced raps on the front door. A guessing game erupted in his head about who it could be. It was too early for their guests.

Jed walked to the window to look outside. Amid the swirling snow sat the deputy sheriff's car, its red and blue lights on but not flashing. His heart began to hammer. The officer wasn't there to sell raffle tickets. He opened the door to a snow-dusted MJ Forester, the young deputy sheriff who'd gone to high school with Nate.

"Good morning, J-Jed. I'm sorry—"

"Come in out of that weather, MJ. And let's skip the pleasantries," he said. "What's happened to Nate?"

MJ removed his hat. His coat was open, the tight-fitting uniform emphasizing his burly build.

"Damn it, MJ. Don't look across the room. Look at me."

"I ju-just left the scene of an accident, Jed. F-First, I want—"

"He's not dead, is he?" A storm brewed inside Jed's head, dismissing MJ's hands, which pleaded with the older man to stay calm.

"No, no. He's not d-dead. He's been in an accident and was t-taken to County Hospital."

Jed got the shakes, but that time it was not because of his abrupt divorce from Mr. Jimmy. MJ's stuttering made the words sound all the harsher.

"What happened?" Jed bellowed. "What happened, damn it?"

"I've seen it done all the t-time," MJ said. "Some people take a ch-chance and pass the snowplow, driving through the snow cloud c-created by the plow."

Jed passed his tongue over his lips and tried to calm his raging thoughts. Nate's young life flashed in front of him, fragmented by eight-second clips of him hanging onto bucking broncs for dear life. *Is he hanging on now?* he thought as he motioned impatiently for MJ to continue.

"The driver of the plow s-stated that the driver of a minivan was not p-patient about passing and hit the berm c-created by the plow. The guy lost c-c-control of his vehicle. He would've met Nate head-on, b-but Nate's quick reflexes made him turn h-hard to the right. Tire tracks show Nate d-drove off the road, preventing c-critical injuries to the f-family in the minivan."

Jed hung his head for a moment, unsure of what to say next. Just then, April walked out of the kitchen. "Oh, no, Jed. What's happened?"

"Shut the oven off and grab your coat. We're heading to County Hospital. It's Nate."

. . .

Carli was at Nate's side when he regained consciousness in the hospital bed. She was gently massaging his fingers when he opened his eyes and gave her a faint smile of recognition.

"Here we are again," she said. Her voice carried a hint from the past. "Just like Pendleton."

"I'm so confused," Nate said, his voice weak. With one eye swollen shut, he had trouble focusing. "What happened? Why are you here?"

"You were in an accident. You avoided another vehicle, and your truck left the road. You're at County Hospital. Your mother and father were here, but you were still out cold, so they took Olivia for ice cream in the cafeteria."

"Is today Thanksgiving?" He groaned and touched the bandage on his forehead, which covered a laceration from the truck's airbag deployment.

"It is. What you did was quite heroic," she said. "You possibly saved a few lives today, and there are several people who are thanking you for that. I'm grateful you're alive and not seriously injured."

He took a deep breath and sank into his pillow, uttering a low moan. "I remember some of it . . . the snowplow . . . a vehicle coming toward me. It was instinct, not heroism. I feel just like I did after Pendleton."

Carli, a bright, beautiful woman with a dark secret, calmly looked down at the man she wanted to share her life with. She warmed inside when she smelled the Western man's lingering scent—the pungent, tangy, earthy smell of alfalfa hay that emanated from him. How could she ever find a more honest, handsome, authentic man, one who loved and adored Olivia the way he did?

Nate had stolen her heart long ago, and she'd suffered enough. At that moment, she began the epic chess game of life, a game played in uncharted territory, sagebrush hills, and wheat fields. She hoped it would lead to a tale of romance and marriage. The fate of the king would be in her hands.

She stroked Nate's arm. "The doctors told your parents they were going to keep you overnight as a precaution. You'll have to take it easy for a few days. How about letting Olivia and me take care of you?"

He was speechless and touched his bandaged forehead again. He looked out the window and then turned his head to look into her eyes.

Carli had no idea how he would respond to her proposal. Seconds ticked by.

Finally, he said, "But your house is small and has only two bedrooms. Besides, my horses need fed."

She replied, "I don't snore, and I know how to toss hay."

He grinned. It was the first time he'd ever looked at her that way. She didn't see him nod, but she felt it.

Chapter 55

Chase had just finished talking with Jed and had learned about Nate's accident. Jed told him they'd have to cancel Thanksgiving dinner. The roads were bad, so Jed recommended Chase stay home. Nate might be discharged the following day under Carli's care.

Chase was extraordinarily surprised, if not shocked, to hear that. *That's a step in the right direction*, he thought. Maybe Nate had heeded his *others* speech after all.

With Thanksgiving dinner canceled, it would be another holiday Chase would spend alone, much like many others since JoAnn had passed. He told himself it could always be worse. He looked out the window and saw his rocker covered in snow. How had he forgotten to bring it in for the winter?

The falling snow carried an atmosphere of dread, a sense of foreboding from being alone in an isolated ranch house. He needed to engage with someone, and the someone he'd become most comfortable with was Tekla. He would call her, wish her a happy Thanksgiving, and let her know of Nate's accident. He also had an idea for Christmas that he wanted to share. He was relieved when she answered the phone on the first ring.

"Chase," she said, "what a nice surprise. Happy Thanksgiving. Not too much pie now." She chuckled, knowing his dislike of sweets.

Judging from her voice, her outlook had changed since they'd talked just after her father's passing. Tiny droplets of cheer were replacing tears of sorrow.

"Happy Thanksgiving to you too. How is everyone doing in Seneca Falls?"

"We have our dark days," she replied. "Then my sister does something silly that makes us laugh, and we see the sunshine again. It's snowing here. Are you at Jed's?"

She coughed explosively, and he wondered if she was coming down with something. "No, I'm home," he said. "Thanksgiving dinner at Jed's was called off. Nate was in an accident this morning. Nothing serious."

"He what?" she asked, alarm in her voice.

"Early blizzard today. He was on his way to Jed's and had to drive off the road when someone wound up in his lane while trying to pass a snowplow."

"Is he okay?"

"He's fine. They're keeping him in the hospital overnight. Then he's going to Carli's and Olivia's house for the long weekend."

"Who's Carli? Who's Olivia?"

Her question stunned him. He couldn't believe it. Nate had never gotten around to telling Tekla about Carli and Olivia. Beneath the many layers of love and loyalty to Nate, who he considered family, a second-degree burn flared inside Chase's gut. Why was he the one who had to let the cat out of the bag? Good gravy!

"Apparently," he said, "Nate hasn't gotten around to telling you about his new family."

"He bought two more horses?" she asked, laughing.

"No-o-o." His voice became brittle, like thin ice breaking. "While we were away in Europe, he reconnected with a lovely woman from his past and the child he fathered with her. It was a shocker since she'd never told Nate that he had a daughter. She moved here and found a teaching job."

The phone went silent for a minute, and Chase figured the news he'd just delivered weighed heavily on Tekla.

"I never saw that coming. Apparently, he didn't either. But I'm happy for Nate. And he's a father too. How about that?"

Her reply was short, but Chase sensed it was heartfelt and deep. He hoped he hadn't made a huge error in telling her. He needed to move on from talking about Nate, from whom he felt momentarily estranged.

A sliver of clear thinking emerged, and the feeling of Paris returned. Finally, he was ready to discuss his Christmas plan.

"I was thinking," he said, "about having a Christmas open house. I wondered if you and your mother would like a Western Christmas. I'll cover the tickets. You two can share the guest house."

"Wow! You bet. That sounds amazing. I'll talk to her. My sister got engaged and will be flying out to D.C. to spend Christmas with her fiancé's family."

"Wonderful. I hope to have a house full, something I've never done."

"Make sure Nate learns a carol on that harmonica."

Nate could learn a few more things, Chase thought. Then he smiled. It was up to Carli now, and he broke into a rollicking laugh, something he didn't do often. "I look forward to seeing you again. I'll be in touch. Take care of your mother."

He hung up and considered where to put the Christmas tree.

Chapter 56

Chase finally had the spot on his lung checked but received no definitive diagnosis. His doctor advised against a biopsy due to his age and instead prescribed steroids for a month, with a recheck the first month of the new year.

With nothing else on his calendar, Chase had a month to prepare for his Christmas Eve open house. Planning an open house was not something he'd ever done, even with JoAnn. First on his list was figuring out where she'd stored the ornaments, especially his favorite German decorations, which she'd bought during their travels.

Good gravy, did he still have them? He didn't know for sure, but he refused to worry about it.

He no longer felt as if stones lined his gut, and his shoulders had relinquished their burden of guilt. He hungered for friendship and felt eager to connect with all those who had shown him warmth during his year of mourning. *Where to begin*, he asked himself.

He certainly wanted the presence of his adjutant with her warm smile and the signature flick of her hair. He also thought about how he might connect with Tekla's grieving mother. *Who knows grief better than me?* he thought. Chase's experience had taught him that grief was like a wound. It took time to heal from such a deep cut. If he couldn't help heal hers, perhaps he could at least put a band-aid on it for the holidays.

Jed and April were usually off duty during the winter, starting the first week of December. But not that year. Chase needed April to make up a second bed in the guest house and help with decorations, a menu, and food preparations. He wanted lots of poinsettias, for sure. Maybe Jed would volunteer to make his elk and buffalo salami as charcuterie selections. He would also order a red velvet cake from Flo. Oh, and he needed ice cream for Olivia. He'd have to ask about her favorite flavor.

Suddenly overwhelmed, Chase sat at the table and put his head in his hands. His mind was filling fast, and his plate was almost full. Maybe he needed a list. Wasn't that what Tekla had told him?

First on his list would be a Christmas tree, a tall Douglas fir cut from the west slope of his ranch. It would be the centerpiece for all the other decorations. The snow was getting deep, but buying a tree from a town lot was out of the question. Nate had been cleared, with no restrictions on his activities. He'd probably need to take it easy for a week, but then he and Olivia could cut a tree as they had planned to do before Nate's accident.

In the spirit of Christmas, he would also do what was once unthinkable to him. He would invite Daisy Grimble. He groaned and gritted his teeth at the thought. If he invited Daisy, why not invite Lexi too? He'd recently written a legal letter for her. Chase hated to admit the possibility, but Lexi could be a buffer in case Tekla and Carli chilled to one another.

What about invitations? And he couldn't forget to write checks to Toys for Tots and the town's food bank.

That did it. His mind was done. No more planning for that day. Besides, he was hungry. He headed for the kitchen, where he made a ham sandwich on stale sourdough and grabbed a cold lager. He ended Thanksgiving by falling asleep on the couch while watching football.

Chapter 57

The Christmas Eve open house was in full swing, and Olivia wanted to finger paint. He had planned for the possibility and set up a spot for her in his office. Chase hadn't been around children since Nate was a toddler. He worried he would be clumsy with her in comparison with Jed's grandfatherly ways.

Carli had tuned into his apprehension when she and Nate delivered the Christmas tree to the ranch house earlier that week. She told Olivia to call him Big Pop, if Chase okayed it. He had readily agreed. Chase wanted to be everything a grandfather could be, unconditionally loving and kind—a wonderful role model. It seemed he was off to a good start. But he did not want to overshadow Jed or rob him of his position as Olivia's grandfather.

Chase escorted the precocious little girl to his office. "Olivia, I set up this table for you so you can paint when you're here. I can't wait to see your masterpiece."

"Thank you, Big Pop." Her voice was high and thin and easy for him to understand.

"You can paint and sing for as long as you want. I'll have your mommy check on you in a while. Watch the mess."

"Good gravy," she said with a giggle.

Laughing at her imitation of him, Chase returned to the festivities and his guests. The house was filled with cheer and Christmas music, but he could not say which song was playing. Tekla had joined Carli and Lexi to form a beautiful trio, all sipping eggnog and laughing in front of the fire. Jed, dressed in his ugly Christmas reindeer sweater, had Daisy Grimble's ear. From the look on his face, Chase knew he was lecturing her about subdividing her property.

Chase had sent Nate outside to bring in more firewood, but he hadn't seen him bring any in. He had a hunch about what was going on and shook his head. April was busy putting the finishing touches on the artisanal beauty of the buffet table.

Tekla's mother stood alone, sipping white wine and admiring the ornaments, which Chase had located after a long search. When she and Tekla had arrived the day before, she'd introduced herself as Natasha, contrary to Nate's suggestion to call her Gnat.

Natasha caught his eye, and he couldn't help but stare back. Her outward appearance did not suggest a woman in mourning or lost in grief. She stood stately and erect. Her voluminous gray hair, which belied her youthful appearance, brushed her shoulders. She wore a pine-green dress paired with ankle boots, achieving an elegant but casual look. When she flicked her hair off one shoulder, just as her daughter did, he grabbed a glass of wine and joined her.

"I'm really impressed," she said with a heavy New York accent. "Your home and all this Christmas cheer. I'm so glad you invited us. I just love it here."

Chase had raised his glass to toast her husband's memory when he saw that Daisy had turned from Jed and tracked him to Natasha. He'd promised himself that he would spend a few minutes chatting with Daisy during the open house, but that was not the right moment.

He was tingling from head to toe. Was that proper? He'd tucked his grief away. Now he was feeling ambushed, not by love but by compassion. However, the prospect of love was looking more and more interesting.

"Merry Christmas, Natasha." Chase's voice covered her like a cozy blanket. "I understand how hard the holidays can be after we lose someone, but it is also a time that asks us to believe in life and hope."

"Thank you," she lamented. "Yes, some days are very hard. I just try not to show it. We didn't get to talk much last night. May I ask how you are doing after that terrible fall?" Her eyes shone with empathy.

"Natasha, would you mind if we moved to a corner? I'm sorry, but I have problems hearing in a room filled with people and music." He had accepted his hearing loss, but he needed to make accommodations for it.

"Of course," she said, speaking directly into his ear. "I have the same problem."

He reached for her hand and escorted the late officer's wife across the room. They eased into gentle conversation and continued until she said, "I need to use the bathroom. I'd like to talk more. Perhaps we can chat tomorrow when Tekla and I are cooking dinner."

Chase wondered if it was a polite move on her part to encourage him to spend time with his other guests.

While she ate, Daisy had been watching Chase with the attractive widow. As soon as the woman left his side, she put down her plate and reached for a wrapped gift under her chair.

Ambushing his attention, she said, "Merry Christmas, Chase. I brought you a little something I bought at the Merc. Lexi recommended it."

"Thanks, Daisy, but I did say no gifts."

"Don't worry. It's not a pie. Go ahead and open it."

Chase felt overwhelmed but in a good way. He took his time, not ripping the paper. When he saw what was beneath the wrapping, he held his breath and her eyes and said, "Thanks, Daisy. It's beautiful."

She'd given him a hard-cover coffee table book, *Forgotten Places Along Montana's Back Roads*. It was a thoughtful gift that spoke to his passion.

"Okay, so I peeked inside before wrapping it." Her slow southern drawl leaked out. "I saw the ghost town of Elkhorn. Some of Clayton's family settled there, and I wondered if you would like to join me in exploring the area some summer day."

He scratched his head and arched his eyebrows at the thought. It would have been rude to say no, but he couldn't say yes slowly enough.

"Only," he said, "if we take my truck."

"That's like giving me bacon without the sizzle."

"That sounds just like Clayton. I'll get back to you on that, but right now I need to speak with Tekla."

What he really needed was a break. Any more conversation with Daisy would give him indigestion.

His beloved traveling companion had just gotten off her phone. Chase savored the memory of their time together and hugged her close, the familiar scent of her hair filling his nose. He had spoken without words, and she replied with a wide smile. He squeezed her as if scared to let her go and said, "Merry Christmas, Tekla."

"Merry Christmas, Chase," she said before whispering in his ear, "I'm happy for Nate."

Nate finally returned and added another log to the fire. He then organized the group to sing *Jingle Bells* while he played his harmonica. When the song ended, the party began to break up.

Christmas was a time for family, and for the first time in his life, Chase DeMers enjoyed the love of a Montana family with whom he shared no blood. Still, he felt a twinge of loneliness after the last guest left.

Chapter 58

Alone in his empty house on Christmas Eve, Chase sank into the couch to relieve the pain in his back. The silence comforted him. The scent of burning logs and the earthy and spicy notes from his Christmas tree provided him with a soothing form of aromatherapy.

As his pain eased, he was able to straighten his back. Carli had told him she cleaned up after Olivia's finger-painting session. His office was hallowed ground, and he needed to make sure it was tidy.

He switched on the light when he reached his office. Carli had done a good job, but Olivia's painting had slid onto the floor where it lay, dry and curled. He picked it up and laid it flat. Then he gasped, and his heart throbbed with joy. Olivia had created a child's portrait of him, dressed in the clothes he wore that day, dark brown pants and a green shirt.

He saw *Medicine Man* staring at him and shook his head to clear the vision. When he shifted his gaze to *River Walkers*, he imagined that one of the mounted braves was signaling to him, waving him onward. There was no doubt in his mind what he would do next. He rummaged in his desk, fished out four thumbtacks, and mounted Olivia's painting next to his two sacred prints. He would frame her artwork later, but that night he gazed, misty-eyed, at one of the most priceless paintings he would ever own.

. . .

Chase had returned to the couch when he noticed headlights approaching and then heard a vehicle pull up outside. He assumed it was Nate, coming back to pick up Olivia's favorite stuffed teddy bear, which he'd found in the office.

The knock that he heard was a firm, compact sound like that of a prisoner pounding rock. "It's open," he yelled.

The oak door did not open. The knock repeated, louder than before.

In a throaty rumble, he said, "Come in, Nate."

Had Nate come back to pick up the teddy bear? No, not on Christmas Eve. He rose from the couch to see why he hadn't come inside. *Was the door locked?*

"Hold your horses," he called out. He set the teddy bear on the kitchen table and walked to the door to discover it was locked, after all. Shaking his head, he unlocked the door and opened it.

"Merry—*grunt*—Christmas, Chase. Sorry I didn't make your party. I guess you're surprised to see me."

Frank Oglesby stood in the pale shadow of Chase's kitchen lights, uncuffed and unshackled.

"No, Frank. As a matter of fact, I've been expecting you for some time."

"You can relax your fists. You knew I was innocent, and now do you think I'm here to hurt you twenty years later?"

Is he being sincere? Chase wondered. He decided to trust his gut. "No, I guess not," Chase replied with a small note of apprehension in his voice. "Come inside where it's warm."

Frank wiped his feet and walked into Chase's kitchen. He took in the magnificent stone fireplace and crackling fire, which made him feel warm and validated. He'd been living in a cramped tin-box camper in a Forest Service campground, keeping warm with a propane heater and piles of used blankets he'd picked up at Goodwill.

The massive elk-antler chandelier and white lights on the glorious fir illuminated his coat's threadbare fabric. He hoped his visit would magically break the pendulum of the grandfather clock he saw and heard in the hall. For twenty years he'd been locked up. He'd spent twenty Christmases in prison. He'd lived by counting the tick-tocks of solitude, but time had never passed for him.

Frank had tried to reconcile his lifetime struggle with the haves and the have-nots of the world. He'd often wondered in dismay how a high school prank and a neurological condition had shaped his life and landed him in prison.

"You've done well," Frank said as he looked around. He couldn't reconcile Chase's living-room comforts with the indignity of being locked in an ugly jail cell. He took in the sepia-colored photos of Chase's ancestors and the shabby, leather-bound books on his bookshelf. He stared at the exquisite Christmas bulbs and ornaments that decorated Chase's tree and said, "I've no heirlooms to call my own."

"Frank, this is sometimes an unfair world. Did I think you were innocent? Yes, I did. But I failed to prove it."

Frank snorted like a horse and sniffed like a bloodhound. He wanted Chase to confess, to ask his forgiveness for the halfhearted defense he'd provided all those years ago. "So, tell me—*grunt*. How did you lose my case?"

"That has troubled me through the years." Chase pointed squarely at Frank's chest and said, "You were the main reason I stopped practicing law. I could not provide reasonable doubt, and it ate at me. You were a tough client, Frank. The jury was bound to view you in a negative light. The world is different now. I believe jurors these days can understand your condition. That wasn't the case back then."

"I sat in my cell and thought, *I'm the only person in this world who knows I'm innocent.*"

"I've come to believe in your innocence." Chase locked eyes with Frank. "I believe it now more than ever."

"Prison in America," Frank said, "is not constructed to offer any form of comfort." He stopped and sniffed twice. "I tackled challenges and experienced loneliness that you could never imagine or handle. Deep, numbing loneliness. You have no clue."

Chase didn't flinch. He put a thumb to his lips and nibbled on his thumbnail, waiting for Frank to continue.

He told Chase that prison had given him a chance to grow and gain knowledge, that he'd taken an online college course in drafting and architecture. He said he'd always liked to build because he could get lost in thought, which reduced his tics. "Education was my liberation," he said.

"I knew you were smart, Frank, but you had a lot of challenges."

"I gained wisdom from all of it. Life in prison—*grunt*—could become a battlefield at any moment." Out of habit, he glanced behind him. "I always had to watch my back. My life improved after being transferred to minimum security, just three miles from Yosemite. But, shit, it was a constant reminder of my wife falling off the ledge."

"I'm sorry, Frank. If there is anything—"

"Forget it, Chase. I've said what I came to say. I don't want or need anything from you. Merry Christmas."

Frank thought about shaking Chase's hand. Instead, he nodded once and stared at Chase with disdain in his eyes. Then he turned and walked into a star studded December night in the Paradise Valley, with only the moon for company. Nothing but the stark and lonely wailing of coyotes in the distance penetrated his silent night.

. . .

Chase watched the man leave. That Frank wouldn't shake his hand felt like a terrible weight, one he could feel in his legs and shoulders. Frank hadn't forgiven him and never would, and how could Chase blame him? The man had wrongfully lived behind bars for twenty years and was used to being confined.

Now Frank was living in confinement once again, this time in a cold and cramped camper in a deserted campground. Frank's hostility, which the man couldn't let go of, was of course the result of being wronged by the criminal justice system but also by Chase's failure to provide a solid defense. Prison would have changed the man or at least made more extreme what the man was.

Even a man from Butte, a fighter, one who wasn't scared of shadows, could become afraid of being alone. Wouldn't any man change in his own way? Was it possible for such a man to believe that someone he trusted, a system he trusted, had failed him and not hold onto that grievance forever—never forgiving?

And Chase wasn't sure Frank should forgive him. Chase hadn't forgiven himself, even if sometimes he thought he had. *Sometimes*, he thought, *we think we have forgiven, or we forgive in the wrong way. We carry the grievance with us forever, though we think we've let it go.*

Chase found himself pulling out a chair, sitting, and reaching for Olivia's teddy bear, his eyes blurred by tears. He wasn't sure why, but it felt like the right thing to do, even if his eyes might not clear for a long time.

Epilogue

Somewhere, in some universe, a man named Chase wonders whether forgiveness is ever possible, while a man named Nate fears he is living a false and dishonest life.

Nate believes his life will improve in time, but he is uneasy with any happiness that comes his way. Olivia can never know that his marriage to her mother is based on a fabrication. His true passion will always be for a wounded warrior with a prosthetic leg. The single memory of making love to Tekla on an early morning in Seneca Falls has not dulled with time, and the recollection of lavender still haunts him.

He wonders if he has chosen the right way to live, but he'll cowboy up, right or wrong. At that moment, with Olivia's arms wrapped tightly around him and her face nestled into his back as they ride Santiago, Nate stares into the wide Montana sky and thinks, *Some things are not meant to be understood.* The horse stops abruptly, shakes its head, and snorts. Nate cannot help but smile.

Miles away, sipping a cup of extra-hot chai, Tekla thinks about the day she met Liam in a train station high in the Swiss Alps. Did she accidentally stumble upon the beautiful life she always dreamed of having? She admits that she is not a woman who conforms. How can she be? PTSD and her attachment issues constrain her, though both conditions have improved. She no longer looks back on her last normal day.

She has downloaded "Folsom Prison Blues" to her phone and plays it when she feels detached, letting the music steal into her emotions, taking her back to the banks of a blue-ribbon trout stream in Montana. Sometimes Tekla thinks life is unfair, but she's learning what love really means, even if she's come by that wisdom the hard way.

Jed, April, and Carli. They live other lives, fulfilling destinies beyond what we can imagine. They travel through love and grievance and forgiveness in ways that feel like happenstance. Human lives are never predictable, after all. They are never fully within our control, whether we are living them or imagining them in a story like this one.